I0615369

Beneath the Skin

The Sam Hunter Case Files

By
Jonathan Maberry

JournalStone

JOURNALSTONE
YOUR LINK TO ARTISTIC TALENT

Copyright © 2016 Jonathan Maberry
Originally published in:
*** Like Part of the Family (Originally published in NEW BLOOD –Padwolf
Publishing, 2010; © 2010 Jonathan Maberry.)
*** Strip Search (Originally published in LIMBUS, INC, -JournalStone Publishing,
2013; © 2012 by Jonathan Maberry Productions, LLC.)
*** Toby's Closet (Originally published in STREETS OF SHADOWS, edited by
Maurice Broaddus and Jerry Gordon for Alleration, Inc.; © 2014 by Jonathan
Maberry Productions, LLC.)
*** Three Guys Walk into a Bar (Originally published in LIMBUS II, October
2014; © 2014 by Jonathan Maberry Productions, LLC.)
*** Dream a Little Dream of Me (Originally published GODS OF H.P.
LOVECRAFT)
*** The Unlearnable Truths (Originally published in LIMBUS III, October 2016; ©
2016 by Jonathan Maberry Productions, LLC.)
*** Goth Chicks – © 2016 by Jonathan Maberry Productions, LLC.; first
publication

All rights reserved. No part of this book may be used or reproduced by any means,
graphic, electronic, or mechanical, including photocopying, recording, taping or by any
information storage retrieval system without the written permission of the publisher
except in the case of brief quotations embodied in critical articles and reviews.
This is a work of fiction. All of the characters, names, incidents, organizations, and
dialogue in this novel are either the products of the author's imagination or are used
fictitiously.

JournalStone books may be ordered through booksellers or by contacting:
JournalStone
www.journalstone.com

The views expressed in this work are solely those of the authors and do not necessarily
reflect the views of the publisher, and the publisher hereby disclaims any responsibility
for them.

ISBN: 978-1-945373-12-1   (sc)
ISBN: 978-1-945373-14-5   (ebook)
ISBN: 978-1-945373-13-8   (hc)

JournalStone rev. date: December 2, 2016

Library of Congress Control Number: 2016957965

Printed in the United States of America

Cover Art – photo images & Design: Rob Grom

Edited by: Sean Leonard

Sam Hunter

Sam Hunter is a PI in the big bad city. When he takes a new case it's like he's accepting the client into his 'pack.' And Sam will do anything to protect the members of his pack. Dogs are like that. So are wolves. And so, too, are werewolves. Like Sam.

Sam is a *benandanti*, an ancient race of werewolves who fight evil. And evil comes in all shapes and sizes; it comes at people from all directions. The cases Sam takes range from saving the world from genetically-engineered super soldiers to saving a young boy from the very real monster in his closet.

The Sam Hunter Case Files gather together the weird, strange, funny, heartbreaking and disturbing adventures of a low-rent private investigator taking on very odd jobs. These stories include cameos by fan-favorite characters from Maberry's bestselling *Joe Ledger* thrillers and *The Pine Deep Trilogy*.

Table of Contents

Who's Afraid of the Big Bad Wolf?

Introduction
By
Kevin J. Anderson

Creative writing teachers always tell their students "write about what you know about."

You hold in your hands a collection of stories about Sam Hunter, a private investigator who also happens to be a werewolf, a guy who works on cases in the seediest, grimmest places you can imagine.

Werewolves and seedy dumps. What does Jonathan Maberry know that we don't know?

I can say for certain that he does know werewolves. Jonathan's first novel to hit the New York Times bestseller list was his novelization of *The Wolf Man*. He's a big guy, intimidating (until you talk with him and realize he's warm and funny and gregarious). I wouldn't go so far as to call him "hirsute," but Jonathan Maberry does have a big beard and more hair than I do (well, a dolphin has more hair than I do).

And as for detectives, he is renowned for his Joe Ledger series, and now he's working on *X-Files* books. That gives him street cred.

As for why he's so familiar with strip clubs, dive bars, and dark alleys...maybe it's better not to ask. ("A dozen beer taps, but none of them were for good beers." Hey, I've been to that place!)

Let's just say that writers do a lot of the hard research so that the armchair reader doesn't have to.

> "You're the private investigator?"
> "Yes, ma'am."
> "Named 'Hunter'?"
> "Yes."
> "That a stage name or something?"
> "No. It's a coincidence, but I've come to embrace the cliché."

That's how clients, and readers, meet Sam Hunter, werewolf private investigator. When Jonathan first asked me to read these stories and write the introduction, the connection was obvious. We've known each other for a decade or so, and Jonathan is a particular fan of my Dan Shamble, Zombie P.I. stories (he even wrote the introduction to my *Working Stiff* collection). A werewolf detective? Who could resist a hardboiled hairball?

Considering the intrinsic potential for humor in the subject matter, I imagined these would be goofy and entertaining romps.

> "I have three ex-wives and I pay alimony bigger than India's national debt. I know how expensive women's shoes are."

And it turns out the Sam Hunter stories do have a lot of humor, mostly from the lycanthropic attitude and the tough worldview that keeps Hunter sane in a grim and twisted world.

> "As it turns out, beings from the outer darkness don't like to be called dickhead anymore than, say, a redneck at a roadside bar."

But these stories aren't slapstick. They are entertaining, but they are not meant to be *fun*. In fact, Jonathan's prose sometimes is so sharp, deep, and visceral it is a literary sucker punch. While reading, I often stopped to marvel at how he puts his fingers on the keyboard and also puts them *right on* the human soul.

Read this, you'll see what I mean:

"Gail was one of the broken ones. One of those women who have been so comprehensively beaten down by life, by circumstance, by financial disappointments, by obligations, by missed opportunities, by fractured families and fair-weather friends that she was one step away from being no one at all. Pale, thin, almost translucent. You could look right through her and see that the world would be here if she up and died and that everything would look the same. Like that. "

Nice.

These stories are engrossing, fast-paced, thrilling, and often thought-provoking. Many are substantial, almost short novels. All of them are excellent.

I have to confess that I read a lot of manuscripts, mostly from writing students, new authors, writers at the beginning of their careers and eager for a blurb from a well-known author. Reading those is just part of my job, and it often *feels* like work. When I printed out the manuscript for *Beneath the Skin*, I went into "work" mode again and rapidly found myself caught up, turning pages and absorbing the story, delighted to remember how enjoyable it is to read a book from a really good writer. And Jonathan Maberry is a really good writer. He knows what he's doing.

I still don't know why he knows so much about strip clubs and dive bars, though. I don't want to know…

Beneath the Skin

Like Part of the Family

-1-

"*My* ex-husband is trying to kill me," she said.

She was one of those cookie-cutter East Coast blondes. Pale skin, pale hair, pale eyes. Lots of New Age jewelry. Not a lot of curves and too much perfume. Kind of pretty if you dig the modeling-scene heroin chic look. Or if you troll the anorexia twelve-steps or crack houses looking for easy ass that's so desperate for affection they'll boff you blind for a smile. Not my kind. I like a little more meat on the bone, and a bit more sanity in the eyes. This one came to me on a referral from another client.

"He actually try?"

"I can *tell*, Mr. Hunter."

Yeah, I thought and tried not to sigh. *What I figured.*

"You call the cops?"

She shrugged.

"What's that mean? You call them or not?"

"I called," she said. "They said that there wasn't anything they could do unless he did something first."

"Yeah," I said. "Can't arrest someone for thinking about something."

"He threatened me."

"Anyone hear him make the threat?"

"No."

"Then it's your word."

"That's what the police said." She crossed her legs. Her legs were on the thin side of being nice. Probably were nice before drugs or stress or a fractured self image wasted her down to Sally Stick-figure.

Skirt was short, shoes looked expensive. I have three ex-wives and I pay alimony bigger than India's national debt. I know how expensive women's shoes are. I was wearing black sneakers from Payless. Glad I had a desk between me and her.

"Your husband ever hurt you?" I asked. "Or try to?"

"*Ex*," she corrected. "And...yes. That's why I left him. He hit me a few times. Mostly when he was drunk and out of control."

I held up a hand. "Don't make excuses for him. He hit you. Being drunk doesn't change the rules. Might even make it worse, especially if he did it once while drunk and then let himself come home drunk again."

She digested that. She'd probably heard that rap before but it might have come from a female case worker or a shrink. From the way her eyes shifted to me and away and back again I guessed she'd never heard that from a man before. I guess for her men were the Big Bad. Too many of them are.

It was ten to five but it was already dark outside. December snow swirled past the window. It wasn't accumulating, so the snow still looked pretty. Once it started piling up I hated the shit. My secretary, Mrs. Gilligan, fled at the first flake. Typical Philadelphian – they think the world will come to a screeching halt if there's half an inch on the ground. She's probably at Wegmans stocking up on milk, bread and toilet paper. The staples of the apocalypse. Me, I grew up in Minneapolis, and out in the Cities we think twenty inches is getting off light. Doesn't mean I don't hate the shit, though. A low annual snowfall is one of the reasons I moved to Philly after I got my PI license. Easier to hunt if you don't have to slog through snow.

"When he hit you," I said, "you report it?"

"No."

"Not to the cops?"

"No."

"Women's shelter?

"No."

"Anyone? A friend?"

She shook her head. "I was...embarrassed, Mr. Hunter. A black eye and all. Didn't want to be seen."

Which means there's no record. Nothing to support her case about ex-hubby wanting to kill her.

I drummed my fingers on the desk blotter. I get these kinds of cases every once in a while, though I stayed well clear of domestic disputes and spousal abuse cases when I was with Minneapolis PD. I have a temper and by the time they asked for my shield back I had six reprimands in my jacket for excessive force. At one of my IA hearings the captain said that he was disappointed that I showed no remorse for the last 'incident.' I busted a child molester and somehow while the guy was, um, resisting arrest he managed to get mauled and mangled a bit. The pedophile tried to spin some crazy shit that I sicced a dog on him, but I don't *have* a dog. I said that he got mauled by a stray during a foot pursuit. Even at my own hearing I couldn't keep a smile off my face to save my job. Squeaked by on that one, but next time something like it happened—this time with a guy who whipped his wife half to death with an extension cord because she wasn't 'willing enough' in the bedroom—I was out on my ass. He ran into the same stray dog. Weird how that happens, huh? Long story short, I already didn't have the warm fuzzies for her husband. We all have our buttons, and when the strong prey on the weak all of mine get pushed.

"Did you go to the E.R.?"

"No," she said. "It was never that bad. More humiliating than anything."

I nodded. "What about after the divorce? He lay a hand on you since?"

She hesitated.

"Mrs. Skye?" I prompted.

"He tried. He chased me. Twice."

"*Chased* you? Tell me about it."

She licked her lips. She wore a very nice rose-pink lipstick that was the only splash of color. Even her clothes and shoes were white. Pale horse, pale rider.

"Well," she said, "that's where the story gets really...strange."

"Strange how?"

"He—David, my ex-husband—*changed* after I filed for divorce. He's like a different person. Before, when I first met him, he was a very fastidious man. Always dressed nicely, always very clean and well-groomed."

"What's he do for a living?"

"He owns a nightclub. *The Crypt*, just off South Street."

"I know it, but that's a Goth club right? Is he Goth?"

"No. Not at all. He bought the club from the former owner, but he remodeled it after *The Batcave*."

"As in Batman?"

"As in the London club that was kind of the prototype of pretty much the whole Goth club scene. David's a businessman. There's a strong Goth crowd Downtown, and they hang together, but the clubs in Philly aren't big enough to turn a big profit, and not near big enough to attract the better bands. So, he bought the two adjoining buildings and expanded out. He made a small-time club into a very successful main stage club, and he keeps the music current. A lot of post-punk stuff, but also the newer styles. Dark cabaret, deathrock, Gothabilly. That sort of thing. Low lights, black-tile bathrooms, bartenders who look like ghouls."

"Okay," I said.

"But this was all business to David. He didn't dress Goth. I mean, he wore black suits or black silk shirts to work, but he didn't dye his hair, didn't wear eye-liner. Funny thing is, even though he was clearly not buying into the lifestyle the patrons loved him. They called him the Prince. As in Prince of—"

"Darkness, yeah, got it. Go on."

"David was more fussy getting ready to go out than I ever was. Spent forever in the bathroom shaving, fixing his hair. Always took him longer to pick out his clothes than me or any of my girlfriends."

"He gay?"

"No." And she shot me a 'wow, what a stereo-typically homophobic thing to say' sort of look.

I smiled. "I'm just trying to get a read on him. Fastidious guy having trouble with a relationship with his wife. Drinking problem, flashes of violence. Not a gay thing, but I've seen it before in guys who are sexually conflicted and at war with themselves and the world because of it."

She studied me for a moment. "You used to be a cop, Mr. Hunter?"

"Call me Sam," I said. "And, yeah, I was a cop. Minneapolis PD."

"A detective?"

"Yep."

"Okay." That seemed to mollify her. I gestured to her to continue. She took a breath. "Well…toward the end of our relationship David stopped being so fastidious. He would go two or three days without shaving. I know that doesn't sound like the end of the world, but I never saw David without a fresh shave. Never. He carried an electric razor in his briefcase, had another at home and one in the office at the club. Clothes, too. Before, he'd sometimes change clothes twice or even three times a day if it was humid. He always wanted to look fresh. Showered at home morning and night, and had a shower installed in his office."

"I get the picture. Mr. Clean. But you say that changed while you were still together?"

"It started when he fell off the wagon."

"Ah."

"When I met him he said that he hadn't taken a drink for over two years. He was proud of it. He thought that his thirst—he always called it that—was evil, and being on the wagon made him feel like a real person. Then, after we started having problems, he started drinking again. Never in front of me, and he always washed his mouth out before he came home. I never smelled alcohol on him, but he was a different person from then on. And he started yelling at me all the time. He called me horrible names and made threats. He said that I didn't love him, that I was just trying to use him."

"I have to ask," I said, being as delicate as I could, "but was there someone else?"

"For me? God, no!"

"What set him off? From his perspective, I mean. Did he say that there was something that made him angry or paranoid?"

"Well…I think it was his health."

"Tell me."

"He started losing weight. He was never fat, not even stocky. David was very muscular. He lifted a lot of weights, drank that protein powder twice a day. He had big arms, a huge chest. I asked him if he was taking steroids. He denied it, but I think he was trying to turn into one of those muscle freaks. Then, about a year and a half ago he started losing weight. When he taped his arms and found that his biceps were only twenty-two inches, he got really angry."

"David has twenty-two inch biceps?" Christ. Back in his Mr. Universe days, Arnold the Terminator had twenty-four inch arms, fully pumped. I think mine are somewhere shy of fifteen, and that's after three sets on the Bowflex.

"Not anymore," said Mrs. Skye. "He lost a lot of muscle mass. Really fast, too. I was scared, I told him to go to a doctor. I thought he might have cancer."

"Did he go to the doctor?"

"He said so...but I don't think he did. He kept losing weight. After six months he didn't even have much definition. He was kind of ordinary sized."

"Was he drinking by this point?"

"I'm sure of it."

"That when he started putting his hands on you?"

"Yes. And he became paranoid. Kept trying to make it all my fault."

"How long did this go on?"

"Well...after the first time he, um, *hurt* me, I gave him a second chance. After all, he was my husband. I figured that he was just scared because of his health. But then it happened again. The second time he knocked me around pretty good. I couldn't go out of the house for a few days."

"Was that when you left?"

It took her so long to answer that I knew what her answer would be. I've done too many interviews of this kind. If self-esteem is low enough then victimization can become an addiction.

"I stayed for two more months."

"How many times did he hurt you during that time?" I asked.

"A few."

"A few is how many?"

Another long pause. "Six."

"Six," I said, trying to put no judgment in my tone. "What was the straw?"

She looked at her hands, at the clock, at the snow falling outside. If there'd been a magazine on my desk she would have picked it up and leafed through it. Anything to keep from meeting my eyes. "He choked me."

"I see."

"It was in the middle of the night. We were…we were…"

I almost sighed. "Let me guess. Make-up sex?"

She nodded, but she didn't blush. I'll give her that. "He'd been sweet to me for two weeks straight without getting mad or yelling, or anything. He acted like his old self. Charming." She finally met my eyes. "David has enormous charisma. He makes everyone like him, and he always seems so genuine."

"Uh huh," I said, wondering how that charm would work on a blackjack across his teeth.

"We sat up talking until late, then we went to bed. And in the middle of the night…things just started happening. You know how it is."

I didn't, but I said nothing.

"I was, um…on top. And we were pretty far into things, and then all of a sudden David reaches up and grabs me around the throat. I thought for one crazy moment that he was doing that auto-whatever it's called."

"Autoerotic asphyxiation," I supplied.

"Yeah, that. I thought he was doing that. He talked about it once before, but we'd never tried it. He's really strong and I'm pretty small. But…I guess I thought he was trying to change things, you know? Create a new pattern for us. A fresh start."

Naivety can be a terrible thing. Jesus wept.

"But it wasn't sex play," I prompted.

"No. He started squeezing his hands. Suddenly I couldn't breathe. It was weird because we were so close to…you know…and David kept staring at me, his eyes wide like he was in some kind of trance. I tried to pull his hands apart, but it just made him squeeze tighter. That's when he started calling me names again, making wild accusations, accusing me of destroying his life."

"How did you get away?"

Her eyes cut away again. This was obviously very hard for her.

"I threw myself sideways and when I landed I kicked him in the, um…you know."

I smiled.

"Good for you," I said, but she shook her head.

"I grabbed my clothes and ran out. Next day I drove past the house and saw that his car was gone. I had a locksmith come out and change all the locks and change the security code on the alarm. I hired a messenger company to come and take a couple of suitcases of his clothes to the club. Next day I rented a storage unit and hired a moving company to take all of his stuff there. I used the same messenger service to send him the key."

"I'm impressed. That was quick thinking."

"I...I'd already looked into that stuff before. Until that last stretch where he was nice I was planning to leave him. I'd already talked to my lawyer, and I filed for divorce by the end of that week."

"What did David do?"

"At first? Nothing except for some hysterical messages on my voicemail. He didn't try to break in, nothing like that. But after a while I started seeing his car behind mine when I was going to work."

"Where do you work?"

"I'm a nurse supervisor at Sunset Grove, the assisted living facility in Jenkintown. Right now I'm on the four to midnight shift. I've spotted David's car a lot, sometimes every night for weeks on end. I've seen him drive by when I'm going into the staff entrance, and he's there again when I get back home."

"What makes you think he's planning to do more than just harass you?"

"He's said so."

"But—"

"He didn't say or do anything at first...but over the last couple of weeks it's gotten worse. About three weeks ago I came out of work and stopped at a 7-11 for some gum, and when I came out he was leaning against my car. I told him to get away, but he pushed himself off the car and came up to me, smiling his charming smile. He told me that he knew who I was and what I was and that he was going to end me. His words. *'I'm going to end you.'* Then he left, still smiling."

"Did anyone see this?"

"At one in the morning? No."

Convenience stores have security cameras, I thought. If this thing got messy I could have her lawyer subpoena those tapes. I had her write down the address of the 7-11.

"That's how it went for a couple of weeks," she said. "But last night he really scared me."

"What happened?"

"He was in my bedroom."

"How?"

"That's it...I don't know. The alarms didn't go off and none of the windows were broken. I heard a sound and I woke up and there he was, standing by the side of my bed. He's really thin now, and as pale as those Goth kids at his club. He stood there, smiling. I started to scream and he put a finger to his lips and made a weird shushing sound. It was so strange that I actually did shut up. Don't ask me why. The whole thing was like a nightmare."

"Are you sure it wasn't?"

She hesitated, but she said, "I'm positive. He pointed at me and said that he knew everything about me. Then he started praying."

"Praying?"

"At least I think that's what he was doing. It was Latin, I think. He said a long string of things in Latin and then he left."

"How'd he get out?"

"The same way he got in, I guess...but I don't know how. I was so scared that I almost peed myself and I just lay there in bed for a long time. I don't know how long. When I finally worked up the nerve, I ran downstairs and got a knife from the kitchen and went through the whole house."

"You didn't call the cops?"

"I was going to...but the alarm never went off. I checked the system...it was still set. I began wondering if I *was* dreaming."

"But you don't think so?"

"No."

"Why are you so sure?"

She fished in her purse and produced a pink cell phone. She flipped it open and pressed a few buttons to call up her text messages. She pointed to the number and then handed me the phone.

"That's David's cell number."

The text read: *Tonight.*

"Okay," I said. "Let me see what I can do."

"What *can* you do?" she asked.

"Well, the best first thing to do is go have a talk with him. See if I can convince him to back off."

"And if he won't?"

"I can be pretty convincing."

"But what if he won't? What if he's...I don't know...too crazy to listen to reason?"

I smiled. "Then we'll explore other options."

-2-

The Crypt is a big ugly building on the corner of South and Fourth in Philadelphia. Once upon a time it was a coffin factory – which I think would have been a cooler name. Less trendy and obvious. The light snow did nothing to make it look less ugly. When we pulled to the corner, Mrs. Skye pointed to a sleek silver Lexus parked on the side street.

"That's his."

I jotted down the license plate and used my digital camera to take photos of it and the exterior of the building. You never know.

"Okay," I said, "I want you to wait here. I'll go have a talk with David and see if we can sort this out."

"What if something happens? What if you don't come out?"

"Just sit tight. You have a cell phone and I'll give you the keys. If I'm not out of there in fifteen minutes, drive somewhere safe and call the name on the back of my card." I gave her my business card. She turned it over and saw a name and number. Before she could ask, I said, "Ray's a friend. One of my pack."

"Another private investigator?"

"A bodyguard. I use him for certain jobs, but I don't think we'll need to bring him in on this. From what you've told me I have a pretty good sense of what to expect in there."

As I got out my jacket flap opened and she spotted the handle of my Glock.

"You're not...going to *hurt* him," she asked, wide eyed.

I shook my head. "I've been doing this for a lot of years, Mrs. Skye. I haven't had to pull my gun once. I don't expect I'll break that streak tonight."

The breeze was coming from the west and the snow was just about done. I squinted up past the streetlights. The cloud cover was thin and I could already see the white outline of the moon. Nope, no accumulation. Typical Philly winter.

I crossed the street and tried the front door. Place didn't do much business before late evening, but the doors were unlocked. The doors opened with an exhalation of cigarette smoke and alcohol fumes. There was probably an anti-smoking violation in that. Something else to use later if I needed to go the route of making life difficult for him.

It was too early for a doorman, and I walked a short hallway that was empty and painted black. Heavy black velvet curtains at the end. Cute. I pushed them aside and entered the club. Place was huge. David Skye must have taken out the second floor and knocked out everything but the retaining walls of the adjoining properties. The red and white maximum occupancy sign said that it shouldn't exceed four hundred, but the place looked capable of taking twice that number. Bandstand was empty, so someone had put quarters in to play the tuneless junk that was beating the shit out of the woofers and tweeters. Whoever the group was on the record, they subscribed to the philosophy that if you can't play well you should play real god damn loud.

There were maybe twenty people in the place, scattered around at tables. A few at the bar. Everyone looked like extras from a direct-to-video vampire flick. The motif was black on black with occasional splashes of blood red. White skin that probably never saw the sun. Eyeliner and black lipstick, even on the guys. I was in jeans and a Vikings warm-up jacket. At least my sneakers and my leather porkpie hat were black. Handle of my gun was black, too, but they couldn't see that. Better for everyone if nobody did.

The bartender was giving me *the look,* so I strolled over to him. He knew I wasn't there for a beer and didn't waste either of our time by asking.

"David Skye," I said, having to bend forward and shout over the music.

"Badge me," he said.

I flipped open my PI license. "Private."

"Fuck off," he suggested.

"Not a chance."

"I can call the cops."

"Bet I can have L and I here before they show. Smoking in a public restaurant?"

Another smartass remark was on his lips, but he didn't have the energy for it. He was paid by the hour and this had to be a slow shift for tips. I took a twenty from my wallet and put it on the bar.

"This isn't your shit, kid," I said. "Call your boss."

He didn't like it, but he took the twenty and made the call.

"He says come up." The bartender pointed to another curtained doorway beside the bar. I gave him a sunny day smile and went inside.

There was a long hallway with bathrooms on both sides and a set of stairs at the end. I took the stairs two at a time. The stairs went straight up to his office and the door was open. I knocked anyway.

"It's open," he yelled. I went inside and as I looked around I hoped like hell that the office décor was not modeled after the interior landscape of David Skye's mind. The walls were painted a dark red, the trim was gloss black. Instead of the band posters and framed *'look at who I'm shaking hands with'* eight-by-tens, the walls were hung with torture devices and S and M clothes. Spiked harnesses, leather zippered masks, thumbscrews, photos from Abu Ghraib, diagrams of dissected bodies. A full-sized rack occupied one corner of the room and an iron maiden stood in the other, one door open to reveal rows of tarnished metal spikes. The only other furniture was a big desk made from some dark wood, a black file cabinet and the leather swivel chair in which David Skye sat. He wore a black poet's shirt, leather wristbands, and a smile that was already belligerent.

"The fuck are you and the fuck you want?"

The man was a charmer. I could just taste the charisma his wife had mentioned flowing like sweetness from his pores.

I flipped my ID case open. "We need to have a chat. It can be friendly or not. Your call."

"Go fuck yourself."

So much for *friendly*.

"That whore send you?" he demanded.

I smiled but didn't answer.

He had a handsome face, but his wife was right when she said that he'd lost weight. His skin looked thin and loose, and he had the complexion of a mushroom. More gray than white.

"Did my wife send you?" he said, pronouncing the words slowly as if I'd come here on the short bus.

"Why would your ex-wife send me?"

His eyes flickered for a second at '*ex*-wife.' I strolled across the room and stood in front of his desk. He didn't get up, neither of us offered a hand to the other.

"She makes up stories," he said.

"What kind of stories?"

"Bullshit. Lies. Says I slapped her around."

"Who'd she say that to?"

He didn't answer. He did, however, give me the ninja secret death stare, but I manned my way through it.

"What are you supposed to be?" he asked.

"Just what the license says."

"Private investigator. Private *dick*."

"Yes, and that was funny back in the 1950s. Why do *you* think I'm here?"

"She's probably trying some kind of squeeze play. The club's doing okay, so she wants a bigger slice."

"Try again," I said, though he might have been right about that.

"Oh, I get it....you're supposed to scare me into leaving her alone."

"Do I look scary?"

He smiled. He had very red lips and very white teeth. "No," he said, "you don't."

"Right...so let's pretend that I'm here to have a reasonable discussion. Man to man."

Skye leaned back in his chair and stared at me with his dark eyes. It was a calculating look and I'm sure he took in everything from my slightly threadbare Vikings jacket to my cheap black sneakers. Put everything I was wearing together and it would equal the cost of his shirt. I was okay with that. I don't dress to impress. Skye, on the other hand, smiled as if our mutual understanding of my material net worth clearly made him the alpha.

I smiled back.

"What does she want?" he asked.

"For you to leave her alone."

"What is she afraid of?"

"She thinks you're trying to kill her."

"What do *you* think?"

"What I think doesn't matter. I'm not a psychic, so I don't know whether you're trying to kill her or if you're playing some kind of mind game on her. Whatever it is, I'm here to ask you to lay off."

"Why should I?"

"Because I asked real nice."

He smiled at that.

"Because it's illegal and I could build a harassment case against you and you could lose your club and sink a quarter mil into legal fees. Because I know inspectors who can slap you with fifteen kinds of violations that will hurt your business. I can have your car booted by *accident* three or four times a week, every week."

"And I could have you killed," he said, the smile unwavering.

"Maybe," I said. "You could try, and I might fuck up anyone you send and then come back here and fuck you up."

"Think you could?"

"You really want to find out?" When he didn't answer, I took a glass paperweight off his desk and turned it over in my hands. A spider was trapped inside, frozen into a moment of time for the amusement of the trinket crowd. I knew he was watching me play with the paperweight, wondering what I was going to do with it.

I put it back down on the desk.

"Really, though," I said, "how long do we need to circle and sniff each other? We don't run in the same pack and I don't give a rat's ass what you do, who you are, or how tough you think you are. We both know that you're either going to stop bothering your ex-wife and go on with your life, or you're going to make a run at her—either because you have some loose wiring or because I'm pushing your buttons by being here. If you back off, we're all friends. I'll advise my client not to file a restraining order and you two can let the divorce lawyers earn their paychecks by kicking each other in the nuts."

"Or...?" he asked. Still smiling.

"Or, you don't back off and then this is about you and me."

"Nonsense. You're no part of this. This is about me and—"

I cut him off. "I'm *making* this about you and me. Maybe I have a wire loose, too, but once I tell a client that I'm going to keep her safe, I take it amiss if anything happens to her."

"'Amiss,'" he repeated, enjoying the word.

"But that's a minute from now. We're still on the other side of it until you give me an answer. What's it going to be? You leave her alone? Or this gets complicated."

"What were you before you started doing this PI bullshit?"

"A cop."

He grunted. "You sound like a thug. An asshole leg-breaker from South Philly."

"Thin line sometimes."

He steepled his fingers. It was one of those moves that looked good when Doctor Doom did it in a comic book. Maybe in a boardroom. Looked silly right now, but he had enough intensity in his eyes to almost pull it off. He gave me ten seconds of *the stare*.

I stood my ground.

His cell phone rang and he flipped it open, listened.

"I'm in a meeting," he said and closed the phone.

His smile returned.

I heard the footsteps on the stairs even though they were quiet.

I sighed and turned. There were four of them. All as pale as Skye, but much bigger. "Really? You want to play that card?"

"It's one of the classics. Though, to be fair, it'll be more than a typical beating. I...hm, am I wrong in presuming you *have* had your ass kicked?"

"That cherry was popped a long time ago."

The four men entered the room and fanned out behind me.

"So, our challenge, then," Skye said, "is to put a new spin on this. Something surprising and fresh so that you'll be entertained."

"Mind if I take my jacket off first?"

"Go right ahead."

I heard a hammer-cock behind me.

Skye said, "You can put your jacket on my desk here, and take off your shoulder holster and put that—and your piece—on top of it."

"Sure, whatever," I said. I shrugged out of the jacket. I bought it the year the Vikings took their eighteenth division title. I'll buy a new one if they ever win the Super Bowl. Or when pigs sprout wings and learn to fly, whichever comes first. I folded it and set it down, unclipped my shoulder rig, set that down. If I was going to ruin my clothes, then at least nothing I was currently wearing had sentimental value.

I leaned on the desk. "Let's agree on a couple of things first, okay?"

"Sure," he said with a grin.

"When I'm done handing these clowns their asses, then you and I dance a round or two."

"That would be fun," he said, "but I doubt I'll have the pleasure."

"Second, if I walk out of here on my own steam, then it's with the understanding that you will leave the lady alone."

"If you walk out of here? Sure. But, tell me something," he said, and he looked genuinely interested, "why do you care? What is she to you?"

"Maybe I'm the possessive type, too. Maybe now that she's asked for my help, it's like she's part of the family. So to speak."

"Part of the family? You fucking kidding me here?"

"Nope."

"You Italian? This some kind of dago thing?"

"I said it's *like* she's part of the family. My family," I said, "and I protect what's mine."

"That's it? It's just a macho thing with you?"

"No, it's more than that," I admitted. I gestured to the torture and pain motif in which his office was decorated. "But, seriously, I doubt you would understand."

"Mmm, probably not. I'm not into sentimentality and that bullshit. Not anymore."

"What happened? What changed you?"

His smiled faded to a remote coldness. "I learned that there was something better. Better than family, better than blood ties. Better than any of this ordinary shit."

"You found religion?" I said.

"It's a 'higher order' sort of thing that I really don't want to explain and I doubt *you'd* understand."

"I might surprise you."

"I don't think that's possible. But *we* might surprise you. In fact I can pretty fucking well guarantee it."

"Rock and roll," I said.

I straightened and turned toward the four goons. They took up positions like compass points. The office was big, but not big enough to give me room to maneuver. They were going to fall on me like a wall, and they knew it. The guy with the gun even snugged it back into his shoulder rig. They were *that* confident, and they were smiling like kids at a carnival.

"You shouldn't have bothered Mr. Skye," said the guy in front of me. He was the guy who'd holstered his gun. He stood on the East point of the compass. "You should have—"

I kicked him in the nuts. I really didn't need to hear the speech.

I'm not that big but I can kick like a Rockette. I *felt* bones break and he screamed like a nine year old girl. Dumbass should have kept his gun out.

I stepped backward off of him and put an elbow into West's face. It had all of my mass in motion behind it. That time I heard bones break and he went down so fast that I wondered if I'd snapped his neck.

That left South and North. South spent a half second too long looking shocked, so I jumped at him with a leaping knee—the only Muay Thai kick I know—and drove him all the way to the wall. By the time North closed in I'd grabbed South by the ears and slammed him skull-first into a replica of a torture rack. Blood splattered in a Jackson Pollack pattern.

I pivoted and rushed to intercept North who was barreling at me with a lot of furious speed; so I veered left and clothes-lined him with my stiff right forearm. He did a pretty impressive back flip and landed face down on the black-painted hardwood floor.

If this was an action movie everything would switch to slow motion as the four thugs toppled to the ground and I turned slowly, looking badass, to face the now startled and unprotected villain.

The real world is a lot less accommodating.

I caught movement behind me, figuring it for Skye going after my gun, so I whirled and made ready to launch into a diving tackle.

Only it wasn't Skye.

It was East and West getting to their feet. West's face was smeared with blood from his broken nose, but he was smiling. As I watched he took his nose between thumb and forefinger and *snapped* it into place, then spit a hocker of blood and snot onto the floor.

North was chuckling as he rose; and behind me I could hear South shifting to stand behind me again. I turned in a slow circle. They were all smiling. They shouldn't have been *able* to. They should have been sprawled on the floor and I should have been giving some kind of smart-ass speech as I closed in to lay a beating on Skye. That was the script I'd written in my head.

What the hell was this shit?

"Surprise!" said Skye dryly.

"What the hell are these fuckers *taking*?"

"You wouldn't believe me if I told you."

"Try me."

"Blood," he said.

"What the—"

And I looked more closely at the smiles. Lots of white teeth. Lots of long, pointy white teeth.

"Oh, balls," I said.

"Yeah, kind of cool, huh?"

"Vampires?" I said.

"Yeah."

"Actual vampires."

Skye laughed. The four—well, let's call a spade a spade—*vampires* laughed with him.

Even I laughed.

"Geez. When shit goes wrong it goes all the way wrong, doesn't it?" I said.

"On the up side," said Skye, "you did win the first round. Nice moves."

"Thanks."

The four of them circled me. My pulse jumped from 'uh-oh' to 'oh shit.' It was cold in his office but I was starting to sweat pretty heavily.

"I guess I shouldn't be surprised," I said. "You're one, too? Am I right?"

"A recent convert," he admitted.

"So…that whole weight loss, going all weird on the missus, that was—?"

"A transition process. It's not like they show in the movies, you know. Takes weeks. The whole metabolism changes."

"No kidding."

One of the vampires faked a lunge to psyche me out and I jumped a foot in the air. I'm pretty sure I didn't yelp like a Chihuahua, but I wouldn't swear to that in court. They all laughed at that, too. I didn't.

"Which explains why you lost all that weight."

"Who needs steroids and free-weights," he agreed and spread his hands. "This package comes with honest to God super strength. I'm like Spider-Man and Wolverine rolled into one. Super strong and I heal from damn near anything."

"Could you be more specific on that last point?"

"Cute."

"Worth a try." I looked at them, at their grinning, evil faces. My nuts were trying to crawl up inside of my chest cavity. I mean...*fucking vampires?*

"Weird thing was," I said, "I was starting to build a case in my head about your wife. You losing weight and getting pale, blaming her for it all, saying you know what she is...is she a vampire, too? Is she the one who bit you?"

Skye laughed. "Christ, no. And she's not a succubus either. She's just a nagging, soul-draining, passive-aggressive codependent bitch."

"Wow. You're really a chauvinistic prick, aren't you?"

"Better than being pussy whipped."

I dropped it. I had bigger fish to fry than trying to bring this macho jackass into the twenty-first century. Namely the fact that I was in a roomful of vampires.

I know I keep harping on that, but really...it's not the sort of shit that happens all the time to me. Or, like...*ever.*

"Say, man," I said to Skye, "any chance we can roll back this tape to the point where we were still friends? I just walk out of here and we all call it a day?"

Skye made a face as if pretending to consider it. "Mmm...no, I don't see that happening."

"You want to make a deal of some kind?"

"Nah," he said. "You got nothing I want. Except the O-positive."

"AB neg," I corrected.

"Never tried that."

"You wouldn't like it. Goes right to your hips."

The wattage on his smile was dimmer. Jaunty banter can buy only so many seconds and then it's back to business.

I tried to keep my face neutral, but my pulse was like a jazz drum solo.

"I'm going to throw something out here," I said. I could hear a tremor in my voice. Fuck it.

"Oh, please." He gestured to the four killers and they started forward.

"Wait! Just hear me out. What have you got to lose?"

The thugs looked at Skye. West gave a 'why not?' kind of shrug.

Skye sighed. "Okay, what is it? Last words? A little begging?" he suggested.

"Mm, more like last threat."

"This I got to hear."

The five of them looked genuinely interested.

"Okay, so here you are, five vampires. That's some really scary shit, am I right? I mean creatures of the night and all that."

He nodded, nothing to disagree with.

"To most people that's enough to make them go apeshit crazy. I mean…vampires. Not your everyday thing. It opens up all kinds of metaphysical questions. If vampires exist, what *else* does? If there are supernatural monsters, does that mean God and the Devil are real? You follow me?"

"Sure. We get that a lot."

"And I'm outnumbered here. Five to one. Tough odds without you fellows being the undead. So…why ain't I scared?"

His eyes narrowed.

"I mean, yeah, my pulse is racing and I'm sweating. But do I look as scared as I should be? I don't, do I? Now…why is that?"

"So you put up a good front. It'll be a good anecdote later," he said. "For us."

"Maybe he's got a hammer and stake," suggested West.

That got a laugh.

"Nope."

My heart rate had to be close to two hundred. It was machine gun fire in my chest.

"Coupla garlic bulbs in your pocket?" asked East.

"Nah. I don't even like it on my pizza."

"You don't have any backup," said North. "And you don't got your gun."

My blood pressure could have scalded paint off a battleship. I wiped sweat off my brow with my thumb.

"Okay, jokes over," snapped Skye. "What's the punch line here? Why aren't you as scared as you should be?"

I smiled.

"I'll show you."

The first time it happened, way back when I was thirteen, it took almost half an hour. I screamed and cried and rolled around on the floor. First time's always the hardest. Each time since it was easier. My grandmother and her sister could do it in the time it took you to snap your fingers. My best time was during a foot chase back when I was with Minneapolis PD. I was running down the guy who'd beaten his wife with the extension cord. He saw me coming and ducked into his apartment, I kicked the door and he came out of the bedroom with a gun and opened up. I went through the change in the time it took me to leap through the doorway. Like the snap of my fingers. One minute me, next minute *different* me.

I tore the shit out of him. I lost my badge and pension and had to make up all sorts of excuses. On the plus side, I didn't die, which *would* have happened if I hadn't managed the change so fast. I'm only mortal when I look like one.

That night in Skye's office wasn't my best time. Maybe third or fourth best. Say, two, three seconds. It felt like an explosion. It hurts. Feels like my heart is bursting, like cherry bombs are detonating inside my muscles. It starts in the chest, then ripples out from there as muscle mass changes and is reassigned in new ways. Bones warp, crack and re-form. Nails tear through the flesh of my fingers and toes, my jaw shifts and the longer teeth spike through the gums. It's bloody and it's ugly and it hurts like a motherfucker.

But the end result is a stunner. A real kick-ass dramatic moment that wows the audience.

I think all four of the thugs screamed. They jerked back from me, looks of shock and horror on their faces. If I wasn't so deeply into the moment I would have smiled at the irony. Monsters being scared by a monster.

I crouched in the center of the room, hands flexing, claws streaked with blood, hot saliva dripping from my mouth onto my chest.

It would have been cool and dramatic to have said "Surprise!" to them the way Skye had said it to me, but my mouth was no longer constructed for human speech. All I could do was roar.

I did.

And then I launched at them.

Vampires are strong. Four or five times stronger than an ordinary human.

Werewolves?

Hell, we're a whole different class.

I slammed into West with both sets of front claws. He flew apart like he was made of paper and watery red glue. North and East tried to take me high and low, but they'd have done better to try and run. I brought my knee up into East's jaw as he went for the low tackle and his head burst like a casaba melon. I caught North by the throat and squeezed. Red geysered up from the stump of his neck as his head fell away. South backed away, putting himself between me and Skye, arms spread, making a more heroic stand than I'd have thought. I tore the heart from his chest. Turns out, vampires *need* their hearts.

Skye had my gun in his hands. He racked the slide and buried the barrel against me as I leaped over the desk. He got off four shots. They hurt.

Like wasp stings.

Maybe a little less.

I don't load my piece with silver bullets. I'm not an idiot.

He looked into my eyes and I would like to think that he saw the error of his ways. Don't fuck with the innocent. Don't fuck with my clients. My clients are *mine*, like members of my pack. Mess with them and the pack leader has to put you down. Has to.

So I did.

-3-

She saw me coming from across the street, her face concerned and confused. I was wearing a different pair of pants and different shoes. My own had been torn to rags during the change. Stuff I was wearing used to belong to the bartender. He didn't need them anymore. He'd been on the same team as Skye and the four goons.

I opened the door and climbed in behind the wheel.

"Are you all right, Sam?" she asked, studying my face. "Are you hurt? Is that blood?"

I dabbed at a dot on my cheek. Missed a spot. I pulled a tissue out of my jacket pocket and wiped my cheek.

"Just ketchup," I said.

"You stopped for *food*?" she demanded, eyes wide.

"It was on the house. I was hungry. No biggie."

She stared at me and then looked at the club across the street. The snow was getting heavier, the ground was white and it was starting to coat the street.

"What happened in there?"

I put the key into the ignition.

"I had a long talk with your ex. I told him that you were feeling threatened and uncomfortable with his actions, and asked him to back off."

"What did he say?"

"He won't be bothering you anymore."

"Just like that? He agreed to leave me alone just like that?" She snapped her fingers.

"More or less. I told him that I had some friends on the force and in L and I, and made it clear that I could make his life *more* uncomfortable than he was making yours. He didn't like it," I said, "but..." I let the rest hang.

"And he *agreed*?"

"Take my word for it. He's out of your life."

She continued to study me for several long seconds. I waited her out and I saw the moment when she shifted from doubt and fear to belief and acceptance. She closed her eyes, sagged back against the seat, put her face in her hands and began to cry.

I gripped the wheel and looked out at the falling snow, hiding the smile that kept trying to creep onto my mouth. I was digging the P.I. business. Fewer rules than when I was on the cops. It allowed me to be closer to the street, to go hunting deeper into the forest.

Even so—and despite what I'd said to Skye—I *was* pretty rattled that he'd been a vampire. I mean, being who and what I am I always suspected other things were out there in the dark, but until now I'd never met them. Now I knew. How many vampires were there? *Where* were they? Would they be coming for me?

I didn't have any of those answers. Not yet.

I also wondered what *else* was out there? I could feel the excitement racing through me. I wanted to find out. Good or bad, I wanted to find out.

I reached out a hand and patted Mrs. Skye's trembling shoulder. It felt good to know that one of the pack was safe now. It felt right. It made me feel powerful and satisfied on a lot of different levels. I knew that I was going to want to feel this way again. And again.

The snow swirled inside the thickening shadows.

Inside my head the wolf howled.

Strip Search

A Limbus, Inc. Adventure

-1-

The card was on the floor. I kicked it when I opened the door.

Not the first time somebody slipped something under my office door. At least this time it wasn't a threat, a fuck-you letter from a girl, a summons, or an eviction notice. Been getting way too many of each of those lately. Economically-speaking, this year sucks moose dick.

This was just a business card. It looked crisp and expensive. The kind lawyers sometimes use.

I have three ex-wives, so I left it there. I do not want to hear from another lawyer. Sure, maybe if there was an estate attorney trying to find me to tell me I'd just inherited a mansion and a vault filled with gold bars. But, since the odds on that were on a par with me getting laid this week, I didn't bother picking up the card.

Instead I went through the ritual. I closed my office door, flopped into the piece o' crap faux leather chair, sorted through the mail for job offers or checks from satisfied clients, found none of that shit, listened to my answering machine, didn't hear a thing worth listening to, opened my laptop and checked my agency email, didn't find anything except a Nigerian prince who wanted to transfer thirty million into my account and an ad for the latest dick pills. Same shit, different day.

I had a mildly masochistic urge to log into my bank account to see how much I had left, but I drank beers until I came to my senses.

Outside it was the kind of spring day that Philadelphia gets a lot of but doesn't deserve. Maxfield Parrish blue skies, a few sculpted white clouds, temperature in the mid-seventies, and low humidity. The city was pretending to be San Diego, and it fooled a lot of tourists, but only those who weren't here in the summer, when the humidity and the temperature jump into the low nineties and refuse to fucking budge. For months. I sometimes think the real reason the Founding Fathers started the Revolution was because they were hot and cranky. When Philly summers really start to cook even a Buddhist monk would lock and load and go looking for someone to shoot.

But it was May tenth.

The day was beautiful. I had windows open and the breeze was perfect.

I sat there, sipping a Yuengling and looking at the door, trying to will it to open at the touch of a client with an expensive job.

Nothing.

I was four beers in and the door still remained closed.

I sighed.

I looked around. I run a one-man investigation office. Industrial, domestic, whatever. I'll look for Hoffa if there's a paycheck in it. I have a secretary who works on a per diem. Right now there was nothing to type or file, so she was at home with a dozen cats and her skewed perception of reality.

I saw the card on the floor. Yup, still there.

Another beer came and went.

The card was still there.

I would have knocked back a sixth but I didn't have one. The only thing left in my little cube fridge was a three week old yogurt that was evolving into a new life form.

That was the only reason I got up to get the card. Boredom and no beer.

Funny how things start.

I bent and picked it up.

Frowned at it.

On the front, printed in black on cream stock, raised lettering.

LIMBUS, Inc.
Are you laid off, downsized, undersized?
Call us. We employ. 1-800-555-0606
How lucky do you feel?

"Balls," I said. I've seen this sort of thing before. Sometimes it's an ad for low-end commission work-at-home crap. Cold calls to sell products people wouldn't want even if it was free. Follow-up calls for people dumb enough to put their email addresses down at a restaurant, hotel or resort. Or time-share pitches. Stuff like that.

If that was what it was.

I turned it over. There was a hand-written note on the back. That was different. Most of these kinds of cards are just the basics. A hook, no real information, and a contact number.

With the 'How lucky do you feel?' thing I wondered if this was a new marketing scheme for second-string call girls.

I'm horny, but I haven't ever been so horny I wanted to pay for ass.

The note on the back said:

2:45, your office.

I looked at the wall clock.

2:43.

Shit.

There was still time to pull the shade, lock the door and turn off the office lights. I wanted a client, not some yuppie entrepreneur trying to see some college-girl tail.

But then I caught a whiff of something.

Literally a whiff. I put the card to my nose and sniffed it.

The odor was very faint, but it was there. Just a hint of it. Like freshly-sheared copper.

The smell of blood.

Human blood, too. And, yes, I can tell the difference. Some people can do that with wine or truffles or chocolate. Me, I can tell you anything you want to know about blood. Other things, too, but in my trade it really matters that I can tell a lot from a little noseful of blood-smell.

Thing is, there was no stain anywhere on the card. Not a drop, not a smudge. Nothing.

Smell was definitely there, though.

I put the card against my nose and took a longer, slower sniff.

There's so much you can tell if you have the knack. My whole family has the knack. My grandmother, Minnie, is best at it. She can tell blood type. I may not be in her league—and really, no one is, old broad or not—but I could tell a lot. If I ever sniffed that blood again I'd know who owned it. Better than fingerprints for me. Back when I was a cop in the Twin Cities I closed a shitload of cases that way. Finding the right perp was the easy part for me. Finding evidence that tied him to the case was harder. Sometimes it was impossible, which frustrated the living shit out of me. Nothing worse than knowing someone did something bad and then having to watch him skate through the courts back onto the street with a free pass to hurt someone else.

Most of the time.

A few of those guys tripped and hurt themselves. Or, um, so I heard.

I tapped the card against my chin, thinking about it. What kind of marketing stunt was this? What kind of—?

Out in the hall I heard the elevator open.

The wall clock told me it was 2:44.

"Early," I said.

But as soon as the visitor knocked on the door the clock ticked over to 2:45. The exact second.

-2-

I went around and sat behind my desk before I said anything. I let the seconds tick all the way to 2:46. Just to be pissy.

The person outside didn't knock again. But I saw a figure through the frosted glass. Tall, dressed in some kind of suit, and definitely female. Her silhouette was rocking.

With my luck, though, she'd have the right curves but a face like Voldemort.

"Come in," I yelled.

The door opened.

She came in.

I actually said, "Holy shit."

She had the kind of face that you read about. The kind of face that if it looked down at you from a movie screen you'd absolutely believe you were on your knees in the Temple of Athena. The kind of face Hollywood women pay a lot of money for and never quite get. You're either born with that face or you spend your life in therapy because it's just not going to happen.

That kind of face.

Pale skin with pores so small it looked like she was carved out of marble. Not white marble, though. She had some natural color that I'm pretty sure wasn't a tan. Couldn't peg her race or nationality. Maybe she was from the same island Wonder Woman came from. I don't know. I never visited that island. I knew right there that I couldn't have afforded the boat fare.

She was maybe thirty, about five-eight. Tall, with good bones and great posture, and enough curves to make my hair sweat, but not so many that it walked over the line into cartoonish. That's a very delicate line. Her hair was a foamy spill of black with some faint red highlights. Her lips were full and painted a discreet dark red. Make-up applied with skill and restraint. Pearl earrings, a drop-pearl necklace that rested half inch above the point where her cleavage stopped. Yes, I looked.

The only flaw—if you could call it that—was a small crescent-shaped scar on her cheek near the left corner of her mouth. If she was a different kind of woman I'd think that it was the kind of scar you can get when someone wearing a ring pops you one. But I couldn't sell that story to myself. This was a class act. But, I like scars. They're evidence that a person's lived.

She said, "Mr. Hunter?"

"Sam Hunter," I said, rising and offering my hand.

Her grip was cool and dry, but she withdrew her hand a half-second too quickly. Maybe she was afraid I hadn't washed. Not an unrealistic thought. I suddenly felt grubby.

I gave her an expectant smile, waiting for her name, but she didn't give it. Some clients are like that. Either they like being mysterious or they have to be careful. A lot of them hedge because they seem to think that if they withhold their names it somehow distances them from whatever problem brought them here. Nobody comes looking for a guy like me unless they've stepped in something. A bear trap, a pile of shit. Something.

"Have a seat," I said, gesturing to the better of my crappy visitor chairs. She sat and smoothed her skirt over her knees. She wore a charcoal jacket that had a pale blue chalk stripe that precisely matched the color of her silk blouse. Her skirt matched her jacket. Her shoes looked more expensive than my car, and probably were.

She sat there and studied me for a long time without speaking.

So, apparently the ball was in my court. Fine. I tossed the card onto the desk between us.

"Yours?"

"Ours," she corrected.

She waited for me to ask, but I didn't. I couldn't tell from the mouth she made if that was a good move on my part or not. She was clearly evaluating me, but I didn't know what kind of yardstick she was using. So I leaned back in my chair and waited.

After a while she gave a single, short nod and said, "We want to hire you."

She leaned on the 'we,' so I guess I was supposed to ask.

"We being…?"

"The Limbus Corporation."

"Who are they?"

"That's not really—"

"No," I said.

"Pardon?"

"You're going to tell me that it's not really important. It's a cheap answer to a question that actually *is* important. You left a card with the company name. You're here as a representative of that company. That puts the company into play. So…who or what is Limbus, Inc?"

She gave me a few millimeters of a smile, but she didn't answer the question. Instead she opened her purse—an actual Louis Vuitton that would have paid off my mortgage—and removed two items. One was a standard-sized envelope with a thick bulge in it that was exactly the right size and shape to make me want to wag my tail. She placed that on the desk and held up the second item. A plain black flash drive.

"Will you agree to help us in this matter?" she asked.

I blinked a couple of times before I said, "Is that a serious question?"

"It is."

"You haven't told me anything yet."

"I know."

"And yet you want to know if I'll 'help'?"

"Yes."

"This isn't how it works."

"This is how it works with us."

"With Limbus?"

"Yes," she agreed.

I drummed my fingers on the desk top. "You have your own car or should I call you a cab?"

The smile widened. Just a little tiny bit. But she didn't answer. She wiggled the flash drive back and forth between her fingers.

I sucked my teeth. "What's on it?"

Instead of answering she handed it over.

I hesitated for a moment before accepting it, but figured what the hell. This would be the world's most absurd set-up for someone trying to infect my computer with a virus. Maybe the flash drive had photos of girls and this broad was a very charming pimp. Or maybe the Jehovah's Witnesses were going high-tech and this was the latest issue of the Watchtower in eBook format.

I took the drive.

Something really weird happened when I did, though. Flash drives are small so it's not unusual for fingers to touch when giving and receiving. When my fingertips brushed the edges of her painted nails, there was a shock as sharp and unexpected as an electric shock. Like the little snap of electricity you get on cold days when you touch a doorknob. I could even hear the crack in the air as the energy arced from her to me.

I snatched my hand back.

She didn't.

She withdrew it slowly, smiling that cat smile of hers. There was an opportunity to make some kind of joke about how shocking it all was, yada yada, but it would have been lame. She wasn't a chatty, laugh-a-minute kind of gal. She also wasn't the kind to waste a lot of her time in idle chitchat.

So, I plugged the flash drive into my laptop, located the device, accessed the menu and saw that there was one Word document and sixteen image files. Jpegs.

"Open the pictures," she suggested.

I selected all of them and hit the preview function.

My computer's preview function acts like a slideshow unless I hit a key to give me static images. By the time the first image popped up I forgot about the keys. I forgot about pretty much everything.

The picture was high-definition and tightly focused. No blur to soften any of the edges. No grain to reduce the impact.

It was a girl.

Or, at least it was girl-shaped.

She lay in the open mouth of a grungy alley, her body partially covered by dirty newspapers. Her mouth was wide open, the lips stretched as far as they could go, tongue lolling, teeth biting into the scream that must have been her last. The scream that was stamped now onto the muscles of her face.

Muscles, I said. Not skin.

She had no skin.

Not on her face.

Not on her body.

Not anywhere.

. Not an inch of it.

The image vanished to be replaced by another girl.

Different girl, and I could tell that only by location—this one had been spilled out of a black plastic industrial trash bag—and by size. She was bigger, taller and bigger in the breasts and hips.

But that was the only way to tell the difference. All other individuality—skin tone and color, scars and tattoos, marks and moles—had been sliced away. All I saw was veined meat.

Another image. Another girl.

Another.

Another.

Another.

Sixteen.

The slideshow ground on mercilessly and I was absolutely unable to move a finger to stop it. The images flicked across my laptop screen. Sixteen young women. At least, I think they were young. Somehow I *knew* they were young.

All dead.

All stripped of more than flesh. Someone had torn away their lives, their individuality and their dignity along with their flesh.

When I raised my head to look over the laptop at her, there must have been something in my eyes because her smile vanished and she physically shrank back from me. Not a lot, but a bit.

"What the fuck is this?" I asked, and I barely recognized my own voice.

The woman cleared her throat, licked her lips, smoothed her skirt again. Rebuilding her calm façade.

"Beyond the obvious—the murder and mutilation of young women—we don't know what it is."

"A serial killer?"

"So it would appear. Sixteen dead girls over a period of roughly sixteen months."

"This isn't happening here in Philly," I said. "I'd have heard something."

"The first girl was found in Seattle. Felicia Skye, seventeen," she said. "Other bodies have been found in nine cities in five states. All girls ranging in age from sixteen to eighteen. They're all runaways, and all of them have worked as prostitutes. Eight have also worked as exotic dancers."

"Strip clubs don't hire kids."

"Anyone can get a false I.D., Mr. Hunter," she said coldly. "You know that."

I pointed at the screen. "Where's this shit happening?"

"The most recent—the sixteenth—was found in a storm drain in New York."

"When?"

"Twenty-six days ago."

"It wasn't in the papers."

"No."

"Why not?"

She took a moment on that. "We don't know. None of these have been in the media. Not one."

"That's impossible. Murders like this are front page."

She nodded. "They should be. This should be all over social media and Internet news, but it's not."

"That doesn't make any sense. If *you* know about it and you want something done, then why don't you take this to the press?"

Another pause. "We have."

"And—?"

"We've contacted six separate reporters in six cities. All six have died."

"Died?"

"Three heart attacks, one stroke, one fatal epileptic seizure, one burned to death after smoking in bed."

I stared at her. "You're shitting me."

"I'm not."

"What about the Feds? If this is happening across the country, then the FBI should—"

"They are investigating it. But they've had some problems of their own with the case. The lead agent fell down a flight of stairs and broke his neck. Freak accident. His replacement was killed in a car accident when an ambulance ran a red light. That sort of thing. The investigation is ongoing but agents have been shying away from it. They think it's jinxed."

That didn't surprise me. Even this deep into the 21st century there was a lot of superstition. Everyone has it—from people who knock wood to baseball players who have to wear their lucky socks. Cops have it in spades, just like soldiers, just like anyone whose day job involves real life and death stuff. When I was on the cops back in Minnesota I heard about several jinxed cases. No one wants to say it out loud because of how it sounds, but people still fear the boogeyman.

I got up and crossed to my file cabinet, opened the bottom drawer, and took out the only bottle of really good booze I owned – an unopened bottle of Pappy Van Winkle's 23-Year-Old bourbon. At two-hundred and fifty dollars a bottle it was way out of my price range, but a satisfied client had given it to me last Christmas. I brought it and two clean glasses back to my desk, and the woman watched while I opened the bottle and poured two fingers for each of us. I didn't ask if she drank. She didn't tell me to stop pouring.

I sat down and we each had some. We didn't toast. You don't toast for stuff like this.

The bourbon was legendary. I'd read all about it. It's aged in charred white oak barrels. Sweet, smooth, with a complex mix of honey and toffee flavors.

It might as well have been Gatorade for all I could tell. I drank it because my laptop was still fanning through the images. And because of that, even if I didn't take this case, those dead women were going to live inside my head for the rest of my life. You can forget some things. Other things take up residence, building themselves into the stone and wood and plaster of the structure of your mind.

I suppose if I was capable of dismissing this, or forgetting it, then I wouldn't be who I am. Maybe I'd be happier, I don't know.

I closed the laptop, finished the bourbon and set my cup down.

"What do you want from me?" I asked.

The woman opened her purse again and removed another envelope. She placed it on the desk and slid it across to me. When I opened I could see the glossy border of a photograph. I hesitated, not wanting to see another mutilated girl. But I was already in motion in this, so I sucked it up and slid the photo out of the envelope.

It was another girl.

This one had her skin.

She was a beautiful teenager, with bright blue eyes and a lot of curves that were evident in the skimpy costume she wore. A blue glitter g-string and high heels.

"Her name is Denise Sturbridge," said the woman. "She's only fifteen, which makes her the youngest of the women in question, but as you can see she looks quite a bit older. She's a runaway from Easton here in Pennsylvania. Abusive father, indifferent mother. Pretty common story, and very much in keeping with the backstories of the other girls. She took off four months ago, got picked up by the kind of predator who trolls bus stops and train stations. He got her high and turned her out to work conventions. She was scouted out of there to work in a gentleman's club near the Philadelphia airport. Fake I.D. that says she's nineteen. She dances under the name of Bambi."

I set the photo down.

"Tell me the rest," I said.

"She went missing two days ago. We believe that she will be number seventeen."

"That's a big leap. A lot of girls go missing."

She nodded. "She fits a type."

I glanced at the closed laptop and the black flash drive. "So the killer is targeting exotic dancers."

"Yes."

"And he's been on the move from Seattle, across the country. Now you think he's here."

"Yes. And there's not much time."

I cocked my head. "Now how the hell would you know that?"

"Because it's been four-hundred and seventy-five days since the first girl died. The coroner in Seattle was able to determine the day she died. We think Bambi will be murdered in the next twenty-four hours."

"How do you figure that?"

"Do the math, Mr. Hunter."

I did.

Didn't need a calculator, either. It was simple arithmetic. Add a day to the span of the killings and divide by seventeen.

I could feel my blood turn to ice.

"Oh shit," I said.

She studied me with her dark eyes and I could see the moment when she knew that I knew that *she* knew. Chain of logic, none of it said aloud.

Seventeen murders. One every twenty-eight days.

A cycle.

Sure.

But a very specific *kind* of cycle. She gave me a small nod.

I didn't need to look at the calendar. Not for the next kill and not for any of the kills before that. The pattern screamed at me.

She slid the first envelope across the desk. "Fee and expenses," she said.

I didn't touch it, didn't look at it. I stared down into the smiling eyes of a girl pretending to be a woman who was a couple of days away from becoming a red horror someone would dump in an alley.

Maybe tomorrow.

"We want you to find this girl," she said.

I said nothing.

"There's a Word document on the drive that has a complete copy of the case file. Police and FBI reports. Coroner's report, lab reports. Everything."

I didn't ask her how she'd obtained all of that.

"What if I can't find her in time?"

The woman shook her head. "Then find who's doing this before there's a victim eighteen. This isn't going to stop, Mr. Hunter. Not unless someone stops it."

"The last kill was in New York. This is Philly. I wouldn't know where to start."

She reached across and picked up the business card I'd found on the floor and held it out to me. "This should help."

I didn't touch it. Didn't have to. I could still smell it. I could still smell the blood.

But now I understood.

The woman stood up.

This was the point where I should have asked 'Why me?' With all of the other cops and private investigators out there, why me?

We both knew that I wasn't going to ask that question. We both knew why me.

Twenty eight days.

I didn't stand up, didn't shake her hand, didn't walk her to the door. Didn't tell her whether I was going to take the case.

We both knew the answer to that, too.

"I haven't said that I'm taking the case," I said.

She flicked a glance at the envelope, then shrugged. "You will if you want to, and you won't if you don't. Our policy is to encourage, not to compel."

"Your policy. You still haven't told me who you are. I mean, what's your interest? What's this Limbus thing and why do you people care?"

No answer to that.

"Okay," I said, "tell me this. The reporters who died. The heart attacks and strokes and stuff. You think any of that was legit?"

"Do you?"

"Was there any investigation?"

"Routine, in all cases. No one connected the cases because there was no evidence of foul play."

"Anyone do autopsies on the reporters who croaked?"

"On heart attacks? No. None of the victims were autopsied except for the man who burned to death, and that was ruled death by misadventure."

"And the stuff that happened to the feds looking into it?"

"As I said, this has become known as a bad luck case."

"Do you believe in bad luck?" I asked.

She gave me a smile that lifted the crescent scar beside her mouth. "We believe in quite a lot of things, Mr. Hunter."

With that she turned, walked out and pulled the door shut behind her.

-4-

I sat there and stared at the closed door for maybe ten minutes. I don't think I did anything except blink and breathe the whole time.

Twenty-eight days.

Bodies torn apart.

I picked up the card and sniffed the blood again. Deeply. Eyes closed. Letting the scent go all the way into my lungs, all the way into my senses. I took another breath, and another. Then I put the card down. I wouldn't need it anymore. That scent was locked into me now. I'd know it anywhere.

Interesting that this broad knew that about me.

We believe in quite a lot of things, Mr. Hunter.

"Shit," I told the empty room.

I glanced at the envelope. Even if it was filled with small bills, fives and tens, it had to be a couple of hundred. I guessed, though, that the denominations were higher. If it was twenties and fifties, then there were thousands in there. It was a fat envelope.

It sat there and I didn't pick it up. Didn't really want to touch it.

Not yet.

I had this thing. If I took the money then I was definitely going to take the case.

Then I opened my laptop, accessed the Word document, and began reading. While I did that I tried not to look at the big calendar pinned to the wall by the filing cabinet. It was this year's Minnesota Vikings calendar. I liked the Vikings but I didn't give much of a warm shit as to who was featured on this month's page. Or any month. The calendar's only important feature was a set of small icons that showed the phases of the moon.

Twenty eight days.

One day to go.

One day for little Bambi.

A single day until the killer took her skin and her life and emptied her of her dreams and hopes and breath and smiles and life.

A day.

One day until the next full moon.

In my blood and under my skin I could already *feel* the moon pulling at me. Tearing, clawing.

Screaming at me.

Howling at me.

-5-

When you don't have a clue you start at the beginning and see if you can pick up the scent. For most guys in my line of work that's a metaphor. Guess I'm a little different.

The case file for Bambi—Denise Sturbridge—said that she worked four shifts a week at a strip-club called *ViXXXens* in Northeast Philly. A quick Google search told me that the place was owned by Dante Entertainment and managed by one George Palakas.

I live in Old City near Front and South, so it was an easy trip up I-95. I got off at Grant Avenue, cut across to Bustleton Avenue and followed that to within half a block of the northeastern-most city limits. Couldn't miss the club. The sign was massive, with a neon silhouette of an improbably endowed woman winking on and off in blue and pink. Beneath the sign squatted an ugly three-story building that looked like it might have been built in Colonial times. Who knows, maybe Washington even slept there. But that was then. Now it crouched in embarrassment. Whitewashed plank siding, smoked windows blocked by beer signs, twenty or thirty cars in the parking lot, and bass notes shuddering along the ground from speakers that were way too powerful for the size of the building.

I parked near a pair of Harleys and got out.

I've been in a hundred places like this. As a cop, as a P.I. Once, when I was in high school, as a patron. Sure, I'm a healthy straight guy, but I'm not the demographic for joints like this. It's not an economic thing or a class thing or even an education thing. I think it comes down to personal awareness. It's hard to sit on a stool, drinking beer after beer, watching a woman you don't know and can't touch gyrate and take off her clothes to bad dance pop, when everyone else is doing the same thing. None of it's really for you. It's for your beer money and tip money. It's about you bringing your friends so they can spend their money. It's about you becoming a regular so you contribute to the profit of both dancer and club. But it lacks anything of true human connection. You aren't friends with the friendly bartenders and you won't have sex with the sexy dancers. You're an open wallet.

So who goes to places like these? Like I said, it's not a class of men. Even before I entered I knew that there would be guys in construction worker boots and denims, and guys in good business suits. There would be married guys and single guys. There would be college grads and high school drop outs. There would be white, black, Asian and Latino guys. What there wouldn't be would be very many guys who were genuinely happy in their lives. The ones who were, probably only came here with buddies. More for their friends than for the silicone tits and painted mouths up on stage. Or guys coming here for their first *legal* drinks, surrounded by fathers, uncles, friends; a big shit-eating grin stapled onto their faces to hide their actual embarrassment.

The rest?

You couldn't even call them lost and lonely. A lot of them aren't. But they're missing something. Some connection, or maybe some optimism. Whatever it is, they either came here looking for a thread of it, or because they gave up looking and the music here was too loud for introspection and self-evaluation.

I drew in a breath through my nostrils, held it, let it out, and went inside.

It was two o'clock in the afternoon and the place was already three-quarters full. Too early for a bouncer, so there was no cover and no hassle. The bar was a big oblong with seats all the way around it and two small square stages inside, intercut by a bank of cash registers and liquor shelves. A dozen beer taps, but none of them were for good beers. Their top brand was Heineken, which was a short step up from dog piss, and Budweiser which was a full step down. No Tröegs, no good local microbrews. You didn't come here to sample a good beer. You came here to drink a lot of beers quickly and cheaply so that you didn't feel weird tucking part of your paycheck into a girl's g-string for no god damn good reason at all.

There were two dancers working the afternoon shift. The one closest to the door was probably pushing forty but she'd had a lot of work done and kept her muscles toned. My guess was that she was a single mother with no college and shaking her ass earned her more cash—particularly unreportable cash—than asking drive-through customers if they wanted their Happy Meal giant-sized. Her eyes flicked around, looking for the kind of guy who would pony up a buck just to have her come closer, or the kind of guy who would toss her a buck to make her go away. There were plenty of both. When her eyes briefly met mine she got no signal that she could use and her gaze swept on. A rotating spot swept across her face and I could see some old acne scars that were nearly buried under lots of pancake. Not a pretty woman, but probably not a junkie or a hooker. Someone willing to do this to put food in her kids' mouths and make as good a life for them as she could.

I moved on and took a seat between the two stages.

The second dancer was half the age of the first. She'd be skinny if it wasn't for plastic boobs and a decent ass. Sticks for arms and legs that had shape only because of high heels and patterned stockings. She wore a red thong and flesh-colored pasties over her nipples. And although she had a pretty face, she was about as sexy as root canal. At least to me, but like I said, I'm not the demographic.

The bartender drifted up and used a single uptick of his chin to ask what I wanted.

I ordered a vodka martini with three olives just to see what kind of expression it put on his face. His face turned to wood.

"Bud," I said, and he curled just enough of his lip to let me know that he appreciated the joke. He drew a Budweiser and slid a mug in front of me. I put a twenty on the bar and tapped it to let him know I was starting a tab on it. He nodded and moved away.

The song that was playing was so gratingly loud that it could sterilize an elk. The lyrics were meaningless pap. Something about 'high school charms,' which gave it all a pedophile vibe.

The other patrons were staring at the dancers. The music was too loud for conversation. One guy was playing video poker and eating fistfuls of beer nuts without looking at them. Two guys in dark suits sat at the far end drinking dark mixed drinks that I'm pretty sure were actually Coke in highball glasses. I marked them in my mind. Strip clubs don't let you sit there and drink soda, which means that these guys were either part of the staff—off-shift bouncers, maybe— or they were friends of the house. I saw them watching me as I watched them. One of them gave me a nod and I nodded back. That's not a friendly exchange, not in places like this. It's one player letting the other player know that they're all in the game.

When the record changed, I left the beer and the twenty as placeholders, turned slowly on my stool until I spotted the entrance to the back rooms. I headed that way, and a short hall took me past employee restrooms, a store room, a fire door, all the way to a door marked OFFICE.

I knocked.

The man who opened the door was a burly forty-something, probably Greek face with a bald head, Popeye forearms, a thick mustache and wary eyes. He gave me a quick up and down and apparently decided I wasn't a cop or someone from L and I. I was dressed in jeans and a Vikings windbreaker over an Everlast tank top. Cops and license inspectors all dress better than me.

"George Palakas?" I asked.

"What if I am?" he demanded, unimpressed.

"Need to talk to you."

Palakas narrowed his eyes. "About what?"

"I'm looking for Denise Sturbridge."

The manager gave me a slow three-count of silent appraisal, then he said, "No." He turned away and started to close his door.

I got a foot out and blocked it. The edge of the door hit the outside sole of my Payless running shoes and rebounded.

Palakas wheeled on me. "Yo, asshole," he growled. "The fuck you think you're doing?"

"I told you," I said mildly, smiling.

"Get your ass out of here before I have you—"

I shoved him. Quick and light, but it caught him off guard and sent him running backward into his office. His ass hit the edge of the desk, the impact spun him and he fell onto the floor, dragging a desk-light and a coffee cup full of pencils with him. He landed on his knees hard enough to make me wince. The lamp and coffee cup shattered.

I closed the door and leaned my back against it.

Palakas looked up at me. His knees had to hurt and his face was turning from a fake tan to brick red.

"You stupid motherfucker," he whispered through teeth that ground together between curled lips. "I'm going to—"

"No," I said, "you're not. Stop trying to scare me to death."

He cursed some more.

I kept smiling.

When Palakas paused for a breath I said, "You hired a fifteen year old girl to strip in your club. We could start there and see how fast I could get you shut down."

"Bullshit," he said, but suddenly his voice lacked emphasis.

"Right now that's all that I know she did here. It's enough for me not to want to take any shit from you."

"Who's she to you?" he asked as he got heavily to his feet.

I shrugged. "Maybe I'm her father."

He actually laughed. "Her old man's a methed-out schizo up in Easton."

"Then maybe I'm her brother."

"She doesn't have a brother."

There was a pack of gum in my pocket. I took it out and popped a couple of pieces out of the aluminum blister pack, put them into my mouth, crunched through the candy coating and chewed the gum. Palakas watched me do all this.

I said, "Does it really matter who I am?"

"It's going to matter when I—"

"I already told you, stop trying to scare me. I want to have a conversation with you and I really don't want to have to wade through a bunch of lines cribbed from old Sopranos reruns. I'm going to ask you some questions. You're going to answer my questions. If I'm satisfied with the answers then I'm done and you can forget I was ever here."

"Why should I tell you a god damn thing?"

"Ah," I said, "this is the part where *I* threaten *you*. You see, if you don't tell me what I want, or if I don't like what you tell me, then I will kick a two-by-four so far up your ass you'll be spitting toothpicks."

"Think you could?"

"We can find out," I said mildly. "And afterward we can have this conversation while we're waiting for the paramedics."

Palakas tried a sneer on me. It was supposed to look fearless and defiant, but this wasn't a movie and he knew that if I was telling him I could hurt him then that's how it would play out. Even if he had my legs broken later on, it wouldn't stop him from taking the full weight now and very few people want to play it that way. Besides, the door was closed and I think he was actually curious.

"The fuck you want to know?" he said, playing it out, though. That was okay. He could posture all he wanted as long as he talked. What he didn't know was that I could smell his fear. Beneath the deodorant, the residual smell of his soap—Ivory, I think—and his cologne—Axe—I could smell the fear stink.

"Denise Sturbridge," I reminded him.

"Bambi. Yeah, so what? What about her?" He stepped over the debris on the floor and sat down behind his desk. I came and stood close to him and we both knew that it was because I wanted to make sure he didn't get cute and pull anything unfortunate from a desk drawer. Small office. Even with a loaded gun I could get to him before he could take a shot. We both knew that.

"I'm looking for her."

"She's not here."

"I know that, numb-nuts. That's what 'looking for her' means. If she was here I'd have already found her." I tapped him on the forehead with my index finger. "I want you to tell me where she is."

Palakas gave a half-hearted swipe at my hand. "How should I know?"

"She works for you?" I suggested.

"No she don't. She missed three shifts in a row. That's her ass as far as I'm concerned."

"You're saying she's missing?"

"I'm saying she ain't here. I don't know where she is and I couldn't give a hairy rat's ass. She stiffs me on three shifts, am I supposed to send out search parties?"

"I'm trying to find her," I said.

"Then go to her damn apartment. What are you bothering me for?"

I shrugged. "Last know whereabouts."

"Look," Palakas said, taking a breath, "who are you? I mean really."

"I'm nobody," I said.

"You're not a cop?"

"No."

"You're not with Vice?"

"I said I wasn't a cop."

"You look like a cop," Palakas said. From the sour shape his mouth made you think the word 'cop' was smeared with dog shit.

"Used to be a cop."

"What are you now?"

"Private."

He stared at me. "You serious?"

"As a heart attack."

"Bambi a bail skip or something?"

"No. She's a kid who should be in school, not showing her boobs to a bunch of degenerate jerkoffs."

Half a laugh burst from him before he could clamp it down. I edged closer.

"You want to tell me what's so funny? Maybe we can both get a good laugh out of it."

Fear flickered in Palakas's eyes. I am not a big guy—pretty ordinary, really. Five nine, one-seventy; but I've been told I have a quality. Even people who don't know what I have under the skin say that. A quality. When I wore the badge, it must have been there in my eyes. It made some pretty serious thugs back off and back down.

Palakas licked his lips for a moment.

"I don't know where she is," he said. "You want her home address? I can give you that."

"I have that. Give me some names. She have a boyfriend?"

"She has a—"

He almost said something smartass. Probably something like 'she has a million boyfriends.' He stopped himself in time. Two or three more syllables and I'd have belted him, we both knew it.

"Do I need to repeat the question?" I asked quietly.

"She don't have a boyfriend," he said. "Actually I don't think I ever heard of her going on a...um...on a real date."

He didn't have to explain what he meant.

"But...?" I prompted.

"But there was this kid she hung out with."

"A girl?"

"No. A boy. Works in the kitchens. Black kid. Queer."

"They hung out together?"

"Pretty much all the time. Name's Donny Falk."

"Is he working today?"

"No."

"Know where I can find him?"

"Same place as Bambi. Windsor Apartments on Red Lion Road. Same building and floor. His apartment's two doors down from hers."

"You have a phone number for him?"

Palakas licked his lips again. "Yeah," he said, and he very carefully opened the top drawer of his desk and removed a sheet of paper. I leaned over to look at it and saw that it was a list of employees—bar staff, bouncers, kitchen staff, cleaners, dancers—along with contact numbers and email addresses.

"You have a copy of that?" I asked.

"Yeah, but—"

I plucked it out of his hand.

"Hey!"

I turned to him.

"Hey...what?"

Palakas gave me a long, disgusted look. "Hey, I guess help your fucking self to whatever you want. You got a P.I. license, which isn't worth the toilet paper it's printed on, but sure, go ahead, knock around a guy who's got a heart condition. You kick dogs, too?"

I folded the paper and slipped it into my pocket.

"Gosh," I said, "I'm really embarrassed that you think I'm a bully. You think I'm being mean? I certainly don't want to convey that impression."

He glared at me, not falling for it.

So I put a button on it for him. "It's just that I'm pretty sure you knew that girl was underage. I'm actually showing a great degree of restraint here, 'cause my real instinct is to wail on you until I feel better. The only reason I'm not is because you're cooperating—after a fashion. And," I added before he could say anything, "because I don't know for a fact that you're her pimp. If I knew for sure that you were making a fifteen year old girl sell herself, then I think we'd have to explore how really mean I can get. Believe me…neither of us wants to let that dog off the leash. You reading me here?"

"Yeah," he said. He meant to say it tersely, but it came out like a wheeze.

I patted his cheek. "Good."

I could feel George Palakas's glare of hatred as I turned and left.

-6-

As I passed through into the bar toward the exit I saw the two men in dark suits watching me, and I saw their eyes flick from me to the hallway that led to the office. They stood up. The guy on the left was about six foot but had to go two-fifty, most of it in his chest and shoulders. The guy on the right was slimmer but also four inches taller. Big and Tall were not giving me friendly looks. Then Big crossed to the hall and disappeared in the direction of the office while Tall stood there and kept his eyes on me.

Not good.

There were too many people around in the bar, so I began walking toward the exit. Tall saw me and started heading in the same direction. My choices were these—I could wait for them to do something here in the bar, which meant risking injury to civilians. Nope. Or I could let them chase me outside, which opened this up to witnesses with cell phone cameras. Also not good.

Or…

The door to the men's room was closer than the exit door. I gave Tall a smile and ducked through the door.

It took Tall about four seconds to come bursting through the door. He had an old fashioned black-jack in his right hand. You don't see them much anymore. It's a big slug of lead sitting on a spring and wrapped with thick leather. You use it with a snap of the wrist. In skillful hands it can brush the skull and send a person into dreamy land and when they wake up they're sick, disoriented and tractable.

Used wrong it's a skull crusher.

Tall was already starting to raise his for a heavy overhand swing before he was all the way into the bathroom. He was going for the full impact.

I stood with my back to him and saw all this in a mirror.

The blackjack whipped up and was just starting the accelerating drop that would have ended me when I turned.

I don't just mean that I turned around. Sure, I did that, too. But when I say I 'turned,' what I really mean is that I changed.

He swung the blackjack at a man.

It wasn't a man he hit.

His eyes flared wide and his mouth opened to scream in total, sudden horror when I crashed into him and dragged him down to the floor.

The music outside was so loud, nobody heard him scream.

Nobody heard me snarl.

-7-

I was thirteen the first time I changed.

The first time took almost half an hour. I thought I was being torn apart. Guess I kind of was. Torn apart and put back together beneath the skin. Muscles melting into jelly and reassembling; bones reshaping, hair jabbing like needles through my flesh; mouth reshaping, new teeth bursting through the gums. And all of it in a paroxysm of screaming, inarticulate agony. Maybe it feels like dying. Maybe it feels like being tortured. While it was happening I begged God or whoever else is at the help desk to kill me right there and then.

My grandmother was with me through it.

She'd been making that change for nearly seventy years, since she was eleven. Almost everyone on her side of the family had been through it. And, yeah, it actually killed some of them. Depends on your blood line, or maybe if you have the right genes. There are several families like ours and whenever possible we've interbred. Not enough to go all Arkansas back-country, we're not looking to turn out a bunch of moon-faced, slack-jawed brother-cousins. Just enough to strengthen the DNA.

What are we?

There's a lot of folklore out there. A lot of legends. Lots of stories about things like me.

Lot of names.

Lycanthrope.

Berserker.

Vargulf.

Loup-garou.

Werewolf.

We call ourselves the Benandanti. That's an old Italian name that means 'good-walker.' It can also be translated as 'those who go well.' Or even those who 'do good.'

Yeah. Werewolf. Good guy. Same package.

They don't make movies about my kind. You don't see them in too many books or comics. We're not like the Hollywood werewolves, but we've left claw marks all through history. One of us, an eighty-year old guy named Thiess from Jurgenburg, Livonia, was even arrested by the Holy Inquisition in 1692 and put on trial. Not my direct bloodline, but we all know about him. He's kind of a hero to us. The Inquisitors used every kind of torture, every manner of 'enhanced interrogation' to try and force Thiess to say that he was a servant and agent of the devil. Lot of people would have cracked and said anything to stop the pain. Lot of people *did*, which probably accounts for every single signed confession of Satan worship those fruitcakes ever obtained.

Not Thiess, though. That one was one tough, stubborn fucker. And he was eighty!

He *admitted* that he was a werewolf. But he also told them that the Benandanti fought evil on the side of heaven. It was what we always did. It was who we were.

That story didn't go over too well, so they really went to town on Thiess. Thumbscrews, hot irons, the rack. All of it, the works. He should have broken. He should have died.

He didn't.

And he never once wavered in his assertion that the Benandanti have been fighting the true 'good fight.' Against monsters.

Actual monsters.

The Inquisitors tried and tried and tried.

And failed.

Eventually they got to a point where they simply ran out of shit they could do to him. It was down to kill him or let him go.

And…they let him go.

The church court issued a letter saying, in effect, that no servant of the Devil could endure the 'tests' imposed on it by the Inquisition.

Thiess, having survived, must have done so with the grace and protection of God Almighty.

Not only did they let him go, but they even gave him a nickname. A label of honor.

The Hound of God.

Not to say that the church was all kissy-face with us after that. The official result of the trial was exoneration for Thiess. The actual result is that they were embarrassed and probably scared of us. So, in secret and way off the record, they began hunting us down. Not for trial but for quick, quiet execution. There were never many of us, and there were a lot of killers working for the Inquisition. We were very nearly wiped out, and for a while the gene pool was so shallow that whole centuries passed before the wolf once more began screaming in the blood.

My grandmother is the strongest of all of us. Sweetest little old broad you ever wanted to meet. Most of the time. Frail-looking dame with blue hair and a bit of a dowager's hump. But...she can make the change faster than you can snap your fingers, and when the werewolf emerges from beneath the wrinkles of the human, anyone giving her problems—or bothering someone to whom she's offered her protection—is literally in a world of hurt.

For me, I can get pretty cranky, too. On both sides of the skin change, but I do everything I can to keep that change from happening. I don't trust my level of control when I'm a wolf. Bad things have happened, things have spun out of control more than once. It's why I'm not a cop anymore.

But there are times...

I'm telling you all of this so you'll understand what happened in the bathroom at ViXXXens. Tall expected to beat the shit out of some schmuck asking the wrong questions of the wrong person. He had every reason to expect to win that fight. He even scored his hit with the blackjack.

It just didn't do him any damn good.

-8-

The blackjack hit my shoulder as I turned. It hurt. I'm a monster but I still have nerve endings, I'm still meat and bone, and I could still feel pain.

It's just that as a werewolf it takes a lot of damage to slow me down. A whole hell of a lot. Decapitation will do it. Fire will do it. Maybe a machine gun, I don't know. It hasn't ever come to that.

A blackjack?

Oh, please.

And pain is like gasoline on a fire. It dials everything up.

I slashed at his arm and the tough double-stitched leather of the blackjack ripped apart. The lead slug bounced off the ceiling and dropped into a sink. The tips of my nails stroked his hand and wrist and blood splatted the metal toilet stall.

I could have taken the guy's head off.

Easily.

But here's the thing about werewolves. In the movies we're ravening, blood-mad, mindless monsters.

In real life, not so much.

Sure, there's rage.

Sure, there's a lot of animal urges. Lots of subliminal kill-kill-kill impulses.

And, sure, there's a big temptation to chow down because we're predators and humans are tasty prey. Yeah, that's gross, I'm well aware of that. And I've had a lot of next-day puke sessions after I've done some chomping. Less so these days because I have more control. At first, though, I went after the bad guys like they were blue plate specials. Live and learn.

It was Tall's good fortune that I had that control now. And that I'd eaten a couple of quarter pounders on the way here. Otherwise he might have been missing some juicy parts.

Instead, all I did was slam him against the wall over the sink. Kind of hard.

He crashed down onto a row of three filthy sinks, ripping two of them off the wall. He crashed to the floor in a quivering heap, covered with porcelain debris, bleeding from a lot of little cuts. Alive, but not enjoying it.

That's when Big pushed through the door.

The first thing he saw was his friend. I was off to one side. He didn't see me until I got up in his face and *made* him see me.

He started to scream.

I threw him into a toilet stall. He hit the back wall hard enough to turn his eyes blank and knock him all the way to the edge of la-la land. I got to him and caught him before he fell.

Even as I grabbed him I shifted back. I jerked the chain on the wolf and made him go away before he did something we'd all regret. Takes a lot of effort to do that, though. The wolf does not like to go back into the kennel. Not one bit.

It was with human hands that I shoved him onto his knees and stuck his face in the unflushed toilet.

I held him there until my personal disgust told me to stop. Maybe three, four seconds. Then I pulled his dripping head out, spun him around and stuffed him down into the corner between the toilet and the wall.

I squatted in front of him, watching a piece of toilet paper slide down his cheek. He coughed and sputtered and stared at me in total confusion. This wasn't the face he'd seen a second ago. His eyes shifted to find the big bad, but he couldn't know that the monster had already left the building.

Oh, yeah…that whole cycle of the moon thing? That's mostly fiction. During the three days of the full moon we're a little more aggressive, our rages are harder to control, but that's all. We can make the change anytime we want. Into the wolf and back to our own skin. Just like that. On a dime.

A few seconds ago there was a snarling monster with black hair and lots of fangs. Now there was a skinny middle-age guy in a baggy Vikings windbreaker. If you don't come from a home life like mine, that's pretty hard to process, and Big was blowing a lot of mental circuits trying to make sense of it.

I crossed to the door and locked it, then squatted down again in front of Big. He was borderline catatonic with fear.

"What's your name?" I asked.

He started shaking his head. Either refusing to answer or in denial of what was happening.

"Your name." I said it slower, but got nothing.

A slap across the chops would probably have helped unscramble his grits, but, y'know, he was just bobbing for turds, so… no thanks.

For his part, he started flapping his arms around. At first I thought he was trying to fight me or fend me off. But that wasn't it.

He made a half-fist, extending his index and little finger so he could fork the sign of the evil eye at me.

Fair enough. Even though he looked more German than Italian, I figured what the hell. He had just seen a monster. Besides, I've met wiseguys and wiseguy wannabes who did that sort of thing. They were every bit as superstitious as cops and ball players.

Then he began mumbling something. At first I thought it was Italian, but it wasn't.

It was Latin.

"*...defende nos in proelio; contra nequitiam et insidias diaboli esto praesidium. Imperat illi Deus; supplices deprecamur: tuque, Princeps militiae coelestis, Satanam aliosque spiritus malignos, qui ad perditionem animarum pervagantur in mundo, divina virtute in infernum detrude...*"

Unfortunately I don't speak Latin. I mean, who needs to? Even priests don't use it much anymore. But you can *tell* when something is Latin. It doesn't really sound like anything else. Sounded like church stuff. Sounded like stuff you hear in movies.

"Hey," I snapped. "Hey, asshole."

He kept rattling on with the Latin. I yelled at him again. No change.

If I hadn't destroyed the sinks I might have belted some sense into him and then washed my hand. Instead I reached around and under him and took his wallet. He didn't try to stop me. He was totally freaked out, kept pointing the horns of his fingers at me, kept muttering church stuff at me.

The driver's license in the wallet told me that Big's real name was Kurt Gunther. German, like I thought. Or German heritage. All his I.D. was American. There was about four hundred in mixed bills in the wallet, a bunch of credit cards, membership cards from everything from Sam's Club to the library in Doylestown. I smiled. Am I prejudiced because I don't expect thugs to have library cards? Not sure.

There was a glassine flap that had something that really caught my eye. There were two items in it. One was a card the size of a credit card, but it was blood red and had no markings on it except a magnetic strip on the back. But as I turned it over I caught a flash of something. I held it close to my eye and turned it over more slowly, and this time I could see a symbol hidden on the front. It was very subtle, a hologram, like they put on driver's licenses. Only this one was red upon red, with but the slightest 3D effect. It was too small to see clearly, but I could tell that it was circular, with a symbol in the center and lots of radiating spokes. There were other symbols between the spokes, but I couldn't make them out. It reminded me of one of those astrological wheels, but there were more than twelve spokes. Although it was difficult to count, I think there were eighteen symbols around the edge.

The other item was a business card. It had the name, business address, email and contact phone number of a broker from one of those big-ticket national chains. Dunwoody-Kraus-Vitalli. The broker's name was Daniel Meyers.

That's not the thing that made me go 'hmmmm'. What grabbed my attention was what was written in blue ballpoint on the back.

A single word.

A name.

Bambi.

I leaned toward Mr. Gunther and showed him the card.

"Bambi," I said. "Where?"

"...*hostium nostrorum, quaesumus, Domine, elide superbiam: et eorum contumaciam dexterae tuae virtute prosterne...*"

"Stop that," I said, "or you'll get to meet your lord and savior sooner than later, capiche?"

He stopped the chanting.

I wiggled the card and repeated, "Where?"

He looked from the card to me and back again. His eyes, which were already pretty well bugged out, bulged nearly out of their sockets. He said, "N—no..."

Behind me Tall was starting to groan and move sluggishly among the rubble.

Outside the music was still pounding, but who knew what Palakas was doing. Calling the cops. Calling more thugs. Loading a gun. I could hear a big clock ticking in my brain.

"Talk," I said. "Or should I let the dog out to play?"

-9-

Turns out, he didn't want to see the dog again.

Didn't really want to talk, either, but we crossed that speed bump without anyone losing a wheel.

Kurt Gunther and his partner, Salvatore Tucci—Mr. Tall—were bouncers. Not a major surprise there. But they didn't work here at ViXXXens. They worked at a place called Club Dante. I'd heard of it but had never been there. It was one of those so-called 'gentlemen's clubs.' Lots of girls with almost nothing on and lots of booze, but they don't consider themselves a titty bar. The girls are prettier—or have more expensive cosmetic surgery—the booze is all top shelf and over-priced, and lap dances cost more than most of the customers here at ViXXXens make in a week. Places like that are usually fronts for the sex trade, but proving it is a bitch. You have to be a member, and anything hinky happens behind closed doors. The clientele are the local rich and powerful, which means the place has a lot of money and a lot of juice. Places like that don't get raided, or if they do, word has already come down and when Vice breaks in everything is A.J. squared away.

"Is Bambi out there?" I asked him.

Gunther started to tell me that she wasn't, that he didn't know who she was, but I reminded him that if I had to show him the wolf again, then the beast was going to take home a trophy. Gunther clearly didn't want to sing in a high squeaky voice for the rest of his life.

He told me that Bambi was hired to work a special party out at Dante's. They had lots of small rooms for parties.

"Who hired her?" I asked.

"Meyers," he told me. "Daniel Meyers."

The stockbroker.

"Where is she now? Where's Bambi?"

Gunther said he didn't know. He and his partner picked her up at ViXXXens and dropped her at Dante's two nights ago, but the manager over there said that she split. They'd come back here looking for her but had so far come up dry. They were hanging around the place hoping she walked in.

I can usually tell when people are lying to me—it's a smell thing—but Gunther was telling the truth. Or, at least as much of the truth as he knew.

I left him there and got out of the bar pretty quick. I caught a quick glimpse of Palakas across the bar talking on the phone. Didn't wait to find out what kind of heat he was calling down.

Bambi's apartment building was close, so I headed over there and parked outside of the Windsor South Apartments. It was a six-story block built like a slab, with balconied apartments front and back. Cheap but not squalid. Lawn out front needed mowing but it wasn't full of crab grass or weeds.

There was no doorman. The lobby had an intercom, but no one answered at either Bambi's apartment or that of her friend, Donny Falk. So I loitered around until someone came in. When they used their key to open the inner security door, I went through with them. I gave a grunt and a nod like I knew them, and busied myself by pretending to look at something interesting on my BlackBerry. We got in the elevator. He got off at four; I went up to six, then found the fire stairs and went down to three. The apartments on the right-hand side were odd numbers, left side were even. Bambi's apartment was 309. Falk's was 307.

I knocked on 309 and heard nothing but echoes.

The hall was empty, the door was locked. I sniffed the door and smelled only those things I expected to smell. Wood, old cooking smells, a little mildew, and dust.

The place even felt empty. It had that kind of vibe. Like a dead battery.

The other doors along the hall stayed shut, so I bent to study the lock. Every P.I. worth his license can bypass a lock without much trouble. The really good ones require a set of lock-picks and maybe three minutes work. This one was a cheap-ass lock, and I opened it with a flexible six-inch plastic ruler I carry for exactly this kind of thing. It pushed the tapered bolt back on its spring and the lock clicked open. I glanced up and down the hall and then stepped inside.

Denise Sturbridge's apartment was neat and small and clean. And empty. I ghosted my way through it. There were dishes in the dishwasher, leftovers in the fridge, some trash in the cans that told me nothing, the usual stuff in the bathroom, and exactly what you'd expect in the bedroom. Drawers filled with cheap but attractive clothes. Dance stuff. Shoes, but not too many and most of them inexpensive. A hamper with soiled items in it. Twin bed, pink sheets, a stuffed turtle.

I touched very little, but I sniffed it all. And, although that sounds intensely creepy, think of it more like a dog and less like a thirty-something adult man.

I catalogued the scents of Denise Sturbridge as a living person. I added that to the already-logged scent of her blood.

There was nothing of note anywhere. A work schedule was posted on the side of the fridge, held in place by a magnet from a pizza shop. There was a TV and DVD player, and most of the discs she had were romantic comedies or Disney stuff.

Girl stuff.

Kid stuff. Like the stuffed turtle.

My heart hurt looking at it.

"Where are you, kid?" I asked the empty apartment. "Give me a little help here."

But there wasn't even a whisper of anything useful.

I wiped off everything I touched and left her apartment. I drifted down to Donny Falk's door and froze in my tracks.

There were splinters on the carpet and when I peered at the frame around the lock I could see where the wood had been cracked. Someone had forced the door and then pushed the splinters and twisted metal back into place as far as it would go. You had to look close to see it. I was looking close.

Which is when I caught the smell.

Faint.

But there.

Sickly sweet and gassy.

Only one thing smells like that.

I put my ear against the wood and listened for any sound of movement. Anything at all.

Nothing.

Shit.

I leaned my shoulder against the door and pushed it open. There wasn't much resistance beyond the friction of the broken lock and torn frame. I stepped inside and immediately pushed the door shut.

Donny Falk was kitchen help in a strip club, and he clearly lived small. Mismatched Salvation Army furniture, plastic milk crates and boards for shelving, posters thumbtacked to the walls, a threadbare rug over worn linoleum.

Maybe that had been enough for him. Maybe he kept the place clean and filled it with music and friends and his own hopes and dreams. Some people cruise along that way. If they don't have much then at least they have some measure of freedom. They make genuine friendships, and they're loving and loyal to anyone who shows them respect and kindness.

Now, though, the place was a wreck.

It looked like a storm had blown through it.

The couch and chair were overturned, cushions slashed, stuffing pulled out, posters torn down, CD player smashed, CDs crushed underfoot, baseball ball rammed through the TV screen, flowers torn out of pots, cereal boxes torn open and spilled, toaster-oven crashed onto the floor, refrigerator door open and everything pulled out and smeared onto the floor. I moved carefully through the debris, careful not to leave footprints in anything sticky or powdery. There was a short hallway leading off from the living room, with a bathroom door on one side and a bedroom at the end. I peered into the bathroom to see the same kind of destruction. Everything that could be smashed had been, everything that could be cracked or spilled or torn was in ruins. I caught a glimpse of fifty different angry versions of my face in the fragments of the shattered mirror. None of those faces looked happy. This wasn't wolf face, but it was every bit as dangerous.

The bedroom door was closed, but the smell was coming from there.

For a moment I felt so old and depressed that I wondered if I should leave the door closed, turn around and go home. I wasn't a homicide cop anymore—not since they asked me to turn in my badge back in the Cities. I was a P.I. with no legal reason to be here, and I couldn't prove that I hadn't been the one to kick in the door and trash the place.

If I walked into that room then I would be tampering with a crime scene.

They could and probably would put me in jail for something like this.

Best thing in the world for me to do was get the hell out of there. I had other leads to follow—the stockbroker and Club Dante. It was a better, smarter choice to walk away.

But then if I was a better or smarter guy I wouldn't be working this job.

I opened the door.

And stood there.

I didn't enter.

Everything I needed to see I could see from where I was.

Donny Falk was about twenty, maybe five-six, one-thirty. I could tell that much.

George Palakas had said that Donny was black and gay. The posters on the wall were all of good looking men in skimpy outfits, so I could make the case for him being gay. As for black?

You'd need to look at his skin to make that call.

And he didn't have any.

The whole room was painted in his blood. Not artistically, but from arterial sprays. He seemed to float in the midst of it, but that was an illusion. His arms and legs were spread wide. Someone had driven big iron nails through his wrists and shins. I would like to think they'd done that after the kid was dead, but I don't think mercy was really any part of this scenario.

I could see why his screams didn't alert the neighbors. You need a tongue for that. His was nailed to his forehead.

And…the killer had torn open Donny's chest and removed his heart.

I forced myself to look around the room, but there was no sign of the stolen organ. The killer had taken it with him.

But the killer had left something behind. Something I recognized.

On the wall, drawn with care in Donny's blood, was a large circle. There was a small symbol in the center, and eighteen spokes radiating out to connect with the big outer circle. Between each circle was another symbol. Each symbol was unique. Each was entirely unknown to me. I removed the Club Dante card from my jacket and held it up at an angle where I could see the hologram.

Same symbol.

If it was astrological, then it was from some philosophy other than the normal one I knew about. Eighteen symbols.

The pattern was strange, alien to me.

Looking at it made my heart hammer and my skin crawl.

Was this killer hunting according to some crazy religious thing? Was this part of some ritual he was acting out? While on the cops I ran into religious maniacs before. Some of them had this view in their heads that they were on the verge of *becoming* something greater than what they were; that they were about to ascend, and that it only required blood sacrifices and an adherence to specific rituals to open that door.

Is that what I had here? Was Bambi waiting to become a victim to the grand designs of someone who wanted to become God?

"Bambi,' I murmured. "Denise…Donny…"

I stood there for a long time as a series of weird emotions crawled through my shocked brain.

Donny Falk was not my client. I hadn't known him, and differences in age and location and profession would probably have prevented us from ever crossing paths, or if we had, we probably wouldn't have anything to say to one another.

And yet…

He was the friend, perhaps the *only* friend of Denise Sturbridge. Bambi. She was a lost little girl pretending to be a jaded woman of the stage and streets. Donny was probably the only 'safe' man in her world. The only one who didn't want to plunder her silky loins or sexualize her beyond her years. And maybe she was an equally safe zone for him. Nonjudgmental, a kindred innocent in a corrupt world.

Bambi wasn't my client any more than Donny was. The unnamed woman from Limbus had hired me to find her. Donny was a side-effect of that search.

And yet…

My brain is wired in a certain way. I know that some of it has to do with my Benandanti heritage—we're pack animals, and you always protect the pack. But I'd like to think that I would have some approximation of that sensibility even if I was a normal man. The desire to protect the pack, to protect anyone who can't protect themselves. When I take on a client it's like they become part of my family, part of my pack. I will do absolutely anything, go to extreme lengths to protect what's mine.

But Bambi and Donny weren't mine. They weren't part of my pack.

Were they? Did the protection I afforded clients extend to people like them? Or was what I was feeling merely the normal outrage a moral person feels in the face of a demonstration of so clearly an immoral act?

Inside my head the wolf howled.

Aloud I said, "No."

I removed my cell phone and used it to take several photos of the symbol, and immediately forwarded them to a woman I knew at the University of Pennsylvania. An anthropologist who'd helped me on another case involving ritual symbols.

Then I backed out of the room, turned in the hall and leaned my forehead against the wall.

Shit.

Who was this maniac?

I looked down at the Club Dante card in my hand. I removed the business card for the stockbroker, Daniel Meyers.

That place and that man were tied to Bambi.

Somebody was going to give me some answers.

I only hoped those answers led me to the monster who tore the skin from these young people. Sixteen girls, one boy. I knew that the girls were all prostitutes, but in my heart they were all children. Innocents. The damaged and discarded ones. A lot of them were victims of abuse at home, or from shattered homes. Drugs were one way out, a way to blunt the jagged edges of the pain and self-loathing. Hooking bought more drugs and it completed the cycle of destruction that often began at home and ended on the streets. When I thought of them as 'innocent' I didn't mean pure. Some of them were willing participants in their own destruction, but I've found that few people are truly self-destructive. Usually self-immolation of the moral kind is an end result, a skill learned from others.

For seventeen of those lost souls there was absolutely nothing I could do. Even revenge or managing to get the killer arrested wouldn't clothe them in their lost skin or breathe life into their empty lungs. Nothing I did would make their hearts beat again or coax a smile onto their dead mouths.

However Bambi might still be alive.

Out there.

Somewhere.

At Club Dante?

I was going to have to find out.

Donny Falk hung on the wall and I couldn't take him down. Maybe the cops could find some evidence in all that gore. I couldn't risk disturbing that process. But there was something I could do.

I closed my eyes and drew in all of the scents of this place. Identifying Donny's, filing it away. Separating out Bambi's. Discarding all of the neutral smells—food, clothing, all of that. Then picking through the commingled animal smells.

Donny didn't have any pets.

The only animal smells had been left by people.

There were two smells that were stronger than the others. Fresh and pungent. Male smells. Not Big and Tall. Other male scents.

I catalogued them the way my grandmother taught me. If I smelled them again, even months from now, I'd know them.

Not one scent, but two.

Two killers?

Those smells were both in the killing room.

Two killers.

There was nothing else to learn here, so I wiped off the wall where I'd leaned my head, smudged any footprints I'd left on the floor, pulled the door shut as I left, and wiped the doorknob.

I walked down the fire stairs with every outward appearance of calm.

Appearances are so incredibly deceptive.

-10-

The offices of Dunwoody-Kraus-Vitalli were in Center City, but by the time I got down there it was after five. I stood at the receptionist's desk and tried to look affable, upscale and charming. In the parking garage I'd changed out of my oversized Vikings jacket and put on a three-button Polo shirt. Like most working P.I.s, I have all sorts of clothes in my trunk. I combed my hair and tucked a pair of Wayfarers into the vee of the shirt.

The receptionist was a snooty brunette with too much eye-makeup and too little warmth.

"Mr. Meyers has left for the day," she said.

"Ah, damn," I said mildly and started to turn away, then paused, snapping my fingers. "Hey, did Mike say he was going to the club tonight?"

The receptionist lifted one eyebrow about a quarter of an inch. My attitude and apparent familiarity with Meyers, along with the reference to a club, was at war with the fact that she didn't know me from a can of paint.

"I...think he said something," she said evasively.

It was enough.

"Cool," I said. "I'll catch him there."

"He may call in. I'll be happy to tell him you stopped by, Mister...?"

I grinned. "Wolf," I said.

"Very well, Mr. Wolf."

I gave her a smile and a wink and headed for the elevators.

Wolf.

Sometimes I crack myself up.

-11-

Two calls came in while I was on my way south to Club Dante.

The first was Jonatha Corbiel-Newton, the anthropologist at University of Pennsylvania.

"Hey, doc," I said. "Thanks for getting back to me so fast."

"No problem. You caught me in my office grading papers."

"You get the images?"

"I did. Where did you take them?"

"They're attached to a case. Something I'm working on right now."

"Are these from a crime scene?"

I was careful to make sure that Donny wasn't in the shots I'd forwarded. "What makes you ask?"

"Well...it rather looks like the medium used to paint the symbol is blood."

"Pretty sure it's paint," I lied.

"It's very dark and viscous-looking."

"Red poster paint. That tempura stuff."

"Uh huh." She clearly didn't believe me, but then again I hadn't contacted her because she was an idiot.

Even so, I sidestepped the topic. "Is that an astrological symbol?"

She took a moment before answering. "Not precisely. It has cosmological connections, but it isn't a chart for any of the common astrologies. It's not the zodiac or the Chinese astrological grouping. It doesn't represent planets, animals or aspects of the natural world."

"Okay, but—"

"However I *do* recognize it."

"Ah."

"It's a symbol used by a group who call themselves the Order of Melchom."

"The who of who?"

"Order of Melchom. There are several versions of the group, some new and some very old. The new groups vary between covens of modern neo-pagans and RPG-ers."

"Who?"

"Role playing gamers. Like Dungeons and Dragons. Those groups have adopted thousands of names and symbols from various arcane sources and used them as backstory for their games. It's all over the Net."

"I'm pretty sure this wasn't posted by geeks playing games," I said. "You said the others were neo-pagans? Do you mean witches?"

"Well, wiccan, of one kind or another. Not the white-energy wiccans, though. This symbol is tied to dark energy."

"You mean evil?"

"Evil is relative. Most modern pagans view the universal forces as white and black, light and dark, or positive and negative."

It wasn't quite the way I saw things, but I kept that to myself.

"You said there was another reference," I said. "Something older? What's that?"

"In Biblical terms, Melchom is often cited as a variation of a god worshipped by the Ammonites, Phoenicians and Canaanites. The more common name is Moloch, which is itself another name for 'king.' The worshippers of Moloch were brutal."

"In what way?"

"In sacrificial ways," said Jonatha. "Devotees practiced a particular kind of propitiatory child sacrifice in which parents gave up their children."

I had to clear my throat before I asked, "What *kind* of sacrifice?"

"The biblical and historical records vary. Most likely the children were burned alive. There's a reference to that in the Book of Leviticus, but other texts include plenty of references to various kinds of mutilation include a 'sacrifice of the flesh.'"

"Which is what?" I asked, though I thought I already knew.

"The sacrificed children were very carefully skinned so that they would be 'unclothed to the soul' and still alive when given up to Moloch."

The day outside was bright and there were puffy white clouds in the gorgeous blue sky. All of that didn't belong in any world in which this conversation was a part. I told myself that, but the bright clouds and the flawless sky mocked me for my naiveté. Lovely skies have looked down upon every despicable thing we humans have done. What's truly naïve is to think that horrors are always hidden away in shadows.

"This Moloch sounds like a charmer," I said.

"He is. He's nasty and he's fierce. The ancients considered him one of the greatest warriors of the fallen angels." I heard her rustling book pages. "John Milton wrote this about him in *Paradise Lost*…

"'…MOLOCH, horrid King besmear'd with blood
Of human sacrifice, and parents tears,
Though, for the noise of Drums and Timbrels loud,
Their children's cries unheard that passed through fire
To his grim Idol.'"

"Nice."

"There's more," she said. "Milton listed him among the chief of Satan's angels, and he gives a speech at the Parliament of Hell to argue for war against God."

"He's an angel?"

"Depending on which source you read," she said, "he's either a fallen angel, a god, or a demon. In his aspect as Melchom, he's the accountant for hell. He holds the purse strings to all of the Devil's gold, and he inspires men to strive for wealth, often by any means necessary. He's a monster in all of his aspects, really."

And that fast something went skittering across my brain. A demon worshipped by men striving for money.

"Sam—?" asked Jonatha Corbiel-Newton. "You still there?"

"Yeah."

"Is any of this useful to you?"

"Christ," I said, "I hope not."

Seventeen skinned teenagers. 'Hope' was a pretty vain luxury.

"What have you gotten yourself into?"

"I'm not sure, doc. I'm still blundering my way through it." I paused. "Tell me something, though...are there any *modern* cults of Moloch? Does anyone still believe this sort of thing?"

She was a long time answering. "Back when I first began studying anthropology I would have said no unreservedly."

"But now?"

"Now I'm not so sure. The more I get out of the office and into the field so I can see what people are actually out there doing, and practicing...I'm not so sure. Especially lately."

"Why lately?"

"It's the world, Sam. There's no peace anywhere. Wars everywhere, the economy falling apart, such extreme political divisiveness, even the return of class wars. People are scared, they're angry and they're desperate." She paused again. "These days people are looking for something to change the way things are going. They're looking for an edge to help them get through all of this upheaval and carnage."

"Geez," I said with a small laugh, "so much for the detached scientist."

She laughed, too, but it was thin and false. "Objectivity is taking as serious a beating as idealism these days."

I saw my exit coming up and drifted off of I-95.

"Sam...what *are* you into?"

"As of right now, Jonatha," I said, "it beats the shit out of me. I've got too much of the wrong information and not nearly enough of the right kind."

"Sam..." she said hesitantly. "That wasn't tempura paint in that picture, was it?"

I drummed my fingers on the knobbed arc of the steering wheel as I waited for the light at the end of the exit ramp to turn from red to green.

"Thanks for the info, doc," I said. "I owe you a steak dinner."

Before she could reply to that I hung up.

The light turned green and I drove on.

Moloch. Melchom.

An ancient cult that involves sacrifices of flesh to an ancient god. Or demon. Or fallen angel. Or whatever the fuck he was.

A sacrifice of the flesh.

How in the big yellow fuck did that make any kind of sense? This wasn't ancient Israel. This wasn't medieval Europe. This was Phila-damn-delphia.

Then I thought about the stockbroker. Daniel Meyers. He was almost certainly a college graduate. I wondered how old he was, and if he used to belong to a fraternity. I worked some frat hazing cases before. Some of those clowns went way over the line. Branding each other, lots of ritual behavior, beatings. Even rape.

Could a group of frat brothers cross a harder line? Was this some kind of brotherhood thing? A Skull and Bones thing, or something worse?

That felt both wrong and right at the same time.

Either way, I was still shooting in the dark.

-12-

Club Dante was a big block nothing of a building from the outside. Tall, stuccoed walls, a pitched roof covered in faux terra cotta tiles, and massive wooden doors that would have looked better on the front of a medieval castle. Twelve feet high, wrapped in bands of black wrought-iron, and lined with chunky studded bolt-heads. The parking lot was behind a fence and a pair of armed guards worked the entrance. I parked across the street and studied them through the telephoto lens of a digital camera. The guards had that thin-lipped, lantern-jawed, unsmiling look of ex-military and possibly ex-special forces. Tough men, and from the way they moved and worked it was pretty clear that they were too good for the job they were doing. You don't hire guys like that to check cars into a strip club parking lot, not even a very expensive strip club parking lot.

Hmm.

The cars were interesting, though. Nothing that looked more than two years old, and nothing that had a sticker price under fifty G's. Some of them were way above that mark, too. Lots of sports cars. That made a certain kind of statement. The kind of guys who over-paid to come to a place like this were the kind who wanted everyone to know—or think—they had a big dick. Expensive clothes, ten thousand dollar wristwatches, hand-sewn shoes, nothing that was ever off the rack, and cars that cost more than my education were all ways of saying look at me and bow to my dick. It was the equivalent of attaching a fire hose to a tank of testosterone and hosing down everyone around them.

And because they made so damn much money, and money really is power in almost every way that matters in this world, everyone with less money dropped down and kissed their privileged asses.

For a whole lot of reasons I am less inclined to kowtow to assholes like that.

Maybe that's why I'm always broke. I won't play those kinds of games and I've never felt any urge to stand in a crowd of moneyed jackasses and pass around a golden ruler while we all measured our johnsons.

I drove slowly around the building, studying the fence from all sides. It was a tall chain-link affair with coils of stainless-steel razor wire along the top. Very inviting. There was no back gate and, as far as I could tell, only a single locked and alarmed red fire door. Odd for a building that size. Couldn't possibly have passed code, which suggested that the owners were greasing the right palms.

There was movement among the parked cars and I saw another armed guard on foot patrol, walking a brute of a Doberman on a leash. Ninety pounds of sinew, muscle and attitude. Black and brown, with a bobbed tail and devil ears. As my car drifted past the Doberman came suddenly to point and focused all of its senses on me. He couldn't see me through the smoked windows of my car, but he *knew* that I was there, just as he knew that I wasn't right.

Dogs always react to me. The ones who aren't alphas tuck their tails between their legs and want to lick my hand. People always smile and tell me that I'm a real dog person.

Yeah, in a way.

The alphas are always instantly wary of me. The ones who are alphas but haven't been trained for combat or patrol will keep their distance and watch me with wary eyes. If I push it I can get them to roll to me, but I seldom want to do that because some of them don't reclaim their mojo afterward. I like dogs, so breaking their will isn't high on my to-do list.

Alphas with guard dog training are a different matter. We've had some issues in the past. Their training is sometimes so intense that they will make choices they wouldn't make in the wild. I'm one-seventy, which means that when I do the change, the wolf is one-seventy, too. That's a lot of wolf. Even the biggest gray wolf is only about a hundred pounds. I'm closer to a dire wolf, the old prehistoric species. Their top range was one seventy. My grandmother thinks that we have dire wolf genes. I don't know. Maybe I'll get that checked one day, if I can figure out how to get a DNA lab to do it without freaking them too much, or outing myself.

When I'm face to face with a trained attack dog, there's usually trouble. I hate to kill a dog. I'll play slice and dice with a person before I'll open up a dog. Yeah, I know, a psychologist could really have fun with that, but there it is.

That Doberman had the kind of focused, barely suppressed aggression that let me know that it wouldn't turn belly-up for me. If I wolfed out, then he'd make a run at me. And I'd have to kill him for it.

Club Dante wasn't filling me with feelings of joy and puppies. Way too much security, the presence of a certain kind of money, and a definite connection to the missing girl. None of that added up to comforting math.

On the other hand it didn't necessarily add up to involvement in seventeen brutal murders. It was, however, the only lead I had.

And in a way that was only semi-rational it *smelled* right.

When I stopped at the light I fished in my pocket for the red membership card. I sniffed it, but all I smelled was that guy Gunther. It was possible that by now he'd called to say that I'd taken the card from him. Was that the reason for the heavy security?

No, I decided. The patrols here had a lived-in look. I was pretty sure this was their regular security.

Hoping that things wouldn't play out that way, I drove four blocks away, parked, hailed a cab and had the taxi drop me at the club. I couldn't risk that the guards would have a list of all of the tag numbers of regular members.

With my Wayfarers on and just enough indolent slouch in my walk, I strolled past the gate and entered through the massive front doors. They had a doorman in a tuxedo right inside. He was roughly the size of Godzilla and I had to lean back to look up at him. He gave me a quick up-and-down appraisal and shifted to stand between me and the door.

"May I help you, sir?"

I pulled the card out and held it up between two fingers. "Been a long day," I said casually, "and I hear a martini calling to me."

He was well-trained. His scowl became an agreeable smile and he stepped aside to allow me access to a key-swipe station mounted to one side of a second set of doors. I kept a bland smile on my face but held my breath as I fitted the card into the slot and swiped it.

The little red light on the station blinked from red to green. There was a faint *click* behind the door, and the doorman's smile became less artificial and more genuine. He pushed the door open for me.

"Have a glorious evening, sir," he said.

"Count on it," I assured him as I stepped through the doors and entered the belly of the beast.

-13-

The club was pretty much as you'd expect. It was shadowy as a closet, an effect insured by low-wattage indirect lights and lots of dark wood. The motif was, apparently, early dungeon. Wrought iron fixtures, low couches, rough stone walls, rich draperies hung from brass rods. As I passed one of these I glanced at it and then gave it a double-take. What I first thought was a hunting scene of mounted riders, a dog pack and a bunch of frightened deer was actually something a lot less enchanting. The riders all wore burgundy-colored robes, the dogs looked half-starved and ravenous, and the 'prey' were men and women scurrying on all fours. Naked, some with antlers tied to their heads. The tapestry was old and woven from thick, rich threads, so it was hard to tell much about the people on all fours...except that the more I stared at them the younger they all looked.

I said, very softly, "Uh oh."

I made myself turn away from the tapestry to study the room.

There were probably forty men in there. Most of them were dressed in expensive suits. A few had loosened their ties; a few others wore Polo shirts like mine. None of the customers were women. This was clearly a men's club. Not sure I'd go as far as 'gentlemen,' though.

The wait-staff were women of a type. Busty, leggy, barely dressed and very young. If any of them was older than nineteen then I was the Tsar of Russia.

I wonder how many of them were even eighteen.

For a few seconds I debated short-cutting this whole thing by making a call to the cops and Child Protection Services. Maybe the press, too. Blow it open. Pedophilia is not a popular crime, not for the common guy on the street. People will sometimes look the other way if politicians or white collar criminals run money scams, or take kick-backs, but when it comes to sex with kids, my fellow citizens have a very admirable tendency toward pitchforks and torches. Look what happened with Penn State. Look what's happening with all those priests.

But what could I prove?

I mean, right here, right now, what could I prove? That there are *possibly* underage girls showing their breasts and serving drinks? The news might like that, but I doubted I could get a warrant happening.

And if Bambi was here, then it might encourage the bad guys to dispose of any evidence. That girl was evidence.

So I drifted through the place and pretended to be a part of the debauch. I obtained a drink as protective coloration. I exchanged a few words with other 'members.' We talked sports, we talked politics. We talked stocks and investments.

Nobody mentioned Moloch. Nobody mentioned dead girls.

I noticed that nobody used names. They didn't offer or ask names.

There was a small stage at the far end of the cavernous main room. When I'd come in, a redhead was beginning a veil dance. She discarded about a dozen of them until she was stark naked. There was some mild applause and she gathered up the gossamer scraps and trotted lightly off. Then the lights changed and I saw a lot of the men shift their attention more seriously to the stage. Two women came out. Twins with masses of blond hair. They wore stylized bullfighter costumes. Then a pair of very large Latinos came out, both of them wearing bull horns. A small band began playing dramatic bullfight music, and the foursome launched into a variation of the *paso doble.* But instead of the man acting as bullfighter and the woman, with her swirling skirts, acting as his cape, the men were the bulls and the women the toreadors. They were all pretty good dancers and for a moment I thought that this was a surprising bit of real art in this place. But then the horns of the bulls caught on pieces of the women's costumes. With each lunge and twist the clothing was torn away, gradually revealing a lot of flesh and turning the women from bullfighters to helpless victims. The bullish men began stripping away sections of their costumes, particularly their pants. I saw where this was going and turned away. I like sex as much as the next four guys, but the theme of this had rolled down hill into a presentation of female defeat and use. I wanted no part of that.

There was a wooden apron that ran around the outside of the main room, with several hallways and doors leading off from there. As the action onstage grew more heated and the club's members became more focused upon it, I faded to the back and began looking for a door I could open.

Movement to my left made me pause and I saw one of the men get up and walk toward the back of the big room. He threw a few glances over his shoulder at the increasingly X-rated action on stage, but I got the impression he was leaving. He didn't head for the door, though. Instead he made for a hallway that cut off out of sight on the far corner. A few seconds later another man followed. And another.

It wasn't an exodus. Only a small percentage of the customers vanished down that hallway. The rest were staring with total attention at the sweaty spectacle on the stage. The timing of it all seemed odd to me. That many guys couldn't need to use the bathroom at the same time; an assumption supported by the fact that the men didn't return. As I moseyed nonchalantly in that direction I could see that there was another guard just inside the mouth of the hallway, and beyond him was a door with the same key-swipe station as outside.

If I had spider sense it would have been tingling.

I watched a couple of guys to see what the routine was. They approached the hall, flashed something to the guard, then swiped their keycard and passed through the locked door. It took me three or four times before I realized that all they were showing was their red cards. Nice.

I waited for a moment when no one else was heading that way and I stepped into the hallway, flashed my red card, got a terse nod from the guard, swiped my card, and stepped through the doorway.

That easy.

As soon as I was inside I met a second security guard. He was even bigger than the Godzilla at the front door. Where do they get these guys? Thugs'R'Us?

He smiled at me. "Good evening, brother."

Since I didn't know what else to say, I returned his smile as I walked over to him. "Am I late? Have they started yet?"

He frowned and looked at his watch. "Uh...no, brother, it doesn't start for another—"

He stopped talking when I screwed the barrel of my Glock into his ear.

People tend to do that.

"Be smart," I told him.

He froze into a statue, eyes wide, sweat bursting from the pores on his face.

"Where's the girl?" I asked. I kept my voice low and level, letting the gun do all of my shouting for me.

I had no idea if he knew anything about anything, but sometimes you go on balls and instinct and a flip of a coin. Most of the time you waste your time. Once in a while though...

"She's still upstairs," he said.

I pressed the barrel harder against him. "Is she alive?"

"Who are you?" he asked.

"Her fairy godfather. Answer the fucking question."

He hedged. "Yes," he said. But there was too much uncertainty in his voice. "They're getting her ready."

It was a simple statement that in any other circumstances might have meant something relatively innocent. But it filled my mind with terrible images and awful potential.

"How many are up there?"

His eyes shifted away and I knew he was about to lie to me. Before he could push us both out onto a ledge, I leaned close and whispered. "I don't mind blowing your head off, slick. You have one chance to walk out of this, but you're on a short fuse here."

"I don't know," he said. "God's honest truth. I only came on shift twenty minutes ago and some of them were already up there. Only about a dozen members have checked in."

A dozen was the number of men I'd seen leaving the action outside.

I moved in front of him and put the barrel under his chin. I wanted to see his eyes better when I asked the next question.

"Do you know what they're going to do to her?"

His mouth opened but it made a lot of shapes before he finally spoke, trying on different answers, seeing if any of them fit well enough.

"I'm just a grunt, man," he said at last. "I just work the door."

I leaned close to him and took his scent, sniffing at his face and chest the way a dog would. The gun stayed in place as I sniffed and I could see the total confusion on his face. He must have thought I was some nutcase. Sniffing like a dog.

I smelled fear on him. I smelled booze and tobacco and hashish. I smelled sweat and sex and blood.

And I smelled Bambi.

Not her blood scent.

Her *living* scent. The subtle perfume of hormones and skin oils and glands. The scent I'd picked up at her apartment.

He'd been close enough to her to get that scent on his clothes.

No blood, though.

No blood.

It was the only reason I didn't kill him right there and then.

But it was a damn close decision.

Instead I kneed him in the nuts as hard as I could. His eyes bulged, his mouth puckered into a tiny 'Oh' and he caved forward, cupping his balls. As he bent down over the pain, I clubbed him on the back of the neck, right where the spine enters the skull. It jerks the brain stem and short-circuits the nerve conduction. In the movies James Bond chops a guy there and the man goes out and wakes up ten minutes later with a headache. I'm not James Bond and this wasn't the movies. He dropped like he'd been pole-axed, and when he woke up—maybe half an hour from now—he'd puke, he'd be dizzy and dazed, and he'd probably have neck problems for years.

Fuck it.

Behind me the door clicked as someone else used their keycard. I lunged toward a set of light switches and slapped them down just as the door opened. A man-shape filled the doorway, pausing in confusion at the unexpected darkness. I grabbed a fistful of his tie and jerked him into the hall, then kicked the door shut. The guy was a businessman in a nice wool suit. About my age, a little bigger, a whole lot richer.

I punched him in the throat.

He dropped, gagging and coughing, clawing at his neck.

The security guard said, "Hey!"

That was all I allowed him to say. I grabbed him by the tie and jerked that as tight as a noose while putting my foot as far through his nutsack as I could manage.

He said, "Oooooof," in a high, squeaky voice. I used the necktie to pull him into the hallway. I took a one-second look to see if anyone in the main hall noticed any of this, but both couples onstage were going at it loud and weird, and the band's speakers were cranked all the way up to eleven. No one saw shit.

I slammed the door, pivoted and kicked the key-swipe station off the wall.

The businessman was thrashing around on the floor trying to breathe. The security guy was on his knees, eyes popped nearly out of his head, face purple. I gave him a little bit of a shuffle side-thrust and he flopped back into bad dreams. Then I turned and kicked the businessman in the jewels and in the face. He groaned, rolled over and passed out.

It was suddenly very quiet in the hallway.

I was doing some real damage here and a small splinter of my mind was watching, aghast. The rest of me was remembering the faceless faces of the sixteen dead women, and the boy who'd been stripped of his life and nailed to a wall. And remembering the smell of Bambi, still alive, on the one guard's clothes.

So, yeah, sure, compassion and all that. But not now and not for these guys. They were lucky I hadn't wolfed out and really gone to town on them, and believe me that was a very strong temptation.

I paused to listen. If anyone upstairs heard the commotion they weren't reacting. There was music drifting down the stairs. Drums and some kind of pipes. Very tribal. Voices, too. Some kind of chanting.

Ever since I spoke with Jonatha Corbiel-Newton my overactive brain had been conjuring a series of ugly pictures of what was going on here at Club Dante. I suppose the most dominant one was of frat boys going through some bullshit pseudo-ancient ritual before gang-banging Bambi and carving her skin off, all in some crazy belief that

Moloch—fallen angel, demon or half-ass ancient god—was going to make them rich.

I shoved the businessman against the door and then dragged the unconscious guards over. That was more than a quarter ton of dead weight. If anyone tried to get the door open they could manage it, but not in the next five minutes.

Better for them if they didn't.

Then I spun around and ran up the stairs.

-14-

I took the stairs two at a time, fast but quiet, thinking to myself, *Hold on, kid. Hold on.*

There was one more door at the top and one more key-swipe. I chopped the card down through it and then made myself slow down. I eased the door open and slipped quietly inside. The chamber was big, as wide as downstairs though with fifteen-foot high ceilings. Lights in recessed alcoves provided minimal illumination, but overall the room was dark. Shadows lay draped across everything. I squeezed my eyes shut for a moment to goose along my night vision.

When I opened them I saw that there were at least twenty men in the room. Most of them were clustered around an open cabinet as one of the staff handed out robes of dark red silk. The men were stripping out of their expensive suits and then pulling the robes on over their naked skin. The expectation of what was about to happen must have been electric because some of the guys had hard-ons. I didn't need to see that.

Music blared from at least a dozen speakers mounted high on the walls. It was the tribal stuff I'd heard downstairs, and the chanting was actually part of it. The guys here weren't chanting. No idea what language the chant was in. Not Latin. Not anything I'd ever heard.

I faded into deep shadows thrown by a tall wooden carving. When I glanced up at it I was surprised to see that it was a bull. Kind of. The body was human, but the shoulders were massively overdeveloped and the head was that of a massive bull with long horns. I glanced around to see that there were other statues like this one. Not exactly like it, and some made out of stone or metal, but all of a gigantic bull-headed man. A minotaur? I wasn't sure. My knowledge of mythology was pretty thin.

Another of the bull statues dominated the center of the chamber. At first I thought it was made of polished brass, but the more I stared at it the more I realized that it was gold. Maybe it was gold paint or gold plate, but somehow I got the impression that there was a serious amount of actual gold there.

And in a strange way it fit with the whole Moloch vibe. A demon who was the treasurer of hell. A creature who the ancient Ammonites and Phoenicians believed would guide certain men toward wealth. Would men like these—the financial kings of this city—have a false idol, one painted with sham gold?

No, I didn't think so.

Somehow that made me a little more afraid.

This was looking a lot less like a frat stunt that got too serious and more like an actual cult. Or, I guess...a religion.

Did people really believe in something like this? *Could* they?

I mean...a cult that required human sacrifices wasn't something you simply joined. Every man here risked life imprisonment or death row. At very least this was felony murder, kidnapping, conspiracy, and a laundry list of capital crimes. I don't care what kind of big-ticket lawyer they trotted out, everyone even remotely attached to this would go down for the hardest of hard falls.

And yet here they were, putting on robes, waving their chubbys around as they got ready to commit *another* murder.

What was the payoff that made this kind of risk worth it?

I mean...how could one member of the club ever sell this kind of thing to a friend?

Shit.

The thing that really chilled my blood, though, was the art on the walls. Spaced at regular intervals around the room were two-by-three foot posters in wooden frames. Women's faces. All very young, all very pretty. Each of them looked absolutely terrified, some looked like they were in terrible agony when the photos were taken.

I counted them.

There were sixteen pictures. And empty frames for another ten.

I could only see a couple of the faces, and they were strangers-- but I'm pretty sure I'd seen them before, but in the pictures I'd seen none of them had their skin. Were these trophy shots, taken during rape or torture? Or at the moment of their deaths?

The wolf began to growl, low and with dark intent, deep inside my brain.

One man, a very tall, thin guy with prematurely white hair, kept glancing toward the door through which I'd entered and then down at his watch. He was probably wondering where the rest of his fellow worshippers were.

My time was running out. Bambi's too.

So where was…?

Suddenly a curtain in the back of the chamber opened and two burly guards came out, supporting Bambi between them. She was dressed in a little tunic that was made from the sheerest of fabrics and belted by a gold sash. The girl was able to walk, but even from across the room I could see that she was totally whacked out. Drugged on something. She seemed to float along with the men, her mouth slack, eyes glazed.

The gathered men all turned and began applauding. Some of them were still naked. They beamed smiles at her and gave her a thunderous greeting, pounding their hands together with enthusiasm that was clearly genuine. One of them started a chant and within seconds the others joined in. Someone cut the tribal music and chants to allow this new mantra to dominate the room.

No real surprise what they chanted.

"Moloch…Moloch…Moloch…"

Balls.

But they were chanting it like frat boys. "Moe-*lock*…Moe-*lock*…"

Made it sound a little silly, but for all that it was still scary as shit.

The man with the white hair nodded to the guards and they half-led, half-pushed Bambi up a short flight of steps in front of the golden statue. Then they used red silk scarves to tie her wrists and ankles to small rings set into the statue.

The gathered men applauded this, too. They were a happy bunch. They laughed and elbowed each other and hurried to pull on their robes.

White-hair looked at his watch again and spoke to one of the guards, nodding toward the door as he did so. The guard immediately began heading toward the door.

My time was up. If the guard went downstairs he'd see the three guys I'd trashed.

What choice did I have?

I stepped out of the shadows and pointed the gun at the center of the crowd. As I did so I yelled to the whole crowd, very loud and very clearly.

"Shut the fuck up."

They did.

They actually froze in place, their chant snapped off like someone had hit a switch, leaving their mouths hanging open. White-hair pointed a finger at me.

"Who the fuck are you?"

It was a reasonable question.

Wasn't one I wanted to answer, though.

"Cut the girl down," I said.

They didn't. They also didn't move or speak. The whole bunch of them simply stood there and stared at me. So I swung my gun toward White-hair, aiming it at his face.

"Cut her down," I repeated. "Right now."

He didn't even bother looking at the gun. Instead he looked at me and a slow smile formed on his face.

Smiles are not what you want to see when you have someone in your sights. You want to see fear and a cooperation born from a desire for self-preservation.

"Who are you?" he asked.

"The fuck does that matter to you?"

"You come in here, waving a gun, disrupting our religious services—we should at least know who you are and why you're here."

"I'm just here for the girl," I told him. "I'm taking her out of here and I'll blow a hole in anyone who so much as blinks."

The rude son of a bitch actually blinked. Deliberately and repeatedly. Smiling all the time.

"You're not a policeman," he said.

"I could be."

He shook his head. "We own the police."

Ah.

"And you're not FBI."

"You own them, too?"

Another shake. "No...but they're too smart to show up alone."

"Now that's just mean," I said.

He chuckled. So did I. The other guys didn't laugh, though there were a few tentative smiles. Most of them were still trying to figure out what was going on. Me, too. Only White-hair seemed to be comfortable with the way things were falling out. I didn't find that comforting.

I cut a look at Bambi. She was still on her feet, but the glazed look in her eyes was intensifying. I wondered if they shot her up with something just before bringing her out. It looked like the drug was still hitting her system. She tugged at her bonds but instead of being alarmed at being restrained she seemed only mildly surprised.

"Look, chief," I said to White-hair, "let's cut the shit. Cut the girl down now."

"Or—?"

"I thought we covered that. I shoot you and take her anyway."

He nodded at my gun. "That's a Glock 17 with an optional floor plate, which gives you nineteen rounds instead of the standard seventeen. That's nineteen shots max and there are more than twenty of us, not counting the guards. Even if you dropped one man with each bullet—and I think we can both agree that's unlikely—the rest of us will drag you down."

"Maybe."

"Definitely," he said.

"You won't live to see it happen."

"I don't care."

He looked like he genuinely didn't.

"Bet you'll feel different when your brains are on the wall."

He shook his head. "If I die then I ascend to the golden halls of Lord Moloch where I will sit on a jeweled throne and have a thousand slaves bowing at my feet."

"Or, you'd be worm meat in a box."

One of the security guards chose that moment to go for his gun. He was to my right and probably thought he had a real chance.

I pivoted and shot him in the chest. I don't care how big your pecs are or how much Dianabol you take, a nine millimeter slug is going to punch your ticket. The round went in beside his sternum and punched its way out through a shoulder bone, taking pieces of his heart with it. Blood sprayed some of the gathered men.

The guard dropped right there and then.

The crowd looked down at the blood on their clothes and skin, and immediately began rubbing at it. I thought they were freaking out and trying to rub it off. But that wasn't it. They were smearing it into their skin, smiling as they did so, laughing as if they were in ecstasy.

The rest of the crowd…*cheered.*

The second guard was also cheering as he pulled his gun. He was standing five feet from Bambi, and I swung around and put one into his chest and a second through the bridge of his nose. The back of his head exploded, splattering the girl and the golden statue with brain tissue and blood.

The crowd began yelling, laughing, applauding.

I turned back to White-hair, who was clapping his hands together with slow irony.

Around us the cheers were turning into a new chant of *Moloch…Moloch.*

White-hair said, "Do you have any idea what's happening here? Do you have any idea what you've stepped into? What you've interrupted?"

"Some," I said. "Bunch of dickheads making human sacrifices to an ancient god in the hopes of getting some divine assistance with your stock portfolios."

He beamed at me. "That's wonderful. Oversimplified and a little naïve, but wonderful."

"So, fill in the blanks," I suggested.

"Why? Are you hoping to join us?"

"I don't know. Let me hear the recruitment speech."

He spread his arms and turned toward the golden statue. "You said it, friend. We're praying to the god Moloch. We sacrifice to him as man was instructed to do—a sacrifice of the children, made in blood and flesh and flame. In return he guides us and protects us and fills our pockets with gold."

"Uh huh. Tell me, sport," I said, "how many of those sacrifices are you *own* kids?"

He snorted. "Our own? Do we look crazy?"

"Pretty much."

He glanced around. "Okay, sure, in the moment, but you came in at the wrong part of the show. If you'd been a little patient you'd have seen the main attraction."

"Which is what, you going all Hannibal Lecter on a teenager girl who can't defend herself? Excuse me but that's hardly a—"

"No," he said. "The life or death of that worthless slut is nothing. You're a man, you should understand that. She's a cow, a piece of meat. If you're here looking for her then you must know her history. A whore and a junkie whose life would never have mattered. If we hadn't given her the chance to *matter*, then she'd have wound up in a crack house giving two dollar blow jobs while marking time until disease and a cirrhotic liver took her down to the hell that is surely waiting for her."

"Oh, right, and you guys are the Salvation Army. Skinning her alive is the best way to save her soul."

"*Her* soul doesn't matter," he said, his smile flickering a bit. "She is a means to an end. Our god is appeased only through the offering of living flesh, and the only flesh that matters is that of the young. That is the pathway to glory. It is through such offerings that every man here—every devout believer in the majesty of Moloch—has become wealthy beyond his dreams." He scowled at me for a moment and shook his head. "You probably can't grasp this. You put on an expensive shirt and think that's going to make you look rich? You stink of poverty, of cheapness, of weakness, so this might all be beyond you."

"Maybe not."

He gave another shrug. "But we were all born to money. We deserve the good things we have. It's in our blood, in our breeding. We are the elite of this world."

The men all applauded this. Some of them gave each other high-fives.

"It is our right to take what we want," White-hair continued.

"Even if it means killing the innocent?"

He spat on the floor between us. "Innocent? That's a bullshit word and it doesn't mean a fucking thing. That girl and everyone like her is a parasite. It's because of people like her that our whole country is on the edge of economic collapse. She's a leech on the system, and who pays for her free food and medical care? Us! The very ones who actually make the money and whose skill and genius made America great in the first place. It's people like her—and you— who want to take it from us."

"Seriously," I said, "you want to turn this into a political rant? Now? With a gun in your face and your guards' brains on your shoes? That's where you're going with this?"

He stopped and cocked his head as if listening to a replay of his own words. Then he sighed.

"Sorry," he said. "I got caught up in the moment."

"Sure," I said.

"Where were we?"

"The girl. You were about to come to your fucking senses and let her go."

"Ah," he said, gesturing to a small table near the golden statue on which were various knives and scalpels. "No. I think I was going to invite you to watch our god accept the sacrifice of flesh and blood."

"I'm pretty sure we weren't going there."

Behind me fists began pounding on the door. They must have broken through into the hall downstairs. My time was up. His eyes flicked to the door and back to me, and his smile returned, brighter and broader than ever.

"Playtime's over," he said.

I shifted around to stand between Bambi and the crowd. White-hair turned with me, so I edged closer to him so he could get a better look at the barrel of my gun.

"You're right," I said. "We're done fucking around. I want you and all of your asshole buddies down on the floor, hands behind your heads, fingers laced. Last man down gets a bullet in the head."

Nobody moved. All the chanting died away and the room fell into silence except for the fists pounding on the door.

Bambi stirred and moaned.

White-hair smiled.

Behind me, Bambi suddenly screamed.

I whirled, bringing the gun up, expecting to see a guard or one of the men trying something fancy, maybe sneaking up behind me.

I wish that's what it was.

But it wasn't.

When I'd shot the second guard his blood had splattered all over the statue. As I turned I saw that almost all of it was gone.

It hadn't dripped or rolled off.

As I watched in absolutely stunned horror I saw the blood vanish as if it was being absorbed, pulled *into* the skin of the golden statue. Bambi screamed and screamed. Not because the blood was vanishing...but because the statue was moving.

Moving.

Moloch, the bull-headed god.

Moving.

Flexing its massive limbs, muscles rippling beneath a skin that glistened like polished gold but which was becoming real, tangible flesh. Still golden, but pulsing with life. Wherever the blood had touched it, the statue's surface became *alive*.

Behind me I heard White-hair say, "Behold the glory of Moloch. Behold the demon-god made flesh through a sacrifice of blood. Behold your death."

-15-

Bambi screamed and screamed.

And I screamed, too.

My mind reeled just as my feet staggered backward. This was impossible. This wasn't some fucked up frat stunt...these men had actually conjured a monster, a demon, from the darkness of the ancient world. It was real.

It was real.

The giant bull head was still immobile, but the blood-spattered chest expanded and the muscles of its abdomen rippled. Then from the open mouth of the statue an impossibly long tongue lolled out, uncoiling like a pale serpent until the tip of it touched Bambi's shoulder. Her whole body was speckled with blood, and the obscene tongue licked it up, drop by drop, hooking gobbets of meat and curling them back into that golden mouth.

The face—the solid metal mask of its face—*moved*. Jaws opened and eyes blinked once and again, losing the blank stare of a statue and flashing with hideous life. Its lips curled into a sneer that was part sensual delight in the taste of human blood and part cruel expectation of a greater feast to come.

The gathered men once more began their chant.

"Moloch…Moloch…Moloch…"

White-hair laughed like a madman as the demon-god drew in a massive lungful of air and then let loose with a roar that was unlike anything I could ever imagine. It was so loud that it knocked me backward. I lost the gun and clapped my hands to my ears. Blood burst from my nose. I landed hard on the floor as the sound smashed me like a fist.

Then it stopped.

I gagged and rolled over onto hands and knees, vomiting onto the hardwood.

"Moloch…Moloch…Moloch…"

My ears were so badly damaged that the chant sounded like it came from the bottom of a deep well.

"Moloch…Moloch…Moloch…"

Out of the corner of my eye I saw White-hair bend down to pick up my pistol. Beyond him the men in robes were crowding the table on which the knives were displayed. Bright steel seemed to sprout from every hand. There was a weird sound like bending metal as the demon-god Moloch began to move its massive limbs.

Bambi's screams were rising to the ultrasonic as the full horror of what was happening pushed through the protective haze of the drugs. Somewhere deep within that scream I could hear the lost sea-gull cry of a little girl. The desperate and utterly hopeless shriek of a child who is being used and used and who knows that no one would ever, could ever come to save her. It was the most horrible sound I'd ever heard. It was the sound of an innocent being destroyed.

I think that's what did it.

Not the threat of the gun.

Not the men with their knives or the pounding of guards' fists on the door.

Not even the first earth-shaking footfall of the demon-god.

It was the sound of the lost child within the woman's scream.

It was primal.

Feral.

And in my mind, the wolf heard the scream and he—it—howled back in unbridled fury. The young of the pack were in danger, and the strongest of the pack had to answer. Had to respond.

Had to fight.

I transformed without knowing I was going to do it.

No…that's wrong. I transformed without resistance. All of me—man and wolf—*wanted* this. All of me needed this.

On one side of a broken second I was a man, smashed to the ground, broken and lost; and on the other side of that second I was the werewolf.

I rose from the floor just as White-hair raised the gun.

I saw the surprise in his eyes. The shock.

The fear.

The doubt.

Even with all of that he pulled the trigger.

Again and again. Each bullet found its target. In my chest. In my heart.

And it did him no damn good at all.

I leaped into the air, closing the fifteen foot distance between us in the space between his third and fourth shot. I took him with my front paws, claws extended. He exploded around me. Arms and legs and head.

His blood was a cloud of red mist that I flew through as I rushed toward the other men.

They had their knives.

They tried.

They tried.

But they might as well have turned their knives on themselves.

I filled the room with screams. Theirs. Bambi's. Mine.

They died around me. Beneath me. In me.

The room shook and I wheeled amid red carnage as the demon-god came toward me. Bambi was still tethered to him, tied wrist and ankle with red scarves. As he reached for me with one massive hand he reached for her with the other.

Most of him was flesh.

Some of him was still metal.

Whatever process of transformation was necessary for him to come from whatever hell he lived into the world of flesh and blood, it was not completed. Maybe there hadn't been enough of the guards' blood. Or maybe adult male blood was not enough. Maybe Moloch really needed the blood of a child sacrifice to gain his full power. Maybe that's why he reached for her, to feed his need, to create the bridge between his world and ours.

Maybe.

Maybe.

But who gives a fuck?

Bambi was still alive. And I was never more alive than I was in that moment. Fully the wolf. Without hesitation or resistance on my part. A monster, and reveling in that.

On the walls all around me were framed posters of women who had died in this room. I could feel their eyes watching me. I looked at their faces. Recorded every image with the clarity of mind that is a gift of the wolf. Every face, every line, every curve, ever scar and blemish. Sixteen beautiful girls, each of whom had been torn apart and had their blood and flesh fed to a monster.

An actual monster.

My ancestors, the Benandanti, fought evil. They fought monsters and demons. Until now I thought evil was a human thing. Entirely human. I thought the whole 'fighting monsters' things was some kind of metaphor, a grandiose way of describing struggles with human corruption.

Moloch, by his fact, by his presence, by his reality, changed all of that. It made the unreal real.

It also made the stuff of nightmares real.

Demon-gods.

Fallen angels.

Blood sacrifices to conjure something impossible.

Gold made flesh.

Maybe being flesh was the only way Moloch could exist in this world. I don't know, I'm not a mystic, I don't do metaphysical questions. All I know is that if Moloch was flesh—or even partly flesh—then it meant that he belonged to this world. And this world has rules.

One of which is that all flesh is vulnerable.

With a howl as loud as the roar of the demon-god, I threw myself at Moloch, slashing at him with my claws.

The golden flesh was tough.

Damn tough.

But flesh is flesh.

I had claws as sharp as razors. I had all of the muscle given to me by whatever power or gene or curse created my family's bloodline.

I had the rage of a werewolf. A Benandanti.

A hound of God.

And I laid into that evil son of a bitch with everything I had.

Golden flesh opened as I raked him back and forth.

Red-gold blood splashed out, striking Bambi, who screamed and screamed. Hitting me in the face, in the mouth. I snarled and drank the blood down as I slashed.

Moloch roared in sudden pain and his surprise was awesome to see.

Maybe in all of his thousands of years of existence he'd never felt pain. Maybe he thought that pain was beyond him, that he was immune to it.

But he chose to be flesh. That's what he wanted from his worshippers. They killed so many girls to give him that gift.

And I used it against him.

I tore at him. I bit into his stomach and pulled out organs and meat. I covered the floor and the walls with the blood of a fallen angel.

It burned my mouth and throat.

I drank it anyway.

When the guards knocked down the door they found shattered pieces of a statue standing in a lake of molten gold. Bambi crouched on a table that had once been covered with knives. She hunkered down, arms wrapped around her head, unwilling and unable to witness this.

I stood in the center, in the hollow of what had been the chest of the bull-god, a golden lump of heart-shaped meat in my hands, muzzle buried in it, feasting.

The guards saw this. They pointed guns at me.

I raised my head and growled at them.

And they dropped their guns and fled.

-16-

Later...

I'm not sure how much later.

I dropped Bambi at the E.R. of the closest hospital. I walked her in. She was catatonic. She had some minor burns from drops of molten gold. She couldn't speak, and the drugs were still in her system. I left her with nurses who tried to get me to tell them who she was, who I was, what had happened.

I walked away and found my car and drove back to my office.

That was six hours ago.

I showered in the tiny bathroom then took the bottle of Pappy Van Winkle's 23-Year-Old bourbon back to my desk, poured a big glass, and drank it slowly. When it was gone I refilled it. And refilled it again.

Around midnight I fished for the card I'd found on my floor and laid it on my desk blotter.

LIMBUS, Inc.

Are you laid off, downsized, undersized?

Call us. We employ. 1-800-555-0606

How lucky do you feel?

How lucky did I feel?

Hard to say.

Hard to really know what to think.

I'd fought something that shouldn't exist. On the other hand, to most people I *was* something that shouldn't exist. Hang both of those on the wall and look at them.

Moloch.

Jesus.

But with all of that, there was something that hung burning in my mind.

After I'd let the wolf out, I'd looked at the faces of the sixteen murdered women. Those images were indelibly recorded in my mind. Every single detail. They were all strangers, women I'd only ever seen as skinned meat.

Except.

There was one face, one woman. A little more beautiful than all the others.

It was the kind of face that you read about. The kind of face that might have looked down at you from a movie screen if she'd been allowed to live, to grow up, to become what she'd wanted to be. Pale skin with pores so small it looked like she was carved out of marble; with good bones and full lips and only a single visible flaw. If you could call it a flaw. A small crescent-shaped scar on her cheek near the left corner of her mouth.

I thought about that face. It had been on a poster, screaming down at me, dying.

Maybe the cops would be able to match it against one of the sixteen bodies in morgues across the country. That scar, though, wouldn't be there. It had been stolen with her skin.

But I'd seen it.

Yeah, I'd seen that scar.

I reached out and touched the Limbus card. I traced each digit of the phone number.

If I called it, I wondered who would answer.

I wondered if anyone would answer.

I sipped some more of my bourbon and wondered about a lot of things.

My cell phone lay on the blotter next to the card. I looked at it.

I poured myself another drink.

And another.

Toby's Closet

-1-

The place wasn't a dive.

Dive is an active word.

This was past tense.

Dove.

There was enough neon left in the sign outside to give you a clue about the name.

Heaven Street Diner.

They didn't do what some diners try, where they call it a 'family restaurant' so they can jack up the dinner specials to twenty bucks for crab cakes that tasted like they were padded with mulch. Nobody would bring the family into this place. No-fucking-body. Not unless they started out with bad directions and took a few wrong turns along the way. And even then it would be to use the bathroom, grab some road coffee and get the hell out of here.

I kind of liked the place.

It suited my personal economy.

And the coffee could defend itself. Tom Waits wrote a song about that, but I forget the words. Point's the same. You don't want the taste of a plate of eggs or a Salisbury steak kicking your coffee's ass. There's already enough heartbreak and disappointment in the world to give up on coffee. My coffee. Real goddamn American boiled, black and bitter diner coffee.

I was on my third cup, perched on the corner stool of the wraparound counter. Four or five other people in there. Sitting alone. Wrapped in their aloneness. I can't call it 'loneliness' because I don't know them well enough. But they are pointedly, even aggressively, alone.

As was I.

Though, I was waiting for someone and I doubt any of them were.

I'd been waiting for about an hour, but that was cool. The coffee was good. I had tomorrow's newspaper and was working my way through the crossword, trying to figure what eighteen across was. Eight letter word for trouble beginning with a 'V.'

It's how I pass the time because when you're a P.I. you have to learn to wait. Surveillance eats up whole days. Waiting for a timid client is another way to kill some minutes. You can't always choose where the client wants to meet, either. I mean, sure, if I was a big ticket firm then they'd come to me. I'd make them. We'd sit in a big air conditioned office and I'd have a secretary take notes. But that's not me. My office is a shithole that currently has no air conditioning and a problem with flies. Temperature inside is three degrees hotter than the surface of the sun. Window fans won't touch it. So, when a client sends an email and asks to meet at a diner that has air conditioning and coffee, I go. You wouldn't believe the kinds of places I've waited and the kinds of people I meet.

In my line you don't meet the pillars of society or the cream of any crop. Nope. You meet the kind of people who wash up against the counter at Heaven Street.

The dinner special was chalked on the board but it was almost midnight. Bacon-wrapped chicken legs, two veg and soup. I had maybe half a pinhole of flow left in my arteries, so I passed. Had a salad.

An actual salad.

The waitress—her name is Ivy—gave me a long five count while she waited for the punch line. When she realized I actually wanted a salad she looked crestfallen.

"You sick, Sam?"

"No," I answered. "Why?"

"Every time you've ever been in here you ordered a steak. Rare steak. Like you wanted it to moo when you stuck a fork in it."

"I like rare."

"There's rare and then there's steak you have to chase around the room."

"You walking toward a point, Ivy?"

She looked down at her order pad and then raised disappointed eyes to me. "Salad?"

"My doctor tells me that my cholesterol numbers are too high."

"Ah."

"She has me on those statin drugs. And I'm taking a water pill, too. My blood pressure could blow bolts out of plate steel."

"Ah," she said again.

"So, yeah...salad."

"And...what? You want light dressing on that?"

"Balls, no. Ranch."

Her smile returned like I was not a completely lost soul. When she returned with the salad it was covered in bacon bits. Big, fresh bottle of Hidden Valley next to it. More coffee. Couple of hot rolls and butter.

Hey, it's not steak. Most of it's green. It's healthy.

I ate it while I read the paper and waited. Occasionally throwing looks at Ivy, who was a cutie. Maybe five years younger than me, though her eyes were older. Way older, like she'd already seen too much before she wound up here. A medium-height dishwater blond with a good smile and great legs. I was thinking of asking her out, but the tattoo made me wonder. Around her third finger, left hand, where a wedding ring used to be she had a band of tiny skulls wrapped in barbed wire. As statements go that kind of thing tends to give a man serious pause.

I sat. I finished the salad. Drank more coffee. The diner emptied out.

Figured out that crossword clue.

Eight letter word for trouble beginning with a V.

Vexation.

Ivy came over and leaned on her side of the bar. The sound system was playing a Leonard Cohen song. Sisters of Mercy. One of those songs that walks the alley between hopeful and sad. I guess bittersweet is the word.

We were the only two people in the place.

"Sorry to make you wait so long," Ivy said. "I thought they'd never leave."

I set down my cup and looked into her deep green eyes.

Troubled eyes.

I said, "Oh."

And she said, "I'm glad you came. I didn't sign the email."

"Oh," I said again. I'm sharp as a razor.

She said, "Can we talk?"

I looked around. There was nothing in any of the booths except shadows.

"Talk about what?"

"I need help," she said.

"Sure. We can talk."

I held out my cup for a refill.

We talked.

-2-

"It's my landlord's son," she said. "Toby."

"Is he bothering you?" I asked. "Hitting on you or—?"

"He's six," Ivy said."

"So, that would be a no."

She said, "He keeps getting hurt."

"Old man knocking him around?"

"His father's gone. Bugged out when Toby was still a bun in the oven."

"'Kay."

"His mom, my landlord, is Gail. She has a four-story place over on Dover Street. Six apartments. Not much of a place, but she keeps the hot water running and keeps the roach population down."

"Better than my landlord."

"Gail's okay," said Ivy. "We're not friends, exactly. Veterans of the same war, if you know what I mean. We bonded over the fact that men, as a rule, suck."

"I've heard. That's why I don't date them," I said.

"Yeah. Funny. Anyway, we've had a few beers, you know? Killed a couple bottles of tequila and talked about why all men are scum." She paused and gave me a low-wattage smile. "Almost all men."

"Thanks," I said. "I think."

She shrugged. "You never try to grab my ass and you aren't obvious about looking down my blouse when I bend over to pour coffee."

"Ah."

"And," she said, "people talk."

"About?"

"About you. You have a reputation. People can go to you."

"That's my job. Private investigator and all. I have cards."

"You know what I mean, Sam. They say that if the cops can't help—or *won't*—sometimes you can do stuff."

"'Stuff,'" I echoed.

She shrugged. "Stuff."

I drank some coffee. "What's happening with the kid? With Toby? Who's hurting him?"

"That's just it," she said. "We don't know."

"He won't tell his mom?"

"He says he doesn't know who's doing it."

"You mean it's a stranger?"

She shook her head.

"Then you lost me. Who's thumping on the kid?"

Ivy took a while on that. It shouldn't have been the kind of question requiring this much thought. She folded her arms and leaned a hip against the counter and looked at me through the filter of what she knew and maybe of what she was willing to say.

I waited her out. Push too hard and you can chase the timid ones off. Some people need to get to it in their own way and time. I wasn't double-parked; my coffee cup was full. So I waited.

She said, "It happens when he's sleeping."

I waited some more.

"He goes to bed without bruises," she said. "When he wakes up he's hurt."

"Every night?"

"No. Some nights. If there's a pattern Gail hasn't figured it out."

"How bad are the injuries?"

"Not bad. But bad enough. Like I said, he's six."

"His mom take him to the E.R.?"

"Sure. Guess what they said?"

I sighed and nodded. "They think it's her."

"Yes. A caseworker's been to the house twice. There's paperwork on it now, and even though they haven't come out and made actual threats, Gail knows that she could lose her kid to the system. Unfit mother and all that. Child abuse."

"Which makes me have to ask…"

"No," Ivy said firmly. "It's not Gail."

"And you know this how?"

"I know."

I shook my head. "Sorry, kid, but that's not good enough. I've met a lot of sweet-faced, innocent-as-a-lamb people who did some pretty extreme stuff when no one was looking. Appearance doesn't count for much when you're talking the way the personality is wired. Ted Bundy was a charming guy."

"It's not her. I'm telling you."

"And I'm telling you that I don't know you well enough outside of this diner to know if you're any judge."

Ivy cocked her head to one side and her eyes hardened. They got even older, if that's possible. "When it comes to child abuse, Sam, I know what I'm talking about. I can look in someone's eyes and I know."

"You know," I said, flatly. Nailing it to the air between us. A challenge, maybe.

"I know."

"So, if you're so sure, and if you know the other people in the building, who do you think looks good for this?"

Her intensity wavered. "I…don't have any idea."

"Ah."

"I mean, I was there one night."

"What?"

"One of the times it happened. I was there," she said. "I came up with leftovers from here, and I brought a sixer of Coors to split with Gail. We all watched a Disney movie on cable. One of those penguin ones. The first one. And then Gail put Toby to bed. The place was locked up, and her apartment's small. The living room's right next to his bedroom. We put on Grey's Anatomy and had some beer and she told me about the people from Child Services. Then, oh I guess it was like ten-thirty, eleven—no, not even eleven because Jon Stewart wasn't on yet—Toby starts screaming."

"Screaming…"

"And Gail all but kicked his door in. I knew that this was going on so I had something in my pocket."

"What?" I asked.

She hesitated, glanced around the empty diner, and then fished something out of the pocket of her waitress uniform. She held it out on the flat of her palm. It was a Stanley box-cutter with a retractable blade.

"We get some sketchy characters in here," she said, putting it away again. "I work a lot of nights."

"Glad you have it," I told her. "So, you barge into Toby's room, Gail's upset, you have your blade and—?"

"And nothing. Toby's all scrunched up against the headboard. Sheets are on the floor. Pillows are on the floor. His pajama top is open and he's got bruises on him."

"What kind of bruises?"

"Hand marks. They were bright red, like he'd been slapped. And…you could see them starting to fade a little. You know how when you touch someone's skin and then let go you can see the blood flow back? Like that, except these were the opposite. They were red and then they faded."

"Completely?"

She shook her head. "No. He still has bruises."

"How big were the marks? Could he have made them himself? Kids sometimes do that. All sorts of psych problems a kid goes through. Broken home, maybe something going on in school. Mom works a lot of nights, so there's always a stranger babysitting. Kids get confused, the world's scary. Hurting themselves isn't—."

"Toby didn't make those marks. No way."

"You're sure?"

Ivy gave me a strange look. "Wait here."

She went into the back and came out with her purse, then fished her phone out. She opened the camera function, brought up the photo stream and then pressed one of the pictures before handing the phone to me.

"I took these. Scroll through," she said. "You'll see."

I scrolled.

I saw.

I said, "I'll take the case."

Ivy gave me the address and it wasn't too far from the diner. Walking distance if I wanted to get the exercise my doctor said I needed.

I drove.

The apartment building was a pile of dirty red bricks that squatted between a five story tenement that Fagin wouldn't live in, and a movie theater that used to show porn flicks and was now a Korean church. Gail's building had bars on all the windows, even the third floor. I walked around back. Fire escape was rusted junk that I wouldn't climb at gunpoint. There was a five-step walkdown to a cellar door. The stairwell was half filled with trash and I doubt that door had been opened anytime since Bush senior was in office.

If someone was getting into Gail's apartment, they weren't doing it from outside.

From the photos I saw, I wasn't all that surprised.

Didn't look like junkies or visits from the neighborhood pedophile.

One odd thing was what I didn't smell.

Dog piss.

Not a drop of it anywhere.

Now, understand, I have this sense of smell. It's one of those extras that come with what I am. Great sense of smell, pretty good ears, outstanding sense of taste—which is why I appreciate good coffee. I'm particularly sensitive to the subtleties of dog urine. I sniff a few drops I can tell you everything about the dog. Breed, age, sex, whether he still has his balls. All of it.

And in a neighborhood like this, you get a lot of dogs running around and they are very territorial. One will piss on a wall, another one who thinks he's King Shit will come along and piss over it. Like gangbangers spray-painting over someone else's tag. Got to say who *you* are and take away anyone else's mark.

Outside the Korean church and all around the movie theater I could make out thirty, forty different dogs. Old and new scents. Couple of alphas, lot of wannabes.

Back of Gail's place? Nothing.

Nothing is weird.

Nothing is...

I cut through the alley to the front, climbed the steps to the front door and rang the bell.

Took Gail a couple of minutes to answer. When she opened the door I understood why Ivy wanted me to help her.

Gail was one of the broken ones. One of those women who have been so comprehensively beaten down by life, by circumstance, by financial disappointments, by obligations, by missed opportunities, by fractured families and fair-weather friends that she was one step away from being no one at all. Pale, thin, almost translucent. You could look right through her and see that the world would be here if she up and died and that everything would look the same. Like that.

Except…

Except there was fresh hurt in her eyes, and hurt is an immediate thing. It's now. Especially when it's stitched to the fabric of that phenomenon called motherhood.

That whole mother thing? Guys can sympathize but they can't really empathize, and it's not just 'cause we have different plumbing. There's something about a mother—a good one, mind you, not some organic machine that drops a kid after nine months of inconvenience. What that something is, I don't know. I saw it in my mom, and in my grandmother and a couple of my aunts. There's a certain change. Maybe it's spiritual, maybe it's supernatural, maybe it's only chemical. I don't know and don't pretend to know. But it's there. This woman had it.

Maybe it was the only real spark of life left in her, but it was there.

She was a mother who was desperately afraid for her kid.

I've met that kind before. A two person pack. Mom and kid. Sometimes the mother—the woman—would let life and circumstances and men push her around and knock her down and drain her dry. Some of those women were so broken they didn't care enough about themselves to duck a punch or file a police report. It's heartbreaking, because that level of defeat is itself a product of systematic abuse.

But go after their kid?

Fuck, man.

If there's anything they can do, they'll do it. If they need to bite your throat out with their teeth, yeah they'll go right for the jugular.

All that stuff about a mama bear protecting her cubs? It's not bullshit and it's not myth.

The fracture line comes when the ferocious need to protect their young is on the other side of not knowing how.

That was Gail North.

"Ivy sent me," I said when she opened that door.

She looked up at me with haunted blue eyes.

"Are you Sam Hunter?"

"Yeah," I said. "I'm here to help Toby."

-4-

We sat in the living room. She called it a parlor. A little touch of the old fashioned that I found charming.

The room was small. A second-hand couch with indifferent springs, two big, old but comfortable-looking armchairs with lots of pillows, a coffee table that matched none of the furniture. A nice TV. When she caught me looking at it, she smiled.

"From Ivy."

I nodded. Ivy played down how close they were so I wouldn't think this was a charity case or an emotional 9-1-1. Fair enough. I might have passed.

On the floor in front of the TV was a stack of DVDs. *Finding Nemo*, *Lion King*. Like that. Old titles, probably bought second hand or in a lot on Ebay. Nice for the kid, though. Maybe nice for the women, too. All of the relationships were uncomplicated and the good guys always won in the end.

She offered me coffee but I settled for water. It was tap, but I'm a long way from being a snob. I sat with the glass cradled between my palms and tried to look earnest and resourceful.

"Did Ivy tell you what was happening?" she asked.

"She told me some. Enough to get me here."

"She show you the pictures?"

"She did."

Gail nodded.

Those pictures. Boy oh boy.

"Let's start at the beginning," I said. "How long's this been going on?"

"A few months."

"How many months?"

"Three. Almost four."

"How many attacks?"

"I…don't know."

I cocked my eyebrow. "You don't know? How's that work?"

Gail pushed a wisp of brown hair out of her eye. "Toby…he…he didn't…"

"He didn't tell you right away?" I suggested, and she nodded.

"But I started putting it together, you know?" said Gail.

"No, tell me what you mean."

She licked her lips again. The tension must have been drying her mouth out. That or it was a regular nervous tic. "After I, you know, *found out*. I mean, after I saw those marks, I started asking him." She turned away, momentarily embarrassed. "Actually I grilled him. I was pretty loud about it."

Her face turned slowly back toward me, but there was a flinch buried beneath a fragile smile. Like she expected me to hit her. Or accuse her.

"You were scared," I said. It's not like me to take someone off the hook or to make it easy for them to talk. Comfort isn't part of my job description. Except when it is.

I guess it's fair to say that I did not for one moment believe that Gail North was hurting her son. Not for a half a moment. If I did, we'd be having a whole different kind of conversation, woman or not. Everybody has buttons. I have mine. Not like I came from a bad home or anything. I didn't. My parents were the best. I have a big family. Cousins and aunts all over the place. No, it's not that.

You see, before I started working private cases I was a cop. Not here in Philly. Back in the Twin Cities. A court-appointed psychologist once told me that I was too emotionally involved in my work, particularly when it came to domestic violence cases. I kept getting written up for being too rough with rapists and baby rapers. With wife beaters and child abusers.

Everyone has their thing.

I don't give much of a wet shit about someone selling crack or rigging poker machines. I'm not Elliot Ness and I'm not Captain Avenger.

Take an electrical cord to a pregnant woman? Send a kid to Emergency five times in eight months? Yes, we could have problems.

It's what got me shit-canned from the job.

Can't say I've made progress with what that therapist called 'action steps' since.

So, no, I looked in Gail North's eyes and I heard her voice, I smelled the chemicals in her skin and could taste the raw fear in the air, and I knew.

She wasn't hurting Toby. And she hadn't beaten the story out of him.

"I kept after him about it, though," she said. "He didn't want to talk about it. But I guess I wore him down. I figured it out. From times he said he wasn't feeling good. Times I thought he was sick or something, but I think he was hurt. And other times, when I saw bruises. At first I thought it was kids at school. He just started first grade. But now I know that's not what it was."

"How many times?"

"Ivy and I spent a whole night on it. Trying to do the math." She licked her lips again. "Maybe seventeen times over fifteen weeks. About every six days."

Six days.

Every six days.

Going back nearly four months.

Christ. The kid must be in hell.

"Always in his bedroom?"

She shook her head. "No. It happened in my bedroom, too. And a couple of times in here."

"How were they getting at him?"

She had no answer to that. Or none she wanted to say out loud.

"Did you ask Toby?" I asked.

"He doesn't like to talk about it. Actually, he won't talk about it."

"Why didn't he want to talk about it?"

She looked away again. This time I saw her eyes fill with tears and that's what she didn't want me to see.

"They said not to."

I waited.

"They told him that he wasn't allowed to tell anyone."

"'They'?" I asked. "Who are they?"

I watched her face in profile. I saw a tear break and roll down over her cheek.

"He...he..."

But even with all of her need, Gail couldn't actually speak the words. She shook her head. And then buried her face in her hands. The sound of her sobs were like punches that hit me in the chest over and over again.

I wanted to go over there, gather her in my arms and shelter her from this. I wanted to tell her it was all going to be okay. That all her problems were over now that I was here.

But I'm not that big a liar.

There are some things I can fix. Lots of things I can't.

"Gail," I said, and even my own voice sounded hoarse, "look at me."

It took her a while. It cost her a lot. But she did.

"Tell me what you think is happening."

Her eyes were big and filled with shadows. She shook her head.

"Gail, if this is happening here, then why don't you move?"

She flinched. You'd have thought I'd raised an angry fist.

"I—I—"

"Go on," I coaxed, "you can tell me anything."

"I did move."

"What?"

"Before we came here, I had a three unit place in Kensington. Before I had Toby."

"And...?"

"Someone killed my two cats."

I said nothing.

"A couple of times they'd be hurt and I thought they were getting out somehow. But then I found Whiskers and he was all torn up. He was right in my bedroom and he was all torn apart."

I said nothing.

"A few months later Spooky died, too. Someone had...had..." She shook her head refusing to describe the carnage. I didn't need the details. She took a steadying breath. "A year later I got a dog. A puppy."

She left it there. Point made.

"Who's doing this?" I asked.

"That's just it—there's *no one*."

I nodded. "Then tell me *what's* doing it, Gail."

She started to turn away again. Stopped. Pulled a crumpled tissue out of her pockets, dabbed at her eyes and stared down into it.

She began to say a word.

"Mon—"

A sound stopped her.

There was a door beside the TV. It opened and a small, pale, round face peered out.

Big blue eyes. Lots of freckles. A scuffle of brown hair.

Toby.

-5-

You want to say that all kids are cute, that they're adorable. That they are beautiful.

Toby wasn't any of that. He was just a kid. No better or worse looking than anyone else's kid. His skin was a little splotchy and his mouth was too small. Maybe he'd grow up to be a movie star, but probably he wouldn't. He'd grow up to maybe work at a convenience store. Or maybe he'd deal weed. Or maybe he'd wriggle his way into community college. He was from this part of town and there weren't a lot of Harvard alumni here. Not a lot of NASA math geeks.

Ordinary folks. Maybe on the poor side of ordinary. Maybe on the slow side of average. There's no crime in it. You play the hand you're dealt. We all do.

The crime is when someone steps on them because they don't seem to count.

That's one of my buttons, too.

"Toby—?" I said, hoisting a smile onto my face. I'm not a good looking guy, either. I'm shorter than average size, thinner than average weight, plainer than average looks. Like Toby, I guess.

Gail looked up and hastily wiped away her tears, slapping on one of those fake it's-all-okay smiles. She held out a hand and waggled her fingers toward him.

"Hey, baby, come on in. It's okay."

The kid hesitated, his eyes darting from her face to mine.

"It's okay," she repeated. "This is Mr. Hunter. He's a friend of Ivy's."

That did it. The kid pushed the door open and stepped into the living room. God, he was a scrawny little thing. Tiny Tim without the limp. He ghosted into the room, made a wide circle around me and glued himself to his mother's side.

The transformation in Gail was immediate and heartbreaking. Heartwarming, too, in its way. As Toby pressed up against her that mother fierceness was suddenly in the room with us. She wrapped her arm around him and pulled him close and kissed the top of his head. Right then if a three hundred pound trucker with a tire iron had come after Toby she'd have gutted him like a trout.

Mothers, man. Gotta love 'em.

I said, "Toby, would it be okay if I looked at your bruises?"

His eyes got huge. He shook his head and pressed closer to Gail's side.

"Toby, honey..." she said. "It's okay. Mr. Hunter's going to help us."

"N-no..." he murmured, turning away from me.

"It's okay..." she soothed.

"They don't want me to."

They again.

"Who, baby?" asked Gail, stroking his hair. "Tell Mr. Hunter who said not to tell?"

"*They* did. They said not to. They said I shouldn't. They said bad stuff was going to happen if I told."

"Nothing bad's going to happen," I said. "Not anymore."

He shook his head. "They said that they'd do stuff if I told."

"What kind of stuff?"

"*Bad* stuff."

"Who?" I asked gently. "Who doesn't want you to tell?"

"*Them.*"

I took a breath. "Toby, where are they?"

He pressed closer. Shut his eyes.

"Toby, if you want me to stop them you have to tell me where they are. How are they getting in?"

He said something very faint, very small.

I don't know if his mother heard it, or if she heard whether she understood. I have really good ears. I heard it.

Toby said, *"They're always here."*

"Where are they?" I asked.

Maybe it was something in my voice, or maybe being that close to his mom gave him a splinter of courage. Hard to say. He didn't say anything, didn't come right out and say it, but he pointed. To the coat closet by the door.

Then to his open doorway.

I turned and looked.

I could see past the bed and the little desk and the rickety chair. The chair was pushed up against the closet door. Stuff was piled on it. Not because the kid was sloppy.

No. Because the kid was smart.

Trying to be smart.

Weighing the chair down.

Making it harder to push.

Making it harder to open the bedroom closet.

I said, "Jesus."

I stood up and turned toward the bedroom.

"Wait!" said Gail. "What are you doing?"

I shrugged. "Nothing much. Going to take a look in Toby's closet."

The boy spun around in his mother's arms and stared at me in total terror.

"No!" he shrieked. "You can't!"

"Why not?" I asked.

"They won't like it."

"I don't care what they like, kiddo. You shouldn't either."

"But they said they'd—" He stopped short, unable to voice whatever threats he'd heard.

"Maybe it's not up to them."

"But they *said*…"

I turned back to him and smiled. "They said. Okay, they said. Sure. And maybe that was scary. Maybe that scared you and your mom, and maybe that's been scary for a long time. But here's the thing, Toby, and I need you to understand me, okay? Can you try?"

He nodded. It was a tentative, uncertain nod, but it was there.

"Sometimes even the big, bad scary things have other things they're afraid of. Like bullies. Most bullies are afraid of something. They teach you that in school?"

He nodded more easily. Bullies were something ordinary and he could stand on the firmer ground of that concept.

"*They*," I said, pointing through the open doorway toward his closet, "are just like bullies. They go after you 'cause you're little. You know what that tells me? It tells me they're scared. They don't come out of your mom's closet 'cause they know she'd kick their butts."

Gail gave me a frightened look as if she thought I was suggesting she do something heroic and dangerous.

She was a mother fighting for her kid's life in the best way she knew how. That was heroic and dangerous enough. I grinned at them both and I showed a lot of white teeth.

Most of the time my teeth are just like regular teeth.

Until they're not.

I didn't show them fangs or fur or any of that, but maybe for a moment they both saw the wolf looking out of my eyes. They recoiled, but they didn't actually turn away.

"There are a lot of scary things in the world," I told them. "And some of them are on *your* side."

Toby's mouth opened and it took him a few seconds to speak.

"But...but...they have claws..."

I could feel the muscles of my face, the ones that kept my smile warm and friendly, tighten. Just a bit.

"Lots of things have claws," I said.

Then I turned and went into Toby's bedroom and closed the door.

-6-

Alone now.

Standing in front of the closed closet door.

The bravado and the bullshit? That's for the clients.

Some of it's real enough. A lot of it is conman patter you dish out to make the shills think you know everything and it's all copacetic.

In my line of work almost nothing's copacetic.

You lie to the clients all the time.

Not because you're running some kind of scam to bilk them out of their savings. Nah, it's not like that. I may not be on the side of the angels but I'm not a total dick. No, for me the conman stuff, the trash talk is because you need them to leave you to it. You don't want interference. And you sure as hell don't want them to try and come along for the ride. If you have to protect someone while doing your job, then your attention is split and your life expectancy is for shit.

I stood there in front of the door and I could feel the shakes start.

Some of it was fear, and yeah, I was scared out of my fucking mind. I had no real idea what was behind that door. Only vague guesses and none of them were sane. None of them promised a happy day for me or the people I came here to protect.

None of them fit into the world that was on my side of the door.

At least not entirely.

Maybe they fit into my world because of who and what I am. Because of what my family is, what we've been for as far back as our family history records. The Hunters. One of a hundred names adopted by my people, and one of the more obvious puns. Hunter? Jeez. Not as bad as my cousins in Kentucky. Bill and Karen Slaughter. Or my third cousin in Italy. Tito Lupos.

You get the picture. For us, in our version of the world, strange stuff happens. Not all the time. Not even a lot of the time, but it happens.

For me it happens a little more often because of what I do. Not so much as a cop, but since I've been a private investigator I've come up against some deeply weird shit. Pretty sure I met a ghost once. Smoking hot, too. Good chance she was a murder victim who hired me to find her killer. That wasn't even the most extreme part of that because the killer turned out to be a group not a person—a bunch of one percenter dickheads who thought sacrificing girls to a demon would make them richer and more powerful.

The fact that they actually conjured a demon? Yeah, that freaked me out.

Totally freaked me.

Still freaks me and it was four years ago.

Met a couple of vampires, too. Wiseguy wannabes trying to create some kind of half-assed Mafia with fangs.

And other things. I've even met people like me. That was wild, because I'd never met a single one of us outside of the family.

Then I went to this weirdo little town north of Philly called Pine Deep. Met all *kinds* of people like me. The fur and fang club. We did not sit around a campfire and bond over how hard it is to be lycanthropes in today's society. We didn't drink wine and braid each other's tail hair.

Nah.

We fucking killed each other.

Well, some of that crowd got killed.

I didn't. Clearly.

Which meant that I was alive and able to stand outside of Toby's closet door and feel every tremor of fear and dread about what was on the other side of it.

Winning a bunch of fights can make you tough, sure. It can prove to you that you're a bad mamba-jamba. But it can also have the opposite effect. Each time you put the other guy down and you get back to your feet you can almost feel another card being dealt from your deck of luck and you wonder what will happen when you have no good cards left to play.

I was wondering that, too.

But, like I said, being scared was only one of the reasons I was standing there trembling, why my hands shook as I pulled the chair from in front of the door and reached for the handle. Being scared is always going to be part of it. I'm not a super hero.

The other part?

Yeah, that was rage.

These fuckers—whoever and whatever they are—they're going after a woman and her kid.

That kind of pisses me off. It makes me angry.

Remember that old show with Bill Bixby? The Hulk? That famous tagline about how you wouldn't like me when I'm angry.

Like that.

I turned the handle and opened the door.

It was a closet.

I stepped inside and closed the door.

Stood in the dark.

Knowing that it was a lot more than a closet.

Knowing that I wasn't alone in there.

-7-

The darkness was all around me.

And it was big.

A lot bigger than a closet. A lot bigger than Gail's whole apartment.

I had no freaking clue where I was.

All I had was a lot of pop-culture references, too many Lovecraft novels, and a misspent youth playing long hours of D&D with my nerd herd.

It was a fabulous, formless darkness. Not my words. I read them somewhere.

It was a vast and maybe timeless place.

An abode of spirits.

Maybe, if I was channeling reruns of Buffy the Vampire Slayer, it was a hell dimension.

Never been to one before. I hope to Christ that I never find myself in one again. I felt naked, exposed, and more alone than it is possible to be anywhere in the physical world and that includes in the middle of Antarctica on a cold winter's night.

I was nowhere.

Which, apparently, is a place you can actually be. Who knew?

This is a moment when you are absolutely sure you are in the presence of some kind of grand power. When you have proof of life beyond our world. Maybe it's a kind of left-handed proof of God. Or something godlike. Not sure. What I did know was that it was a time for awe. For reverence. A time to be humbled by the infinite possibilities of this dimension beyond the known.

So, I guess what I should have done was say something nice. A prayer. A plea. A politely worded entreaty.

What I said was, "Hey, dickhead!"

And I said it very loud.

-8-

As it turns out, beings from the outer darkness don't like to be called dickhead anymore than, say, a redneck at a roadside bar.

They get pissed.

Kind of the point of saying it, though.

I could feel him coming.

Him, them, it. Whatever.

Suddenly I wasn't alone in the big black nothing. I could feel something there. Bigger than me. Close to me. Breathing on me.

Breathing.

Its breath was awful. Cold and rancid. A mélange of stinks and chemicals. Ozone and sulfur. Rotting fish and adrenaline. Sweat and piss.

"Jesus H. Christ," I said to him. "You fuckers have your own pocket universe and you can't buy some Tic-Tacs? Seriously?"

The roiling darkness seemed to pause.

I grinned, hoping I was aiming that grin in the right direction because I couldn't see a thing. I figured *it* could.

He told.

It wasn't a spoken voice so much as a thought that appeared in my head. Telepathy or something like it.

"Who told what?" I replied.

The boy, spoke the voice in my head. *He told you about us.*

"What if he did?"

We told the boy what would happen if he told.

"Yeah," I said, "about that. Three things occur to me."

Who are you to speak to us?

"Does it matter?"

There was a pause before the big voice answered. *You are meat for us. As the boy is meat. As his mother is meat. As—*

"Yeah, I got it. Everyone's meat. Point made. Now listen to me, 'cause I want to share those three little insights. I think you'll find them important because, hey, I think they're crucial talking points for us here."

Sweat ran down in lines beneath my clothes. My frigging scalp was sweating. I could smell my own fear, which meant *they* could, too.

Speak, said the voice, and there was amusement in his voice.

Fine.

Asshole.

I said, "First thing, the whole monster in the closet thing is sad. I mean it. Sad. It's so 1950s. It's not even retro cool. It's just silly. Have you seen *Monsters, Inc*? You're a fucking Pixar film."

You mock us.

"Pretty much," I agreed.

We will tear your flesh and—

"Okay, okay. Stop yelling. I'm already scared of you. You're in my head, can't you tell?"

There was a silence and I thought it was significant. Maybe they *couldn't* tell. Maybe transmitting their voice into my head was in their skill set, but not reading minds. Cool.

"Second thing," I said, "is that you picking on little kids and house pets tells me something. It tells me a lot, actually. A whole lot, when you think about it."

I could feel the thing moving. The exhaled breath was on my face, then on the back of my neck. In my mind I could see the pictures Ivy showed me on her phone. The marks left behind on Toby's skin. Not slap marks or punch marks. Not cigarette burns like you see on some abuse victims. Not even claw marks.

The kid's chest and back had been covered by rows of round marks.

Sucker marks.

Like the kind of thing you see on a fish that an octopus has killed.

Whatever this was, it had tentacles.

I think that's how it fed. It wrapped them around the kid and took what it wanted from him. Maybe it was fear. Maybe it was life force. In the folklore of supernatural predators there's a lot of cases to be made for both. The books on the subject talk about monsters that came in by night and stole the breath from a sleeping child. Maybe it wasn't breath. Maybe they fed on fear itself. Maybe *Monsters, Inc* had it right. Who knows, maybe the guy who wrote the movie was working through his childhood issues.

Creatures that feed on the fear of innocent children.

That's some sick shit right there. It's a whole different kind of bullying.

Out loud I said, "I don't hear about you asswipes picking on grownups. Why's that?"

I didn't think he'd answer, but he did. Not the answer I wanted, either.

The flavor is wrong. The older the bottle, the poorer the wine.

I said, "Oh."

If he was telling the truth, then apparently my logic was flawed. Shit. I was hoping I was facing a pussy of a monster. Someone who didn't have the stones to go after a grown-up.

Not good.

The darkness seemed to writhe and boil around me. It exhaled its rotting fish breath so close to me it ruffled my hair and stung my eyes.

Tell us, taunted the beast, *what is the third thing that you came all the way here to tell us.*

Now it was in front of me again, even though I couldn't see it. The breath blew straight into my face. It was so strong, so powerful that I gagged on it. I had to turn away and gulp in some air to keep from throwing up.

The fact that there was air here mattered a whole lot to me.

I told him that.

"The third thing," I croaked, "is your breath."

Our…breath?

"Yeah. Like I told you before, it stinks. Really and truly stinks. Like horse shit on a hot wind, and I don't mean that in a nice way. Every time you breathe on me I want to hurl."

There was a sound in my head. Maybe it was laughter. Hard to say in all that darkness.

We are so sorry to offend you. But have you wasted your last breath to tell us this?

"Sorry, no, that was kind of a digression," I said. "I'm getting to my point but I felt I had to say that, you know? To put it out there."

More of that laughter.

"What I really wanted to say was that I find the whole breathing thing to be a major talking point for us. A sticking point, in a way."

Explain this nonsense.

"Sure. Happy to," I said, and now my whole body was shivering and shaking. I could feel this thing getting even closer. Slimy coils of blackness brushed up against me, and snaked around me. There was a sucking sound and I wondered how it liked the taste of my fear. Maybe I was the wrong vintage for it, but the thing was taking a sip. "You're not the first monster I've met."

We are not a monster. We are gods.

"Whatever," I said, "my point is that you're not the first supernatural being I've met. You're not even in the first dozen."

Then you understand that the universe is greater and darker than the other cattle think. Understanding is the key that opens the door to fear.

"Well, yeah, understanding is clutch. No doubt. Here's the thing, though," I said, forcing my voice to sound calm. "Everything I've met, everything weird and unnatural and supernaturally fuck-ass wrong that I've dealt with is like you."

A pause, even in the movement of the tentacles.

Nothing is like us.

"I'm not saying they're all Cthulhu wannabe tentacular abominations, which—I'll admit—is something you're rocking pretty hard. No, what I'm saying is that there are a few common things about all of them."

No.

"Oh yes. First, they all fucking breathe. Even vampires, and that one surprised the crap out of me. They breathe. Just like you're breathing."

As if to both agree with me and mock me, it exhaled a blast of sulfur and fish rot at me. I staggered backward and it was only the presence of its unseen coils that stopped me from falling on my ass.

The thing laughed at me.

The laughter rang inside my head. Hurting me. I felt warmth in my nose and touched it, smelled my own blood.

"Hey, sparky, I'm not done," I said, my voice thick because of the blood running down the back of my throat. "The thing I've been getting to is that anything with a body, anything that *breathes*, is mortal."

We are forever.

"Not talking about lifespan, dickhead. I'm talking about flesh. You are flesh, and that makes you mortal."

We are not mortal. We are monsters.

It took the word a child would use and tried to mock me with it.

I grinned. I could play kid games, too.

"I know you are," I said, "but what am I?"

You are human. You are cattle.

I wanted to say 'no,' to fire back some cool witticism, but at that moment I changed and my throat was no longer built for human speech. I can do the change really fast now. A second. A heartbeat.

Bang.

Scared man one minute.

Wolf the next.

Big freaking wolf. Lots of claws. Lots of teeth,

Pissed the fuck off because this motherfucker was trying to eat the life of a little kid.

Here's the really funny part.

Monsters in the dark—yeah, they can be afraid, too.

They can scream, too.

This one screamed.

He cried.

He even begged.

Not sure, but he might have even--right at the last--called out for his mother. If that word even applies to this thing. It was that kind of call, though.

Loud, wailing, plaintive.

And futile.

I threw my head back and drowned the sound of it with my own howl. It was the loudest cry I'd ever made, and I wanted it to echo in the darkness for a long time.

-9-

I found the doorknob.

It was right there behind me.

I staggered out and collapsed onto the floor.

I was naked and covered in black oil that was probably blood. I smelled like dead fish.

I was me again. The wolf was sleeping. Satiated. Content with what it had done.

On all fours I crawled over to the bed and dragged the sheet off, wrapped it around me. Huddled there on the floor for a long time, shivering, trembling.

The wolf isn't afraid of anything.

I am.

Afraid and human. My mind was almost frozen in gear trying to accept what just happened.

When Gail knocked and came in, she saw me and almost screamed. The closet door stood open. It was filled with toys and clothes.

"I…think I need a shower."

"Oh my god!" she cried, dropping to her knees but not actually touching me. "What happened?"

"D-doesn't m-m-m-matter," I said, my teeth chattering. "It's ov-over. I have extra clothes in my trunk. Car keys are on the table by the couch."

Past her, peering around the edge of the door, I saw Toby. Just part of him. One big eye.

He looked at me and I looked back. Maybe there was some shared awareness that certain people have. He saw me and he *knew* that I knew. That we shared that bit of knowledge.

I smiled at him, and I nodded.

"It's okay now," I said.

The smile he gave me was slow in coming, but it was brighter than anything I'd ever seen. It pushed back the memory of darkness in my mind.

-10-

Got showered. Got dressed.

Hugged the kid. Left my card with Gail.

She didn't have much money, but I told her that it was already taken care of. I figured Ivy wouldn't be asking me to pay for omelets and coffee for a while.

I hugged Gail, and that became a group hug with Toby. Kid's a good hugger. Puts his heart into it.

Then I left.

And, yeah, before I got into my car, I went around back. There was a mutt back there pissing on the wall. I let him finish then went over, unzipped and pissed over top of his splash. Wolves do that, too.

Then I got in and drove away.

Back to the diner.

I needed some strong damn coffee.

Three Guys Walk into a Bar

A Limbus, Inc. Adventure

-1-

The card was tucked into the cleft of a crack in the vinyl of my old Ford Escape's dashboard. The car was locked, the alarm functional but silent.

Card was still there.

I hovered there in the open doorway of the car and looked at it. Whoever had placed it there crinkled the end so the card folded back to make it easy for me to see what was printed on it.

LIMBUS, Inc.
Are you laid off, downsized, undersized?
Call us. We employ. 1-800-555-0606
How lucky do you feel?

"Balls," I said.

-2-

I plucked the card out and threw it on the shotgun seat, got in, fired up the old beast, and headed out of the parking lot of the medical offices of Dr. Frieda Lipschitz.

She's a great doctor, but, seriously, no one should ever have a name like Lipschitz. I know it doesn't mean what it sounds like it means. Dr. Frieda—and I have to call her that or I can't keep a straight face—makes a point of telling everyone that it's a bastardization of Leobschütz, the German name for the Polish town of Głubczyce. Okay, sure, fine, nice history lesson. Change your name. Go with Lefkowitz or Lipstick or anything.

I mean, if you're a proctologist you have a certain responsibility to your clients. It's a thing. Go with it.

So, there's me, driving away from Dr. Frieda's office after her telling me that I need a colonoscopy because I'm looking at fifty close enough to read the fine print and guys my age who eat like I do and drink like I do and generally act like overgrown frat boys like I do need to have someone stick a hose and a flashlight up their ass. Not how she put it, but words to that effect.

I told her I'd think about it.

She then browbeat me for twenty minutes and somehow I wound up agreeing. But…I really don't know if I could or should do it. There are complications with guys like me going under general anesthesia. Those complications could be life-changing for anyone in the E.R. if I have a bad dream.

Funny thing is, the thing she harped on the most was my cholesterol.

"You eat too much red meat," she said.

I tried to make a joke and tell her that it wasn't by choice. She didn't get it and, let's face it, it's not like I could explain.

So, she stuck her fingers in my butt, told me my prostate was okay, and cut me loose with a date for the procedure and a prescription for stuff that would 'cleanse my bowels' the night before.

Given a choice between marathon pre-procedure bowel evacuation and, say, getting mugged by an entire hockey team, I'll take my chances with the hockey team. Sticks and all.

This is what I was thinking about as I drove.

The card was still on the seat next to me.

Still saying 'Limbus' on it. Still reminding me of the last card with that name on it I'd had.

What was it now? Three years ago and change.

One of the nastiest cases I ever worked. Some psychopaths skinning young girls.

Yeah. Skinning.

Turns out, when I finally ran it down, the skinning wasn't actually the worst thing that was happening to those girls. I know, you're thinking how could it get worse than that?

There are more things in heaven and earth, Horatio.

Some of those things come into my life dragging a lot of very ugly baggage.

That case haunts me.

Absolutely fucking haunts me.

Sometimes in the middle of the night I wake up and see those dead girls standing around my bed. Naked of flesh, stripped of humanity, bloodless and lost.

I know I'm dreaming, but I think I'm awake. The things those girls say...

When I really wake up, I try to remember their words, but I can't. Not really. It's like the dead speak in a language that the living can't really understand. Can't, and shouldn't try.

What scares me the most is that the older I get, the more I think I'm starting to understand a few words of that language. It's becoming more familiar.

I leave night lights on now.

Me. Sam Hunter. Ex-cop, occasional bodyguard, working private investigator. Whatever else I am. Tough and scary.

A night light.

Shit.

The card refused to evaporate or fly out the window even though there was a breeze whipping through the car. As if it was anchored there. As if it didn't want to leave.

Limbus, Inc.
How lucky do you feel?

I stopped at a red light and watched a father cross the street while holding the hands of two little girls. Twins. Maybe four years old. Curly blond hair on one, curly red hair on the other. Otherwise identical.

The little girls looked at me. Both of them.

They smiled at me.

I smiled back.

Innocent little kids. Pretty, happy. Their whole lives ahead of them.

The group of assholes I hunted for Limbus flayed the skin from girls only a dozen years older than these two. Girls who also expected to have lives, a future. Happiness.

Dead. Destroyed.

Consumed.

The father shepherded his daughters to the other side. The little redhead kept looking back at me.

And, as the light turned green, she gave me a single, silent nod.

It was such a weird thing. Not a kid thing. It was an adult gesture, and for a flickering moment her blue eyes were filled with a much older light.

Then she turned away and the guy behind me beeped his horn.

I hit the gas too hard and jerked the Escape forward, cursed, adjusted the pressure on the pedal, and drove away from the moment.

The card was still right there.

When I pulled into the slot outside of the creaky old building where I have my office, I left the card where it was. I didn't want to bring it inside. It would mean that I was at least considering giving them a call. No way that was going to happen.

I locked my car, went up into my office.

Read the mail.

Most of it was bills. Some of it was junk.

Some of it was threatening letters.

Usual stuff.

I made some calls. Did some Net stuff for clients.

Didn't think much at all about the card.

Except that's a lie.

I couldn't *help* but think about the fucking card.

I was thinking about the card when Stevie Turks walked in with two of his goons. Card went right out of my head at that point.

Here's the thing about Stevie. His real last name is Turkleton, and he's a six and a half foot tall lump of ugly white boy with more biceps than brains. I was warned about him when I took a missing persons case last year. Stevie likes young chicks. Ideally fifteen or so.

He gets them high, gets them naked, and videotapes them having sex with him and some of his crew. The video files are uploaded to a server in the Netherlands and sold to foreign buyers. I found this out while looking for a ninth grade girl who was last seen in Stevie's storefront business—a video game shop on Broad Street near Girard. The girl's mother let me look around the kid's room, and that allowed me to pick up her scent. Everyone has a distinctive smell. Even kids with good hygiene. Most people can't tell.

I'm not most people.

It took me a week to find the kid. Unfortunately by then Stevie had spent way too much time with her. The kid was so far out on the edge of a heroin high that she didn't know what day it was. Barely knew her own name.

They'd been busy with her. Three video sessions a day. Different outfits. Schoolgirl clothes, cheerleader uniforms. Shit like that.

I am no prude. But I have a very clear set of rules. Rape is, to me, no different than murder. It kills a part of the victim's soul. I've seen it way too many times. As a cop in the Cities and as a P.I. in Philly.

And when it comes to the rape of a child? When it comes to white slavery? Sex trafficking? Forced addiction?

Well…

Stevie was in the hospital for three months. Did that without changing, either. Just me, a blackjack, and a lot of moral indignation.

Would have been worse if I'd let him see the real me, but I actually wanted him to stand trial.

He lawyered up, of course, and they're taking their sweet time getting the trial started. Jury selection is next month.

Honestly, though, I did not expect him to be stupid enough to come here, to my office. He thought he was being smart by bringing two guys who were as big as he was. The three of them looked like bridge supports. Muscles on top of muscles.

Stevie opened his jacket to show the gun tucked into his belt. One of the goons closed the door. It was after hours, there was nobody else in the building. Again, they thought they were stacking things in their favor.

I stood up from behind my desk.

Stevie pulled his gun and pointed it at me. "You don't want to fucking move, dickbag."

-3-

The killer moved through the shadows. Running low, running fast. The winding ribbon of the game trail twisted and turned, whipsawed and plunged down the backs of the hills. Night birds screamed and fled the trees, flinging their ragged bodies into the cold sky. The last of the season's crickets held their noise, their insect minds unable to process anything other than the concept of danger.

Of death.

A brown bear raised her head and sniffed the air. Then she pulled her cubs close and sheltered them with her bulk. The bear closed her eyes, not wanting to see what it was that passed so fast and so close.

The killer was aware of these things.

It drank in the intoxicating richness of sight and sound, of smell and taste. There was no drug that could match this rush. Not even the most powerful psychotropic pill or magic mushroom. Nothing came close.

It reveled in the thousand things that flooded in through its senses. The enormity of the information had been staggering at first.

At first.

Now…

Now it was greater than a sexual thrill. Greater than anything.

Almost anything.

There was one thing that sent an even more potent thrill through the killer's dark mind.

It raced toward that experience now.

With claws that tore the soft ground.

With teeth that gleamed as the killer smiled and smiled and smiled.

-4-

I stayed where I was. "You really want to do this, Stevie?"

"No, I'm still fretting over whether it's a good idea."

We both grinned at that. It was a good comeback.

"They already have my deposition. On video. I signed the transcript in front of witnesses."

He shook his head. "Don't mean shit. It's your word against mine. And that little slut isn't going to be worth shit on the witness stand. My lawyers will rip her a new asshole. Not that her last asshole wasn't good. I tapped that shit. Damn if I didn't. Tight? Holy shit was she tight."

"Stevie," I said quietly, "you'd do yourself a big favor to shut the fuck up right about now."

He chuckled. "Why? Thinking about that tight little brown-eye giving you wood?"

"Stevie…" I said.

"Fuck this guy, Stevie," said one of the two goons. He had a big nose that looked like it wanted to be punched.

"Yeah, fuck him," agreed his colleague, who had no noticeable chin. "Let's do him and get the fuck out of here."

Stevie shook his head. "I'm not in a hurry. I spent three months thinking about this. This asshole suckered me and stomped me when I was down, and I need him to appreciate the consequences of his actions."

"Who writes your dialogue?" I asked. "I'm serious. Joe Pesci couldn't sell lines like that. You sound stupid, Stevie. No, let me correct that, you sound cheap. You're a third string kiddie porn asshole and your father would have done the whole world a favor by jerking off instead of banging your mother. Now you come here and try to lay some tough guy Goodfellas rap on me like I'm supposed to go all knock-kneed. Are you kidding me?"

He brightened. "Wait, you think I'm putting this on? Really? 'Cause I think that you're going to realize just how wrong you are when I cut your dick off and stuff it in your—"

And that was as much of this bullshit as I could take. It wasn't a good day to begin with. Doctor sticking both hands and one foot up my ass. That damn card from Limbus. These assholes. The memories of the hurt in the girl's eyes when she was done with rehab and sitting with the cops to tell them what she remembered. A hurt I was sure would always be there, polluting her life, darkening her skies.

I know I said I wanted Stevie to go to trial.

I really did.

Past tense.

I jumped over the desk at him.

He wasn't expecting that.

Not a knock against him that he wasn't expecting it. The average person wouldn't be primed to make that kind of intuitive leap.

I was only a medium-sized, middle-age man when I started the jump.

I was something else when I hit him.

I saw the way his eyes changed as he realized just how much trouble he was in. As he realized exactly what tough really was and how little judgment he possessed. As he realized that the world was so much different than what filled his limited understanding.

He'd come with superior numbers and overwhelming force to kill a man.

He did not bring enough of anything to kill the wolf.

-5-

A solitary headlight cut through the forest and the killer stopped.

He froze into the moment, becoming absolutely still. The breeze blew past it, rifling hair, but the killer was now part of the vast and complex darkness of the woods. Beneath the canopy of oak and pine boughs, the floor of the forest was as impenetrable as the deepest part of the ocean. Not even a spark of moonlight fell through that ceiling.

But the headlights...

They moved along the serpentine fire access road, pushing the engine buzz in front of it.

The killer watched the light, amused by it like a traveler seeing a will-o'-the-wisp. The road the bike drove came from the southeast and curved around toward the northwest.

Toward where the killer waited.

The killer felt drool worm its way from between his lips, hang pendulously from his chin and then fall. He could hear the release of the ropey spittle. Could hear the splash as it struck the grass. He could hear everything.

The sound of the motorcycle and the glow of its light ignited a burning hunger deep in the killer's mind. His mind, first. Then in his chest, and then in his stomach.

Always in the mind.

That's where hunger began.

That's where lust lived.

The killer turned, peeling itself out of the featureless black of the forest as it stepped onto the winding road.

To wait.

-6-

It takes a long, long time to bag three grown men.

Takes even longer to clean up the mess.

My office is prepped for it, though. Everything is waterproof. Everything is cleanable. I keep a bucket and mop, bleach, paper towels, rags, soap, sponges and brushes in the closet. A big box of heavy-duty contractor black plastic bags. And a wheeled mail cart.

Took me nearly five hours to clean everything up.

Played Tom Waits and Steely Dan really loud while I did it. Sometimes you got to play loud music to distract you from what you're doing. And, yes, I have playlists for this sort of thing.

My life is complicated.

I killed two more hours driving to a landfill I knew of and dumping the bags, then driving back. Tried not to look at the card while I was driving. Still hoping it would blow out the window. Still didn't. Came back to the office, drank some beer. Watched a DVR of the All-Star game and fell asleep on my couch.

I didn't start thinking about the card until I woke up. Took a poor-man's shower standing in front of the sink and washing myself with paper towels. Thought about coffee and decided to go find some.

The card was still in my car when I came outside at a quarter to seven in the morning.

Except it wasn't where I left it.

It should have been on the passenger seat. Instead it was tucked into the cracked vinyl where I'd found it the first time.

But this time it was turned backward so I could see what somebody'd written in blue ballpoint. One word.

"Now."

I looked at the card.

I got out of the car and looked around the area. The usual suspects were doing what they usually do. Cars passed on Street Road, heading everywhere but where I gave a shit. No one was looking at me. No one looked like the kind of person who'd leave this kind of card.

I didn't want to call the number. They might as well have printed *'nothing but trouble'* in red embossed typeface.

I said, "Fuck."

I went back into my office.

And called the goddamn number.

-7-

The motorcycle rounded the curve in the road and the light splashed its whiteness ahead. The pale light painted the figure standing in the road.

The driver tried to stop in time.

He swerved.

He braked.

The bike turned and began to slew sideways toward an inevitable collision. One that would break bone and burst meat and splash the landscape with blood that would be black as oil in the night.

The killer did not move.

Not right away, at least.

As the bike and its driver skidded and spun toward him, the killer rose up from four legs to two. He bared his teeth and with red joy reached out to accept the gift that was being given.

It was not just meat and blood that fed him.

He feasted on the screams as well.

Oh, how delicious they were. And he made sure they lasted a long, long time.

-8-

The voice that answered did not belong to the beautiful woman who'd hired me last time.

The voice was male.

Nasal, high-pitched, fussy. If a Chihuahua could talk it would be like that.

Funny and cute if it was a cartoon. Less so on a business call.

Instead of saying "Hello" or any of that shit, he picked up halfway through the second ring and said, "Mr. Hunter."

My name, not his.

"Who's this?"

"We're delighted that you called, Mr. Hunter."

"I'm not. Who is this?"

"Limbus," he said.

"No, your name."

A pause. "My name is Cricket."

"First or last?"

"Just Cricket."

"Jeez."

"And, as I said, we're delighted you called."

"Why?"

"My employers were very satisfied with the manner in which the last matter was, mmmm, handled."

The humming pause was for effect. He wanted me to know that *he* knew exactly how that case was handled. I had to use some irregular methods. Irregular for most P.I.s. Only semi-irregular for me.

"Can I speak with the lady who hired me before?"

"Mmmm, which lady would that be?"

"Don't jerk me off."

Another pause. "That person is no longer a part of this organization."

"What happened to her?"

"She is, mmmm, engaged in other work," said Mr. Cricket. "And before you ask, Mr. Hunter, I am not at liberty to discuss the matter."

"Balls."

To be fair, it was what I expected. I would have been genuinely surprised if I ever saw her again.

I sighed. "Okay, so what do you want?"

"Are you, mmm, familiar with the town of Pine Deep, Pennsylvania?"

"Sure. In Bucks County, on the river."

"Have you ever been there?"

"No. I heard it burned down."

"There was some trouble," Cricket said diffidently, "but that was a number of years ago. It has been, mmmm, substantially rebuilt."

"Big whoop. How's that matter to me?"

"We would like you to go there."

"Why?"

"To conduct an investigation."

"What would I be investigating?"

"There have been a series of, mmm, attacks."

"What kind of attacks?"

"Murders."

"Murders? Plural?"

"Five murders," he said. "And one person seriously injured."

"That's too bad. Correct me if I'm wrong, but don't even one-Starbucks towns in Bucks County have police departments?"

"They do."

"Maybe you haven't heard, but unless you're in a movie, it's pretty rare for anyone to hire a private investigator to go anywhere near a police matter. Cops, as a rule, take that sort of thing amiss."

"Amiss," he repeated, apparently enjoying the word.

I waited.

Cricket said, "You used to be a police officer."

"'Used to be' is a phrase you should look at more closely."

"You're *still* an investigator."

"Private. And let me reiterate that P.I.s do not—I repeat, *do not*—interfere with active police cases. Cops tend to get cranky about that. Cranky cops can make life very difficult for working P.I.s, even small town cranky cops. If I interfered, I could get my ticket pulled."

"I do not believe that would happen in this case, Mr. Hunter."

"Why, are you cats going to pay for my lawyer?"

"Mmmmm, no."

"Are you going to run inference between me and local law?"

"No."

"Then have a swell day."

"Mr. Hunter, the reason you won't have those kinds of problems is that the Pine Deep Police have requested our assistance."

I said nothing.

"They have, in point of fact, requested *your* help."

"Me?"

"Well, perhaps I should clarify…your actual name was not included in the request."

"Then what—?"

"Well, mmmm, through various channels the chief of police in Pine Deep has been searching for an expert in a certain kind of crime."

"I'm no expert. More of a general practitioner. Jack of all trades, master of none," I said, trying and failing to make a small joke.

"Forgive me, Mr. Hunter, but we disagree with that assertion. You are exceptionally well qualified for this particular kind of crime."

"How so?"

"Because of the unique nature of the murders."

That's when I got the first real tingle of warning. Small, but serious. The smart thing to do would have been to simply end the call. No goodbyes, no polite refusals, just hit the button, put the cell phone in the bottom drawer of my file cabinet, and go to the multiplex to watch a movie about things blowing up. Maybe get some Ben and Jerry's afterward.

That's what I should have done. I knew it then, and I sure as shit know it now.

Instead I felt my mouth speak, heard my voice say, "What do you mean?"

I swear to Christ that I could *hear* him smile. Like a fisherman who knew that his last tug had set the hook.

"The victims," he said after the slightest pause, "were torn apart and partially, mmmm, consumed."

"Oh," I said.

"And at the scene of each crime the forensics experts took castings of an unusual set of prints. Do you, mmmm, care to guess which kind of prints?"

I pinched the bridge of my nose. "Not really," I said.

"Just so," he said.

There was a very long silence on the line. Mr. Cricket did not seem interested in breaking it. He wanted me to jump out of the water into his little boat.

And, damn it, I did.

"Tell me the rest," I said.

-9-

The killer sagged back from the orgy of his feast.

Sated.

Swollen.

His mouth tingled from the hundreds of tastes present in fresh meat and blood.

His cock was turgid from the frenzy of the kill.

His eyes were glazed from the intoxicating beauty of it all.

He rolled over and flopped onto his back, letting the night breeze cool the blood on his skin and mouth and hands.

Hands now. Not paws.

He lay there and stared up through the trees. They were sparser here above the road and he could see a few stars.

He could see the moon.

It was a sickle-slash of white. So bright. So bright.

-10-

After the call was over, I sat slumped in my chair staring a hole through the middle of nowhere.

Cricket hadn't told me much more, saying that the local law in Pine Deep would give me the whole story. He suggested I familiarize myself with that troubled little town. The story was readily available on the Net.

When we finally got to the question of my fee, Cricket made his mmmm-ing noise again and said, "Third drawer down."

After which the line went dead.

I pushed my wheeled chair back from my desk and looked at the bottom drawer. It was closed, the way I'd left it, and I hadn't checked it since getting back. The wall clock ticked its way through a lot of cold seconds while I sat there. I hadn't told Cricket I was taking the job. We had no formal agreement. And whatever was in that drawer did not constitute acceptance on my part. Not unless I put it in the bank.

So, I could just leave it there.

Or I could mail it back to them.

Except that there was no address on the card. Just the number.

I drummed my fingers very, very slowly on the desktop.

The minute hand had time for two whole trips around before I opened the drawer.

The usual stuff was there. Yellow legal pads, box of disposable mechanical pencils, extra rolls of Scotch tape, plastic thing of staples, a dog-eared Jon McGoran thriller I was rereading.

And the envelope.

Placed very neatly and squarely in the exact center of the drawer's interior space. Fussy. Like I imagine everything was on Cricket's desk. I think he even straightened the stuff in my drawer.

"Mmmm," I said in acknowledgment.

The envelope was a standard number ten, off-white, with nothing written on the outside.

I could tell right away that it wasn't a check. Checks are flat. The contents of this envelope distorted its shape. Bulged it.

I sighed and reached for it. Hefted it, weighed it in my hand.

Heavy.

Heavy is nice. First nice thing about this matter.

I tried to judge how much would be in there. If it was fives, tens and twenties, it could be five hundred. Half a week's income for me, on a good week.

I tore open the top and let the bundle of bills slide down into my hand.

The top bill was not a five, a ten, or a twenty.

Mr. Benjamin Franklin smiled at me with a smug awareness as if to say, "Yes, son, we all have a price."

I took a breath and folded down the corner of the top bill.

The next one was a hundred, too.

So were the next thirty-nine.

My scalp began to sweat.

The stack didn't end there, though.

There were six bills with the face of someone I'd never seen on a piece of paper currency. Read about him, but never actually looked at one.

William McKinley.

The denomination insisted that this was a five hundred dollar bill.

There were six of these.

Six.

I turned on my computer and did a search to see if these were even in circulation anymore.

They weren't. The last five hundred dollar bills had been printed in 1945.

These were all from 1934. All crisp and clean as if they'd never been used.

I did a second search to see if they were still worth five hundred.

They were not.

Not even close.

I found auction sites that listed them, that sold them.

My scalp was sweating even more. So was every other part of me.

I called the number for one of the auction houses, a place in Doylestown. The receptionist transferred me to the rare coins guy. When I explained what I had, the man snorted and asked me if I was making a prank call. I assured him I was not.

"And you have *six* such bills?"

"Yes," I assured him.

"Would you mind reading the serial numbers to me?" The skepticism was thick in his tone.

I read the numbers. They were all in sequence.

He made a sound somewhere between a gasp and a growl.

"Please," he said, "assure me that this is not a joke."

"Not unless someone is playing one on me. But, look, just tell me…are these still good? I mean, could I deposit them in my bank?"

He made that sound again. Much louder this time.

"Please, sir, do not even *joke* about that. If these are legitimate bills, and if they are in the condition you describe, then they have considerable worth."

"Yeah…I saw something on your site that they might be worth fifteen hundred or—"

"No," he said abruptly.

"Oh," I said, deflated, "then—"

"If these bills are real then they are worth a great deal more than that."

"Like…how much more?"

"Do you have any understanding of rare currencies?"

"Not beyond that fact that it's rare for me to *have* currency."

He gave a polite little laugh. Enough to tell me that I wasn't as funny as I thought I was, or maybe that this was no time for jokes.

"Rarities of any kind are what drive the passion for collection. Art, coins, stamps…they have value based on a number of factors. Condition—even a scratch can take hundreds off of a rare penny, and—"

"Right, I understand that part."

"Condition is one factor in determining value. The actual degree of rarity is another. Take, for example, the 1933 Saint-Gaudens Double Eagle. When the Depression was in full swing, President Roosevelt took the country off the gold standard and recalled all gold coins for melting. About a dozen of that particular coin never made it back to the mint or were smuggled out again by enterprising government employees. One of those coins resurfaced in 1992 and was confiscated by the Secret Service but was not melted down. In 1933, it had a face value of $20; in 2002, it was sold at auction for over seven million dollars."

"Jesus Alexander Christ."

"Exactly."

"Now the third thing that can influence the value of an item is provenance. You know what that is?"

"Sure—who owned it, when they owned it, how it moved from owner to owner. Like that."

"Like that, yes. In the case of the 1934 Five Hundred Dollar Bills, there is a sequence of them that were part of a private collection of rarities. The entire collection, by the way, was appraised in 1973 and at that time valued at just under nine million dollars. It would be worth considerably more now."

"And these bills?"

"They are all from the missing sequence. There were ten bills in sequence. One turned up in Lambertville, New Jersey in 2006. The rest have remained completely off the radar since the owner of that collection died."

"Who was he and when did he die?"

There was a pause. "Excuse me, Mr...?"

"Hunter," I said. "Sam Hunter."

"Excuse me, Mr. Hunter, but would you be willing to engage our firm to handle any auction for these bills? I can assure you that no one else would be able to get you a higher price for them, or a quicker sale."

"If I decide to sell them," I said, "we can talk. Right now I need to know more about the bills. That'll help me decide what to do."

"I understand."

"What's your name?" I asked.

"Milton Peabody," he said. It seemed about right. He had a Milton Peabody kind of voice.

"So who owned the bills?"

"They were part of the private collection of a foreign gentleman who moved to Eastern Pennsylvania in the late nineteen sixties. His name was Ubel Griswold."

That name rang a very faint bell. Not a nice bell, either, but no matter how hard I scrabbled for details there was nothing in my memory. I wrote it down so I could do a search later.

"And where did this Griswold guy live?"

Mr. Peabody said, "He lived in Pine Deep. And that is where he was murdered."

-11-

The killer got slowly to his feet. He stumbled once in the dark. The man could see less than the beast. He longed to revert, to stay in the other shape. Always.

Always.

Always.

But that other mouth was not made for speech, and he needed to speak.

He was naked, but around his neck was a small metal disk on a sturdy chain. The chain was painted a flat black so that it caught no light. The disk had a single button.

He caught it between thumb and forefinger that were sticky with blood. He pressed the button.

"I..." he began, then coughed and spat out a wad of clotted blood. "I need a cleanup team."

He did not speak in English.

-12-

So, yeah, I took the case.

Cricket told me that an email with some case details would be in my inbox. It was. Somehow, though, Cricket had blanked out his own return email address. Like most P.I.s, I know some tricks about tracing emails. I hit a dead end right away. Whoever these Limbus people were they were very tech savvy. They left me nowhere to go.

So, I opened the email. There was no text, just an attachment with five photos. I opened them and sat for a long time looking at the pictures. Five people. Two men, two women, one child.

They were all dead. They had all been torn up.

These were morgue photos rather than the more useful crime scene photo. Two of the victims were in pretty good shape—

relatively speaking. They had massive chest and throat wounds, but were otherwise intact. Whole.

The other three were not.

Whole, I mean.

Each of them had been torn to pieces. Actual pieces.

"This was no boat accident," I said in my best Richard Dreyfuss, but there was no one around to get the joke.

I zoomed in on the photos and studied the wounds. I'm no forensic expert, but I know how to read wound patterns. To guys like me they tell a very clear story. Flesh torn by bullets and flesh torn by knives tell one kind of story. Friction injuries of a certain pattern can indicate a motorcycle accident or a fall down a mountain. There are distinct differences in dog bites, rat bites, and snake bites. You simply have to understand human tissue and bone, something of physics, something of anatomy.

What I was seeing told a very specific story. Maybe a coroner might have some problems with it because of the angle of certain wounds, the depths of the bite marks, the apparent bite strength needed to crush bones like the humerus and femur. Me? I could read this like a book.

Personal experience is a great teacher.

I saved the images to my computer and thought about the money.

The money would go into my bank, but not riding a deposit slip. Before I did that, though, I ran a high-res scan of each side of each bill and sent the files to myself via DropBox.

I also sniffed each bill.

I do that. I'm not weird the way it sounds. I'm weird in a different way. My sense of smell is better than most. Better than most dogs, if you want to make a point of it. Sniffing the bills told me a lot.

First, I could tell that they'd been handled by someone, but not recently. It was an old scent, just a trace. And that's really interesting because it meant that no one has handled that money recently, and by recently I mean in years. The scent was really old, barely there. How had those bills then been placed in the envelope? The hundreds were mixed bills, most of them relatively recent. Late nineties into the early 2000s. Stuff that's still in circulation. The same human scent was on them, too.

That scent and no other.

"Curiouser and curiouser," I said to the empty room. I did not for a moment believe that the scent was that of the mysterious Mr. Cricket. There was also no residual smell of latex from gloves. What had they used to stuff the envelope? Plastic tweezers?

I spent some time going over the envelope, but if there was anything to find, then not even my senses could pick it up. That was very disturbing.

And, also...intriguing.

Before I left for Pine Deep, I spent a few hours on the Net reading up about Ubel Griswold and the troubles in the town. A lot of it was new to me. I used to live in Minneapolis and Pine Deep is a rural suburb of Philadelphia. Griswold, according to the news reports, had been a foreign national who'd moved to America in the 1960s. His name was German but one reporter implied that the man was either Russian or Polish. Or maybe from Belarus, from back when that little country was known as the Byelorussian Soviet Socialist Republic. Either way, Griswold move to the States, bought some land and set himself up as a small-time cattle farmer in a section of Pine Deep known as Dark Hollow. In 1976, the area was rocked by a series of particularly savage killings. There was a whole slew of them and it was believed they were the work of one man, whom the papers nicknamed 'the Reaper.' Reporters love titles like that.

The manhunt for the Reaper was intense and the leading suspect in those killings was an itinerant day laborer and blues musician named Oren Morse. Known locally as the Bone Man because he was as thin as a scarecrow.

Ubel Griswold vanished on a—you guessed it—dark and stormy night, and his body was never found. The locals apparently ran Morse to ground and lynched him. The killings stopped at that point, so it seemed pretty clear they'd killed the killer.

If the story ended there it would be weird and sad enough, but there was a second part. Thirty years to the actual day of the Reaper killings, another psychopath came to town in the person of one Karl Ruger. He was a real piece of work. A former mob button man who'd gone way off the reservation into Hannibal Lecter territory. Apparently Ruger had ties to a local group of radical white supremacist militiamen and they put together a terrorist attack that still stands as the worst example of domestic terrorism on U.S.

shores. You read about it in the papers, maybe saw the movie they did. Or read the books. The Trouble. That's what they call it.

Ruger and the other assholes spiked the town's water supply with hallucinogens during a big Halloween festival. Pine Deep was wall-to-wall with tourists. Everyone went apeshit nuts. Eleven thousand people died.

No matter how many times I read and reread that number it still hits me in the gut.

Eleven thousand.

Three times that many were injured, and more than half the town burned down.

The Trouble.

According to the Net the town was trying to come back. Some of it was already back, though it was no longer a Halloween tourist spot. It was settling back into being a blue-collar farming community with a scattering of craft shops and some galleries.

That's what I learned from web searches.

So, while I drove out there, I tried to make sense of those events—forty years ago and ten years ago—and how they might connect with recent murders. There was damn little about the new killings in the press, and every story I read suggested that each of the victims died in a violent car crash or farm-related accident. Not one word of anything criminal. The news stories didn't mention anything about animal attacks either, which means either that was squashed or the reporters out there are dumb as fuck. My guess was the former.

I hit Route 611 and turned north.

-13-

The killer watched the big man in the woods.

The man was dressed in dark clothes. Battle dress uniform, boots, a shoulder rig with a holstered pistol. A Beretta. A knife clipped to the inside of the right front pants pocket.

The killer crouched on the thick oak limb and leaned down to watch.

The big man walked around the wreck of the motorcycle. He touched nothing. He stood for long moments studying it. He walked the perimeter of the crash scene, then out to the road, then back.

Occasionally the big man spoke out loud even though he was alone.

The killer strained to hear.

"Bug," the big man said, "looks like we got another one." He read the bike's license plate number. He gave a physical description of the driver. Or what was left of the driver. He stood as if listening. "No, tell Top and Bunny to check out that car crash in Lambertville. I'll call if I need them to come a'running."

He listened again.

"No. I think I'm going to have to talk to the locals on this. Yeah, I know the chief. Ornery little bastard. Okay. Cowboy out."

The big man suddenly straightened as if he'd heard something. His gun was suddenly in his hand. It was like a magic trick. The man was fast.

So fast.

He crouched and turned, bringing the gun up into a two-handed grip, eyes tracking at the same time as the gun barrel. The man was sharp.

Very sharp.

He even looked up at the surrounding trees.

For one fragment of a moment he looked directly at the killer.

But he did not see him.

The camouflage was too good, the intervening foliage too thick, the place of concealment too well chosen. So the narrowed eyes of the big man moved away. Reluctantly, though, as if the big man's instincts were not in harmony with his senses. As if his instincts were sharper, more primitive. Limited by the sensory awareness potentials of the modern human.

The killer smiled.

He could understand that.

He did not move at all.

But he watched every single thing this big man did. This was a dangerous, dangerous man. This was a killer in his own right. That much was obvious. His speed, the confidence he demonstrated as he turned to face the unknown. As if he'd faced — and fought — things that came at him from unexpected directions. Many times.

He had that kind of aura.

The killer in the trees watched the killer with the gun.

He wanted so badly to fight this man.

To battle with him in the most primal of ways.

To revel in defeating him.

To taste the blood of another predator.

To eat a warrior's heart.

-14-

Pine Deep is a triangular wedge of fertile farmland and mountains in Bucks County. It's bisected by Interstate Alternate Extension Route A-32, lying hard against the Delaware River that separated Pennsylvania from New Jersey and framed on all sides by streams and canals. A-32 wavers back and forth between the two states, across old iron bridges and up through farm country and then plows right through the town. To the southwest was the much smaller town of Black Marsh, and above Pine Deep was the even tinier Crestville. A-32 was the only road that cut all the way through those three towns. All other roads inside the triangle led nowhere except someone's back forty or to the asymmetrical tangle of cobblestoned streets in Pine Deep's trendy shopping and dining district. Bigger and more prosperous towns like Doylestown, New Hope, and Lambertville were pretty close, but Pine Deep felt more remote than it was. Like a lot of farming towns in America, it covered an astounding amount of real estate for the number of people who lived there. Some of the farms had ten thousand acres of corn or pumpkins or garlic and maybe a dozen people living in the farmhouse and related buildings. Migrant workers did a lot of the labor.

I rattled across the bridge and drove into Pine Deep in the middle of an afternoon that was hotter than the weatherman said it would be. The trees were heavy with lush growth, and the brighter greens of spring had given way to the darkness of summer leaves. Towers of white cumulonimbus clouds rose like the pillars of heaven, but the distant western sky was softer, painted with cirrus clouds in brushstrokes of gray-white. There were birds up there, and at first I thought they were hawks, but they were too big. Probably turkey vultures.

I slowed to a stop on the shoulder of the road and leaned out to look up at them. Counted them.

Thirteen.

I tried not to make anything of that.

Spooky town, meaningless coincidence.

I kept driving.

A-32 rolls on for mile after mile and I didn't see a single living soul. The corn was half-grown and stiff and tall. The pumpkins were only pale knobs. Way off in the distance the farmhouses looked like toys from a Monopoly set. I drove past a tractor sitting at an angle in the middle of a fallow field, the engine rusted to a bright orange. A threadbare crow stood on the curve of the seat-back, his head turning slowly to follow the passage of my car. Flies swarmed in the air over a dead raccoon whose head had been squashed flat by a car tire.

I turned the radio on to find some music to lighten the load. Couldn't get reception worth a damn except for some religious blood and thunder stuff. I dug a CD at random from the center console and fed it into the slot. Tom Waits began growling at me. Song about a murder in a red barn.

"Balls," I said and almost turned it off.

Didn't though.

Drove on, listening to Tom's gravelly voice spin dark magic under the blue summer sky.

-15-

The highway wandered around between some hefty mountains and then spilled out at the far end of a small town. Kind of a Twin Peaks vibe to it. One main street. Lots of crooked little side streets. Low buildings, lots of trees. From the crest of the hill I could look down and count all five of the streetlights.

I took my foot off the brake and let the car find its own way down the hill, coasting, in no hurry to get there. As I reached the main drag I switched the CD player off and drove in silence through the center of town. There were people here and there, but you couldn't call it 'bustling' without lying. Most of the houses and stores had been rebuilt or repaired, but here and there I could see some blackened shells. Even after ten years the town still wore its scars.

Eleven thousand people.

Were there eleven thousand ghosts haunting these hills and this sad little town? I sure as shit wouldn't buy real estate here. Not at a penny an acre.

According to the Wikipedia page for the city of Pine Deep, there were currently two thousand one hundred and nine people living here. In town and on the farms. It was hard to believe. I'd have guessed maybe five, six hundred.

I tried to imagine what it must be like to live in a place like this. It had been devastated by domestic terrorism. It had taken a worse hit than New York on 9/11 in terms of deaths. Maybe worse still when you considered that it hadn't been done by enemies of our country or religious fanatics. This terror was home grown. It was brother attacking brother. That's some hard shit to accept, hard to get past.

As I drove down the main street I saw the haunted looks on the faces of the people of Pine Deep. Some looked furtively away, unwilling or unable to meet the eyes of a stranger. Fear, paranoia, shame. Hang any label on it you think will fit.

Others stared at me, their eyes dark and intense, their attention focused and unwavering as I rolled past. I don't think I saw a single smile. I don't think I could blame anyone for being that grim, that detached. I sure as hell would be if this was my town.

I passed the Saul Weinstock Memorial Hospital, but the place was only half built. Creeper vines had crawled over the stacks of building materials and there were no lights in any of the windows.

Halfway through town I saw the sign for the police department. It was a storefront place with big ceramic pots with dead evergreens beside the door. I nosed my car into an angled slot and killed the engine.

The sign on the glass door read:

PINE DEEP POLICE DEPT.
Chief Malcolm Crow

Turn around and go home, said a little voice inside my head.

"Too late for that," I murmured, and got out. As I did, a woman came out of the office. Tall, with short black hair and dark blue eyes. Slim and very pretty in a no-nonsense country way. Around fifty but fighting it and winning. A touch of make-up and a mouth that looked made for smiling, but which wore no smile. She stopped five feet in front of me and gave me an up and down appraisal. Impossible to tell what she read from my scuffle of brown hair, JC Penney sports coat over jeans, Payless black sneakers. Probably not much.

But something flickered in her eyes and she half turned, opened the door to the police office and called inside. "He's here."

She left the door ajar.

I pasted on a friendly smile. "Are you with the police?" I asked.

A little smile flickered on her mouth. "I'm married to it."

"Oh. Then you're Mrs....um...Crow?" I ventured.

"Val Guthrie. I kept my maiden name." She offered her hand and we shook. Her hand was hard and dry and strong. She didn't go for a manly bully-boy handshake. She was strong the way women are strong. This one had zero interest in defining herself by comparison to a man. I liked that. I liked her.

"Sam Hunter," I said.

"You're the private investigator?"

"Yes, ma'am."

"Named 'Hunter'?"

"Yes."

"That a stage name or something?"

"No. It's a coincidence, but I've come to embrace the cliché."

That upped the wattage on her smile as she reappraised me. "You're a smartass."

"Says so on my business card. Sam Hunter, Professional Smartass."

She laughed. "You're going to get along fine."

She patted me on the shoulder and, still smiling, walked toward a parked Ford F-250 pickup whose bed was piled high with burlap sacks of seed. I watched her go, admiring both the straightness of her posture, and the curves that went with the whole package. Smart, sexy, and powerful. Nice.

I turned to the open office door and wondered what kind of a husband a woman like that would have. My guess would be someone who looked like Thor from the *Avengers* movies. Some big, tanned Nordic son of a bitch with muscles on his muscles and maybe a bit of aw-shucks in his voice. Or one of those redneck giants who bench press Hereford cows. Probably politically to the right of Sarah Palin. Rural Pennsylvania bears a lot of resemblance in attitude and culture to the less progressive back roads of Mississippi.

As I went in, the man I saw behind the desk was the precise diametric opposite of my guess.

He stood up to meet me, a wide grin on his elfin face. He was shorter than the woman who'd just left—call it five-seven and change. Slight build, curly black hair that had gone mostly gray, a sallow tan crisscrossed with white lines from old scars. His nametag said CROW.

"Mr. Hunter?" he asked, extending his hand.

-16-

The killer followed the big man back to the road, then hid behind a rhododendron while the man got into a black SUV and drove away. The killer noted the license number, but if this man was what he thought, that plate number would likely be a dead end.

That was fine.

The big man was hunting now.

Hunting him.

The killer wanted to make very sure that the big man found his prey.

-17-

"Sam Hunter, sir," I replied, taking the chief's hand. For a little guy he had a good, strong hand. Shooter's callus on his index finger, and a ring of calluses all the way around to his thumb. Only other guy I know with those kinds of hands trained with those Japanese swords. *Katanas.*

"How can we help you?"

"I was asked to come here and—"

Still smiling, Crow interrupted, "Let's see your driver's license, P.I. ticket, and any other I.D. you'd like to show me. That's it, spread it all out on the counter."

I did as he asked, and he scooped it up and took it over to his desk. He did not offer me a chair. Cops have a right to ask private dicks to jump and to ask how high on the way up; and if we don't jump the right way they can get a judge to pull our license faster than you can say Sam Spade. At best, P.I.s are an irrelevant fact of life to cops; at worst we are flies to be swatted. I did not feel like being swatted.

I stood like a schoolboy in the principal's office while he studied my cards and then typed my information into his computer. Crow made a few calls and I watched his face. He frowned, he grunted, his eyebrows arched. He'd be a lousy poker player. Finally he sat there, lips pursed, for maybe fifteen seconds. I wondered if he was jerking my chain and decided he probably was. A wiseass comment struggled to get past my lips, but I clenched my teeth and kept it trapped inside.

"Okay," Crow said, rising and crossing to the counter that served as the intake desk. He placed my stuff down and slid it across to me. "No wants, no warrants."

I nodded and put the cards back into my wallet.

"I called Minneapolis P.D. and some buddies in Philly. You don't have a lot of friends out there."

"Hoping to make some here," I said.

He grinned. "Let's see how that works out."

We stood there and smiled at each other for a moment. Then Crow waved me past the counter to his desk, nodded at the patched and creaking leather guest chair and sank into a slightly bigger one on the other side.

"Chief," I said, "before we begin—"

"Crow," he corrected.

"Hm?"

"Everybody calls me Crow. I don't like 'Chief' 'cause it makes me feel like I should be wearing feathers, and I don't like 'Mister' 'cause my dad was Mr. Crow and he was kind of a dick. So, Crow."

"Fair enough. I'm Sam."

We nodded to seal that.

"Crow, before we begin I'd like to understand why I'm here."

"Me, too," he said.

"Um…what now?"

He went to a Mr. Coffee and poured two cups, handed me one. "You go first. How'd you get here?"

I sucked my teeth for a moment, then decided to tell him the truth. Most of the truth. I left certain parts out, as I'm sure you'll understand.

"Limbus," he murmured, echoing the word.

"They said you reached out to them. That you were looking for some help on a case."

"Is that what they said?"

"More or less. They said the Pine Deep P.D. did. I guess that's you, right?"

"Mostly me. Couple officers hiding somewhere, sitting speed traps, generally fucking off. And my best guy's out at a crime scene."

"Related to this?"

"To be determined."

"Okay," I said, "but *did* you call Limbus or not? Didn't you ask them to bring in an expert?"

"Not exactly."

"Then what?"

He opened his desk drawer and removed a business card, looked at it for a moment, then handed it to me. I didn't need to read it. I already knew what it would say.

LIMBUS, Inc.
~~Are you laid off, downsized, undersized?~~
~~Call us. We employ.~~ 1-800-555-0606
How lucky do you feel?

However someone had drawn neat straight lines through most of the text.

"Look on the back," he suggested, and I turned it over.

In very neat script someone had written a note: *We can provide a consultant familiar with matters of this kind.*

Before I could ask, he opened his desk and removed a second card. And a third. They were identical, front and back.

"I found one of these near each of the crime scenes."

"Near?"

Crow studied me for a moment. "Near. One was in my cruiser, apparently placed there *after* I arrived on the scene. My cruiser was locked."

"Ah," I said.

"Ah *what*?"

I explained where I'd found mine.

He gave a sour grunt. "The others showed up pretty much the same way. I even had an officer watch my car. He did and no one approached it that he could see."

"How sharp is your officer?"

"Sweeney?" Crow's smile was thin and wide and weird. "He's pretty sharp. Nothing gets past him."

"Except someone did."

Crow gave me a crooked smile. "That note on the back. Want to tell me what it means?"

I shrugged.

"Sorry, Sport," said Crow, "but I'm gonna need something more than a shrug. Explain to me how you are an expert."

"I never said I was an expert."

"You're here as a 'consultant,' though."

"Sure. Why not?"

"Exactly what do you consult *on?*"

That was the question I'd known was coming but didn't really know how to answer. I'd hoped that he would have been in some way clued in about me, but it was pretty clear he wasn't. Or maybe in place of a good poker face he was a bluffer. If so, I couldn't read him.

So, I reached into my jacket and produced a set of color prints I'd made from the email attachments Cricket had sent me. I spread them out on Crow's desk, neatly, side by side.

"The news reports say these were accidents," I said.

"So do my official reports."

I shrugged. "But we both know different."

He looked at me instead of the pictures. "And you're certain these were murders?"

"I am."

"What makes you so sure?"

"Because," I said, "I've seen these kinds of murders before."

Crow nodded, gathered the photos up and handed them back to me. "So have I."

-18-

The killer heard another car coming, and he faded deeper into the shadows as a police cruiser came bumping and thumping, trailing a plume of dust.

An hour ago this same cruiser had been out here, but the officer had abruptly left minutes before the big man had arrived. The killer now understood. The big man had somehow lured the police officer away so he could have a few minutes alone at the crime scene. Now the officer was returning.

The killer shifted downwind so that he could not be detected and then climbed another tree. He settled in, drew his camouflage cape around him, and watched. The officer who got out of the car was not the same one who was here before. That first officer had been a redneck with a beer gut. This new arrival was lean and hard-muscled. Very tall. With red hair and sunglasses that he never took off, not even when he walked through shadows.

The breeze was blowing past the crime scene toward where the killer hid, and that allowed him to take the officer's scent.

Suddenly all of the alarms inside the killer's mind began to ring.

This officer was not at all what he seemed.

He was something much more.

Something powerful.

Something very like the killer.

Very much like him.

-19-

Crow told me he wanted to take me to the most recent crime scene. We took his cruiser, which was a battered Ford Interceptor SUV that looked like it hadn't seen the inside of a car wash since Bush was president. As I got in I peered at the side panel of the door.

"Is that a bullet hole?" I asked.

"Good chance," he said.

I got in. There was a hole on the inside too. A through-and-through. "You didn't get it fixed?"

He shrugged. "Air conditioner's busted. Gives a nice cross breeze."

"Uh huh."

As we drove he talked about everything except the case. The Phillies and the Eagles—teams I didn't give a fuzzy rat's ass about since my heart belongs to the Twins and the Vikings. I said "Uh huh" a lot. He talked about his wife's farm, which was now the fifth largest independent garlic farm in Pennsylvania. I asked him if he had kids. He didn't answer and didn't say anything for a couple of miles. Then he started a new conversation about what he liked on TV. As if I hadn't asked the question.

So, fuck it, we talked about TV. *The Walking Dead. Game of Thrones. 24.* We both liked typical man stuff. Monsters, guns and boobs. Big surprise. He was a closet fan of *So You Think You Can Dance.* My dirty secret was *Downton Abbey.* Total tough guys.

For most of the drive we were backtracking the route I'd taken to get to town, but then he made a turn down a small side road. I caught the name on the sign.

Dark Hollow Road

It was a name I'd seen in the news stories. There had been murders here. And that murdered rich guy, Ubel Griswold, had lived in Dark Hollow.

I asked him about Griswold.

And Crow goddamn nearly drove us off the road and into a tree.

-20-

The killer watched the big police officer.

The cop spent several minutes taking photographs and measurements.

Then the officer abruptly stopped, stiffened and turned in a slow circle. It was very much like what the other man had done earlier.

Except the officer raised his head and sniffed the air.

-21-

The Ford slewed around and kicked up gravel and leaves, barraging a weathered fence and nearly knocking the slats out. He threw it in park and wheeled on me, took a fistful of my tie and jerked me forward so that we were inches apart.

"How the *hell* do you know about Ubel Griswold?" he snarled.

His face was insane. I mean it. Like bugfuck nuts. There was nothing in those eyes but a wild madness that scared the living shit out of me.

The moment stretched and I could feel the heat of each of his ragged breaths.

When I didn't answer he leaned an inch closer. "Listen, dickhead, this is not a game you want to play. Not with me."

"What the fuck?" I said. And I said it slowly.

Crow shoved me back against the door. His hand rested on his holstered pistol. "I'm going to ask once more. Real nice. And believe me when I tell you that this is not an opportunity for wiseass comments or calling for a lawyer. This is you and me here in this truck and we are going to have an open and frank conversation, am I making myself crystal fucking clear?"

I held my breath.

I had an escape hatch for when things really hit the fan, but I didn't want to use it. Not on a stranger, not on a cop. And not on someone who might actually be an innocent. Not sane, by any stretch, but probably not a villain.

Besides, if the wolf came out to play there was no way to ever reclaim the moment.

So I had that ace but knew I couldn't play it. I'd be alive but in jail, or in the wind, and I didn't want to live the rest of my life that way. On the other hand, he was a cop, a stranger, and, clearly, a fucking lunatic. Or something close to it. He could mess up my entire life.

When I didn't answer, he snapped, "Do you understand me?"

I nodded. "Loud and clear. It's your game, man. Just calm down."

"I'll calm down when I have a reason to. And don't you tell me what to do. You're on the wrong side of the badge to do that. Now...let's try this one last time—how do you know Ubel Griswold?"

"I don't know him."

"How do you know *about* him?"

"From Google. I looked him up."

"Why? What's your connection to him?"

I said, "Limbus."

He frowned. "What?"

"Limbus. That's how I know about Griswold."

"No," he said, shaking his head. "Give me more than that."

You have to develop good instincts about people if you're going to shoot hoops in the kinds of playgrounds I frequent. My nerves were telling me this guy was half a keg short of a six-pack. My senses told me that he was scared out of his goddamn mind. And that he was primed to attack. I could smell the adrenaline. I could almost taste it.

My gut, though...

My gut told me he really was one of the good guys.

Call it instinct, call it whatever.

I held up my hands in a no-problem way.

"Okay," I said. "I'll tell you, but you're scaring the shit out me with that gun."

He looked down at his hand, at the fact that he'd unsnapped the holster. He made a little grunting sound. Surprised at what his hand was doing while he wasn't watching.

"Fuck," he said.

"Fuck," I agreed.

Didn't snap the holster though. Instead he laid his hand on his thigh. A token gesture that lowered my blood pressure by maybe half a point.

"Talk," he said.

I took a breath, and told him about Limbus, about Cricket, and about the envelope of money.

Crow didn't say a word the entire time. Didn't ask a question. Instead he sat there and chewed on his lower lip and looked strange. Older. Confused. Tired. He took his hand off his lap and rubbed his eyes, then spent almost a full minute looking out the window.

"Shit," he said.

I cleared my throat. "Don't suppose you want to tell me what the hell's going on? 'Cause, Chief, I'm pretty sure I've never been this confused before."

"Welcome to Pine Deep," he muttered.

"Huh?"

"Nothing."

We sat there for another minute. Doesn't sound like a lot of time until you're peeling the seconds off one at a time while seated next to an armed crazy person.

Out of the blue, Crow asked, "What do you know about the Trouble?"

I shrugged. "What everyone else knows. Maybe a little less. I mean, sure, it was big news for a while. Domestic terrorism, over ten thousand people dead. Worst day in U.S. history. Got that. I didn't hear Ubel Griswold's name in any of that, though, except in a footnote about a coincidence. Him getting killed thirty years to the day before the Trouble here."

He nodded. "Yeah. You ever see the movie they made? *Hell Night*? Or read the book?"

"No. I read a review when it came out. Saw it on Redbox but didn't get it. I heard they changed the story around. Made something supernatural out of it."

"Something like that."

"So? Why are we talking about it?" I asked.

He looked out the window at the cornfields to the right side of the road and the deep, dark forest on the other.

"If you weren't here because of that Limbus card I wouldn't be saying what I'm about to say," said Crow.

"Um…okay."

"The story about the white supremacists spiking the town's water, driving everybody crazy?"

"Yeah?"

"Kind of true."

"*Kind* of?"

"Kind of. It was a cover story."

"Wait," I said, "are you saying there was a government cover-up?"

Crow shook his head. "Not exactly. Not the way you're thinking. The Feds *did* cover some things up, but there was a group of white supremacist dickheads operating in town, and they did, in fact, dump a bunch of hallucinogens into the water. Fritzed everyone out. They also planted bombs to blow up the bridges, knock down the cell towers, take out all phone and cable service, and generally turn the main part of town into World War III."

"I don't—"

"That happened," he said. "But the tricky thing is that all of that was itself a cover for something else."

"Wait, the white trash dickheads were covering up for someone? Who? I don't understand. And, if that was a cover-up, why'd the Feds use that story, too?"

He smiled at the windshield. No visible humor in it, though.

"Because the cover story was something everyone could sell. Domestic terrorism. White power. Racism. Drugs in the water. That's doable. That makes sense. That's something, scary as it was, tragic as it was, people could live with. The rest of the country, I mean. Maybe the rest of the world. They could live with that story, especially since all of those militia assholes died that night."

"You lost me a couple of turns back, man."

"No," he said, "I just haven't gotten to the part where it makes sense. Or, maybe I should say I haven't gotten to the truth. 'Cause unless you're who or what I think you are, this isn't going to sound like the truth and it isn't going to make any fucking sense at all."

"You are scaring the living piss out of me here," I said.

He nodded. "Yeah, being scared is absolutely the appropriate response. I was scared then. More scared than I've ever been in my life. But I have to tell you, Mr. Hunter, that I am starting to get that scared again."

"Why?"

"Because I'm afraid that what was happening then is happening now. That it's happening again."

"Okay...but what did happen back then? If there was a cover story, then what was it covering up?"

That's when he finally turned to me and I saw all sorts of dark lights glimmering in his eyes. If he'd looked crazy before, then he looked absolutely lost now.

"The whole thing, the drugs, the violence, all of that was done to hide the fact that there were monsters in Pine Deep."

I had to take a moment on that. "When you say...'monsters'...?"

"I mean monsters. Vampires and..."

When he didn't finish, I pushed him.

"And what?"

He looked me right in the eye.

"And werewolves."

-22-

To which I said, "Oh shit."

To which he replied, "Yeah."

-23-

We sat there.

Talk about the elephant in the room.

I said, "You're looking at me funny."

He said, "I guess I am."

"Am I going to regret asking?"

"Depends on how this conversation goes," he said. "Could play out a bunch of different ways."

"You're making a lot of assumptions. You know how that usually turns out."

He shrugged. I noticed he'd placed his hand on his lap again. Very close to the gun.

Again.

Balls.

"I'm going to say a word," he said. "It's a word that the Limbus guy used. He didn't explain what it was. He figured I already knew. Which I do."

"Okay."

"I'm going to say it and then you're going to tell me the first thing that comes to mind. Fair enough?"

"I don't like games," I said.

"Not a game."

I said, "Shit."

Then I said, "What's the word."

His hand moved an inch closer to his pistol.

Let's face it, I expected the word to start with a 'w.'

Instead he used a different word. A lot more precise. A word that changed the entire dynamic between us.

He said, "Benandanti."

I looked at him, at his face, his eyes. At the expression he wore.

I took a breath and said, "Yes."

He closed his eyes.

And said, "Thank God."

-24-

Without another word, he turned in his seat, restarted the car, put it in drive, and hit the gas. We drove for maybe a mile before he said anything. I sure as hell wasn't starting any conversations.

Crow said, "Tell me."

"I don't talk about this with anyone."

"Tough. Tell me."

"You used the word," I said. "You know what it means."

"Sure," he said, "I know what the word means. 'Goodwalker.' I want to know what it means to you."

"I think you already know."

"That's not what I mean. I want some background on you. Because if the stuff that's happening is what I think it is, then there's only two sides. Black and white. No gray area at all."

I nodded. He was being very cagey about it. So was I. We were dancing around it because, hell, this really isn't the kind of conversation people have.

I mean, I do, but only at home, when I'm around my aunts and my grandmother and my cousin. They're like me. They're exactly like me. Families tend to keep secrets like this. I've always kept it to myself. Usually the only people who find out about our family secret do so on their last and worst day.

On the other hand, I think I can say for certain that the people at Limbus—whoever or whatever the fuck they are—know. Why else would I be here? Cricket knew that I'd recognize the bite and claw patterns in those photos.

He was right.

"This has to go two ways," I said. "If I show you mine, you got to show me yours."

"You comfortable with the way that came out?" he asked.

"You know what I mean."

"Yeah. And...yes, this is a two-way street. Kind of has to be, don't you think?"

So, after another mile I began talking. Trees whipped past. The sky above us was blotted out by the canopy of fall foliage.

"It's a family thing," I said. "Going back like...forever. My bunch is more or less Irish-English mutts. Been here since five minutes after the Mayflower. But we have roots in Italy going back to Etruscan times. Like six, seven hundred years B.C., you dig?"

He nodded.

"We weren't always what you'd call saints, but I guess in our own way we've always been on the side of the angels. Not literally, 'cause that would be a little New Agey even for me. But in spirit. White hats, no matter how battered and stained those hats were."

"Nice to know," he said, then threw me a curveball. "Any relation to Theiss?"

I took a moment on that, then figured in for a penny, in for a pound. "Direct descent," I said.

"Wow."

"Wow," I agreed. "Not sure which version of the story you heard. The one that makes the history books is that back in 1692, in Jurgenburg, Livonia, a Benandanti named Theiss was arrested and put on trial for being...well, for being what he was."

"Say the word," said Crow. He cut me a glance out of the corner of his eye. "Really…say it."

I sighed. "Okay. Theiss was arrested for being a werewolf."

He took a deep breath, held it, let it out, then he picked up the story I'd started. "Theiss's defense was that at night he and the members of his order—"

"Family," I corrected.

"Family. Okay. He and the members of his family transformed into werewolves in order to fight demons and other kinds of evil. Witches, pernicious spirits. Like that. He was whipped for superstition and idolatry and let go."

"To paraphrase you," I said, "that's the story they sold to the press."

"And the real story?"

"He was tortured for a long damn time. They wanted him to confess to being an apostate of Hell and an enemy of God. But…Theiss was a tough old motherfucker. They tried it all on him. Thumbscrews, the rack, dunking. The church is nothing if not enthusiastic."

"They couldn't break him, though?" prompted Crow.

"No. In the end they let him go because they figured that he couldn't possibly endure all of the torture if he didn't have God's grace. Yada, yada, yada. So they let him go. They even gave him a nickname. You seem to know the story. What'd they call him?"

Crow smiled thinly. "The Hound of God."

"Right. The thing is, a lot of the history books get it wrong. They don't always connect the Benandanti with werewolves. Mostly 'cause there are a lot of new age lamebrains who use that name like the Celts use 'wicca.' There are plenty of Benandanti in Europe today who come in to bless a new baby or sage a new house. Like that."

"Don't mock," said Crow. "They might be doing something useful."

"Maybe they are, but that doesn't make them true Benandanti."

"Ah," he said, "pride goeth before a fall."

"Yeah, well fuck you, too."

"Point taken."

We both smiled at that. Not sure what it meant, though.

"So," I said, "are you going to ask me the obvious question?"

"Do I need to?"

"I don't know. You tell me?"

"Sam," he said, "I knew what you were when you walked into my office."

"Why? Because Cricket told you?"

"Nope."

"Then how? I didn't wear my *'I'm A Werewolf, Ask Me How'* button today."

He didn't answer. We rounded a bend and on the other side was a parked police cruiser, lots of crime scene tape strung between tree trunks, and a big kid in a deputy's uniform leaning against the fender of the car. Maybe twenty-two. He was massive. Six-six, with more muscles than is necessary on any human being. He had his arms folded over his chest, a kitchen match between his teeth, and a scowl as dour as a country parson at a peep show.

I took one look at him and I knew why Crow knew what I was when he met me. This was his deputy.

And damn if he wasn't playing for the same team as me.

Shit.

-25-

Big Bad

The killer climbed another tree and hunkered down in the crotch, his body completely concealed by camouflage, his face painted green and brown. He had a pair of binoculars whose lenses were covered with a filter that would not reflect light. His clothes were daubed with a paste made from ground bird feathers, squirrel urine, owl feces, and insect larvae. Not even a bloodhound could smell him through that.

Not even one of his brothers could smell him.

Not unless they were very close, and the killer was six hundred feet away and fifty feet up a towering oak.

He watched the three figures below.

The smallest of the three men was strange. The killer knew him, had seen him many times in the town. Had read about him on the Internet. Chief of Police. Alcoholic. Husband to a farmer.

And, very likely, a killer, too. A man who was more dangerous than his size and age suggested.

The biggest of the three men was even harder to categorize. He was a monster, even by the killer's standards. Man, wolf and something else. There was a darkness in him that ran all the way to the soul. The killer feared him for reasons he could not name.

The third man looked weak, but wasn't. Middle sized, middle aged, thin and haggard. He looked like a salesman, and not a successful one. He looked tired and frail.

But the killer could smell the wolf in him.

It was a strong wolf.

A true hunter.

The killer wanted to fight him. To see which of them was stronger.

To see which of them deserved to live.

He would have to arrange that.

He knew, in fact, that he would have to face all of these men. And maybe the big man he'd seen earlier. He would have to kill them all.

He...and his family.

The slaughter would be so delicious.

-26-

We sniffed each other.

I'm not proud of it.

And, don't get the wrong idea. We didn't sniff each other's asses. We're strange but we're not weird. We stood a few feet apart and took the air. His expression never flickered. Him I definitely wouldn't play poker with. If he was like me, he was cataloging everything he could from my smell. I sure as hell was.

He was bigger and stronger than me, but the wolf in him was younger. A lot younger. It was more savage than mine. Less controlled. I could feel it wanting to come out. The kid had some iron goddamn control, though.

"Okay, okay," said Crow, "you two are weirding me out. So cut the shit."

"He's the consultant?"

"Yes. Officer Mike Sweeney meet Sam Hunter, and vice versa. Shake hands and mind your manners. Both of you."

He didn't budge, so I took the cue and offered my hand. Sweeney looked at it for a moment, then without haste took it. And held it.

"Crow," he said, "this guy had blood on him. Been in a fight. Couple of different guys. No…three different guys."

My mouth went dry. No one's ever read me that way. The way I usually read people.

Crow came and stood beside Mike. "I won't ask if Mike's telling the truth," he said, "'cause Mike doesn't make those kinds of mistakes."

"Private matter," I said.

"Which you're going to tell us about," said Crow.

I shook my head. "I plead the fifth."

"No," said Crow.

"No," said Mike.

"Then we have a problem," I said. "I didn't come here to be blindsided by Sherriff Andy and Barney Fife."

"Who?" asked Mike.

Crow said, "Sam, I think it's fair to say that a lot of what's going on here isn't going to make it into any official report. If you're going to work with us, then it has to be by being straight up."

"You could arrest me."

"Pretend for a moment that I won't."

We stood there inside that moment, none of us budging.

"He killed someone," said Mike. "He changed and he killed someone."

Crow nodded. "Is that true?"

I shrugged.

"Did they need killing?" asked Mike.

I tilted my head to one side. "You hear about that case last year? Guy doping little girls and making rape porn?"

"I heard about it."

I shrugged again.

"There's not going to be a trial," said Crow, "is there?"

"Doesn't look like it."

Mike Sweeney took a step closer and sniffed again. Then he nodded and stepped back. "More than one guy."

"Even total assholes have friends."

"Had," he corrected.

"Had," I agreed."

He smiled then. A very small, thin smile. It was the kind of smile nobody—and I mean nobody—would ever want to see. There was no trace of humanity in it. No fragment of mercy.

"Fuck 'em," he said. "You're here as a consultant?"

"Yeah."

"Then consult."

With that he turned his back on me and walked toward the crime scene.

Crow sighed.

"What was that all about?" I asked.

"Mike had a complicated childhood."

"I can imagine."

He shook his head. "No, I really don't think you could."

He turned to follow Mike, and I, feeling more awkward than I had since my first middle school dance, trudged along in his wake.

-27-

I ducked under the yellow crime scene tape and moved into a space that was dense with shadows. A motorcycle was wrapped around a tree. Front wheel torn open, gas tank ruptured, seat dislodged, headlight glass twinkling in a thousand pieces. There was dried blood everywhere, though for once I had to rely more on sight than smell because of the presence of the spilled gasoline.

Mike took an iPad from a briefcase he'd laid on the edge of a plastic tarp near the crash site, called up an image folder and handed it to me.

"The body was transported last night. These are the photos."

I looked at them one at a time. High-res digital photography is very stark, very detailed. Artless and cruel. The body of a man lay partly atop the bike, partly on the grass. And partly fifteen feet away. He was literally torn to pieces. It was a very brutal kind of thing, and a very familiar kind of thing.

I tried my Richard Dreyfuss line again.

"This was no boating accident."

Crow chuckled. Mike didn't.

"Sam used to be a cop," Crow said to Mike. To me he said, "Walk the scene. Tell me what you see."

I did. There were tire tracks that curved off the road and right into the tree. There was dead grass around the spilled gas. There was blood spatter. There was the ruined machine.

"This is bullshit," I said.

Crow and Mike exchanged a quick look.

"Walk us through it," said Crow.

We went back to the road and I reconstructed it for them. "Here's what is supposed to have happened," I said. "It rained last night, right?"

"Until ten."

"Ten. Okay. And when was the crash?"

"Passing motorist called it in at ten-twenty-one."

"Uh huh. So, the story is this. Guy's tooling down this black as fuck road in the middle of a rainstorm at night. Loses control, goes into a skid, wraps his bike around the tree at high speed and goes splat."

Crow put a stick of gum into his mouth and began folding the little foil wrapper with great care. "Uh huh," he said.

"Bike had to be going at high speed and for some reason the driver didn't throttle down when he lost control."

"Uh huh."

"To do that much damage, he had to be going at least a hundred or better."

"Uh huh."

I looked at him. "All of which amounts to a yard-high pile of total bullshit."

"Why?"

"Let's start with the road. Why would anyone be on this road at night? Does it even go anywhere?"

"It's a fire access road and it's used by the forestry service," said Mike. "Kids come up here to make out."

"Not in the rain," I said. "And not on a bike. It's not a dirt bike, either."

"No."

"In the photos, the guy's wearing jeans and a sweatshirt. In the rain?"

Crow spread his hands.

"Where's his helmet?"

"He wasn't wearing one," said Mike.

"Again I say, in the rain?"

No one bothered to answer that. I squatted by the tire tracks. "No way these were made during the storm. Look at the ridges in the mud. Even if it was drizzling they'd be smeared more than this."

They nodded.

"And over here," I said, moving from the road onto the dirt, to a point halfway to the impact point. "See how deep it is here? The bike accelerated right here. Right when the bike was lined up with the tree."

They nodded.

I went over to the bike now and bent over it, touching various points on the fractured frame. "This is all wrong. It looked like the bike was starting to tilt away from the line of impact, like the driver was trying to avoid collision by ditching sideways. That would be the natural thing, even if you lose control in the dark. But look at the underside of the frame, right here. That's crumpled the wrong way. It should be pushed up but it's pushed in. That means the bike, while slewing sideways, was starting to stand back up."

"And what does that tell you?" asked Crow.

"It tells me that whoever was riding this bike jumped off right before it hit. Jumped off with a hell of a lot of force, enough to nearly stand the bike up while it was falling over. If that was the case, then the body should have landed over here. He wouldn't have been *on* the bike when it hit. At most, he'd have gotten a leg trapped under it, but he wouldn't have hit the tree hard enough to be splattered."

Crow said, "That's pretty good. What else?"

I bent over the bike again and spent some time with it. I've seen a lot of car and motorcycle accidents, accidental and criminal. I've also seen some faked accidents before. I've been in court plenty of times to hear expert testimony on the physics of high-speed vehicular impacts. What I was seeing here didn't square with my understanding of cause and effect. I said as much to them.

"This isn't something you probably want to put in your official report," I began, "but I think someone *bent* this bike around the tree."

"Bent," said Crow.

"Bent."

"That would take a lot of muscle."

"It would."

"Could *you* do it?"

I thought about it for a moment. "No. Under certain, um, circumstances, I could mangle it pretty good, but some of these bends...no. I couldn't."

"Which brings us to our problem, Mr. Consultant."

"Yeah."

"Mike and I walked this site together and we came up with the same read on it that you gave us. Nice work, by the way."

"Thanks."

"Once the forensics guys were gone, I asked Mike to see if he could duplicate those bends."

I stared at him. And at Mike, who continued to make his matchstick bob slowly up and down. "Well," I said, "that must have been interesting."

"It was instructive," admitted Crow. "Mike was able to bend it a little. But that was with the frame already fatigued and cracked. And, trust me when I say this, Mike is a very, very strong young man."

"Knock it off, Crow," said Mike.

"I'm making a point here."

Mike looked at the trees and sighed slowly.

"So," continued Crow, "what I'm wondering is whether you and Mike working together—under, as you say, certain circumstances— could do that kind of damage."

It was an interesting question.

We all stood there and thought about it.

I shook my head first. Then Mike.

"No," I said, "not even together."

Crow nodded. "What I thought. But someone did. And either it was one very, very, *very* strong son of a bitch—someone way outside of the normal range. Or...whatever passes for normal with you guys."

I said nothing.

"Or we're dealing with something even worse. Something that's stronger than two werewolves."

I said, "Well, shit."

Mike Sweeney grinned. "Yeah, and isn't that interesting as all shit?"

-28-

The killer moved away from the kill site.

He was confused by the presence of two others like him. That was wrong. That made no sense. There should only be one wolf in these woods. The big, red-haired one. The one who seemed to belong here.

But now this other one was here.

The killer did not like it.

He wasn't afraid, though. Fear was not a factor in the killer's life. Not now anyway. He was beyond that now.

He faded into the woods and vanished.

-29-

"The victim," I said. "The wounds in those photos…what's the coroner going to say about it?"

"Exactly what I want him to say," said Crow.

"He, um…knows?"

"He's the coroner for Pine Deep, Pennsylvania. He's come to accept certain realities."

"Shit."

"Tell me about it."

"But we all know those aren't injuries sustained in a crash."

"My guess," said Crow, "is that the body was torn up pretty good by whoever our Big Bad is, and then dropped off a roof. There are visible impact injuries."

"Unless they're stupid they'd have to know that an autopsy would—"

"We can assume they didn't choose Pine Deep by accident."

"Meaning you can keep secrets?"

"Meaning we've had to keep secrets."

Mike snorted but didn't say anything.

I walked past the scene into the woods and stood there for a while, letting the smells and sounds tell me whatever they wanted to share. After a few moments Crow and Mike joined me.

"Shame it rained so hard last night," Crow said. "No scent to follow."

I glanced at Mike. "You tried?"

He shrugged. "Sure. Lots of scents, but they're all mingled. Rain, you know?"

I nodded. "Makes me wonder if the rain was part of an agenda. Not just to fake the slip and slide crash, but to wash away any useful spoor."

Mike grunted and nodded.

"What were the other crash sites like?" I asked.

"Similar," said Crow. "In each case there was some kind of accident—car wreck, farm accident, house fire—but the details don't completely square. Especially the pathology. Someone's killing people and doing a slightly better than half-ass job covering it up."

"Yeah, but how would a regular police department be reacting to this?"

Crow nodded his approval. "I did some checking to see if there are any similarly troubled cases."

"And?"

"There were four suspicious fatal accidents in upstate New York last August, in the Finger Lakes district. All ultimately ruled accidental, but with notations about anomalies in the case files. Another two in Cape May, New Jersey in December. Same conclusions. And three out near Pittsburgh this past May. The pattern is the same. A couple of the investigating detectives have been sharing case information in hopes of getting somewhere, but there's so little conventional evidence that they keep hitting a wall."

"Because they don't have certain specialized knowledge," I suggested.

"Yup."

"This is interstate," I said. "That makes it Federal. A serial killer?"

"Maybe."

"Shame there isn't really something like the *X-Files*. Fox Mulder would go nuts for something like this."

"Can't call him, can't call the Ghostbusters," he said. "If wishes were horses."

We stood there and looked at the huge forest. Oaks and sycamores and pines, with underbrush so dense it seemed impenetrable.

"What do you know about the vics?" I asked.

Crow fielded that. "No obvious connections. Not between the victims here in Pine Deep or between ours and those in other towns. I have someone doing background checks—a computer geek friend of mine—but so far we got bupkis."

"Balls," I said.

"Balls," he agreed.

-30-

The killer ran through the darkening woods, exulting in the power that rippled through his muscles. The solidity of his bones. The song of hunger that shouted in his blood.

He would find something to kill.

Anything.

Animal.

Human.

Even a bear.

Anything that would scream.

Thinking red thoughts, he ran.

-31-

We spent the rest of the afternoon going over the crime scene, which yielded a lot of information, none of which seemed particularly useful. Then we went back to the station and Crow walked me through the rest of the case file. Again, lots of forensic information—photos, hair and fiber samples, casts of tire tracks, coroner's reports, the works.

Bottom line?

Well, shit. We knew there was one or more werewolf killing people.

They were doing it in bunches and, apparently, moving on.

Motive? Unknown.

Identity? Unknown.

Anything of actual use?

Impossible to say.

"Have you reached out to the FBI about this?" I asked.

"I filed a report."

"And—?"

"You familiar with the word 'obfuscation'?"

"Ah."

"What about your own investigation? Do you have any leads?"

"Beyond guesswork on the nature of the killers?"

"Beyond that, yes."

"Nope."

"Oh."

"But," he said, "I've been hearing about strangers in town."

"What kind of strangers?"

"Unknown. I have my people running that down right now. All I know is that there have been a few out-of-towners around. One of them was over at the Scarecrow Inn asking questions about the accident. And either the same guy or a different guy asking questions at some of the farms."

"You have a description on him?"

"Big, blond guy. The one local I talked to said he looked 'mean.'"

"That's it?"

"Getting information from stubborn farm-country folk is like pulling your own teeth. You'll get it, but there's a lot of unpleasant effort involved."

"Ah. This guy flash a badge of any kind?"

"Not so far."

"You think he's a Fed?"

"Maybe. Who else would be asking questions?"

I thought about it. "Could be another P.I., maybe hired by the family of one of the victims."

"Our vics were locals."

"A vic from another town."

Crow pursed his lips, nodded. "Maybe. I'll bet a shiny nickel it's a Fed."

"There's another possibility."

"What's that?"

"Could be someone related to the killings asking around to see what the locals know."

"Or suspect," he suggested.

"Or suspect," I agreed.

We poked at it for another couple of minutes and got nowhere. Then I suggested we retire to the local bar and drown our sorrows in some beers. Crow smiled and shook his head.

"Gave up drinking. I go to meetings now."

"Balls."

"Mike doesn't drink, either."

"He in the same Twelve Step?"

"No. He's a purity freak. Organic foods, no drugs, no alcohol. Won't even take an aspirin."

"How come?"

Crow sucked his teeth for a moment. "He has some health concerns. He wants to make sure he stays ahead of them."

"Like…?"

"Like it's his business and there's no second half to this discussion." He said it pleasantly enough, but there was a finality to it.

"Well, shit," I said. "*I* need a beer. Maybe six or eight of them."

I left him at his office and walked up the street until I found a place called the Scarecrow Inn. It wasn't exactly a dive bar. Dive is an active word. This was more like '*dove*.' Past tense. Dark as pockets. Bunch of little tables with old wooden chairs that didn't match. Visible ass-wear on the stools. Sawdust on the floor, like they do down south. Half the people were ignoring the No Smoking sign, including a table full of fat guys with cigars. A wooden bar that was probably two hundred years old, and a bartender who looked to have been here since the place was built. Tall, cadaverous, comprehensively wrinkled. Big jar of hard-boiled eggs by the beer taps. Country music on the jukebox. Travis Tritt, I think, but I'm not a country fan so what do I know.

I found an empty stool, ordered chili and a schooner of Yuengling to go with it. Dug into a bowl of peanuts while I was waiting.

Crow let me take the case file, so I made my way through the chili and two beers while reading every single word. I had a few pages of notes, mostly outside-chance connections I'd run down when I was in front of a computer again. I'd brought my iPad, but— big surprise—there was no WIFI in the Scarecrow Inn. Too modern for them. They're probably still grousing about those newfangled electric lights.

As I read I became very slowly and subtly aware that I was being watched. At first I passed it off as the usual stranger-in-town thing, but then my spider sense really began tingling. So I used taking a sip of beer to check the room out in the mirror behind the bar. Everyone was a stranger, so that wasn't very helpful. There were about two dozen people in the place, either dressed for work on a farm or in casual clothes.

Then I spotted the two people who didn't belong.

They were seated alone at tables on opposite sides of the place, and they were so totally different from one another that it looked like they were here to make a statement. White guy, black guy. White guy was big in a jock ballplayer way. Not big like Mike Sweeney or the goons I danced with yesterday. Muscular, mid-thirties, blond. All-American looks. Kind of like the guy who plays Captain America in the movies. Mean looking son of a bitch, though. Could be a cop, could be a soldier. Could be a freelance shooter. Something very dangerous about him. I could tell that right off. Sat there with half a smile on his face, nursing a beer, using the same mirror I was using to watch the other guy and, every once in a while, me.

The other guy was a black twenty-something. Short, skinny, bookish, with thick glasses and a fringe of beard. Not the only black guy I'd seen in Pine Deep, but one of maybe three or four. Gave off a pop-culture geek vibe.

The Geek was looking at me; the Jock was looking at him. And me.

I adjusted the way I was sitting so my gun was a little easier to reach.

The Geek caught me looking at him and looked away.

Then he looked back.

He did that a couple of times, and I kept looking at him until he caught and finally held my stare. I nodded. After a long five-count, he nodded back.

So, I figured fuck it. I picked up my beer and walked over to his table. For a moment I thought he was going to bolt. He sat straight as a rake handle and looked up at me. I'm not that big, and I'm not what you'd call physically imposing. I've been told, however, that I give off a certain vibe. At times.

Like now.

He cut a look to the front door and then back at me. At close range I figured him closer to early twenties.

But here's the thing.

At close range, I could tell something about him I couldn't tell from across a smoky bar.

The kid had a certain scent.

A familiar scent. The kind I spent a lot of time every morning, with shampoo, skin creams and cologne trying to mask.

A smell most people can't smell.

Except guys like Mike Sweeney.

He looked up at me, and before I could even ask, he said, "I think we need to talk."

"Yeah," I said. "I think we'd better."

"Not here."

I nodded to the door. "Let's go."

-32-

The killer smelled the hitchhiker before he saw her.

She smelled young.

She smelled afraid.

He knew that she would taste wonderful.

He knew that she would scream.

The young ones always screamed. They have so much to lose.

He raced down a hill and up the other side, then down again to the road. This was a lonely stretch. A stupid place for anyone to hitchhike. She couldn't have known that or she wouldn't have come this way.

-33-

I stood aside to let him go first. If this was some kind of elaborate set-up I didn't want to be the first guy through the door.

It wasn't.

The kid stopped in the middle of the pavement, hands in his pockets. He wore a long black coat over jeans and a t-shirt with the words OBSCURE POP-CULTURE REFERENCE stenciled on it. He looked nervous. Maybe scared.

"There's a park up the street," he said, and we began walking that way.

"Let's start with the basics," I said. "Name?"

He hesitated.

I said, "Would you rather I held you down and stole your wallet?"

"Antonio," he said. "Antonio Jones."

"Real name?"

"Sure. Why?"

"Sounds like a stage name."

He shrugged. "Antonio Jones."

"Fair enough. I'm Sam Hunter."

"You're a cop?"

"Not anymore. Private investigator," I said as we crossed the street. There were only two traffic lights in town and they both blinked yellow continually. Either they were trying for a Twin Peaks thing, or all small towns are creepy like that. Yellow means 'caution,' so I figured a subtext was implied. Besides, it was that kind of a day.

Antonio said, "Working for the cops, though?"

"Why do you want to know?"

"I saw you with Chief Crow and Iron Mike."

"'Iron Mike'?"

"That's what people used to call him. In school, I mean. When he was little. Before the, um…"

"Before the Trouble?"

"Before that, yeah."

"Why? Was he always a body builder?"

"Huh? Oh…no. Mike used to be in his head all the time. Always dreaming up stuff. One day he'd be a Jedi, the next he'd be Sheriff Rick. Or Conan. Whatever. He spent a lot of time like that. Playing by himself. Daydreaming in school. Not sure if he started calling himself Iron Mike or the other kids did."

"You went to school with him?"

He shook his head. "Two years behind."

We crossed a side street and entered the park. Like most of the town of Pine Deep, the park was seedy, untended, and dark. Broken slats in the benches. Overflowing trash can. Beer bottles lying among the weeds. Indifferent lighting.

"Nice place for a mugging," I said to my new friend.

He stopped and looked at me. "I know," he said.

Which is when I felt the icy mouth of a gun barrel press into the base of my skull.

"Don't try anything funny," said a male voice. "And I'm pretty sure we both know what I mean by 'funny.'"

-34-

The killer stalked her because stalking was fun.

One game was to see how close to the edge of the woods he could get without the hitchhiker seeing him. Then to make small, odd sounds so that she became aware of something. But unaware of what was in those shadowy woods.

That game was fun.

Then he changed his own rules. He ran ahead and stepped out of the woods. Very briefly. Just long enough for the girl to see him. A quick glance, then he was gone.

The way her lithe young body stiffened was very appealing. She had long legs and long hair and tiny little breasts. She was maybe sixteen, but young for it. Bruises on her face. Running away from a heavy-handed father, perhaps.

The girl stood there, uncertain, without a plan and without a direction, staring in the direction of the big, dark thing that had watched her from the road ahead.

She turned around, considering the road she'd walked. It was empty and it led back in a direction she could not go. Not if something had been bad enough to put her out alone on a road like this.

The girl waited for almost five full minutes, looking at the road, looking under the trees, seeing nothing because the killer allowed her nothing to see. Not even when she was looking directly toward where he crouched. She had human eyes and they were so weak.

He waited until she began walking again. Hesitantly at first, and then at a rapid clip. The girl wanted to be past this stretch of road.

The killer circled around and came out of the woods behind her. He crept onto the asphalt and moved up behind her. Taking his time, waiting for that exquisite moment when the girl would inevitably turn to check behind her.

That was a new game.

He loved the way this one would end.

I stood absolutely still.

No matter how fast I can do the change, it's not fast enough to dodge a bullet. Besides, little known fact about werewolves. Head shots? Pretty much does it. Head shots will pretty much flip the switch on everything. Vampires, zombies, me.

So, no, I didn't try anything funny.

I stood there.

"You carrying?" the voice asked.

"Shoulder holster," I told him.

"Take it out with two fingers. Hand it to Antonio."

I did. Antonio took it like it was radioactive. He looked scared and nervous and embarrassed. If this was a mugging, it wasn't following the right pattern.

"What else?" asked the guy with the gun.

"Blackjack. Rear pocket."

"Okay. Remove it the same way. Ditto for your wallet. Hand them to the kid."

"Got thirty bucks in my wallet," I said, just to see how he'd react.

"Cute. See that bench? Put your hands in your pants pockets and go sit down. Do it real slow and we'll stay friends."

I did what he asked and as I turned to sit, I got my first look at him. He was an All-American jock type. Six-two or so. Blond hair, blue eyes, white smile. Looked healthy but there was something in his eyes. Like maybe there was something freaky going on behind them. Something crazy, something dangerous. Something very, very dangerous. I discreetly sniffed but his scent was one hundred percent human.

Not a wolf, but definitely an alpha.

"What's the play?" I asked.

He ignored me and spoke to Antonio. "You sure this guy's playing for the same team as you?"

Antonio paused, sniffed the air in my direction, paused again. "Pretty sure."

"Check his I.D."

The kid did that. "Sam Hunter," he said, reading my driver's license. "Oh, hey. He has a private investigator's license."

"Read me the numbers."

He did.

The guy with the gun held his Beretta 92F in a rock-steady hand. He looked at me, taking stock. "Okay, Mr. Hunter," he said, "we're going to have us a nice chat."

"Uh-uh," I said. "I showed you mine, now you show me yours. Who the hell are you?"

"What, you don't think this is a mugging?"

I snorted.

"What would you say if I told you I was a cop?"

I shrugged. "You look the type. I used to be a cop."

"Where?"

"Minneapolis."

"What happened?"

"Got kicked out."

"Why?"

"I don't play well with others."

"Other cops?"

I shrugged again. "It's possible a couple of perps got dented while resisting."

"What kind of perps? This a racial thing?" he asked.

"No," I said. "I don't like bullies. Not too crazy about guys who hurt women and kids."

I watched his eyes while I said that. You can tell a lot from the way a guy reacts. Dickheads tend to grin. Closet-abusers get self-righteous about due process. By the book cops are merely disapproving. Guys who've walked some dark streets tend to connect with you on a purely nonverbal level—but the connection is there. Even guys who are good poker players always have a tell in moments like that.

This guy did.

There was the tiniest thinning of his lips. Not a smile. Nothing like that. More like a predatory smile. There are different kinds of predators. There are the kinds who target the weak. And there are those with more of a Dexter vibe who don't lose sleep if a child abuser has a hard time on the way to the station.

"Any of this going to come up if I run a background check on you?"

"My dismissal letter makes for quality reading," I told him.

"Okay," he said, though he didn't lower the gun. "New subject. What are you doing in Pine Deep?"

"What does it matter to you?"

"Not a two-way conversation, Sparky. Answer the question."

"I'm here on a case."

"What case?"

"A police case. I'm working with local law on a series of unexplained deaths."

"Who's your contact here?"

"The chief of police. Malcolm Crow."

Keeping his gun pointed at my forehead, he tapped his ear. "Bug, you get all this?"

I didn't hear anything, but the guy did. "Copy that."

"'Bug'?" I asked. "You wearing a wire?"

He ignored me and stood in an attitude of listening. I couldn't see his earbud or mic Had to be high-tech stuff if it was that well-concealed. Which changed my estimation of him from cop to some kind of federal agent. FBI or higher. Which made some sense if someone in the Justice Department was taking these deaths seriously. If there was any evidence to link the kills, then it made this a federal case.

Didn't explain why he was holding a gun to my head.

"Okay," he said, "thanks, Bug. Hit me with anything else you dig up."

The jock looked me up and down for a few moments longer, then he lowered his gun. Lowered it, not put it away.

"You had a colorful career in the Cities," he said. "Samuel Taylor Coleridge Hunter. How the fuck did you get hung with a name like that?"

"My parents read a lot," I said. "And they're a little weird."

"Uh huh."

"You got my background that fast?"

"I have good people."

"How long have you been tailing me?"

"Since you left the Scarecrow."

"Why'd you pick me?"

He nodded to Antonio. "My friend tagged you."

"He wearing a wire, too?"

"Does it matter?"

I changed tack. "You want to tell me who you are and why you pulled a gun on me?"

He glanced around at the darkened trees, then shrugged and holstered his piece.

"Joe Ledger," he said.

"FBI?"

"Same league, different team."

"Care to tell me which team?"

"Not really." He grinned at me. Son of a bitch had great teeth. I wanted to punch them down his throat.

"Can I have my gun and wallet back?"

"Antonio," said Ledger, "give the man his wallet."

The kid handed it to me and I slipped it into my pocket. I held my hand out for the gun.

"Let's pretend you don't need it right now," said Ledger.

I lowered my hand.

"Okay, Mr. Mysterious. How about you tell me what in the fuck is going on."

"You first," he said, "why don't you tell me why you're here in Pine Deep."

"I already told you."

He gestured to the bench. "You gave me a headline, now give me the story."

We sat, the two of us. Antonio stood a dozen feet away, my gun in his pocket. He fidgeted and looked like he wanted to be anywhere else but here.

I looked at Ledger. "The chief said there was someone asking questions around town. That's you?"

He shrugged.

"If you're already looking into these deaths, then you must know what's going on. You know about me. Not about my background, but, you know…"

"You get weird and fuzzy," he said, "yeah, I know. Still borderline freaked out about it, but I know."

"Which means the government knows?"

"Some parts of it do. Most don't."

"Am I about to get myself onto some kind of watch list? You guys have an X-Files thing for real?"

"X-Files is fiction, and it's FBI," he said. "I personally don't give a fuck about the things that go bump in the night unless those bumpy things have a political agenda."

"I don't."

He touched his ear. "So I'm told. You're a lapsed Independent. You haven't voted since you left Minneapolis. Never been arrested at a rally. You're not a person of interest in any way that matters to guys like me."

"So why this set-up? You had Knick-Knack here lure me to where you could blindside me. Very slick, and I fell for it. But as your mysterious Bug must have told you, I'm not a player in anything political. I don't even watch the debates. I think everyone in Washington needs a good foot up their ass, but I don't have any aspirations to be the one doing the kicking. Is there any chance you're going to stop being Mr. Cryptic and get to the fucking point?"

Ledger laughed. "Fair enough. This clandestine shit always makes me feel like a jackass."

"See it from my side."

He nodded. "But this isn't a discussion, Sam. This is me interrogating you. This is you cooperating without reservation. This is me—much as I hate to do it—waving the Patriot Act in your face and not having to play quid pro quo. Sorry, but life's a bitch like that."

"Why don't you just go ask the fucking chief of police?"

"I will. But he's lower priority. And, he's kind of a dick," said Ledger.

"You know him?"

"We've met. Besides, he's an ordinary guy. You're not. You're definitely not, if Antonio is certain."

"Absolutely," said Antonio. "He's like me."

"I'm neither short nor black," I said.

We all laughed.

Ledger said, "So, I want you to tell me why a werewolf private investigator—and I'm having a hard time saying those actual words—is in Pine Deep, Pennsylvania. I want to know what you know about the person or persons who committed these murders. I want to know if you have any connection to them, because I'm pretty damn sure you're all members of the Hair Club for Weirdos. So, talk."

"I think this conversation would make more sense if we included Chief Crow," I said.

"I don't."

A voice behind him said, "I do."

And there was the unmistakable sound of a pump shotgun being jacked.

-36-

The girl turned around.

She saw the killer.

Of course she did. It was what she was meant to do.

He was fifty feet behind her, moving on all fours, grinning with all his teeth.

She screamed.

She screamed so loudly.

A shrill, piercing note that the killer was positive would live within his personal treasure trove of superb screams. It was a girl scream. A girl-woman scream. Filled with all of the dark imaginings of the child. And all of the understanding of the adult. It was as perfect as she was, this girl on the edge of womanhood. She, in all of her desperate, bruised beauty. Her defiled innocence. Her ripeness.

She ran.

Of course she ran.

He would have been disappointed, crushed, if she had not.

She dropped her backpack and her cheap little purse, and ran.

He let her run.

Another fifty feet. A hundred.

Two hundred.

And then he ran after.

-37-

Joe Ledger turned. Slowly, without real concern.

Malcolm Crow stood twenty feet behind him, a Remington pump snugged into his shoulder.

Ledger smiled, got up, walked over, bent and picked up an unfired shell from where it had landed on the grass.

"Much as I appreciate the dramatics of pumping the shotgun—it's a real nut-twister—it's done purely for effect. You wouldn't have come out here without a shell being already in the breech. Which means you had to eject one to make your entrance."

He reached past the barrel and tucked the shell into the chief's pocket.

Crow sighed and lowered the gun.

"It scares the piss out of most people," he said.

"Hey," said Ledger, "I'm not saying it didn't work on me. I'll probably have a pee stain on my Joe Boxers. Just making an observation. You see that on TV?"

"Yeah."

"They always do it on TV. Saw one episode of *The Walking Dead* where a guy racked his gun twice."

"Nice."

They smiled at each other.

"Howdy, Chief Crow," said Ledger.

"Howdy, Duke."

I said, "Duke?"

Crow nodded. "First time we met he introduced himself as Marion Morrison. John Wayne's real name."

"Oh."

"Flashed an FBI badge."

Ledger shrugged. "It was convenient."

Crow pushed past him and walked over to Antonio. He held out a hand and waited as the kid looked for and received a nod from Ledger. He handed my gun to Crow, who exhaled through his nose and handed it to me.

I considered how much fun it would be to pistol-whip Ledger, but frankly didn't like my chances. Not without changing. He looked like a happy-go-lucky dumb jock, but there was something behind that façade that troubled me. I had the feeling he could turn mean as a snake if he wanted to. I didn't want him to.

Crow turned back to the agent. "We are going to have a frank conversation, Agent Whateveryournameis."

"Joe Ledger."

"Agent Ledger. Fine. We're going to have a pow-wow and if I get even a whiff of obstruction—"

"Or obfuscation," I amended.

"—I will kick your ass out of Pine Deep. And before you ask, yes I think it can be done and no I don't give a cold shit what kind of federal juice you have or which agency you belong to. Am I making myself clear?"

"Crystal," said Ledger, though it was also clear he was amused.

"Good. Let's all go over to the Scarecrow."

"Not your office?"

"No. The coffee sucks moose dick. Artie at the Scarecrow makes the best coffee in town."

I said, "You don't mind that it's a bar?"

"Son," he said, giving me a weary, pitying smile, "everyone I've ever met in this town drinks like a fish. Seeing it isn't going to knock me off the wagon. This is Pine Deep. Besides, you two ass-clowns could use a few beers. Maybe it'll help wash off the testosterone."

"I'm in," I said.

We all looked at Ledger.

"First round's on me."

Crow nodded to Antonio. "You want to do me a favor?"

"Um…sure."

"You know Mike Sweeney?"

He swallowed and nodded.

"Go find him. Tell him where we are."

Then Crow laid the barrel of his shotgun over his shoulder and nodded toward the lights of town. "Gentlemen, shall we—?"

-38-

The killer ran at half speed most of the way.

He didn't want to catch her.

Yet.

Where would the fun be in that?

He loped along, watching her legs pump, watching her hair bob. Watching her.

Aching for her.

Hungering.

In other times, in older times, he would have taken her a different way. Like he'd done in harbor towns throughout Southeast Asia. Like he'd done when crossing this country. Like he'd done more times than he could remember. Back then, when it was his old flesh that he wore and his weaker senses that he used, he still loved the chase, the catch, the tearing of clothes, the tearing of skin, the tearing of screams from young throats. Screams of fear. Screams of desperation. Screams of despair when they reached that critical moment when all fight and all flight were clearly failing. Screams of use. Screams of invasion. And screams filled with pleading as they tried to hold on to the bottom rung of life.

That had been different. Good for what it was, but not what it was now.

Now the killer wanted something different. Sex was fine, but it no longer thrilled him. It was too easy to get and too shallow a thing. No, what he wanted was the blood. The meat. The crack of bones between his teeth. The taste of all of the several parts that made up a human life. Oils of different pungencies. The flavor of skin on the hand and how different it was than the flavors of thigh and breast and hip and throat.

She ran so hard. She tried so much to be part of her own future.

But she could not run that fast.

Because he could run so much faster.

-39-

So, three guys walk into a bar.

Pint-sized badass of a town cop. Scary jock government agent. And me. Werewolf ex-cop P.I.

Life has gotten very strange.

Even by my standards.

-40-

We took a table in a corner that was so dark I needed my cell phone light to read the menu. I ordered a Philly cheesesteak, fries, and a beer. Ledger liked that and asked for the same thing. Crow had a Diet Coke.

"Okay," said Ledger, "cards on the table time."

"That'd make a refreshing change," observed Crow. "Let's start with your real name and official status."

There was no one seated within earshot, but even so Ledger lowered his voice. "Captain Joseph Edwin Ledger," he said. "I work for a specialized group operating under executive order."

"Name?"

"If I told you I'd have to kill you." Ledger smiled as he said it.

"Not joking here," said Crow. "I'm a half-step away from arresting you. I don't care if you could squeeze enough federal juice to beat an obstruction of justice charge. I'm the chief of police and you have to identify yourself."

Ledger nodded. "I used to be a cop," he said. "In Baltimore. Worked homicide and then I was attached to Homeland. Mostly sitting on my ass working wiretaps. Then I caught the tail of something and when we yanked on it there was a dragon at the other end. I was in on the bust, which went south when everyone thought it would be fun to be stupid with guns. After that I was scouted by a group called the Department of Military Sciences."

"Never heard of it," said Crow.

"You wouldn't. We fly pretty much below the radar."

"Part of Homeland?"

"Parallel. A lot smaller, less red tape and bullshit. We target groups with cutting-edge bio-weapons and other tech. Designer pathogens, man-portable nukes, that sort of thing."

"Mad scientists?" said Crow, amused.

"The maddest."

"So," I said, "you're James Bond."

Ledger shook his head. "No laser-beam cufflinks. No ejector seats. And I prefer lagers to martinis."

Crow sipped his diet pisswater. "Which doesn't explain why you're here. Again. Last time you were here you pretended to be FBI and you brought two thugs with you who claimed to be Federal Marshals. Which they weren't."

"Not as such, no."

"You brought a lot of bad people to my town. You turned a farmhouse into the Battle of Bull Run."

"I didn't deal that play. We had a guy in witness protection who did something very stupid. Tried to reach out to some very bad people in hopes of uncovering some terrorists on American soil. Brought a lot of cockroaches out of the woodpile. Things got creative and the good guys rode their horses into the sunset." Ledger paused. "I never did thank you for stepping in on that."

Crow ran his finger around the rim of his glass. "I had no official involvement in that case. There was, I believe, no evidence of my ever having been there. Perhaps you're mistaken."

"Uh huh," said Ledger. "Your nose grew two full inches when you said that."

They sat there and looked at each other, and I had the impression that there was a lot I didn't know about them. Not sure I actually wanted to know. I was already creeped out and probably way out of my depth here.

"Guys…going on the assumption that I have no idea what the fuck you two jokers are talking about, how about we circle around to the matter at hand?"

Crow leaned back in his chair, effectively breaking the connection. "All cards on the table," he said.

"All cards on the table," echoed Ledger. "Tell me about your investigation and then I'll tell you why I'm here. I think we'll find we're working two ends of the same case."

Crow nodded and went through it all. The murders in other towns, the deaths here. The lack of any visible federal investigation. Ledger said nothing. He ate his cheesesteak and listened. I noticed Crow glossed over the part about who and what Mike Sweeney was. When he got to the part about Limbus, Ledger began asking questions. He wanted to know everything either of us knew about that organization. Unfortunately we didn't know much.

When it was my turn, I told them about my previous case with the mysterious organization. Naturally I omitted a few details— namely the nature of the real enemy in that case. I was still having nightmares about that.

I had my Limbus card with me and he used his phone to photograph it and send the picture to his office. His contact there— presumably the 'Bug' he'd been talking to earlier—got back to him and Ledger relayed the information to us. We didn't like it.

"The number is fake. My guys traced it and it dead-ends. Understand something," Ledger said. "We have some pretty nifty toys and we can trace darn near anything. We can't trace that number. And it's not re-routing tech. Our pingbacks tell us that there is nothing at the end of that line. Database searches on Limbus came up empty, too. There are some obscure references to various groups using that name going back more than a hundred years, but so far we can't tie any of it together."

"You got all of that this fast?" asked Crow.

"Like I said, we have nifty toys. My people will continue to work on it. Maybe we'll come up with something. We have to assume, though, that your office is bugged, Crow. And maybe this Limbus group has some informants in town."

It was the logical answer, but Crow shook his head. "I don't think so," he said.

"Has to be," insisted Ledger.

Crow shrugged. "Not sure it does."

Ledger let it go for now. The fact that he did made me wonder if he'd run up against other stuff that was equally weird. I sure as hell have. Ever since I went into business as a P.I. I've found that this world is a lot bigger, darker and stranger than I ever thought. Werewolves are far from the only thing going bump in the night. And in my day I've met things I don't understand and things that terrify me.

Crow had that look, too.

So did Ledger.

The three of us lapsed into a brief silence. We ate, we drank, we avoided each other's eyes.

Finally, Ledger said, "Super soldiers."

Crow paused, his glass halfway to his lips. "What now?"

"Super soldiers."

"That's what we think this is about."

"Super soldiers," repeated Crow.

"Super soldiers?" I asked.

"Super soldiers," said Ledger.

And when he said it, I could see it.

"Jesus Christ," I said.

-41-

The killer dragged the girl into the woods and ate her.
Not all of her.
Just the good parts.
He nearly wept for the beauty of it.

"We inherited this case," Ledger said. "The first attacks happened in a small town near Saskatoon, Saskatchewan. Local law was called in when a couple of joggers running back roads to prepare for a marathon smelled something nasty. Mounties checked out an abandoned warehouse and—"

"Seriously?" I asked. "An abandoned warehouse?"

"I know. It's cliché, but you have to respect the classics. Anyway, they found two bodies pretty much torn to beef jerky. Been there about a week. Back door was open, so the locals had to conclude that the corpses had been bitten post-mortem by animals."

"Let me guess which *kind* of animal," said Crow dryly.

"Wolves aren't entirely unknown in Canada," said Crow. "Even if they're not exactly common in Saskatoon. The coroner's report, though, cited blunt force trauma as the cause of death. Murder weapon unknown, but presumably heavy and soft."

He looked at me. So did Crow.

"What?"

"If you wanted to arrange a crime scene in a way that would muddy the investigation, how would you do it? Specifically, you."

I felt my face getting hot. I don't like to be put on the spot and I have never once in my adult life had anyone call me out for being what I was. Ledger was doing exactly that. It was so fucking weird. What was weirder still was that neither of these guys looked particularly freaked by this line of questioning. They weren't spooked by it. I was.

So fucked up.

I cleared my throat. "Um…well, I guess I'd, you know, *change*, and you know, maybe, um, hit the guys and, well…"

Crow and Ledger burst out laughing. They howled. Ledger slapped his thighs. Crow put his face in his hands and his whole body shook. My face was actually burning now.

In a creaking, wheezing voice, Crow said, "He's embarrassed by being a were…were…"

The rest of it dissolved into laughter.

Joe Ledger began singing *Werewolves of London*, and Crow joined him for the "Wahoooo" chorus.

"I am going to kill both of you," I said.

That made them laugh harder.

"Seriously. Headshots. Bury you out in the country."

There were tears on Crow's cheeks.

I glared at them.

"Yeah, well...fuck you."

Then I was laughing, too.

-43-

The killer heard something and he raised his head. He'd been cradling the girl's head, sniffing her hair, but now there was a sound in the woods.

The killer tossed the head into the bushes and rose to smell the breeze. He was covered in blood, and the smell of the girl's life was like strong perfume, blotting out most of what was exhaled on the forest's breath.

He moved away from the kill, going deeper into the woods, following the sound. Smelling the air. He changed halfway so that he had arms but still had claws, and he climbed a tree.

There.

Way over there, a mile away or more, was the big red-haired policeman.

The local wolf, he thought.

Coming this way.

The killer shimmied down the tree, turned away from the half-eaten girl, and ran.

Was this local wolf blunted to the subtleties of the hunt? He wondered that as he ran.

He dared the wolf to pick up his scent. He dared him to follow.

He dared this pup to find him.

-44-

Eventually Ledger got back to his story. More beer was involved. The other patrons at the Scarecrow moved even farther away from the three loud, obnoxious crazy people in the corner.

"Anyway, anyway," said Ledger, bringing it all down to earth, "there was a second set of murders in Manitoba. A third on Prince Edward Island. In each case there were two or more corpses. All mutilated. Each one in situations where there was another *convenient* possible cause of death. Industrial accidents, car crashe3. You get the picture."

"Who put it all together?" asked Crow.

Ledger smiled. "A computer. We have a great pattern-recognition software package. It trolls interagency databases. Mostly used to scout for terrorist activity, but every once in a while it coughs out something that's simply weird."

"Even so," I said, "what was the connecting factor? There are a lot of strange, violent deaths."

Ledger nodded his approval. "Location, location, location. In each case, the deaths occurred within twenty miles, give or take, of a known—or suspected—lab."

"What kind of lab?" I asked.

"Bio-weapons research."

Crow shook his head. "Then your computer is wonky, 'cause there's nothing like that in Pine Deep. Nothing even remotely like it."

Ledger gave him a long, hard look. "How much of your pension would you like to bet on that?"

"Wait," said Crow, "what?"

"Yup, there is a bio-weapons R&D facility in your own little slice of rural heaven."

"Run by whom?"

"That's a different question. It's sure as hell not run by the U.S. government. I know that for a fact."

"Are you talking about a private lab?" I asked. "Something attached to a pharmaceutical company?"

"No. We don't have those here, either," said Crow, who was getting very angry now.

"Then what?" I asked. "Private sector working on something they want to sell to Uncle Sam?"

Ledger shook his head. "I wish. No, gentlemen, I think what we have here is a clandestine and highly illegal lab. Probably funded by a terrorist group. And one that's highly mobile. I think it's been moving around North America doing research on the fly."

We digested that, and it was a hard pill to swallow.

"How sure are you?" I asked.

"Pretty sure."

"Based on what evidence?" demanded Crow.

"Based on a shitload of supposition and some negative reasoning," said Ledger. He drank the last of his beer and signaled for another. "Let's look at the facts, shall we? We have a series of murders in rural areas. Each murder has been orchestrated to look like an accident. Because of the nature of the injuries, they haven't been able to totally sell it, but enough so that no one in authority has been enthusiastic enough to start an international or even interstate investigation. Right now there's too much room for doubt."

Crow and I reluctantly agreed.

"Whoever these folks are, they have access to, or have somehow created, lycanthropes."

"Look at you using technical words," said Crow.

"I went to college," said Ledger. "We can suppose that they have more than one, because of the nature of the crime scenes. There's signs of evidence tampering that could not have been done in the absence of hypernormal physical strength."

"How did you make the jump from that to, um, *lycanthropes*?" I asked.

Ledger smiled. "Rumors in the pipeline." When it was clear that Crow and I wanted more than that, he explained. "There's been talk about this for a while now. Ever since Dr. Broussard found the lycanthropic gene and—"

"Whoa!" I said immediately. "Doctor who found what?"

"Ah," he said, "I would have thought that someone of your kind would have known about that. No? Okay, well Broussard is a French molecular biologist working with a team in Switzerland. They've been indexing the genes that are known in the tabloids as 'junk DNA.' Turns out, they're not junk. You guys up on your genetics? No? I'll try to flatten it out for you. In genomics they've found that about 98% of our DNA is what they call 'noncoding.' Some of this noncoding DNA is transcribed into functional noncoding RNA molecules, while others are not transcribed or give rise to RNA transcripts of unknown function. Follow me?"

"I have no idea what the fuck you just said," I admitted.

"Lost me on the first curve," said Crow.

Ledger grinned. "Yeah, a couple of years ago I didn't understand any of this shit. It's become a kind of job requirement."

"Weird job," I suggested.

"You have no idea. Anyway, the amount of this noncoding DNA varies species to species. Like I said, 98% of the human genome is noncoding while only about 2% of, say, a typical bacterial genome is noncoding."

"I think I almost understood that," said Crow.

"At first, most of the noncoding DNA had no *known* biological function—emphasis on *known*—and someone hung the nickname 'junk DNA' on it. But there are teams all over the world working to unlock the secrets of those genes. Dr. Broussard's team has been working on chimeric genes and—"

"On what?"

"Chimeric. Genes that change their nature, or that change what they code for. They're a brand new branch of evolutionary science. Broussard's pretty much ready to prove that a lot of theriomorphic phenomena in world folklore—and that means things that change shape—"

"I know." Crow and I said it at the same time.

"—are not part of some weirdo supernatural shit," continued Ledger, "but are evidence that genetics is a much, much bigger field than we thought. It's Broussard's belief that werewolves are a genetic offshoot of good ol' *homo sapiens sapiens*."

We said nothing.

"And, before you ask, there are other examples of chimeric genes. I had a tussle a couple of years ago with *Upierczy*."

"That's a kind of Russian vampire," said Crow quietly.

"*Homo vampiri*," said Ledger. "Now fully documented, though we haven't released that to the press yet. The *Upierczy* are some nasty fucks. They call themselves the Red Knights and even though they're not supernatural, they are still every damn bit as scary."

"You don't believe in the supernatural?" asked Crow.

"Not really," said Ledger, but his tone was mildly evasive. It was clear he didn't want to travel down that side road.

"How does that connect to an illegal bio-weapons lab in my backyard?" asked Crow.

Ledger shrugged. "Most of the labs doing illegal bio-weapons research tend to be either offshore or hidden."

"Hollowed-out volcanoes?" I suggested.

"Close enough. A few are on ships in international waters. Or hidden in oil refineries. Places where they can hide science teams, where people come and go, and where large shipments of supplies are routine. We busted one in a container yard in Baltimore last year and another on a freight train operating out of the Pacific Northwest. We've found mini-labs in RVs, in mobile homes, and in your generic abandoned or short-leased warehouses. Computer and lab equipment is getting more compact every day and it's easier to have a grab-it-and-go lab than before. And there are what amounts to virtual labs, where everyone is networked through WI-FI so they don't all have to be in the same physical location. I think that's what we're hunting for here. Someone is messing around with lycanthrope DNA. Your basic *homo sapiens canis lupis*. Broussard's term, not mine."

"Even so, how'd you get to werewolves?" asked Crow.

"Hair and fiber recovered from victims. We, um, *hijacked* some of the lab reports and sent it to Broussard's people for sequencing. Rang all the right bells. And the genes show clear signs of after-market manipulation. Transgenics, gene therapy, all sorts of stuff." He leaned forward and rested his elbows on the table. "Our theory is that someone is trying to build a better werewolf. I don't know about you gents, but that pretty much scares the shit out of me."

-45-

The killer ran and the local wolf ran after.

They chased each other through the woods for long minutes, and then the killer broke and ran through a stream and shed his pursuer like a snake sheds a skin.

After ten full minutes of running, the killer stopped and went to high ground. He searched in all directions for the local wolf. For the pup.

And found nothing.

He sneered in contempt.

A wolf that could not follow a living scent was no wolf at all. He deserved to be gutted and left to rot.

The killer made a mental promise to see that done.

-46-

"Why the fuck would someone want to do that?" I demanded.

"Two words," said Ledger. "Super soldier."

"Like Captain America with fur?" suggested Crow.

"More like Captain Russia or Captain North Korea, or something like that," said Ledger. "But in broad terms, sure. Why not? If you can make the science work, and if that science isn't all that expensive—and if you're starting with actual werewolves it wouldn't be—why not give it a shot? Of course, it's more cost effective and logistically sound to do something like this, to draw from the local populace of your enemy. If you can find lycanthropes within a target country and recruit them, then it reduces the likelihood of political fallout. It's always easier to disown a traitor than explain away a spy. Plus, given that there actually *are* werewolves, then imagine the psychological and religious implications. That kind of thing would do real harm. Actual monsters."

Crow and I sat there and chewed on that. Kind of choked on it going down.

It also made me review some of my own encounters with what I've always thought were supernatural elements. Was Ledger right? Were these things really part of a much bigger version of 'natural science'? Like the way physics has had to expand to embrace both Einstein's relativity and Max Planck's quantum physics, and was being stretched further to take in chaos theory, string theory and other crazy shit that I can't even begin to understand.

Vampires? Sure, the ones I met didn't turn into bats or command storms. None of that nonsense. And me? The phases of the moon didn't mean dick to me. Maybe it was all evidence that Mother Nature was a freaky bitch.

Demons and ghosts? Jury would have to deliberate a little longer on that. And that wasn't a topic I wanted to float with Ledger. Or Crow, though I was beginning to suspect that he knew more about this than all of us.

"What about that kid, Antonio?" I asked. "Is he part of this mad science bullshit?"

Ledger shook his head. "No. He's a friend of a friend."

Crow made a twirling motion with his index finger, indicating that he wanted more of an answer than that.

"One of the guys that works with me, a computer super-geek, travels in some of the same circles as Antonio. When the Broussard thing came up, this friend of mine did some covert Net searches. Very much on the D.L., and based on message board posts, Facebook searches and other data, he made a list of people who might actually be lycanthropes hiding within regular society."

"More NSA spy shit?" asked Crow, but Ledger ignored that.

"How many names?" I asked.

"A few," said Ledger, but he wouldn't go any deeper into that. All he said was, "Antonio Jones popped up on the list, and it happened to be that my friend knew him from some sci-fi and horror conventions. The kid's Facebook photo was of him in full make-up as a werewolf, except—"

"Except it was real?"

"Yup."

"That's nuts," I said, but I found it funny, too. "Hiding in plain sight."

Crow grunted. "Kind of makes you wonder."

"Yes it does," Ledger agreed.

"So where does all this leave us?" I asked. "I mean, I can kind of buy this werewolf super soldier thing, and I've seen firsthand the kind of damage these assholes are willing to do, but...what now? We have a theory and no facts. Do you Mission Impossible cats have any leads?"

Ledger sighed. "Not yet. I was kind of hoping you fellas could help with that."

"Why us?" asked Crow.

"'Cause, you got a werewolf working for you."

"Meaning me?" I asked.

"Meaning your deputy," said Ledger. "Meaning Officer Michael Sweeney. Meaning your adopted son."

Crow said nothing. His expression was completely blank. He hadn't mentioned Mike Sweeney.

So I asked. "What makes you think that?"

"Antonio," said Ledger.

"Balls," said Crow.

"Funny old world," said Ledger.

Which is when Crow's cell phone rang. He looked at it and made a face.

"It's him."

He held up a finger for silence as he took the call. Mostly, he listened.

Then he said, "Stay right there. Don't do anything. You hear me, Mike? You stay right where you are and wait. I'm bringing plenty of backup. No, I don't mean Otis and Farley. Don't worry, we'll be there in a hot minute."

He closed the phone and got to his feet.

"What is it?" Ledger and I both asked.

"Mike thinks he found them."

-47-

Ledger's car was right outside. A Ford Explorer that had gotten some kind of upgrade. The engine was quiet as a whisper, but the fucking thing could move. Crow rode shotgun, I was in the back.

"Buckle up, kids," said Ledger. He wasn't joking. He drove it like a getaway car.

"I only have two spare magazines," said Crow.

Ledger laughed at that. "I got enough shit in the back to invade Iran. Now tell me about Sweeney. What exactly did he find?"

Crow said that Mike was hunting the woods, trying to pick up the trail of the werewolves who'd wrecked the bike. He picked up a fresher scent, and for a while thought he was going to run another wolf to ground. Didn't happen that way, though, and he followed that to a blockhouse in the woods that was sometimes used by the EPA when they sent their teams in. Some universities leased it for use, too. There's some oddball flora and fauna in the woods near Pine Deep.

"Mike said that the trail led to a shed attached to the blockhouse, and he thought that the rear wall might be phony. That's when he backed out and called me."

"You know this blockhouse?" asked Ledger.

"Sure." Crow gave him precise directions out of town, then began calling turns onto small side roads. Pretty soon we were driving roads so narrow and overgrown that weeds and branches brushed both sides of the car.

"I bet the last guy to use this road wore feathers," complained Ledger.

We went deep into the state forest and way off the grid.

As we drove, Ledger caught my eye in the rearview. "This lycanthrope thing is pretty much new to me, and I'll be the first to admit that it's freaking me out."

"Doesn't show," I said.

"Feels it on the inside. My nuts crawled up inside my chest cavity and they don't seem to want to come down."

"You afraid of me?" I asked.

"Of course I am, you freak. You're a fucking werewolf. I have a fucking werewolf in my car. I am driving to meet *another* werewolf who is waiting to lead me to a nest of super soldier werewolves. So, yeah, I'm afraid. I'd worry about anyone who said they weren't scared."

I grinned at him.

"Don't do that," he said. "You look like Hannibal fucking Lecter."

"Sorry."

"Tell me something," Ledger continued. "When you do that, um, change... how much of you is you and how much is the wolf?"

"One and the same."

"That's not enough of an answer, man. I need to know if I have to keep an eye on you. I mean, do I need to worry about you looking at me and thinking I'm on the menu?"

For some reason I couldn't adequately explain, I found that to be moderately offensive.

"No," I said.

"You're sure?"

"I'm sure."

He gave me another look. A hard one. "*Be* sure."

We drove the rest of the way in silence.

-48-

Crow had Ledger pull off onto a side road that ran fifty feet and dead-ended in the woods.

"It's a mile from here," he said. "Best if we go in on foot."

We all agreed to that.

Ledger popped the back of the Explorer and opened a big, flat metal box. Inside there were handguns, rifles, shotguns, boxes of rounds, and even some grenades.

"Party favors," said Ledger.

"Sweet Mother of Pearl," said Crow as he selected a bandolier fitted to hold a dozen loaded magazines. His sidearm was a Glock .40 and there were plenty of magazines for him. Ledger put one on as well, with mags for his Beretta. He also took an A-12 combat shotgun with a big drum filled with buckshot and Frag-12 fragmentation grenades.

"For when you want to send the very best," said Ledger. I saw him check the spring of his rapid-release folding knife, too. Then he glanced at me. "What about you?"

I had my gun and two magazines, but that was all I needed. "Less I carry, the less I have to go back later and find. But...any chance you have an extra pair of sweat pants or something?"

"I have BDU pants. My size, but you can roll up the cuffs. Why?"

"Because I tend to ruin my clothes when I change, unless I strip out first. And if we walk away from this I doubt you want me going commando on your back seat."

He grinned, took the rolled-up extra pants and tucked them into the back of his belt.

We moved off into the woods. Crow texted Mike to let him know we were coming. Ledger was good in the woods. Fast and silent, like me. Crow knew how to move through nature, too, but he had a limp. We had to slow down to let him keep pace with us. Even so, a mile was nothing and it fell away in a few quick minutes.

I smelled Mike before I saw him.

But he was closer than I would have liked. He was smart enough to come at us downwind. I turned a split second before he deliberately stepped on some dry grass. A moment later Crow and Ledger turned, too.

Mike waved us down behind some dense bushes. Beyond it, built into a downslope of a long hill was a box made from cinderblock. Boring, utilitarian, and stained by forest rains and insect slime. The structure was sixty-by-ninety, with a small shed built onto the east corner. Mike pointed to a clump of pines and in the shadows we could see three cars. An SUV and two sedans. Then he dug into a pocket and produced a handful of important-looking wires. Those cars weren't going anywhere.

The young officer nodded to the building. "I picked up a scent in the woods and followed it. Lost it a couple of times because I think he knew he was being followed. He went into the stream for a while, but I found him again. Stayed downwind and tracked him here. Saw him go inside the shed, but when I checked he wasn't there. It's rigged to look like a tool shed, but the back wall's a dummy. Couldn't find the lock or handle, though."

Ledger nodded. "That's good police work, kid."

Sweeney gave him a stony go-fuck-yourself look. Crow patted him on the shoulder.

We watched the building for a few minutes.

"Don't see any security cameras," I said.

"Could be hidden," mused Ledger. "But I don't think so. I think this is a temporary set-up. The fact that it's half a mile from No-fucking-Where is their security system. It'll be different inside. Guys like this always have lots and lots of guns."

"So do we," said Crow.

"They also have super soldiers."

"So do we."

Ledger nodded. He cut a look at Sweeney and at me. "And people wonder why I drink."

"Okay, coach," I said to Ledger. "This seems to be your ballgame. What's the play?"

Before he could answer there was a sound behind us. Very small. Very furtive.

We spun around, guns coming up. The wolf that lives inside of me nearly jumped out. Must have been the same with Sweeney.

A small figure staggered out of the brush behind us.

Antonio Jones.

And he was covered in blood.

He reached out a hand toward us. His mouth worked as he fought to speak. Then his eyes rolled up and he pitched forward.

-49-

Ledger and Sweeney moved at the same time. They closed on Antonio so fast it was like they blurred. With Mike I could understand the speed. The wolf was right there beneath his skin, it glared out through his eyes all the time. Ledger was just a man, but moved with a speed and economy of motion that called to mind an expression I once read in an article about Jesse Owens. 'Oiled grace'.

He reached Antonio first and caught the kid as he fell and lowered him to the ground. We all huddled around him.

"Jesus," I breathed.

The kid was a mess.

Someone had beat the shit out of him. They'd cut him up. There were long ragged gashes in his face and chest and stomach. His hands were bloody, his knuckles visibly broken. Whatever had happened, he'd put up one hell of a fight.

Ledger wiped blood from the kid's eyes and mouth. Crow took his pulse. Mike pulled off his own uniform shirt and began ripping it into strips that I pressed against the worst of the cuts. Antonio's eyelids fluttered and opened.

"What happened, kid?" asked Ledger, bending close.

"I…I…" The young man's voice faltered. "I…tried to…stop…"

He coughed and blood bubbled at the corners of his mouth.

It took a while, but the kid mastered himself through an admirable effort of will. Sometimes you find strength in the strangest of places. This kid had some grit.

He told us that he saw the three of us leave the Scarecrow and was hurrying down the street to catch up, but we drove off. Then he saw two men hurry out of the bar, get into a car and follow. Antonio didn't like the look of them. Or the smell. He got his scooter and tailed them. The car was well behind Ledger's Explorer, and once out in the country it turned off and went up a logger's road. Antonio might have let it go, but he was positive that at least one of those men was a werewolf. So he followed. When he described the road, Crow and Mike nodded. The logger's road changed to a Forest Service road three miles outside of town and then crossed into the state forest. Antonio, thinking that these men might be heading for the hidden lab Ledger had told him about, kept following.

He lost the car twice, and when he found it a third time, not more than a mile east of where we all knelt, the men were in the process of hiding the car with boughs they cut from the trees. They heard the scooter, and before Antonio could turn it around and get the hell out of there, the two men changed into wolfshape and ran him down.

There was one hell of a fight.

Antonio was sure he injured one of them pretty badly, but he took too much damage to keep fighting. The other one—a big son of a bitch that Antonio described as 'maybe Indian or Asian'-- was the one who took the kid apart. He slashed and bit him and beat him nearly to death. To get away, Antonio threw himself down a steep hill, fell into a river and damn near drowned. The men gave up the chase, probably figuring him for dead. Antonio managed to get to the bank. When he climbed up the hill on the other side to try and find a road, he saw Ledger's car drive past with us in it.

He followed and found us here.

We exchanged looks. This was one impressive young man. Tougher than he looked, with big, clanking balls.

Antonio, spent from telling his tale and nearly ruined by the fight with the other werewolves, passed out and lay silent.

Ledger leaned close to me. "You know this lycanthrope stuff, Sam. Aren't you guys supposed to be able to heal fast? Some kind of hyperactive wound repair system? Or is this kid going to die on us here?"

I hesitated. We Benandanti have a lot of specialized knowledge. Things about who we are and what we are. My mother, grandmother and aunts were all very specific about keeping that information confidential. About sharing it with no one outside of the family. Not even with other werewolves.

So, naturally I had to give that a little thought before I answered. I glanced at Mike.

He shook his head. "I never had anyone to teach me how this all works," he admitted. "I've been hurt a few times. I know how fast *I* heal, but I'm not the same as Antonio. Or you."

His eyes were a strange and artificial blue. He reached up and pinched his eye, removing a contact lens. Then another. The eyes that were revealed were no human eyes at all. Nor were they werewolf eyes. They were as red as blood and ringed with gold.

Joe Ledger said, "What the fuck?"

I didn't say shit. Not sure I could have. Whatever he was, Mike Sweeney was a lot more than a werewolf. I was damn sure he wasn't even remotely human.

Ledger edged back, shaken and pale. "What in the wide blue fuck are you?"

Sweeney smiled. A rare thing for him. It was not the kind of smile you ever want to see. On anyone. Not even in a horror movie.

"What am I?" he asked, and for a moment even the timbre of his voice was all wrong. Too deep. Too strange. "I have no idea."

Crow touched Mike's shoulder but looked at us. "Mike's family tree is moderately complicated. Maybe one of these days we can talk about it."

"Or maybe not," said Mike.

"Or maybe not," agreed Crow. "Right now, though, we got to help this kid. You have anything, Sam? Benandanti are supposed to be the secret keepers of the werewolves. Or something like that, am I right?"

"Something like that," I mumbled.

They all looked at me. I looked down at the kid.

Poor little bastard really put his ass on the line. Tried to make a difference.

"Sorry, grandma," I said.

"What?" asked Ledger.

"Nothing." I held my hand out to him. "Give me your knife."

He didn't hesitate, but instead reached for the rapid-release knife, snapped his wrist to lock the blade in place, and offered it to me, handle-first.

I took it and looked at my reflection in the polished steel. "Understand something," I said. "I'm going on what I've been told. I've never actually done this before."

"Kid's going to die," said Ledger.

"This is a gamble," I said. "This might kill him faster."

Crow shook his head. "A small chance is better than none at all."

Ledger and Sweeney nodded.

"Do it," said Ledger.

I put the edge of the knife against the heel of my left palm, took a deep breath to steady my nerves, and let the wickedly sharp blade do its work. Bright red blood welled from the small cut.

"Open his mouth," I said, and Mike put two fingers between the kid's teeth and then splayed them to push open Antonio's mouth. I clenched my fist to increase the blood pressure and when the blood began rolling over my hand and down my wrist I extended my arm and let the first fat drops fall. They splashed his lips, his teeth and then vanished into the darkness of his open mouth.

The old ritual says to use seven drops.

Seven, the number of heaven.

I gave him seven and one to grow on and then put my cut hand into my own mouth and sucked off the last drops of blood. When I removed my hand, the cut was already closed. Kind of freaky. Grandma hadn't told me about that part.

Ledger, who had gone pale earlier, went milk-white now.

"That," he said thickly, "is some weird-ass voodoo bullshit."

I grinned at him. I probably still had blood on my own teeth. "Welcome to my world."

Crow smiled, too. "Welcome to Pine Deep."

Mike Sweeney said nothing, but his red eyes burned into mine.

On the ground Antonio Jones groaned once, twitched.

And died.

-50-

We tried everything.

CPR.

Mouth to mouth.

Everything.

But the kid's body settled into a terminal stillness. No pulse. No nothing.

I turned away and felt tears in my eyes. I balled my fist and drove it into the top of my thigh. Over and over again.

Son of a bitch.

Son of a motherfucking bitch.

This wasn't right.

It wasn't fair.

When I turned back, no one would meet my eyes.

Crow looked old and tired. Sweeney got up and walked back to the line of shrubs that separated us from the blockhouse. Ledger, he sat there looking down at the kid, shaking his head slowly.

He was the only one who said anything, though. "You tried, man. At least you tried."

Before I even knew I was going to do it I grabbed a fistful of his shirt and pulled him halfway to his feet. "Fuck you, asshole. You should never have brought a kid into this. This shit is on you."

Ledger looked at me. If he was afraid of me, it no longer showed. He placed his hand on mine and pressed two fingers into nerve clusters. He did it without effort and my hand popped open. Just like that. Ledger gently pushed me back.

"Don't ever do that again, Sam." His voice was very calm. It wasn't a request and it was somehow more than a threat. He walked forward very slowly, which made me walk backward. Ledger got so close that his forehead and mine were touching. It might have looked like an intimate moment. Two close friends, two brothers, two mourners at a funeral.

But this wasn't that. This was alpha and wolf. His voice was very soft.

"You're letting emotions get in the way of your better sense. Don't. That's what happens to people when they get caught up in this kind of thing. They need to assign blame and because the bad guys are usually out of reach they lash out at whoever's close. The thing about that is—it's what those assholes want. They count on it. Terrorism isn't about overwhelming force. It's about fear. It's about grief. It's about confusion."

"This isn't terrorism—" I began, but he cut me off.

"The fuck it isn't. That's the *only* thing this is about. These sons of bitches killed that kid. They fucked us all up in doing it."

"It's not right!" I growled.

"Shhh. Quiet now," he said. "No, it's not right. None of this is about right or wrong. None of it. It's about evil. It's about darkness. That's what this is about. These fuckers want to shut out all the lights. Everyone's lights. They want to be the boogeymen in the dark. That's what they do so they can feel powerful."

I said nothing. Ledger moved his head back a few inches so I could see his eyes. They were cold and they were hard, but I saw a bottomless pain there. Endless hurt. I could feel Crow and Sweeney watching us.

"Sam, the guys who did this are the same ones who killed the guy on the motorcycle and all of those other civilians. That's what they do. They don't have the balls to go to war with warriors, so they try to cripple us by targeting the innocent. The civilians. The ones who can't protect themselves. If you lose your shit, then that guarantees a win for them. Is that what you want?"

"No," I said hoarsely.

"No," he agreed.

"This...this isn't my sort of thing," I said.

"What *is* your sort of thing?"

"When I take on a client, it's like they become part of my..." The word stuck in my throat. I wanted him to understand. I didn't want to sound like an idiot. But I said it anyway. "When I take on a client, it's like they become part of my pack."

He studied me, and nodded slowly. "And you'll do anything for your pack."

We looked at each other for a long moment.

I nodded.

He took his wallet out, removed a dollar bill and stuffed it into my shirt pocket. "Consider that a retainer from Antonio Jones. He's your client. When this is over, if we're both standing on our feet, you can bill me for the rest."

"I've already been paid."

"By who?"

"Limbus."

"Fuck Limbus. They're not here. That kid is. You're working for him. And if there was ever a client who deserved to be in your *pack*, then he's it."

I shook my head, but even I didn't know if that was a denial of his words or a refusal to accept all of this bullshit.

"So what's the alternative?" asked Ledger. "We could fall back and wait for reinforcements and hope that these bastards don't slip away while we're waiting."

"No."

"Or we can cowboy up and go in there and *prove* to these motherfuckers that they don't have a right to do these things. That they aren't allowed to do this. That there is punishment for it."

I cleared my throat. "We could be walking right into a trap. We don't know what's waiting for us in there."

Ledger smiled. His smile was every bit as alien and as awful as Mike Sweeney's had been. "Maybe," he conceded. "But they don't know what's waiting for them out here."

It took me a few seconds, but then I felt a smile growing on my own face. I couldn't see it, but I was sure it wasn't one I'd want to look at in the bathroom mirror.

-51-

Ledger put a call in to his people and told them to come running. But best estimate was forty minutes. We couldn't risk that kind of time.

We decided to hit the place ourselves.

Ledger mapped out a plan. It was ugly, dangerous as hell, probably insane, and definitely suicidal.

We all agreed to it.

It had somehow become that kind of day.

-52-

We crowded into the shed.

Ledger took some goodies from his pockets and explained them as he set to work. The first thing was a pocket sensor that identified which wall of the shed had a door hidden behind it. That was easy. Finding the lock and door handle took a little longer, but Ledger found it. There was a knot in the wood of the back wall. It was phony and hid a pressure switch. Ledger produced a second gizmo that would let us know if the door was wired with bombs. It wasn't, which provided less of a relief than I would have thought. Then he took what looked like a Fruit Roll-Up from a metal tube, flattened it out, peeled off a plastic cover and pressed it in place over the switch. He pushed a small electronic detonator into the putty-like material.

"Blaster plaster," he explained. "Very high-tech pressure-reactive chemical explosive." He held up a small trigger device. "Let's get out of Dodge."

We went outside and over the edge of the hill.

"Once I trigger it we're committed. We go in hard and fast and it's fuck you to anyone inside. Anything past that door is no longer American soil and whoever's in there is to be considered an enemy combatant."

"Is that legal?" asked Crow.

"Do you care?" Ledger said.

"On the whole, not much."

Ledger nodded. "It'll get loud and smoky. Everyone keeps their shit wired tight. You check your targets. I do not want a bullet up my ass."

"What do we do if they want to surrender?" I asked.

"We let them," said Ledger. "We're not murderers, Sam. For right now we're soldiers. Rules of engagement apply. You good with that?"

We all were.

We were all scared, too.

Even Mike, though it didn't show. I could smell it. Faint, but there.

Ledger was the coolest, but he had a fine sheen of sweat on his forehead. No doubt. After all, this wasn't a cell of al-Qaeda. These were monsters. Scary monsters. Scarier than me, and I have my moments. Super soldier werewolves. If there's a worse-case scenario that trumps that, please do not fucking tell me.

Ledger held up the trigger. "Good guys win, bad guys lose."

We nodded.

As the Bible says, we girded our loins.

He pressed the trigger.

The blast was impressive.

The shed stopped being a shed and became a rapidly expanding cloud of splinters and dust that blew over and past us. The door disintegrated and a big chunk of the interior wall blew inward.

Ledger was up and moving before the first echo of the blast could bounce back at us from the surrounding trees. He had his pistol up, laser sight stabbing through the smoke. He bellowed through the thunder.

"Federal Agents! Put your weapons down. Put your hands in the air. Do it now! Do it now!"

It was rhetoric. It was like saying hello.

None of us expected them to comply.

And, fuck it, they didn't.

-53-

We crowded behind him.

Crow and Mike Sweeney.

Me.

All of us with guns.

We ran into dense smoke and burst through into the blockhouse, none of us really knowing what to expect. I had a kind of Doctor Frankenstein thing in my head. Arcane science, secret experiments.

It wasn't like that.

There were two folding tables on which were laptops. And a third table crowded with some scientific junk. Open metal cases, high-pressure injection guns, alcohol swabs, IV bags. That was it. The whole shebang could have fit into the trunk of a midsized sedan. No exotic machinery, no bubbling vats or towering electrodes. This was twenty-first century micro-science. Transgenics on the go.

But the equipment wasn't important to us. Not at the moment.

The occupants of the room were.

We were expecting two, maybe three of them. A handful at the outside. Some science geeks and a couple of their pet monsters.

Yeah, that's what we were hoping for.

Fuck.

There were fifteen people in the room.

Two of them were Korean. Both in lab coats. Both pencil-neck geeks. North Korean, as we later found out.

The others were home grown. Twelve men, one woman. Americans and Canadians.

And every single one of them was a werewolf.

Every.

Single.

One.

Ledger put the red dot of his laser sight on the chest of the nearest man. A guy who looked like a baseball player. Fit, long-legged, rangy. The man was ten feet from Ledger.

"Hands on your head right now!" bellowed Ledger.

For just a split second it all held together. A tableau. Them and us, with ghosts of smoke drifting around us.

Then the man grabbed the shoulder of one of the Korean scientists and hurled him at Ledger.

Not shoved him.

Hurled.

The scientist went flying into the air, well off the ground, arms pinwheeling, legs kicking, right at Ledger. The agent was able to twist out of the way and the screaming Korean hit Crow. They went down hard.

Then all hell broke loose.

The crowd rushed at us, and even as I swung my gun toward the nearest, he stopped being a man and became a wolf. It was the fastest change I'd ever seen, and I've seen my grandmother do the shift. She could do it in the space of a finger-snap.

This guy was faster.

In a heartbeat he stopped being a man and became a thing.

When I change, I usually go the whole way into pure wolfshape. Most werewolves do. We're faster as wolves. We have four feet and keener senses.

He did not.

None of them did.

They shifted into wolfmen. A horror movie halfway point between man and wolf. He leapt at me and swatted the pistol from my hand. Claws like daggers dug into my chest and if I hadn't begun the change as soon as he leapt, I'd have died as a man, right there and then. The man has more vulnerabilities.

He smashed me back and down, and immediately we were tearing into each other. Teeth and claws. Spit and blood.

I heard gunfire and didn't know who was shooting. Ledger, maybe.

Crow, too, if he could.

I doubt Mike Sweeney was still human.

There was a scream of fury that was higher and stranger than any wolf cry, and I knew at once it had to be him. It was almost the shriek of a jungle cat. What *was* he?

The wolfman who bore me to the ground was strong. Goddamn strong. He gripped my forelegs and tried to tear them apart. His grip alone was crushing. Pain exploded through my legs and shoulders. There was no way I was going to wrestle free. He was easily twice as strong as me.

Super soldiers.

What was it Ledger said? *Someone's trying to build a better werewolf.*

Yeah.

Shit.

So, fuck it, I stopped fighting a fight I couldn't win, and instead darted my head forward and bit his throat. I was in full wolfshape, and if my muscles weren't as powerful as his amped up physique, my jaws were. Wolf jaws were always stronger than wolfman jaws. My family's genetics don't go back to *canis lupis*. Most werewolves do, we don't. We Benandanti are in a direct genetic line from *canis dirus*. The massive, prehistoric Dire Wolves. No canine predator in history had a stronger bite. And as werewolves we get something extra added to the package.

He tried to tough it out, to muscle through my bite.

Fuck him.

He didn't.

His throat tore away between my teeth.

Blood exploded from him with fire hose pressure, smashing into my face, hitting the wall. The evil bastard died right there. His strength evaporated and his powerful and scientifically enhanced physique became so much cooling meat. I threw him off of me and rose to four feet with bloody meat and fur hanging from my jaws.

The rest of the room was a madhouse.

Crow had his back to the wall and had Mike Sweeney's combat shotgun in his hands. He fired, pumped, fired, pumped, over and over again. I've been hit with shotgun shells before. Buckshot hurts. Bear shot will put me on my knees, but it won't kill a werewolf. Not unless you scored a headshot and blew apart the motor cortex or the brain stem.

The rounds in that shotgun were explosive.

He blew arms and legs off. He blew holes through chests.

Hard as balls to shake off a ten inch hole through your sternum, supernatural or not.

Ledger didn't have his gun. It was somewhere on the floor.

Instead he had his rapid-release fighting knife in his hand and he was tackling two of the wolfmen at once.

He should have died. Right away. On the spot, end of story.

He was cut and bleeding, but damn it if that son of a bitch wasn't holding his own. He fought on the attack and with counterattacks. Nothing defensive. They came at him and he went for them. He didn't stab. Stabbing is for suckers who want to die. Ledger used lightning-fast slashes, jabs and picks to open up dozens of wounds in arms, legs, bellies, groins and faces. The wolfmen were the ones on the defensive. Maybe it was their arrogance, maybe they'd never fought a warrior before, but they were losing what should have been a nothing battle.

It couldn't last, though. Ledger was human. He'd tire.

They wouldn't.

And even as I watched I could see some of their wounds beginning to close.

This could only end one way.

I began making my way toward him. On the other side of the room, Mike Sweeney—or what had been Mike Sweeney—was fighting with the largest of the wolfmen. Two giants colliding. Both standing on two legs and slashing with clawed hands. Sweeney and the giant were well-matched and there was no way to tell who was going to win that fight.

Before I could help him or Ledger, the only female werewolf in the room rushed at me. She was tall for a woman, and dishearteningly fast.

She laughed as she slashed at me.

If you haven't heard the cruel laughter of a werewolf, I hope you never do. It's so wrong in so many ways. There's no humanity in it. Just malicious glee and a red anticipation of what's to come.

She raked me from shoulder to hip as I tried to evade, the slashes burning like acid. I hissed and snapped at her, but she danced away, lithe as a dancer. Her riposte was a slash across my forehead that filled one eye with my own blood.

Bitch.

I darted in and she danced back, she slashed and I jumped sideways. And that started our gavotte. She caught me more times than I evaded. I nipped her twice and did no damage at all. Unlike the first wolfman I'd fought, she used cunning and speed rather than relying on her strength.

She was faster than me. By a mile.

I needed to get close enough to use my bite strength.

She did not let me.

So I changed the game; I played hers.

As she lunged for a long slash, I shifted from wolf to wolfman. I pivoted and whipped out my hand and caught her wrist. Then I clamped my teeth around it as I shifted back to werewolf.

Bite strength, baby. Nothing beats it.

Bones collapsed, meat burst, and then I had her hand. She screamed so loud I thought it would blow out my eardrums. I reeled, but it was all noise. She clutched her maimed arm to her body, trying to staunch the flow of blood that jetted from the stump. She backed away, the fight taken out of her.

I had other plans.

As she turned to flee, I hurled myself onto her back and slammed her down onto the floor. As we landed I buried my fangs in the back of her neck. I could feel the vertebrae break apart. I could taste the cerebral spinal fluid as it filled my mouth. I could feel the life as it fled from her like steam from a ruptured pipe.

I almost howled. Like a wolf does after a kill. Almost.

But there was too much going on.

Ledger was being pushed back now. Bloody cuts crisscrossed his body. But amazingly, one of the wolfmen lay dead at his feet, the rapid-release knife buried to the hilt in the top of the creature's skull. Ledger had no weapon. All he had was speed and training and whatever angels protected him.

He was going to die, though. I could see that without question.

He was also fifty feet away and I was never going to be able to get to him in time.

Crow was down on one knee, his whole side glistening red. The shotgun lay in pieces around him, but there were three dead werewolves, too. As I watched, Crow fumbled his pistol out of his holster and raised it. His hands trembled with pain and fatigue. And fear. I could see in his eyes that he thought he was going to die, too.

Maybe we all were.

I'd taken a hell of a lot of damage.

I started in his direction, but then my entire back exploded with searing, unbearable, blinding pain. I could feel nails rake across my spine and ribs. The force of the impact knocked me down and sent me sliding across the floor, riding a red carpet of my own blood. As my body spun, I saw a figure that I hadn't seen before.

A fourteenth werewolf.

Tall. Powerful.

He shifted back to his human aspect, standing there naked and indomitable.

With a face like an American Indian. High cheekbones, black eyes, straight black hair.

This was the werewolf who'd killed Antonio.

I was certain of it.

And, just as certainly, this was the alpha of this pack.

He exuded power.

Across the room, Mike Sweeney vanished beneath a pile of wolfmen. Blood geysered up around them and screams filled the air.

My pistol was on the floor near Mike's feet. He bent and picked it up, dropped the magazine to inspect it, slapped it back in, racked it. The round that had already been in the chamber went arcing over his shoulder. The man looked around the room. His mouth turned down in a frown. Not of unhappiness at how many of his people were dead. It was a sneer of contempt. Everything he saw—us, his own pack, all of it—was nothing to him. He was a monster among monsters. I could *feel* that. I knew it to be true. We werewolves have certain instincts. I knew that this man was as close to death personified as ever walked the earth. Maybe he was the pinnacle of the twisted research being done in this place. Maybe he was the superior soldier that they were looking for. An unstoppable force.

The pain in my back was excruciating, but I had to move. I had to try to fight. This wasn't just a bad guy, not some child abuser I was hunting or a bail skip I was paid to nab. This wasn't the kind of scum I chased for small bucks as a P.I. This was the kind of evil I became a cop to oppose. Actual evil.

Was this what the people at Limbus wanted stopped? They'd put me in the path of a monster before, and I'd nearly died fighting it. This time I was pretty sure that I *was* going to die. Limbus seemed so prescient, but as I struggled to get to my feet, I knew that their faith in me was badly misplaced.

The big man raised the pistol and pointed it. Not at me. He pointed it at Ledger. His mouth curled into a small and very cruel little smile.

"No!" I snarled in a mouth was not constructed for human speech. I flung myself at him. I tried to gut him with my claws. Tried to bite him with my teeth. But all I managed to do was bump against him and spoil his first shot. The round vanished into the smoke above Ledger's head.

The alpha grunted and clubbed me with the butt of the pistol. Once. Twice.

Again and again.

Beating me down. Breaking me.

Killing me.

And he wasn't even in wolfshape.

I collapsed onto the ground.

The man gave a single little nod and raised the pistol again.

This time there was nothing I could do to prevent that shot.

Nothing.

I didn't have to.

There was a flash of movement. A blur, as fast as when Ledger and Mike had moved. Faster.

The hand holding the gun leaped into the air, trailed by rubies. The gun fired, but the barrel was pointing nowhere. The bullet struck the body of the dead werewolf woman, adding neither insult nor injury. Her flesh quivered but a little.

The alpha howled in agony. He spun around, and in doing so changed from bleeding man to maimed wolfman. The thing that had attacked him, the creature that had taken his hand, landed ten feet beyond me. It whirled and bared its bloody teeth at the towering killer.

It was another werewolf.

Smaller than me. Darker fur. Eyes as hot as hell's furnaces.

It stood on four legs, claws flexing with such fury they scored the concrete floor. Hair rose along its spine, its ears were back. It was the picture of savage rage, of a total commitment to hate.

The killer looked into those eyes.

So did I.

I think we both recognized them.

I spoke the name.

"Antonio."

I didn't ask how. The blood. The old ritual I'd performed had done its work. Its magic. It had brought this young man back from the dark place. It had restored him, healed the terrible wounds that had been torn into his flesh. It had brought him to the peak of his feral power. Maybe to a greater peak than ever before.

Even maimed and bleeding the alpha was still twice his size. He'd beaten this young man before. Easily.

He bared his teeth and in that leer there was a promise of even greater harm and humiliation. The alpha suddenly rushed at him and though Antonio tried to dodge away, the killer was insanely fast. He struck Antonio with his stump, and it was like being smashed with a club. The younger werewolf yelped in pain and slammed into me so hard we rolled over and over. Blood welled from his mouth and nose and splashed my face.

Then he scrambled to get off of me, slashing me by accident as he sought to evade the next blow. The alpha caught him on the hip and sent him slewing sideways.

I snapped at the alpha and caught his ankle. With all of my rage I tried to bite hard enough to cripple him, but he squatted, twisted and struck me on the side of the head hard enough to knock the world off its hinges.

Everything went dark.

I felt like I was falling from a great height. Falling through smoke for an endless time. I spun sideways and lay on the floor. Through shadows and blood, I saw the fight between Antonio and the alpha.

It was heroic, what that kid tried to do. He gave as good as he got for as long as he could. Tearing and slashing. Leaping and biting. Fighting with fury. Fighting like a Benandanti. Had my blood given him that edge? If so, it was not enough.

Not enough.

Which is a damn shame, because that was one hell of a comeback. One hell of an entrance. Heroism of that kind should be rewarded. Not pissed on. I wished I could help. I wished I had something left. All I could do was lay there and feel myself die. I could feel Antonio's blood seep into my mouth. I could feel my own blood leak out. I could feel the coldness creep in.

Except…

Except that wasn't what was happening. The taste of blood in my mouth was strange. It was his blood, but it tasted familiar. Like my own. It burned. It burned its way through the flesh of my mouth and into my blood. It burned through my blood.

It burned so goddamn bad.

And it burned so goddamn good.

The fire tore through me. It felt like there was acid in my veins. Lava. I screamed so loud blood flew from my lips.

I was wolf.

I was a human.

I was both.

I screamed as I changed and changed and changed.

The alpha swatted Antonio aside and turned to see what was happening. He frowned again. This time in doubt. I changed and changed and changed and changed.

And all the time I burned.

I had no idea what was happening to me. It was ripping me apart. Burning me at the cellular level. Destroying me.

Except…

The burning stopped. Just like that. Like a switch being thrown. I collapsed onto the bloody floor, gasping, human, naked, covered in blood and sweat.

The alpha watched me with narrowed eyes.

Antonio, gasping on the floor, watched me.

In the reflecting surface of the pool of blood beneath me I watched myself. I saw my human face. I looked for the cuts. The slashes. The exposed bone.

And I saw none of it.

What I saw was whole skin. Painted with blood, but no longer gaping, no longer bleeding.

On the floor, Antonio shifted back to human form. His eyes were bugged in amazement. But he was also smiling.

The alpha was not.

This was not the science he knew. This was not the work of some super soldier formula. This must have looked like sorcery to him.

Magic.

Pretty much was like that for me.

Except that I understood it. As I lay there, whole once again, I understood it. Antonio's blood in my mouth. Somehow in performing the ritual on him I'd changed his nature. From *canis lupis* to *canis dirus*. He was a Dire Wolf now. Not sure if that made him a Benandanti, but definitely a cousin. Enough so that his blood did for me what mine had done for him.

I rolled onto my hands and knees, and in doing so raised my head to look up at the alpha.

"Surprise, surprise," I said. My voice was filled with ugly promise. Fine.

"You were dead," he said.

"Yeah, well, fuck it," I said.

And I launched myself at him.

It was the man who started that lunge, it was the wolf who buried his teeth in the alpha's throat.

He tried to change.

He tried to make a fight of it.

As the saying goes, that ship had sailed.

Beside me I saw Antonio struggle to his feet. He shifted back into wolfshape and raced across the room to help Joe Ledger.

I killed the alpha.

God, did I kill that son of a bitch.

I tore him to pieces.

Pieces.

Never in my life had I ever felt that powerful.

Across the room I heard a howl of agony. I looked up from the steaming corpse and saw a badly wounded Mike Sweeney struggling with two of the wolfmen. I saw Crow crawling toward a pistol that lay out of reach. Still alive, both of them.

There were more of the wolfmen in the room. The odds were still not in our favor.

And right then, at that moment, it didn't matter.

The wolf in me had never been this strong before. Maybe it never would be again. I threw back my head and howled. The howl of an alpha triumphant. It shook the walls. It knocked plaster from the ceiling. It shocked everyone and everything in that room into silence and stillness.

I howled again, louder still. The alpha. The master of this pack. I screamed at them. And one by one, the remaining wolfmen stopped their attacks. One by one, they lay down on the bloody ground.

And goddamn it if they didn't roll to me.

In a pack, when the other wolves do that, the alpha bites them gently on the throat or belly, establishing dominance. Adopting them into the pack. I came to them and bit them. One by one. You couldn't, by any definition, call those bites *gentle*.

No, you couldn't.

When it was over there were only five members of the pack. Two of them were human. Mike Sweeney and Antonio Jones looked at me. I lifted my head and howled.

And they howled with me.

-55-

Joe Ledger and Malcolm Crow were in bad shape.

We left Mike at the crime scene, but Antonio and I had to get them to the hospital, so we broke a lot of traffic laws doing it. We almost didn't make it in time.

While they were still in the E.R., a black helicopter landed in the parking lot and three men came into the hospital. Two were clearly military, in unmarked black BDUs and wires behind their ears. One was a tall, blond-haired guy with lots of muscles. One was a black man in his early forties who looked like he ate crocodiles, uncooked. The third guy, though, was in his sixties, wearing a very expensive suit. Tall, blocky, with dark hair shot through with gray. Even at night he wore tinted glasses. He exuded a kind of personal power I have never before encountered. I would not have wanted to match my alpha status against his. No sir, I would not.

He introduced himself as Mr. Church. No badge, no I.D.

He told me to wait for him, and he left the other two guys with me in the waiting room. Mike Sweeney was still at the crime scene. Antonio was in the waiting room with me.

The two military guys didn't say a fucking word. They stood waiting. They exchanged a few looks. They studied me. One chewed gum, the other didn't.

After twenty minutes their boss came out of the E.R. and motioned for his men and Antonio to leave. When the door was closed, Mr. Church sat down opposite me.

"Captain Ledger will survive," he said.

I let out a breath I hadn't realized I was holding. "How is he?"

"He's had worse," said Church. No trace of sympathy in his voice. No trace of anything.

"He's a good guy," I said. "But this wasn't his kind of fight."

Church eyed me. "And was it your kind of fight?"

I said nothing. Church nodded.

"What about Chief Crow?"

"He'll have some challenging rehab, but they expect him to make a full recovery."

"Guess we got lucky."

"Apparently so."

I chewed my lip for a moment. "Did you talk to Ledger?"

"Briefly. He's been sedated."

"Did he tell you what we found?"

"He did."

"Tell me something, Mr. Church," I said. "I know this isn't my business and you can pull rank and tell me to go piss up a rope. I'm Joe Nobody to you."

"Ask your question."

"That science...the, um, super soldier stuff?"

"What about it?"

"What happens to it? I mean, from what Ledger said this is some kind of foreign terrorist thing."

"Multinational," agreed Church. "Funded covertly by North Korea."

"Okay. But it was terrorist science. What happens to it? I mean, does our government take it and start making its own monsters? Is that how it works?"

He leaned back in his chair, fished a small packet of vanilla wafers from his coat pocket, tore it open and offered me one. I passed. Never been a vanilla wafer fan. He took one and bit off a piece, chewed, and studied the remaining cookie for a long few seconds.

"What do you think we should do with it, Mr. Hunter? This is science that could put superior soldiers into battle against an enemy that is both relentless and determined to see America burn. That science could give us an edge. What do you think we should do with it?"

"Are you really asking or jerking me off here?"

"Asking."

I crossed my legs and stretched my arms across the backs of the seats to either side of me. "I think you should burn it. I think you should destroy whatever's in there. Burn it down and scatter the ashes. There are enough monsters in the world already."

"Not all monsters are the enemy, Mr. Hunter."

"Maybe not, but should we be in the business of making more?"

Church finished his cookie. He brushed a stray crumb from his tie, rewrapped the package and put it into his coat pocket. Then he stood up.

"Wait," I said, "is that it? You never answered my question."

Church reached for the door handle, then paused. "Fifteen minutes ago a Black Hawk helicopter fired four hellfire missiles at a blockhouse in the state forest. The news reports will all say that this was done to destroy a rogue laboratory making weaponized anthrax."

"That's bullshit."

"It's a useful story. And it will explain why that building and all of its contents have been reduced to hot ash." He opened the door, but paused one more time. "The world has enough monsters already, Mr. Hunter."

"Wait," I said, rising to my feet. "What about this Limbus thing? They must have known about that lab and what was in it. You need to find them and find out how they know what they know. You need to find out who they *are*."

His eyes glittered behind the tinted lenses.

He smiled faintly. "Thank you for your assistance in this matter."

And he went out.

An hour later Joe Ledger was medevac'd out of there. I knew that if I tried to find him or Mr. Church, I'd find nothing but shadows.

Antonio was in the hall, and we walked together to the doors to the E.R., then followed the gurney with Crow to his new room. We sat there all night. Crow's wife came in, glared at us, and went in to be with her husband. Hours passed.

We didn't say a word.

Not one fucking word.

The night seemed to last a million years.

In the morning, when Crow was awake, I said my goodbyes and left Pine Deep. All the way home I blasted music because I didn't want to listen to my own thoughts. As I neared the bridge out of town, I saw a police cruiser parked by the side of the road. Mike Sweeney leaned against it, big arms folded. He had bandages on his arms, his throat, his face. They did not make him look weak or injured.

He stared at me with eyes that burned like fire.

He nodded to me.

I nodded to him.

And I drove out of Pine Deep under a morning sky that was dark with clouds and offered nothing but the promise of coming rains.

Dream a Little Dream of Me

A Sam Hunter Adventure

-1-

Some people are weird and some are so weird they abuse the privilege.

This guy was a classic example.

Oliver Boots was the kind of person they invented the word 'geek' for. Nearly seven feet tall but I doubted he weighed two hundred pounds. With narrow shoulders and narrower hips that made him look like a regular-sized person who'd been pulled on until he was all stretched out. Long, lugubrious face, huge brown eyes, and a beaky nose. Nothing about him was balanced. His nostrils were too big and his eyes too wide-set. Swollen lower lip beneath an almost nonexistent upper one. Lots of gums, tiny teeth. Hair that did not seem to understand the logic of the whole combing process, mostly black but streaked with brown. His complexion was strange. I know a lot of black guys, and I've seen every shade of skin from pale like Larry Wilmore to a true African skin tone that's so dark brown it really does look black. This guy was blacker than that. Funny thing is, I wasn't at all convinced he was African or even of African descent. He looked painted or dyed. Like some old Vaudeville guy wearing blackface. Talk about off-putting. I almost dismissed him as one of those fruitcakes who wants to *be* black but isn't and goes about it the wrong way.

The more I looked at him, the less I thought that was the case.

I have a really good sense of smell. Better than yours unless you're like me. I can smell make-up and most of the time I can name the brand. Cover Girl, for example, doesn't smell anything like Maybelline. When a client comes in I let my senses tell me as much or sometimes more than the person says about themselves. And I could tell you that he used tea-tree oil shampoo and Camay soap and had just a hint of Polo Blue spritzed on. I could smell salmon almondine on his breath and the gin brand from his last martini. Boodles. Very nice. What I could not smell, however, was the dye he used to turn his skin black. Not dark brown. *Black.*

Like I said, this guy was rocking the weird thing way over to the edge.

Understand, I'm not the kind of social misfit who usually stares at people—unless they're Claire over at Nick's Taproom, because you *have* to stare at Claire. I mean, c'mon!—but it was hard as hell not to gawp at Mr. Boots.

Even that. *Boots.* What kind of last name is that? It's a noun.

When he came into my office he had to duck under the doorframe. And after I waved him to a chair he sat down in a way that reminded me of one of those wooden clothes hanger things that someone folded wrong.

Even without the fraudulent black skin, tell me you wouldn't stare.

So, yeah, I stared. A bit.

He gave me the kind of look that said he was used to it, accepted it as a matter of course, and was waiting for the point where we got past it so we could get down to business. He had a neat trick for refocusing my attention, too. He placed a brown leather briefcase on the corner of my desk, popped the locks, positioned it so that when he opened it I couldn't see what was inside, and removed a yellow interoffice mail envelope that was intriguingly thick. He then placed this on the blotter at an exact distance between us. It drew my gaze from his Black-Hole-of-Calcutta nostrils and brought me to point like a hunting dog.

"Ten thousand dollars," he said.

"Hello," I said.

"Twenties, fifties and hundreds."

"Three of my favorite flavors."

He reached out and nudged it one inch closer to me. "This is half. The balance on completion of the assignment."

Sure, I wanted to grab the envelope and bear it away for some private time with my stack of outstanding bills. There was also a Bettinardi Model 2 Matt Kuchar blade-style putter that I wanted almost more than I wanted a blowjob. But I left the envelope where it was and sat back in my chair.

"When you say 'assignment,'" I said, "what exactly are we talking about?"

"Can we first agree that you'll work for me?"

"No, we can't. I want to know what I'm signing on for."

He cocked his head to one side, like an ostrich examine a bug he might eat. "Does it matter?"

"Sure it does."

He made a show of looking around my office. Drab furniture that was fourth- or fifth-hand when I bought it from a thrift store. Wallpaper that was probably pasted up when Jimmy Carter was president. Some house plants dying a slow and horrible death. Low lights that tried and failed to soften the edges of the squalor. And me. Short, skinny, semi-tidy, with too much stubble and thinning hair. His eyes drifted back and locked on me. He wore a thin, knowing smile.

"And you're in a position to be selective about the kind of jobs you accept, Mr. Hunter?"

"I am, Mr. Boots," I said.

"Even for twenty thousand dollars?"

"Even for twenty million dollars."

We both smiled. He thought I was joking. I knew I wasn't.

Mr. Boots took a handkerchief from his pocket and dabbed at his lips, then neatly folded the cloth and put it back.

"It is my understanding that private investigators often provide additional services."

"Depends on the investigator," I said. "And it depends on the service."

"I'm looking for someone to champion my cause."

"Yeah, that means nothing to me. You're beating around the bush, Mr. Boots. How about you stop doing that and actually tell me what you'd like me to do for that much money. You have to know that it's a tad above my normal rates."

"There are private investigators who would walk into hell for that much money."

That was true enough. I know some P.I.s who will beat up a nun for a lot less. Israel Bohunk comes to mind. A professional rival who is arguably the least humane human being I've ever met. He sometimes provides protection for a dog-fighting ring run out of South Philly. His office is every bit as seedy as mine, I'll admit, but we have different reputations if you look close enough. I don't think there's anything he wouldn't do for money. No joke. And although I do have my more extreme moments once in a while, which resulted in me burying a few bodies in a landfill or in a swamp over in the Jersey Pine Barrens, my motivation isn't the same as Bohunk's.

There are others, too. The worst were the skip tracers and bounty hunters. They all run under nicknames they think make them sound cool. Bugsy the Mummy, Abel Cain, Dr. Snatch. Like that. Maybe it's that nobody has either the heart or the courage to tell them that their nicknames are stupid as shit.

"What kind of job?" I repeated, saying it slow, spacing the words.

"We would like you to pick up something and deliver it safely."

"What kind of something? I don't courier drugs or stolen goods."

He smiled. "It's a religious artifact. We want it delivered very quietly and without incident."

"Is it stolen?"

"Yes," he said.

-2-

"No," I said.

"Don't you want to know who it was stolen *from* before you turn us down?"

"Not really."

His smile widened. "Are you sure?"

I sighed. "Okay. Impress me."

"Nazis," said Mr. Boots.

I blinked. "A religious artifact stolen from the Nazis? Now I'm thinking you have me confused with Indiana Jones."

"Hardly."

"Nazis?" I said, studying him.

"Nazis," he said.

I sighed. "Okay, tell me."

-3-

Mr. Boots said, "During the Second World War the Nazis, as you've no doubt heard, went to great lengths to, um, *appropriate* a great deal of art, and there are legal battles ongoing even now to settle claims of ownership. The same is true of a variety of holy relics and objects of importance from various cultures. The Spear of Longinus, believed to be the weapon that pierced the side of Jesus Christ, is one such item. Others include clippings from the beard of Muhammad, a tooth from the Buddha, the bones of Orestes and Theseus, the Holy Belt of the Virgin Mary, the Grapevine Cross..."

"The Ark of the Covenant?" I suggested.

"Oh, no," he said and gave a casual flick of his hand. "That's in an Orthodox church in Axum, Ethiopia. The Thule cultists never took possession of it."

I stared at him, waiting for the punch line of the joke, but he appeared to be serious about that statement. Wild.

Boots said, "The Thule Society was behind much of the Nazi drive to possess sacred objects that they believed had true mystical or spiritual power. During the war many of these objects were, regrettably, lost. There was a Thule repository in Dresden that was utterly destroyed by the Allied firebombing. So many powerful things were incinerated to the enduring loss of all."

I said nothing.

"I represent a group of individuals," said Boots, "who have gone to great lengths to recover some of these objects and return them to their rightful owners. We are privately funded and we are determined to remain discreet, even clandestine."

"Okay," I said.

"Although the war ended more than seventy years ago and most of the original Thule Society members are either dead or in nursing homes, the society itself lives on. With any group of hateful extremists there is never a paucity of people willing to take up the standard and continue this ugly work."

I nodded. I knew that to be true enough. Not specifically with the Thule Society, which I'd heard of but only in books, but with other kinds of cults and secret societies. "World has more than its share of fucktards," I said.

"Fucktard." He repeated the word, enjoying it. "Eloquent."

"I'm nothing if not eloquent."

We smiled at each other like we were just a couple of guys.

"So," I said, "you're telling me you stole something from neo-Nazis and you want me to pick it up from somewhere and deliver it somewhere?"

"In a nutshell."

I made come-along motions with my fingers. "More. That's not enough information."

"Fair enough. The Thule Society is still active, though it is naturally covert."

"Oh, naturally."

"Alas they are also very, um, aggressive," said Mr. Boots. "They are covetous people, oh dear me yes. And they are vengeful."

"What is it you stole that's got them so pissed off?"

He cocked his head again. "By way of answering that question, Mr. Hunter, let me ask this. What do you know of the Dreamlands?"

"As in Little Nemo?"

"That's Slumberland. I refer to the Dreamlands described in the writings of Howard Phillips Lovecraft. Are you familiar with that writer's works?"

I shrugged. "Some, I guess. But I don't read a lot of monster stories."

He arched an eyebrow. "Oh? Considering your, ah, *reputation*, I would have figured you to be quite a fan of Lovecraftian stories."

Now I cocked my head at him. "And what exactly do you mean by my 'reputation'?"

I was pretty sure we both knew what he meant. It's just that there aren't a lot of people who know who and what I am. My family knows, of course, because the apple doesn't fall far from the tree in the Hunter clan. A few close friends know. Some trusted clients. Mind you, there are some bad folks who *knew* but they are past tense. That's an occasional side-effect of me being what I am.

Boots fished for a way to say it without saying it. "I know," he said.

I shook my head. "Give me a keyword so I know you're not dicking me around."

Mr. Boots considered. "Wolfsbane?"

"Aconite," I corrected. "I put that on my salad. Try again."

"Full moon?" he ventured.

"Good for night fishing. But otherwise it don't really mean shit. It's Hollywood stuff. Keep trying."

"Do I need to say the word?"

I grinned. "Why not? Are you afraid of the big bad wolf?"

He shrugged. "If I was afraid of you, Mr. Hunter, I would not be here."

"Which makes me wonder why you are here. If your group was strong enough or clever enough to steal the item in question from these Thule asswipes, then why do you need me—or anyone—to deliver it somewhere? I mean...shit, hop in a cab."

"Ah, and so we get to it," he said, leaning forward to place his incredibly bony elbows on his knobby knees. "The other party in this matter has engaged the services of a skilled retrieval specialist. He is someone we do not care to run afoul of. He has a certain reputation that I have been led to believe is in no way exaggerated."

"They hired a bounty hunter?"

"In a word, yes. It is someone with whom you are, by all accounts, familiar."

I sighed. "And will you tell me this guy's name?"

"Bohunk," said Mr. Boots. "Israel Bohunk."

I drummed my fingers on the desktop and frowned at him. I looked down at the thick envelope of delicious tens, twenties and fifties, and then back up at Mr. Boots again.

He said, "While I understand that Mr. Bohunk has a reputation for always getting whatever he goes after, I was reliably informed that you were appropriate to a task of this kind. Was I misled?"

It was a fair question and I took a moment to consider how to answer it. I knew a lot about Bohunk but had never gone up against him. Actually, I've never been alone with him. I've seen him in crowds, in clubs, in bail bond offices, and even in court buildings, but that's it. We've probably said fewer than a hundred words to each other. Most of our exchanges have been the kind of gunslinger nods guys like us use when we don't want to give anything away but at the same time want to send a certain message. Or, messages, really.

One message, *I see you.* The other, *I need you to see me.* There's a shit-ton of subtext to each. With certain people a small look, a lift of an eyebrow, a tightening of the lips, a half smile—they speak volumes.

Bohunk's probably heard some wild stuff about me. Some of it's true, depending on who's doing the telling. And if even half of the stories I've heard about him were half true, then he was not the kind of person anyone ever wants to go up against. Mind you, there are people who say that about me. But Bohunk's different. He's come through situations that he shouldn't have, which means that he has something else going for him besides the obvious brutality and noticeable lack of human compassion. And you can add to that the fact that he looks like the Hulk's bigger brother. He also has a crew of thugs that he runs with who could probably overthrow the average mid-sized country.

Boots frowned very deeply. "Are you going to opt out, Mr. Hunter?"

"No," I said. "I'm in."

"If it is not inconvenient, I need you to actually say that you accept this assignment. In those words."

"Sure. Fine. Whatever. I hereby formally accept this job. And the money. I definitely accept the money."

He looked greatly relieved. "And we have found our champion."

"Let's not get too hasty," I said. "I still need some background and you got us off the subject. What does any of this have to do with H.P. frigging Lovecraft?"

Mr. Boots bent and straightened the leg of his pants, smoothing the expensive cloth over his stick-thin leg. "My colleagues and I are of the opinion that H.P. Lovecraft's stories may not be entirely the stuff of his lurid imagination. It is our belief, in fact, that Mr. Lovecraft was something of a savant who did not dream up his stories in the way 'dreams' are viewed by the average person, but in fact wrote stories based on actual visions."

"Hunh," I grunted.

"*Religious* visions," he said.

"Wow," I said. "So...you're all batshit crazy. Is that the takeaway from this conversation?"

"Hardly. Nor is this a cult thing," said Boots. "This is a legitimate religion believed by more people than you would imagine." He paused and gave me an enigmatic little smile. "Many more people than you would imagine."

I said nothing.

"And these beliefs predate many of this world's most highly regarded and, um, *popular* religions."

"Okay," I said. "So what? You say this like you're a deacon of the church of Cthulhu. I mean...that is what we're talking about, right? Big guy, mouthful of tentacles, tendency to drive his worshippers batshit crazy. That guy?"

If it is possible for someone with skin as black as pitch to go pale, then that's what happened to Mr. Boots. He turned the color of a charcoal briquette. A dusty black. He recovered quickly, though. I'd said what I'd said half to be a smartass—because I like being a smartass—and half to see if I could get a rise out of him. To see where he stood. And apparently Boots stood foursquare inside the church of the bugfuck weird. He also got a little upset with me. Fair enough. I was trying to be offensive. It's a great way to gauge how serious a person was on a given subject.

Mr. Boots was clearly very serious, and pretty soon he had me convinced that this was his actual religion. I know, that takes a lot of open-minded acceptance because...hey, Cthulhu, y'know?

But as Hamlet was so fond of saying, "There are more things in heaven and earth, Horatio, than are dreamt of in your philosophy." Or words to that effect.

He made me a believer. Not in his faith but in the fact that he believed.

"What's the actual job?" I asked. "You keep sidestepping that. What is the actual object? What kind of relic is it?"

"It is a small statue," said Boots. "It is carved to represent the mountain Ngranek, a holy place on the isle of Oriab in the southern part of the Dreamlands. There is a minute map etched onto the base of the statue, written in the language of the guardians of that place, and it includes a spell that will open a doorway that will allow the faithful to travel from this world into that one."

"Uh huh," I said.

"You must understand, Mr. Hunter, that this is an item of great importance and great power. This is a place where great magic exists and where great magic can be learned. It is a place of infinite possibility, a place where the waters of many realities and unrealities merge and blend."

"Uh huh," I said again.

"It would be a terrible thing should the Thule Society appropriate this map. Therefore, we want you to go to where it is being kept, remove it, and protect it."

"Protect it? I thought you wanted it delivered."

Boots smiled. "In a manner of speaking. We want you to safeguard it using your, um, *particular* skill set. There is a very crucial planetary alignment occurring tonight. Gateways between worlds will be fragile at best. We want you to take possession of the stone and keep it safe overnight."

"You mean keep it with me?"

"Yes. Keep it with you and do whatever is necessary to keep it safe. As I say, we have been hoping to enlist you as our champion."

"Just keep it overnight?"

"Yes."

"And then what?"

"Then return it to us in the morning," said Boots. "By then the alignment will be shifting and the gateways will firm up. It is doubtful the Thule Society will be able to manage to open the doorway to the Dreamlands after the sun has risen."

I sat there and studied him. He sat there and studied me. The clock on the wall ticked its way through a whole bunch of empty seconds.

"You realize that I think you're absolutely out of your fucking mind," I said. "I mean you *get* that, right?"

His smile was very small on his very black face. "Have you ever required that your clients function on the same level of subjective sanity as yourself?"

"No, I suppose not."

"Nor do we." Mr. Boots uncrossed and recrossed his legs. "Now let me tell you the details."

-4-

The set up seemed pretty straightforward. The object was in the wall safe of Mr. Boot's office on Walnut Street in Center City. He recited the combination and had me remember it. He said that he could not go and get it himself because Bohunk and his crew were watching the building and if they accosted him they might force him to open the safe. He didn't come out and say that he feared Bohunk might kill him to get the artifact, but it was clear that's what he meant.

So, my goal was to slip in as discreetly as possible, make my way to the eighteenth floor office, open the safe, hide the object on my person, and get the hell out of there without being spotted. Then maybe go get lost for a few hours. Drive to Cape May and watch the sunrise. Take the turnpike to the Poconos and hang out at a casino. Whatever. Basically get lost, get off the radar, so Bohunk couldn't find me. It doesn't sound easy and I knew it wouldn't be easy. Not with Israel Bohunk guarding the place.

The timetable was tight, but not so tight that I didn't have some elbow room to do research. After Oliver Boots gangled his bony ass out of my office I cruised the Net and made a few calls.

Private investigators spend most of their careers doing background searches. It's a lot of computer stuff. Back in the day it used to be actual paperwork, poring over ledgers and poking through public records. Now just about everything has been digitized. It makes the world less interesting in some ways, but it makes my job a hell of a lot easier. Instead of wearing out the soles of my shoes and sweating my ass off in the July heat I sat in my office eating Popeye's chicken out of a tub, drinking Fanta and listening to old Tom Waits songs on my iPad, all while searching the endless databases, records, and websites. There are services and utilities P.I.s can subscribe to for deeper access than Joe Public will ever get. If you like your privacy that should scare you. Given enough time I can find out your pin number, routing number, shoe size, which prescription medicines you take, which porn sites you hit, how much debt you have, which charities you donate to, how many parking violations you have, how much mortgage or rent you owe, what your credit rating is, what your politics are, who your real friends are on Facebook and Twitter, where you spend your disposable income and what TV shows you binge-watch on Netflix. There are ways to keep guys like me out, but most of them don't work all that well.

The good news is that I'm not a stalker or a creep. I don't judge people. If some schmo wants to watch Italian midget biracial porn with golden showers, then God love 'em. I don't give a shit. On the other hand, if that same guy is embezzling money from his employer or buying dirty pictures of little kids, then yeah, we may have a problem. Depends on who's hired me, and it depends on what pushes my buttons. If I'm hired to get the goods on a cheating spouse, I'll get those goods, hand them over to the client, cash the check and forget about it. No judgment. If I'm hired to find actionable evidence on, say, a group of pornographers who are making fuck films of tweens? I may become more directly involved than just turning in a report. I might pay a visit to the video team and have a meaningful discussion with them. I've done that in the past. Like I said, I have buttons.

This thing with Boots wasn't pushing any of those buttons, but it was giving me a bad itch between the shoulder blades. Israel Bohunk was a very, very bad man and I had no desire whatsoever in determining which of us was the baddest dude in Philadelphia.

So I did some research to determine just what in the twinkly chartreuse fuck I'd gotten myself into.

I researched Boots first. There wasn't a whole lot. No birth record, no school. His name began appearing in articles related to the rare art and antiquities world. He was quoted in a few pieces—never with accompanying photo—in several magazines like *Aesthetica*, *Parkett*, *Tate Etc.*, *Art Business Today*. Like that. And *The Journal of Conservation and Museum Studies*. Plus a bunch of incomprehensible trade journals for universities, religious groups, and purveyors of *objet d'art*. So, professionally at least, he seemed legit. Odd that he had no background data. It suggested that he wasn't born as 'Oliver Boots.' I wished I'd thought to ask for a look at his driver's license. From that I could have backtracked to get his Social Security number and maybe found his birth name.

The one thing I did verify is that he belonged to a group called the Dreamland Conservancy. So maybe he really did believe in the stuff Lovecraft wrote about. Truth to tell, I kind of lean toward believing, too. As the saying goes, I've *seen* some stuff.

Weird, weird stuff. Over the last few years I've seen things that have made me a whole lot less likely to dismiss the things that go bump in the night as figments of my—or anyone's—imagination. After all, look at who I am. At what I am. I'm one of the things that bump around in the dark. The fact that I happen to be a good guy— or, good-*ish*, at least—doesn't change things.

After I ran dry on Boots I switched to Bohunk.

There was a lot about him on the Net. Turns out his name is, no joke, Israel Bohunk. I'd always thought it was a South Philly nickname. Like Nickie Grapes and Harry the Spoon. Nope. Israel Stallo Bohunk is the name on his driver's license and Social Security card. And on the copy of his birth certificate I found a scan of. At fifty-three he was older than I thought. He looked mid-thirties. I found some photos of him online and studied them. He is conspicuously large, with bodybuilder biceps, a massive chest, and a head that looked like a beer keg dressed up in a Halloween mask. Lots of coarse dark hair on his head, face, chest and forearms. And his complexion was, in its own way, as strange as Boots's. Where the tall skinny guy was pitch black, Bohunk was the color of stone. Gray as slate.

His criminal record was cleaner than I expected. He was picked up twice for questioning but no charges ever filed. That did not mean he was innocent. My guess was he was careful and had good lawyers.

Bohunk spent eight years as a private military contractor, which is a sanitized euphemism for 'mercenary.' Bohunk worked for Blue Diamond Security, a company that made Blackwater look like the Campfire Girls. They had ties to all sorts of shady groups including the Jakoby family, Hugo Vox and others. Bohunk spent time in Iraq, Afghanistan and elsewhere. The 'elsewhere' part was buried under some 'need to know' seals and even nosy private dicks don't 'need to know' some things. Didn't matter. What I did find confirmed what I suspected. Bohunk was smart, well-trained, dangerous and very experienced.

But something was wrong. When I looked up info on his office I saw that he was no longer in a seedy hole like mine. He was now operating in style. Real style. He now had a large suite of offices in a respectable building on Market Street near City Hall. Wow. I hacked his tax returns and found that he employed twenty people. Way more than I thought. Two secretaries, three computer research specialists, a receptionist, and the rest were listed as 'general support staff.' When I ran some of them I found that this was another euphemism. In this case 'general support staff' meant 'hired muscle.' Some of them had criminal records. All of them had military backgrounds. A few belonged to wacko militia groups who are preparing for the day when the American government invades itself. Or something. I've never been able to sort out that kind of conspiracy paranoid bullshit.

My sense of unease about this case deepened the more I studied Bohunk's organization. I mean…I'm pretty tough but he has actual trained soldiers with combat experience and lots of guns.

My last search before heading out was to find out about the Gogol Building, which was on Walnut Street and Fifth. It was a big brown and tan monstrosity of a place that reminded me of Dana's apartment in the original Ghostbusters movie. An ugly, overly ornate thing left over from the excesses of the *art deco* era. Lots of unusual angles, pitches, arches, and gargoyles. Not the tallest building in Philly, but in the top ten. It was once the world headquarters of the Gogol Trust, a banking and investments corporation, but it had changed hands twenty times in the last century. The current owner was—surprise, surprise—the Dreamlands Trust. Oliver Boots had a suite of offices one flight down from the top.

The good news was that there were half a dozen banks of elevators and twenty stairwells. Bohunk could not watch all of those. The trick would be to find out which routes were being watched and then take one of the others. I figured the elevators would all be watched because who in their right mind would want to run up fifty-six flights of stairs?

Who, I ask you?

Sigh.

I'm not as young as I once was, and my body is a prime example of the phrase 'it's not the years, it's the mileage.' The odometer on my knees and lower back has been around the dial way too many times. Which means that to do this right it would have to be the wolf and not the middle-aged dumpy man who made that climb. That came with its own set of problems.

I got up from my desk and prowled my office, nervous and jumpy. I paced for a few minutes, thinking it through, imagining all the ways this could go wrong. All the ways I could fail. All the ways I could get killed. It was a dishearteningly long list.

I locked the door, went into my phone booth of a bathroom, changed into one of the sets of clothes I keep on hand for jobs where I need to blend in. I chose a set of khaki shorts and a shirt that bore the embroidered patch from one of the world's foremost delivery companies. I added rubber-soled shoes and a billed cap. I slipped a heavy blackjack into my right front pocket. No gun, no knife. If things got that complicated I had other weapons. The sap was for persuasion of the obstinate. Useful in certain circumstances and, in a way, a kindness. The alternative was less pleasant.

I futzed around the office until I realized that I was stalling. I didn't want to take this job. It felt weird. Wrong in some way I couldn't quite describe. But there was an envelope in my office safe with a lot of very nice money in it. Money I needed. I had bills. I had alimony. I wanted to buy myself that putter, god damn it.

"Get your ass in gear, dickhead," I said to my reflection in the mirror next to the door.

So, yeah, I got my ass in gear.

-5-

I drove to Center City and parked three blocks away, and walked toward the Gogol Building. I had pictures of most of Bohunk's people on my phone—lifted from their service records online—and I had a lot of data about them memorized. Pretty sure I'd know them on sight. Wish I had something from each so I could have memorized their smell. Even in normal form I have a killer sense of smell. My spider-sense, more or less.

It was a blistering hot day in Philadelphia. Temperature and humidity both locked at 96. I felt like I was melting into the sidewalk. It was the kind of day that makes your whole body feel heavy and slow and stupid. There was a cart selling Italian water ices and I bought a cherry snow-cone and ate it while I cased the joint. It's hard to look threatening while eating a snow cone. Only way to look less threatening is to go out walking a golden Labrador puppy. The vibe I was projecting was delivery guy trying to find a slice of chill on a day when the furnace doors were all open.

It was pretty easy to find the first five of Bohunk's team. They were sitting in cars with the motors running, windows up, air conditioning blasting. Any one person like that and you think he's waiting for someone to come out of the building. But when you see five big guys who might as well be wearing THUG t-shirts sitting at precise positions near entrances, you start to see the pattern. I risked walking past a couple of the cars so I could take a sniff. Sweat, testosterone, cheap cologne, inadequate deodorant, Coca-Cola, some residual weed, gun oil, and…

Incense?

That was weird. Smelled like temple incense, the kind they use at yoga centers. And I smelled it on two different of Bohunk's men.

It was a weird enough thing to jolt me. Plans are made based on an analysis of information. Intel, they call it in the military. Most things in life are predictable, which allows you to draw a plan of action even in the absence of total knowledge. When you encounter an anomaly it tends to make you pause, step back, and reconsider. Sometimes the anomaly is nothing, a momentary and unrelated weirdness. Had the incense smell only been on one of the thugs, I'd have noted it but not thought much about it beyond that. Maybe the thug did yoga. Or, more likely, he was sleeping with a woman who did yoga. But on two of them, though?

So I risked it and cased the other three cars with close walk-bys.

Incense. On all of them.

Exactly the same kind, and it wasn't a faint trace, not like you'd get if you stepped inside a head shop or a store selling New Age stuff. This was a heavy hit of it on all of them. They'd been inside a room with a lot of incense in the air, and they'd been in that room for a considerable time. My guess was at least an hour. It was soaked into their clothes and hair.

Yeah, I can tell. I told you already.

I fell back and went into a Starbucks to reconsider my plan of attack. Under what circumstances would these guys be exposed to incense? Boots had said that Bohunk was employed by the Thule Society to obtain the artifact. The Thules were a semi-mystical organization, and that suggested rituals. Rituals and incense go together like Philly cheesesteaks and high cholesterol. Did that mean that Bohunk was *part* of the Thule Society? If so, was it possible these thugs were more than Bohunk's muscle? Maybe they were all part of that relic-grabbing, Hitler-worshipping crew of scary ass-hats?

Sure, that's a jump based on smelling incense, but a private investigator without gut instincts should consider another line of work.

Did that change my plan?

No, not really. I was pretty sure I hadn't been made, which meant that my FedEx cover was probably still good. I stayed in the

Starbucks—which was cool and had a nice view of the Gogol Building—until one o'clock. That's when all of the employees who had flooded the streets for lunch began to trudge back in. Crowds make great protective cover. I left the café, crossed the street without hurry, carrying the faux package I'd been toting around all morning. It's an empty box with a false spring-loaded bottom that I'd taken away from a shoplifter once upon a time. Very smart, and there was enough tension on the spring that you could handle it and not realize there was a false trapdoor in the bottom. High-tech for a guy like me.

I heard the crowd utter a collective sigh as they moved from the furnace heat of the streets to the mortuary cool of the lobby. They swarmed into the elevators and I went with them, looking nonchalant, but keeping alert. I saw two more of Bohunk's men in the lobby and there was one on the elevator with me. More incense smell. I left the elevator on the fifteenth floor because there were still plenty of office workers in the crowded car. I didn't want to wind up as the last person sharing the car with the Thule lackey.

The fifteenth floor was shared by a dozen small firms. Patent attorneys, accountants, and an actuary. I walked with purpose toward whatever office was at the end of the hall, conscious of being visible to the people on the elevator. When I heard the doors close, I turned around and ran back to the entrance of the fire stairs, which were on one end of a T-junction close to the elevator bank. No guards. No alarms on the doors. I eased the door open and spent ten seconds letting my nose do my reconnaissance for me. I had to shift a bit to maximize that. Half human, half wolf. I'd have gone all the way but I would have had to strip out of the clothes, or tear them. Didn't want to do either.

The stairwell was clear, but not all the way to the top.

There was a man up there. I could smell the meat of him. And the incense.

Bohunk was smart. He'd positioned a guard near the top floor. Not sure why he didn't just kick his way into Boots's office and crack the safe. Even with modern alarm systems there are ways. I know a couple of safecrackers who could probably steal Donald Trump's toupee collection without rousing Donald from his dreams of avarice. Boots said that there were alarms, and had given me the code, but he hadn't said they were anything special.

That had been niggling at the back of my mind all along.

What was keeping Bohunk's team *outside* of the office? What was making this so hard for them?

I seriously considered bagging this whole thing, going home, calling Boots for more information and trying it again tomorrow.

But...

Fuck it, I was already here.

I began climbing the steps from floor fifteen to floor forty-five.

-6-

First rule, cardio?

I know, I know. Go fuck yourself.

-7-

I went slowly. Partly to save my breath and avoid a coronary and partly to keep Bohunk's minion from hearing me. Even in human form I know how to move without making noise. Actually honed that skill set back when I was a cop in the Twin Cities. Noisy, clumsy cops get shot a lot more often than stealthy, careful ones.

I stopped on the fortieth floor to catch my breath and reassess. The thug was up there on forty-three, pacing in the narrow confines of the landing. He must have had an earbud in, listening to AC-DC. My ears are good enough to catch the spill from one of the earbuds, so I figured he had one in and the other bud dangling. He probably thought that was a smart move because it didn't totally block his hearing. It's not a smart move. The placement of one creates a confusion for human hearing. It reduces perception of what is being heard, especially if you're bored and if you like what you have on your iPod.

Stupid mistake.

He never heard me coming.

Not until I whipped the heavy lead blackjack across his ankle tendons. I was four steps down and he was looking at the closed fire door and not down the stairs. I caught him as he was pivoting for a turn in his pacing cadence. The blackjack is one of the old-school cop varieties—a heavy wafer of lead sewn between two paddle-shaped pieces of thick leather. Heavy and brutal, and apart from the crushing weight of the lead there is a stiff edge running around the business end of the weapon. Hold it one way and you have very precise blunt force trauma; but held at an angle you can rip an ugly trench through skin.

I gave him a little of both.

You don't man it out when you get clipped by a blackjack in the hands of an expert. You go right fucking down, and you go down hard and you go down hurt.

I caught him as he fell and helped him fall harder by jerking him face-forward toward the concrete landing. Things broke. Chin, cheek, teeth.

The thug never had a chance to make any sound louder than a grunt before he was out. He'd need some reconstructive work on the face. Maybe later I'd try to dredge up a little regret about that. Maybe, but probably not. Bohunk was a scumbag and I doubt he hired saints. This guy was one of the faces I memorized. A former soldier who had been thrown out of the army for messing with underage Afghani village girls. Hired by Blue Diamond because they only hired assholes like him.

So...sweet dreams, lumpy.

The smell of his blood, fresh and hot and reeking like freshly sheared copper, hit me hard. If I focus my senses on it I can get high, like someone getting second-hand stoned by being in a room where someone's smoking a blunt. I had to force my mind to focus as I patted him down.

He was armed to the teeth. A Sig Sauer with two extra magazines, and a small-frame .32 pistol in an ankle holster. A Buck lock-knife with a four-inch blade in his right front pants pocket. I sniffed it and smelled blood on that, too. Four, five days old. Female. Young. The wolf beneath my skin wanted to take a bite out of this shithead. His throat looked yummy. But now was not the time.

He wore a stone on a silver chain around his neck and I tore it off and held it up. At first I thought it was just a chunky lump of unshaped turquoise, but when I bent to study it I saw that it was a figure of what looked like Neptune. Or some similar kind of burly sea god. Heavy bearded face, fish tail, trident and attitude.

That was interesting as hell. I placed it on the landing next to him. Then I pocketed the .32, checked to make sure the goon was still breathing, and crept up the final flight of stairs.

The fire door was not locked. Useful. I opened it an inch and peered outside. There was a long, carpeted hallway, soft indirect lighting, some framed art. No people. No alarms, either. I left the stairwell and moved quickly and silently along the hall. There was only one door at the end and it was a very heavy slab of oak that Boots had told me had a steel core. The walls were also reinforced. No one was kicking that door in or using a sledgehammer to punch through the walls. A brass plate was affixed to the door at eye level.

THE DREAMLAND CONSERVANCY.

I bent close to the door and sniffed. Smelled wood, smelled metal, smelled the oil they used on the hinges. Not much else. So I dropped to a push-up position and sniffed at the bottom, but I struck out. The door had a rubber gasket along the frame that formed a tight seal, and the petroleum rubber blocked out anything from inside.

I got to my feet. There was a keypad mounted to the left of the door. Oliver Boots had provided the code but I sniffed the keys before I punched them.

Which is when I smelled something weird.

Incense.

Temple incense. Same kind. Fairly fresh.

I stepped back from the door and considered the possibilities. One was that one of Bohunk's men had tried to fudge his way past the combination. Another was that they *had* the combination and had already gotten inside. Maybe they were waiting for me in there. Other options suggested themselves, but I dismissed them as absurd.

The door remained shut and unhelpful. The guy I'd decked was still bleeding in the fire tower. Someone was going to find him eventually.

What was it Boots said? *We have found our champion.*

"Fuck it," I said.

And punched in the code.

The little red light on the keypad flicked over from red to green and the door lock clicked. No alarms rang. I pushed the door open and then faded to one side in case someone was in there prepared to shoot.

I waited.

No shots.

I went inside very quickly, moving left and ducking down behind a heavy armchair in the reception area. There was no one behind the desk, so I crossed to the glass door that led inside. Opened it. Expected to find cubicles or a set of offices with maybe a shared hall or common waiting area. That's not what I stepped into. It was a huge room with a high ceiling and tall, arched windows. No desks, no office equipment. The floor was made of rare polished marble that seemed to swirl with smoky grays, pale pinks, deep purples and inky blacks. Rich tapestries hung from the wall between each of the windows, and the embroidery was alive with representations of monsters and gods. There was something that looked like a stone altar, inlaid with turquoise, carnelian and lapis lazuli, and trimmed with filigrees of gold and silver. Set into the stone wall so that it bisected the stone altar was a heavy wall safe.

I was alone in the room and everything was still.

But everything was wrong.

-8-

The first thing I smelled was incense.

Yeah, *that* kind of incense.

And we're not talking trace amounts left behind by Bohunk or one of his goons. Sticks of it stood fuming in brass holders that had been placed on marble pedestals. There were maybe a dozen of them positioned around the room. The curling smoke filled the air like writhing snakes. Instead of electric lights there were braziers—actual goddamn braziers—filled with burning coals.

I looked around and said, very clearly and distinctly, "What the fuck?"

My words echoed strangely in the empty hall and lunged back at me in odd and meaningless shapes.

Nothing was currently making sense. Once again I nearly turned around and left. Bohunk and his thugs could *have* whatever this was. Oliver Boots had freaked me out pretty well when he was in my office, but now that I was standing in *his* office I was lost. I mean… what was this place? Definitely not an office.

Was it a temple? A church?

The creatures depicted on the tapestries were strange. A goat-headed monster who rose like a giant above a mass of worshippers whose bodies were torn and broken. A fish-god rising from the deep as if in answer to the prayers of the people in a crooked church perched on the craggy lip of a sea cliff, yet the very arrival of the invoked god brought with it a tsunami that was poised to destroy the entire coastline. Another was a gray blob of a thing that looked like it was covered with festering sores. There was a giant spider with a human face, and something that looked like a pterosaur standing on a field of ice. One of them looked like a zombie but had webbed feet and eyes that burned with coal; there was a monstrous black goat around whose twisted legs clung hundreds of its deformed spawn. And there was something that looked like a gelatinous creature with innumerable humanlike eyes and mouths within its black mass. Others were less clearly defined—glowing orbs of light or darkness, or creatures that were shown to have one shape in half of the tapestry, but as they passed through a wall or dimensional veil, they changed into something else equally horrific.

A few of those images tickled a memory in the back of my mind. I hoped—even prayed—that it was a memory of some book I'd read or a monster movie I'd seen. But it didn't feel like that. It felt more like a much older memory. Something conjured from the primitive fears of the lizard brain. And even though the tapestries were cloth and metal wire and silk thread, they repelled me. I did not want to draw any closer to examine the images. No sir, not one step.

Instead I turned and ran over to the altar. I wanted to get that relic and get the hell out of this weird-ass version of Dodge.

The stone altar was split to allow the safe to be built into the wall. Each side of the altar was ten feet long, with a flat top. There were thick iron rings set in the four corners of each side.

The safe was massive, one of those huge old-style bank-vault doors that stood eight feet high. It had a big spoked wheel and a smaller combination dial. As I inched closer I saw there were designs carved onto the face of the altar, and those designs continued onto the metal surface of the vault. It was a very subtle but highly detailed landscape that showed a series of mountains rising in steps, each larger than the other. Waves crashed against the steep walls on one side, but between the mountains on the other side was a lush valley filled with strange trees bearing no resemblance to anything I recognized. A burning sun hung in the sky, but also representations of several moons and of distant worlds, some with rings like Saturn.

I knew what I was seeing was an artist's interpretation of the Dreamlands, that strange dimension created by H. P. Lovecraft for his story cycles. This whole room—this church, I suppose—was dedicated to a genuine belief in such a place, as well as in its strange gods and other creatures whose celestial designation I couldn't label.

A voice in my head told me to hurry. The rational part of my brain insisted that I make tracks because someone was going to find the guard I'd suckered. But that lizard brain whispered the truth. This room *scared* me.

Yeah, even a guy like me.

I reached for the combination dial and began turning. The code was simple. Eight to the left, fifty-one to the right, eleven to the left. But the second I touched it I snatched my hand back and stared at my fingers as bright red blood welled from a thin cut. There was blood on the dial, too, and I had to shift to allow the firelight to sparkle on the razor-sharp edge of a splinter that had been gouged from the dial.

"Fuck," I snarled, sucking the blood from my index finger.

Careful not to cut myself again, I dialed the numbers. The tumblers clicked.

Click.

Click.

Click.

And I heard a sound deep within the mechanism. Not a click this time. It was different. Weirder. Almost organic.

Like a sigh.

Sweat broke out on my face and ran in lines down my cheeks.

I grasped the big wheel and, as instructed, spun it counter-clockwise one full turn.

Another of those deep sighs.

And then the door shifted. Moved, almost as if pushed. Even so it took a lot of effort to pull that door open. It must have weighed three tons. The hinges squealed as if they were in pain and as the whole thing opened, trapped air inside blew out. It felt strangely moist and warm. Like breath.

Jesus Christ. Just like breath.

It smelled of rotting fish and salt.

I gagged and turned away for a moment. Sweat stung my eyes.

Hurry, screamed the voice in my head.

It took real effort to turn back, to pull the safe open the rest of the way, to step inside.

There wasn't much within the vault. A polished block four feet square that looked to be made from volcanic rock. On top of that was an envelope. Nothing else.

I burned five seconds just staring at the envelope. My name had been written across the front in flowing script.

"Oh, shit," I said aloud.

I picked up the envelope. It was heavy and expensive stock, unsealed. I removed the card from inside, leaving behind a bloody fingerprint. The card had a note written in the same elegant hand.

Thank you for being our champion.
Your courage and sacrifice are appreciated.

It was right about then that I heard the laughter from outside.

-9-

I dropped the card and whirled around, rushed to the vault doorway and gaped at what I saw.

The chamber outside was no longer empty. Several of the tapestries had been pushed aside to allow concealed doors to open. Figures emerged from the shadows. At least a dozen of them. Men and women. All very tall. All with intensely black skin. All wearing white silk robes. All of them smiling big smiles that showed lots of white, white teeth.

And directly in the center of the room, thick arms folded across a massive chest, stood Israel Bohunk.

He was laughing.

Everyone was laughing.

Except me.

-10-

"Sam motherfucking Hunter," said Bohunk as I stepped out of the vault.

I said nothing.

Every single one of the black-skinned people looked like Oliver Boots. Even the women. They were all the same height, same build.

"Feeling stupid yet?" asked Bohunk.

"Pretty stupid," I agreed.

Bohunk was really huge. His skin was that weird gray and he looked like you could break baseball bats off of him without raising a welt. His forearms were as big around as my biceps, and his biceps were insane. I've dated women with narrower waists. I bet his chest, fully expanded, was six feet around if it was an inch. Guy was a fucking brute. And he had that big, ugly bucket of a head.

He also had a Glock in a clamshell shoulder holster.

"I heard you had at least half a brain, Hunter," he said, "so I'm kind of surprised you didn't figure this out."

"Must be one of my slow days," I said. A line of cold sweat was running down my spine and pooling inside my tighty-whities.

"Have you figured it out yet? You know what's going on?"

"I know I've been fucked."

"*Are being* fucked," he corrected. "Present tense. This isn't the happy moment where we let you in on the gag and we all have a good laugh."

"Yeah, I'm getting that," I said. "But I didn't get the CliffsNotes on this, so help a brother out. What in the chartreuse fuck is going on?"

"Trap," he said.

"Yeah, pretty much figured the whole 'trap' part. What's eluding me is the 'why'? If you're in on this, then why hire me to sneak in here and get the relic?"

One of the tall weirdoes detached himself from the crowd and walked up to stand next to Bohunk.

"Boots?" I asked.

"Good afternoon, Mr. Hunter," said Oliver Boots. "We are so very delighted that you could join us."

"First," I said, "let me just say—and I mean this in the nicest possible way—go fuck yourself."

Everyone had a good laugh about that. The crowd of weirdoes laughed like crows. It was an ugly thing to hear. Bohunk had a deep bass rumble when he spoke but his laugh was a donkey bray, and he bent over and slapped his thighs.

Boots wiped a tear from the corner of his eye. "I deserved that, I suppose."

"You did," I said. "Care to tell me why I'm here? If it's not to protect the relic from ass-face here—" I pointed at Bohunk "—then what's the what?"

"I told you. It was all about protecting access to the Dreamlands."

"You said there was a relic…"

"Well, there is, but I may have misled you as to its size."

"You said it was carved to represent the mountain Ngranek on the isle of Oriab in the southern part of the Dreamlands and…" My words slowed and stopped. I turned and looked at the altar and the vault door.

"Ah," I said, "shit."

"Exactly. This altar is the relic and the map which describes the access is one of our greatest treasures."

I shook my head. "But you already *have* it."

"We have the doorway," said Boots, "and we know the way. Our problem is that the doorway is open and we want it shut. That is what we live for, protecting our world from those who would cross over from *your* world and bring with them their diseases and pollution."

"You lost me around the last bend. Why not just shut the freaking door?"

"They can't," said Bohunk.

"Why not?"

"Because the Thule Society wedged it open."

I looked from Bohunk to Boots and back again. "Huh?"

"Long story short," said Bohunk. "There really is a Thule Society and they really are a bunch of assholes who try to steal anything with even the stink of magic on it. All sorts of shit. You wouldn't believe what they've stolen over the last eighty-odd years. Can't keep their lily-white hands off of other people's shit."

"Uh huh. And you are an upstanding defender of the righteous."

Bohunk shrugged. "I never broke any laws that matter."

"Mr. Bohunk has been a cherished employee for many years now," said Boots. "He is a most efficient field operative. This entire operation was his idea."

"You're going to make me blush," said Bohunk.

"If the Thule Society wedged open the doorway, why hire me to steal the map for how to…" I stopped again, shaking my head. "No, none of this makes any sense. If the altar is the map and the door's already wedged open, then why the hell am I even here? Why is any of this happening? Are you fucktards planning on sacrificing me on that altar or some shit?"

"There's that delicious word again," said Boots. "'Fucktard'. So descriptive and useful."

The others of his kind tittered.

Bohunk took a step toward me and I backed up. A nervous reaction, sure, but it was also the wolf inside of me wanting to make sure lines of escape were clear. Bohunk held up his hands, palms out in a calm-down gesture.

"First off, sport," he said, "all this Lovecraft-Cthulhu-Dreamlands stuff? Crazy as it sounds, it's real. I mean it's *all* real. R'lyeh, the Mountains of Madness, the Necronomicon, Nyarlathotep, all of it. Real. Names were changed, sure, but otherwise this is all going on. Elder Gods, Outer Gods, Great Old Ones. Dude, the universe is a shit-ton bigger than you think it is. Worlds within worlds, worlds next to worlds. It can make your head spin. I mean… I used to have to drop acid to even *think* about this stuff, and my people buy into the whole 'larger world' thing anyway."

"Your people?" I echoed.

"Sure." He rapped his knuckles against his forehead. It sounded like stone banging on stone. "You think I got to look like this because of—what? Inbreeding? Having a crack-addict mother? A birth defect? Shit. You're not the only supernatural motherfucker trotting around and cashing in on the more lucrative aspects of his nature. No sir."

I licked my lips. "Which makes you…what? A golem?"

"Do I look Jewish?"

"Um…?"

"Ogre," he said, smiling with pride. "My whole family line is descended from Orcus, the Etruscan man-eating god. And, yes, before you ask, I do eat the occasional person. Only guys who fuck with me, though. And I cook them, because uncooked people are disgusting. I like a good rub to tenderize and bring out the—"

"Mr. Bohunk," said Boots, interrupting gently. Bohunk blinked.

"Oh, yeah, sorry. Caught up in the moment." He smiled at me. "Your people go back to Etruscan times, too. The *Benandanti*, the good wolves, am I right? What'd they call you during the

Inquisition? The Hounds of God? Goody two-shoes werewolves? Kind of cool, I guess. Not as cool as Ogres or Nightgaunts and—"

"The hell's a Nightgaunt?" I asked.

"Oh," said Mr. Boots, "that would be us."

His brilliant white smile broadened as he reached up and took hold of something on the back of his head. Then with a sudden jerk of his arm he tore off his face, his skin and his clothes. I heard a ripping sound that was suspiciously like Velcro, and then Boots flung aside his disguise.

Beneath it all he was still as black as polished coal.

But he had no face at all.

None.

Behind him and around us the others tore away their skins, flinging them to the floor to stand revealed as the monsters they were. These things, these Nightgaunts, had skin that was slick and rubbery. It looked more fake than their false disguises had. They had no mouths, no eyes, no noses. The only feature on their heads was a pair of horns that curled around so the tips pointed toward their otherwise featureless foreheads. They had long fingers that ended in very sharp claws, and thin wings that fluttered from their shoulders. Long barbed tails whipped back and forth behind them.

I said, "Oh shit."

They laughed like carrion birds.

"So," said Bohunk, "what you are, is totally and completely fucked."

-11-

"But why?" I demanded, taking two more backward steps. I was almost hard up against the altar. Not the place I'd prefer to be, but the Nightgaunts had spread out to form a wide ring around me. "What do you *want*?"

"Here's the thing about being part of the supernatural side of the universe," said Bohunk. "Rituals. There's all these goddamn rituals. Everything has to be complicated. Cthulhu, Nodens and all of those gods, man oh man do they have a hard-on for rituals. And, hey, it's not like the Jews and Catholics and Scientologists and everyone else don't get into the act, too. Everyone likes to make things complicated. No one can just *believe* and let it go. My people, the ogres? We got our thing, too. We can't eat anyone who's not an enemy. It's stupid, but if we do it's like having irritable bowel syndrome. I shit razor blades for a week."

I said nothing because, really, what do you say to an ogre who's complaining about problems with his colon?

"So, to understand the nature of the ritual you're tied up in," he continued, "you got to understand who the Nightgaunts are and what they do. Their whole shtick is protecting that mountain, Ngranek, on the isle of Oriab. Travelers from all kinds of worlds, including some unlucky cocksuckers from *our* world, keep trying to go there. Don't ask why. Something to do with the living heart of their god and the sixteen sacred toadstools or some such shit. I don't know. Every time they try to explain it, I just tune them out."

"Mr. Bohunk, please," said Boots. And that was weird because he no longer had a mouth. But I'd already given up trying to make sense of today. That ship sailed, caught fire, hit an iceberg and sank.

"Okay, okay," said Bohunk. "Long story short, it's important for there to *be* a doorway—something about the energetic lifeblood of the universe—but it's supposed to be shut except under certain circumstances."

"Like the planetary convergence?" I suggested.

"Like that. Only Bootsie lied to you. It's during that convergence that the doorway *can* be shut. Or, shut properly, I guess."

Boots nodded his confirmation of this.

"The Thule dickheads managed to get it open," continued Bohunk. "Me and my boys were around and we fucked them up but good. They were delicious, too. We had a pig roast and my boy Denny made this barbecue sauce that—"

"Mr. Bohunk!" snapped Boots, his patience wearing thin.

"Right, right. Anyway, as far as the doorway, it was damage done. Fucking thing's stuck open. And all sorts of things are getting into the Dreamlands."

I frowned and turned to look at the vault. "I don't—"

"No, the doorway is—whaddya call it, Bootsie?"

"Pan-dimensional," supplied the Nightgaunt. "Once open on this plane it opens on all planes. We have not been able to break the Thule spells. They used very powerful black magic. And that has forced us to use a dangerous and ancient spell. One that requires the willing sacrifice of a great champion of pure heart and great courage."

"Which," said Bohunk, giving me a big stage wink, "brings us to you."

I said, "Um...willing? Sacrifice? Champion?"

"Yeah," said Bohunk. "Bootsie tells me you took the job. Guess that's obvious 'cause you're here."

"Pure heart?"

"Well, there's always wiggle room," said Bohunk, and the Nightgaunts tittered.

"No, let's go back to the willing part. I agreed to a job, I never agreed to sacrifice anything."

"You did," said Boots. "You gave your word and you sealed the bargain with your own blood. There is no greater bond in this or any world. It is a blood bargain."

"Bullshit. You guys can take your bargain and your bag of tricks and shove them up your asses. Provided you have asses."

"They don't, actually," said Bohunk. "Weird, I know. And kind of disgusting. My point is that you are screwed, Hunter. Your blood is on the vault door, and the door is the relic. So...sucks to be you."

"And I'm just supposed to stretch out on the altar and let you cut my throat?"

Boots said, "No, Mr. Hunter, we expected you to fight us. You are, after all, a champion. And because you have a certain reputation for ferocity. Because you are a lycanthrope your blood and your soul energy will help us seal the doorway across all of the infinite worlds. You have a magnificent soul and it shines like a sun for those who can see it. All of that energy, that purity of purpose, that honesty and integrity, the *ferocity* that has earned you the reputation for being a true champion for the helpless, for the innocent...my oh my, that is a degree of spiritual force greater than anything we have used in ten thousand millennia. It is an honor to accept your sacrifice. You humble us."

"You," I said, "can go fuck yourself. I quit."

"You can't," he said, sounding almost sorry. "You gave your word."

"My word doesn't mean shit," I lied.

"You shed your blood to seal the deal."

"I cut my finger on a splinter. Which, by the way, was a cheap shot and a sneaky piece of bullshit."

"Nevertheless, a deal is a deal, and any deal made here on the altar is sealed across all of time and space."

"Save the Doctor Who bullcrap for someone who gives a rat's hairy balls."

"Ah, I'm so sorry you feel this way," said Boots. "But it is to be expected. It is a rare thing indeed for a person's soul force to be in alignment with their outer personality. But, no matter, we will help you live up to your agreement. We have asked Mr. Bohunk to assist us in completing the final part of the ritual."

"He can try."

"Oh, it's a done deal," Bohunk assured me, and all the Nightgaunts nodded. Their wings fluttered and creaked like leather. "And, for the record, sport, it's more than just you getting your throat cut. Nah. We got to cut your eyes out, cut your balls off. The more pain you're in, the more you suffer, the more noble your sacrifice is. That's bigger energy. Sucks for you but great for what Bootsie and his crew need. Great for the universe, I suppose."

"You're going to cut me up?" I said, feeling the blood drain from my face.

"Sure. There's a whole lot of cutting on today's program, and because you're a werewolf you'll actually live through almost all of it. Sucks, but there it is. We got silver chains, though, so..." He let it hang.

I glanced at the iron rings on the altar.

It was all there. Twelve Nightgaunts and one ogre. And me. Medium-sized guy who could become a medium-sized wolf.

As odds go, mine blew.

-12-

"You're going to have to earn it," I said, putting a little bit of the wolf's growl in my voice.

Israel Bohunk contrived not to faint from terror. "Yeah," he said, "that's why I'm here. You know, ogre and all."

"Never fought an ogre," I said, putting my hands in my pockets and trying to look like I was calm, cool and collected. "Didn't even believe in them until five minutes ago."

"Life's full of surprises," he said.

"Yes it is. You ever fight a werewolf before?" I asked.

"Nope, but I heard you guys taste great."

He laughed, I smiled. My heart was racing.

I asked, "You're not afraid I might cut *your* balls off?"

"Not really. My skin's as hard as granite. You'd break your little doggy nails. Sorry, sport, but this is how it ends."

"I didn't know ogres were that tough. Claw proof? Knife proof, too?"

"Sure. Bullets, too. They just bounce off. Not that it matters to you," he said. "From what I heard you don't even carry a gun."

"I'm thinking of taking it up," I told him.

And I drew the stolen .32 and shot him in his left eye.

-13-

Here's the thing…

I don't care how tough you are or how strong you are. I don't care if your skin is made of rocks or you're wearing a suit of armor. That's all well and good but I've found that a bullet in the brainpan will do 'er for just about everyone.

And eyes? Go on and tell me what kind of creature, natural or supernatural, has bulletproof eyes. You want to know how many?

Not one.

Not one fucking thing on earth or in any dimension you care to name.

The bullet punched through Bohunk's eye but it couldn't break through whatever the hell his skull was made of. So, instead, it bounced all over inside his skull and turned his brain to Swiss cheese.

Boo-fucking-hoo.

Bohunk fell backward against one of the Nightgaunts and dragged him down. The rest of them, including Oliver Boots, stood there and stared at their hired muscle. Blood leaked like tears from the burst eyeball.

Then Boots looked at me. Or…turned his face to me. Without his disguise he didn't have eyes. Or a mouth. Or anything.

I shot him in the face. Three times.

As it turns out, Nightgaunts aren't bullet proof at all. Not even a little bit.

The bullets blew out the back of his skull and splattered the creatures behind him. One of the bullets clipped the top of another Nightgaunt's head and blew a quarter pound of brains across the floor.

By then the others were beginning to shake off their shock.

They came at me, tearing the air with their claws, their barbed tails whipping, wings lifting them so they could dive-bomb me.

I emptied the .32 and then let it drop because the hand holding it was no longer shaped for that sort of thing. No proper trigger finger, no opposable thumb. Just claws and fur.

Distantly, as if off to one side of my mind, I could hear my clothes rip as my body changed. There was pain and there was blood. There always is. But there was also a lot of rage.

No. Let's call it by the right word.

There was hate.

Pure animal hate.

They came at me and tried to kill Sam Hunter the man. They tried to complete their sacrifice. To tear me apart. To use me, body and soul, to close the door. They tried to rip me apart and use me. They tried to destroy the man who had accepted the role of their champion.

But that man was gone.

Now it was only the wolf.

And, my oh my, the wolf was pissed.

-14-

As it turns out, Nightgaunts taste pretty good.

Like chicken.

The Unlearned Truths

A Limbus, Inc. Adventure

-1-

Sam Hunter

Philadelphia, Pennsylvania

I picked up the phone on the fourth ring. Goddamn thing would not stop ringing. I'd let it go to voicemail five times and hadn't listened to the messages and now whoever it was kept calling.

The caller ID said 'unavailable.'

Since it seemed pretty apparent someone didn't want me to sleep in on a Sunday morning, I finally reached out from under the covers, grabbed the phone, dragged it back in where it was warm, and punched the green button.

"Go fuck yourself," I mumbled, and hung up.

I was on that edge of sleep where you know you can not only dive back in, but step right into the dream you'd been pulled from. This was a good dream. It involved a lot of Scarlett Johansson and not a lot of clothes.

The phone started ringing again.

If I was more awake or, possibly, smarter, I'd have simply turned off the ringer. I was neither, at least not in the moment.

I pressed the button.

"Seriously," I said, "go fu—"

"Mr. Hunter?" interrupted a voice. Very female, very smoky.

So, I said, "Yeah...?" But I left it a question in case I needed to pretend I wasn't Sam Hunter.

"We need you," she said.

"It's Sunday. Need me tomorrow."

"Tomorrow will be too late," said the woman. I figured her for early thirties. There was a quality to her voice that made it clear that she was young but not a kid.

"If it's that pressing," I told her, my own voice thick with sleep, "call 9-1-1."

"We don't work with the police, Mr. Hunter. We prefer to work with you."

I rolled over onto my back. It had been a very good dream and I had a very inconvenient morning erection. And a very full bladder. But the bathroom was on the other side of the arctic tundra that is my apartment.

"Who is 'we'?" I asked.

And she said, "Limbus."

I hung up the phone again.

She called back seven more times.

I had braved the tundra and was on the toilet when I answered. I *told* her that I was on the toilet, hoping that would disgust her into hanging up. Not so.

"We need your help," she said, ignoring my comments and any pictures it might paint for us both to look at. "You've worked with us in the past and—"

"And regret having done so," I told her, then held the phone near the tank while I gave it a courtesy flush.

"You did superior work for us."

"Flattery doesn't do much for me on a Sunday morning."

There was a very brief pause. "What does ten thousand dollars do for you?"

I closed my eyes. I really hate working for Limbus. I've been messed up—inside and out—twice now. I made enemies in very bad places both times. I have nightmares. Yes, even people like me have nightmares, and not all of them are about taxes or middle-age prostate issues.

And, let's face it, I have to work a lot of hours doing intensely boring shit to come up with ten grand. On a good week I pull a thousand dollars doing investigations, chasing bail skips, snapping pictures of philandering spouses, or hunting for runaway kids. That's a good week. Want to know how many good weeks I have in any given year? It's a sad, sad number.

But...*Limbus*?

Fuck me.

"No," I said.

She said, "And the other half on completion of the assignment."

"Wait...what?"

"Ten up front and ten at the close," she said. "And five on top of that if you can resolve this in less than twenty-four hours."

I said nothing. Twenty-five thousand dollars? Holy rat shit.

She was quiet for a few moments, letting my greed go to work. Letting me think about my need to pay bills, my assessment of multiple alimony payments, rent, car repairs, and maybe even a Sony PlayStation 4 for my office.

I took a deep breath and girded my loins as well as someone can while he's on the crapper.

"Thirty," I said. "Half up front. All cash."

She paused again, but I don't think it was because she needed to count her pennies. More likely it was to take time to smile over the fact that she knew the hook was now firmly set in my underlip.

"We can do that."

"If I like the job."

"Oh," she said softly, "I can guarantee you, Mr. Hunter, that you won't like the job."

"Shit."

"So I'll have twenty in small nonsequential bills delivered to your office within the hour," she said, "and another twenty ready at completion."

"Plus the bonus. Another five."

"Another *ten*," she said, selling it.

Fuck.

"Okay, damn it," I said. "What's the job?"

She actually had the courtesy to laugh out loud before she told me. I laughed, too, even though we were both laughing at me.

-2-

Mr. Priest
Town of Poliske
Chernobyl Nuclear Power Plant Zone of Alienation
Kiev Oblast, Ukraine
Six Years Ago

They moved like phantoms through a city of ghosts.

Mr. Priest and his four companions were dressed in form-fitting gray radiation suits. The latest design, and far more flexible even than the MAR 95-3. Very expensive, with an integrated charcoal weave infused into flexible PVC, lightweight air scrubbers, goggles with protective polycarbonate lenses, and chem-tape over all the seals. Wired with real-time telemetry that flashed data onto the big plastic over-hood, including rad count, mission clock and maps.

Priest stopped at an intersection and looked up and down the streets. The blacktop was cracked and pernicious weeds had grown up and grown strange in the cold wasteland of this town.

"Lovely," he muttered. His real name was Esteban Santoro, but he preferred to be called Mr. Priest, or just Priest. His business associates and even his enemies called him that. Unlike his real name, Priest was not on any warrant or watch list.

He did not consider himself to be evil, though he knew others did, and they could make a compelling argument. Priest considered himself to be a realist in a world that did not reward those who cling to illusions. National and international laws were subjective, created by specific groups to suit their own ends; they were not cosmic laws and therefore choosing not to obey them did not equal sin. The god Priest believed in—and he was deeply invested in the Old Testament—was a right bastard. Bloodthirsty, vindictive, duplicitous, occasionally malicious, and very violent. Priest admired those qualities in his god and cultivated them in himself. His long association with certain militant groups buried deep inside the skin of the Roman Catholic Church shared many of those views, and even expanded upon them. Ask the Crusaders, the Templars, the pope who slaughtered the Templars, and the Inquisition. Priest's grandfather had been a cardinal during the Second World War and had worked hand-in-glove with the Nazis.

Priest admired power as much as he admired knowledge. The development of power and the search for knowledge were sacred to him.

Which is why he was in Ukraine with his team. A very powerful and very rich American industrialist had paid Priest a lot of money to locate and recover some very ancient knowledge. It was so immense an undertaking that it felt very much like a sacred quest. No grail at the end of the journey, of course, but something much more real and much more powerful.

A book.

One of many that he had been hired to obtain.

It pleased Mr. Priest to have his specific skill set acknowledged and admired. And paid for. Oh yes, his employer, Mr. Oscar Bell of Long Island, had dug deep into his personal fortune to underwrite this expedition. And, should this one be successful, there would be others. Bell had given him a deliciously long shopping list.

His current lover, Katrinka Favreau—known as Rink—had accompanied Priest on a few smaller missions in the past, but nothing like this. She was convinced that he was some kind of archeologist in the vein of Indiana Jones. Rink was brilliant but immensely naïve when it came to people. She was, however, a superb cultural anthropologist and research scholar, and that was useful to him. Priest was moderately sure that he loved her, but love was a fragile thing to him. If she became less useful or in any other way inconvenient, he would abandon her in whatever town was handy. And if that didn't work, well…

Rink came to stand next to him. She was much shorter than he was, and her goggles were equal with his chest. As she so often did, Rink slipped her hand in his, their gloved fingers entwining.

"This place gives me the creeps," she said.

"This place would give Satan himself the creeps," he agreed.

Frigid winds blew debris and pieces of dead plant matter past them. Boris, Keppler, and Hiro clustered behind them, silent, in awe of the spectacle.

"Looks worse in person," said Rink, and Priest nodded. They'd studied maps, photos, and videos of Poliske, but none of that really captured the desolation.

When reactor number four at the Chernobyl Nuclear Power Plant exploded, this entire part of Ukraine was flooded with radioactivity. Even so, the residents of this town were not evacuated until forty hours later. By then many of the people who had lived and worked here had been exposed. Cancer had chased them out of Poliske and dragged many thousands into early graves. Now that specter of death seemed to whisper to them in the howling wind. It loomed above them in the lichen-covered brickwork of gray buildings. It reached for them with fingers of diseased plants and stunted trees.

Poliske was dead but it wasn't resting in any kind of peace.

That was fine with Priest. He didn't bring his team here for the nightlife, and he didn't care much about ghosts. Some, but not much.

Other things, maybe, but that fear was closer to excitement, and it was something he kept private, even from Rink. As far as she knew—as far as any of them knew—they were here to loot an old Soviet lab. That was scary enough for them.

One of the other team members came to stand with Priest and Rink.

"Call it, dude," said Hiro Tsukino. He was an urban explorer who'd gained international fame as the point man for the *Tengu*, the UE team from Japan. They'd conducted scavenging hunts into several of the most dangerous *haikyo*—abandoned buildings. Their level of skill, inarguable courage, and apparent fearlessness had made them an Internet sensation. As a teen Hiro had gone into the ruins of several department stores within hours of the Tōhoku earthquake of 2011. While aftershocks sent jagged cracks running up the walls, the *Tengu* had gone deep inside and returned with money and jewelry from the stores. His subsequent arrest for looting had sparked a media frenzy, and parties interested in Hiro's bravery and skill set had financed a particularly brutal team of lawyers. Since then the *Tengu* had disintegrated, as many small anarchist groups will, but Hiro rose to solo stardom. Despite the dangerous and illegal nature of his adventures, he received huge endorsements from international companies, including GoPro and Under Armor.

When Priest reached out to him to join the Poliske trip, Hiro had jumped at it. Poliske was legendary. A city in the shadow of Chernobyl. Not just ghosts, but nuclear goddamn ghosts. Hiro was in before Priest told him what his fee was. When they did get to the fee, Hiro was seriously jazzed, but the allure of Poliske was even greater than all those zeroes. The urban explorer was a true daredevil. He was also, as far as Priest could tell, truly fearless. Cautious, yes, but that was more about being smart than blind and reckless. Priest and Rink had interviewed the scavenger and concluded that Hiro was apolitical and a borderline anarchist. That was good. That was fine. Anarchists, even those who still clung to some of their social connections, were useful.

Psychopaths like Boris, Priest's bodyguard, were different. Boris' skills were limited to things he could hurt and things he could kill. Useful, but neither Priest nor Rink—or Hiro for that matter—would burn up calories shedding tears if Boris didn't make it home. As long as Boris kept them safe until they were out of this dead fucking town and this dreary fucking country.

The last member of the team, and the only woman besides Rink, was Inga Keppler, a Swiss nuclear science grad student. Priest would have preferred having a Ph.D. on the team, but Keppler was available, she was intensely brilliant, and she could be bought. That was a winning combination. She also looked like a bridge troll, so Rink never got jealous about having her around.

"The shoe factory is over there," said Priest, pointing to a building down the street to their left. It was a squat three-story pile with a damaged façade and crumbling brickwork, grimed windows and piles of trash heaped against the rusted metal door.

The five of them began moving toward the building. Boris translated the sign outside, "'Three Brothers Shoes and Leather Goods.'" He turned to Priest. "Are you sure about this? How good is your intelligence, *tovarisch*?" His accent was thick, but Priest was used to it by now.

"No doubts," he told the group. "It's there."

They reached the building and looked around. There was dirt and mud from recent snowmelt on the ground. Boris squatted down to examine it and then nodded.

"It's good. No one's been here in a long time."

"How long?" asked Rink. She was nervous and kept looking up and down the street as if expecting Russian or Ukrainian troops to appear out of thin air.

"Meh," said Boris shrugging, "this mud is two, three weeks old. Can't tell more than that, but nobody's gone in or out today." Even so he unslung his rifle as he stood. He carried an AK-103 with the stock folded down and two magazines taped jungle style, one fitted into place and the other reversed for an easy swap-out in a firefight. Privately, Priest thought the double taping of the mags was probably something Boris did to impress the rubes. It was amateurish and clumsy, but it looked cool. Boris was playing his role of professional soldier to the hilt.

"You're up, Hiro," he said, and the former leader of the *Tengu* nodded and approached the door.

There are a lot of ways to approach a new site when doing urban exploration. Hiro was bold but he was also smart. Going over the schematics and floor plans of the old shoe factory was the smart way to go. Taking risks was part of the game; being stupid was not.

"We need to be careful in there," said Hiro. "There's been years of rain and snow with no one to repair weather damage. The floors could be rotted out; the ceiling could be ready to collapse, if it hasn't already. Don't trust anything until I've checked it out first, okay?"

The others nodded, except for Priest. He'd brought Hiro along mostly to field-test the man's attitude, not because he thought this particular hunt was going to require his skills. After today, though, Priest would know whether Hiro could be trusted. Even so, he let the urban explorer have his moment of authority.

The door was slightly ajar and yielded to a light touch.

"Lock's been forced," observed Hiro.

Boris bent to look and nodded, then sneered. "Probably one of those samosely pieces of shit. They're worse than rats."

Despite the radiation, dozens of illegal 'self-settlers' had moved into Poliske and the other abandoned towns in the Exclusion Zone. They were mostly old, poor people who could not afford to live anywhere and had been drawn like flame-dazed moths to all those empty buildings. Sometimes their corpses were recovered and buried by workers of the State Agency of Ukraine on the Exclusion Zone Management; and sometimes they were left to rot.

"How could they even live here?" asked Rink.

Keppler shrugged. "The radiation isn't as bad as all that. I mean, it will kill you, but not right away. Not for years. If you're old…" She shrugged again, as if to say 'who cares?'

Priest and Rink exchanged a brief look. He knew that Keppler tended to underestimate the danger because she didn't want to scare anyone off. Her bonus was contingent on completing this mission. On the other hand, she had insisted on the very best protective equipment including the decontamination units in the van that was parked at the outer edge of the thousand-square-mile Zone. Keppler had also insisted on a timetable that would get them out of here well before the radiation eroded the integrity of their suits.

"Let's get a move on, yes?" suggested Priest. "Tick-tock. There are satellite fly-bys of this area and we have a three hour and fourteen minute window."

"We should think about getting out of here sooner than that," advised Keppler.

"That is the plan. But we leave when we've found what we came for."

Hiro nodded, unclipped his flashlight, and stepped cautiously into the warehouse. The others followed and they moved through a vast space of old machines, rows of industrial sewing machines, bins where rolls of material like the stuff outside was rotting away. Animal bones littered the floor and Priest thought that some of them looked very strange. Too many legs, deformed skulls, spines mottled with odd lumps of calcium. Evidence of the radiation's mutagenic horrors even on creatures as stalwart as rats.

"I hate this place," whispered Rink.

"We're not shopping for a summer home, darling," he told her. "Come on, Hiro, this is taking too long."

"No, it's not," he said as he entered one of the offices. "Come on, I think I found it."

They hurried in after him.

"I don't see nothing," said Boris, looking around at a desk and chair that were badly warped by dripping water. There was a row of file cabinets along one wall and lots of framed pictures of men and women in old Soviet uniforms. They stood in front of the row of file cabinets. Diagrams and measurements flashed on the inside of his hood.

Hiro used his flashlight to tap on the cabinets and on the wall behind them. "Yeah, this is definitely it."

Priest clapped him on the shoulder. "Perfect."

"What?" demanded Boris. "It's old office furniture? So what?"

Priest shook his head. "The floor plan I got from my contact in Moscow said that this whole block of buildings was erected over an old coalmine that had played out in the 1920s, right? But who would build a factory town over a coalmine? Just from the perspective of structural engineering it makes no sense. You'd have to either fill in the mine or otherwise reinforce it."

The others stared at him like studious school kids.

"The specs on this place are nonsensical if you are trying to understand it from any direction except one in which the coalmine is *still* in use. Or, *was* in use before the reactor blew at Chernobyl. The orientation of the buildings, the power grid, the population numbers, even the location of railroad tracks and a landing strip." Priest bent close to examine the cabinets. "I hired a forensic accountant to tear apart the billing records and manifests of building materials sent out here. For it to make sense there would have to be five times as many buildings, and they'd all be in better condition than what we've seen. There are records of premium-grade steel alloys, timber and other stuff. Incredible amounts of expensive materials. Why would a shoe factory like this need six super computers? Why would almost two percent of the electrical power generated by Chernobyl come here? Two percent. Do you know how much power that is?"

"Let me guess," said Boris. "Two percent?"

"Amusing, but no. It's enough to light up twenty cities of this size."

Keppler nodded. "Maybe more."

Boris frowned. "Then what—?"

Instead of answering, Priest nodded to Hiro, who began pulling out the cabinet drawers. Most of them were crammed with old papers, and for a moment Priest's heart began hammering in his chest as doubt flared. Then the top left drawer rolled out differently than the others. It came too far out, as if the cabinet was far deeper than the wall against which it was set. He reached inside and fiddled with something the others couldn't see. There was an audible click and one half of the row of cabinets seemed to lean out toward them.

"Help me with this," said Hiro. Priest and Boris took hold of the handles and pulled. It was immediately clear that the cabinet was a dummy set on hidden casters, but rust made it improbably heavy. "Might have opened electrically. God, it weighs a ton."

Boris gritted his teeth, made a sound like an angry bear and pulled. The rusted wheels made pig-squealing noises as the cabinet moved. The whole row moved outward with dogged reluctance and then stopped, revealing a darkened cleft two feet wide.

"Light, light," called Priest, snapping his fingers impatiently, but Hiro was right there. He aimed the beam inside and they could see that there was a short hallway beyond the cabinets, beyond which a flight of stairs dropped into utter darkness.

"What the fuck?" asked Boris. "How'd you know about this?"

"A little birdie told me," said Priest. "What does it matter? The only thing I care about is what's down there."

"What is down there?" asked Keppler. "Is it something to do with what happened at Chernobyl?"

Priest laughed. "Oh, no," he said as he squeezed inside, "this is a lot more dangerous than that. And a lot more beautiful."

-3-

Sam Hunter
Philadelphia, Pennsylvania

The woman told me her name was Acantha. Greek in origin, I think, though her accent was generic American. No last name given, even when I asked really nicely.

When she got around to telling me about the job it was pretty clear why she was willing to dig deep to hire me. Understand something, she wasn't just looking for a P.I. who isn't afraid to bend the rules a tad, but specifically Samuel Theiss Hunter. Limbus, whoever the Christ they were, knew who and what I was. The jobs they brought me before were not something one of the bigger and better run investigations agencies would have taken or could have handled. I'm not saying I'm better, because...hey, let's be real, but I am different. Limbus hires me for oddball jobs because of certain qualities I bring to the mix. Not talking about my snarky wit or roguish charm.

No, I'm talking about the whole fangs and claws and fur thing.

As for Limbus...I haven't been able to discover much about them except for a few things. First, they have the most enigmatic and annoying fucking business cards I've ever seen. Nice paper, embossed printing, quality work, but this is what their cards say:

LIMBUS, Inc.
Are you laid off, downsized, undersized?

Call us. We employ. 1-800-555-0606
How lucky do you feel?

Sounds like a recruiting ad for a hooker, or maybe a thug to guard a brothel, and not in the good part of town.

The first job I took for them involved the hunt for some rich assholes who were skinning innocent young women alive. Why? Aside from the fact that they thought their money and family connections gave them license to piss on anyone lower on the social ladder, these particular privileged dickheads were trying to appease a demon.

Yeah. Be with that for a minute. Their game plan boiled down to conjuring a demon, appeasing the demon, *enslaving* the demon in order to get it to grant them a lot of wishes including even more money and maybe bigger dicks.

Whatever.

Bottom line is that we had words. Me and them, and me and the demon. Actual demon. Scared the piss out of me when I realized that these ass-clowns had conjured a real demon. No, check that…it scared me to know that demons were real and not something from bad horror movies. My life's been pretty weird but I thought there were limits, you know? There were already enough things going bump in the night. But, I don't get to make that kind of an existential call. So, yeah…demon. Fuck me.

But, fuck *him* too. Turns out, he could bleed. That was a bit of a game changer because up to then I figured I was totally screwed. I mean, demon, am I right? That's usually the point at which you figure it's game over.

But if something can bleed, then it can die. That, as it turned out, is something of a cosmic verity. When the universe turns out to be both bigger and badder than you think, it's nice to know that there are rules.

My second Limbus job was last year, and it involved a team of North Korean wacko scientists trying to create lycanthropic super soldiers. No, I am not making this up and I am not drunk. Okay, well, maybe I've had a couple-three beers today, but everything else is straight. Werewolf super soldiers.

So, my life is complicated. To which you might say, *no shit, Sherlock.* Fair enough. But I'm telling you all of this because it'll help you frame your mind for what Acantha told me about the job.

I took the phone with me through the door that connected my crappy apartment to my crappy office. It was small, cramped, untidy, unwelcoming, uncomfortable and probably unhealthy. I'd prepped the coffeemaker before I went to bed so that all I had to do was hit a button. If I could have gotten a coffeemaker with an IV drip to start the caffeination process that much quicker I'd own one. I knew that Acantha was still waiting on the line through all this even though she hadn't said anything. She called me, so fuck it. Coffee first.

When the magical process of coffee making was in full swing, I plopped down on the creaky leather chair behind my desk. I flipped open my laptop and logged in.

"Okay," I said, "hit me with some details."

She started off by asking me a question. "Mr. Hunter, have you ever heard of the Unlearnable Truths?" When I was a little slow in responding she said, "Stop Googling them."

"I'm not."

"I can hear you typing," she said. "Don't bother, they're not on the Internet."

I stopped one-hand typing the words into Google. "Okay," I said, "then what are they besides an obvious contradiction in terms?"

"Are you familiar with the phrase '*Librorum Prohibitorum*'?" she asked, then quickly added, "Please don't look it up. Just answer me."

"Um," I said, "I don't speak much Latin, but I can take a swing at it. Prohibited book? Something like that?"

"Very good, Mr. Hunter."

"Do I get a cookie?"

"We'll see. The *Index Librorum Prohibitorum* was authorized by Pope Paul IV in 1559. It contained a list of books deemed by the Catholic Church to be heretical, lascivious or anti-clerical."

"Naughty books."

"Naughty books indeed," agreed Acantha. "And, yes, you can find mention of it on the Net. Look under 'Pauline Index.' However what you'll find is the wrong list of books. You see, the *Index Librorum Prohibitorum* contained two separate lists. The Pauline Index was a list of books the general public were allowed to know about but not allowed to have. Books that were decried by the church and sought by the Inquisition."

"Okay. And the second—?"

"Ah, that is a very special list," she said. "We call them the Unlearnable Truths. And they are the most dangerous books ever written."

"Oh come on…"

She ignored me. "Even the titles of those books were kept secret from everyone except for a special and very covert office of the church and their field agents, who are known collectively as the *Ordo Fratrum Claustrorum.*"

"Order of something-something," I said. "Who are they?"

"The Brotherhood of the Lock. They are an ancient order of warrior priests," she said, and there was a quality to her voice that I found both intriguing and alarming. She sounded genuinely scared. "They are the most intense and dangerous arm of the Inquisition."

"You keep talking in the present tense but we're discussing something that happened a long time ago, right?"

"Not entirely."

"Hate to break it to you, sister, but I'm pretty darn sure the Inquisition is yesterday's news."

She sighed. "There is so much that regular people don't know about the world, Mr. Hunter. Even people like you. And, let's face it, the general public don't believe you could possibly be what you are. Or that you're from an ancient family of lycanthropes who can trace their unique bloodlines back to Etruscan times."

"Okay, okay, fair enough," I said. "Tell me the rest."

"The *Ordo Fratrum Claustrorum*—the Brotherhood—were created by a papal bull, but you won't find that on the Net, either, or in any official church records. They were always kept secret. Only a few cardinals know of them, and most popes, including the current one, know nothing about them. Their mission is to search the world for the Unlearnable Truths."

"And do what with them? Burn 'em?"

"If possible."

"How could that not be possible?"

"We'll get to that," said Acantha. "It was the mission of this Brotherhood to seek out the Unlearnable Truths and to protect humanity from the secrets they contain. This they did by any means necessary. It's not much of an exaggeration to say that rivers of blood have been spilled. Many heretics were burned or butchered by the Brotherhood because, after all, sacrifices must sometimes be made to protect the flock."

"You sound like you're in favor of the Brotherhood's game plan."

"One can agree with the end result without agreeing with the motives or methods."

I didn't comment on that but encouraged her to tell me more.

"The creation of the *Index*," she continued, "and the formation of the Brotherhood happened centuries ago. The Pauline Index has, for the most part, become a footnote in history. However the search for the Unlearnable Truths continues, as does the mission of the Brotherhood. They are real, they are dangerous, and they are relentless."

"What does that have to do with me?"

"I'm getting to that. Until the early twentieth century the names of the Unlearnable Truths were unknown to all except the most devoted occult scholars, and then something happened, something that brought the titles into the public consciousness."

"What do you mean?"

"We...don't actually know how or why it happened," said Acantha, "but during the twenties and thirties several writers of pulp fiction—predominantly horror and science fiction writers—began mentioning the titles of those books in their stories. Luckily the contents of the books formed no part of the text of these stories, but it was devastating to discover that even the titles should be so casually mentioned."

"Mentioned how?" I asked. "I don't follow."

"Have you ever heard of a writer named Howard Philips Lovecraft?"

I sighed and it turned into a shiver. "H.P. Lovecraft. Sure. The name's come up."

"Have you read his stories?"

"Yeah."

"And—?"

"And what?"

"Do you think they are entirely fictional?" asked Acantha.

I sat back in my chair and put my heels up on my desk, crossing them, trying to convince my body that everything was casual and cool. However I was sweating under my clothes. Last year—on a gig that didn't involve Limbus—I'd had a run-in with a group who seemed to have stepped right out of a Lovecraft story. They were not products of some asshole writer's lunatic imagination. I wish to Christ I could say they were, but I'm still having *those* nightmares.

"I try to keep an open mind," I said carefully.

There was a sound that might have been a small, quiet laugh. "Have you read any of the writings of Lovecraft's colleagues and those influenced by him, particularly the stories collectively known as the *Cthulhu Mythos*?"

"Some of them."

"August Derleth, Robert Bloch, Robert E. Howard..." She rattled off a dozen or so names. I knew most of them, though I hadn't read all of them and told her as much. "In those stories the writers make mention of forbidden books. Do you recall any of the titles?"

"Um...only the main one, *The Necronomicon*."

"Ah, yes. That is one of them."

"One of...which? Are you saying that *The Necronomicon* is one of these Unlearnable Truths?"

"That is precisely what I'm saying, Mr. Hunter."

"Oh," I said. "Shit."

"There are many other titles on the list. *The Book of Azathoth, The Cloister Manifesto, The Book of Eibon, The Book of Iod, The Celaeno Fragments, The Cultes des Goules, The Eltdown Shards, The Revelations of Gla'aki, Incendium Maleficarum, On the Sending Out of the Soul, De Vermis Mysteriis*...and a dozen others."

"Shit," I said again.

"Over the last five centuries the Brotherhood obtained many of these books, Mr. Hunter. Some were destroyed, others were locked away in the vaults of churches and other sacred places."

"Why weren't they all destroyed?"

"Because some can't be destroyed."

"Why not?"

"There are protections."

"I don't like that word much," I admitted. "Are we talking magic spells or something?"

"Or something. It varies with each book."

"Shit."

"Which brings us to the purpose of my call," said Acantha. "For the last century or so the Unlearnable Truths have been inert. Contained, you might say. Or lost. There were some tremors of course when the pulp fiction writers began naming them, and how and why they did that remains a mystery, but the books themselves did not appear. That, however, has changed. Limbus has learned that there are several parties actively seeking these books. Great money has been invested in finding them, and there are several competing teams."

"Teams?"

"The Brotherhood, of course, and some groups of what appear to be special operators working for highly secret and deeply illegal groups within various world governments. That includes your own."

"My own? You're not American?"

"I'm not anything," she said. "I work for Limbus, Inc."

"Which means what?"

She did not answer that question. Instead she said, "It has come to our attention that one of the most dangerous of these books is being brought to America. It will arrive via cargo ship in a Baltimore port in a few hours. We want you to intercept the people who are in possession of the book and recover it for us."

"Uh huh. Explain to me exactly why I should risk my ass to get a magical book and then turn it over to people I don't know and, quite frankly, don't really trust? You sound like a smart lady, Acantha...sell that to me."

-4-

Mr. Priest
Town of Poliske
Chernobyl Nuclear Power Plant Zone of Alienation
Kiev Oblast, Ukraine
Six Years Ago

"It's probably unstable," said Hiro as they gathered together at the top of the darkened stairs. "Let me go first. Nobody moves until I give the word, and then only where and when I say, okay?"

"Whatever, *tovarisch*," said Boris with a snort. "Do you want to shake my dick when I take a piss, too?"

"Didn't bring tweezers," said Hiro.

Rink and Keppler burst out laughing. Boris shot them evil looks.

"You think that's funny? How about you suck my dick and see if it's too small to choke you."

"I—" began Rink, but Priest clapped his hands once, loud as a gunshot, and everyone jumped. "Okay, that's enough. Why don't you all shut the fuck up, yes?"

Silence fell hard and fast.

Priest gave the group a single, curt nod. "Everybody's here to do a job, and keeping us alive down here is Hiro's. If he says be careful, you be careful. End of discussion."

Boris said nothing but he wore a dismissive smirk. Rink and Keppler nodded. So did Hiro. Without another word he began descending the steps, following the beam of his flashlight.

"Careful, Hiro," said Rink. "Those stairs could be totally rotted out."

The urban explorer stopped three steps down, then crouched and touched the surface of the stair. Priest heard him grunt in surprise. "This is weird."

"What?" asked Rink, shrinking back.

"No, it's okay," said Hiro. "It's just that this is wrong. The floor plans said that the basement was framed in wood, which means the stairs would be wood, too. That's normal, even for factories like this. The basement is supposed to be small, for utility only. All of the storage is on the first floor. But look at these steps." He widened the beam of his light to show a broad set of dusty white stairs. "These are concrete. Heavy-grade, too. And look over there. See that ramp? That's for forklifts."

"So what?" demanded Boris. "So they did renovations. Big deal. My uncle Uri installed a fuck pad in his basement, with a vibrating bed, mirrors on the ceiling and a fully-stocked wetbar."

Hiro shook his head. "No, dude, what I mean is that this design is military."

Boris grunted.

"Military?" asked Keppler. "How can you be sure?"

"See those big conduits on the wall heading down there?" asked Hiro. "Those are ultra high capacity electrical lines, phone lines and bundled Internet cables. I've seen this all over the world. We do events at a lot of decommissioned bases, and this is how they build it when they're setting up an underground installation."

Boris scowled. "There was no military here except a standard checkpoint."

"Oh yes there was," said Priest. They all looked at him.

"Why?" asked Keppler, confused. "What is this place? The building upstairs is falling down but this…this looks recent."

"Not recent," corrected Priest, "but very well-made. It was built in 1934 but completely *rebuilt* in '85."

"What was rebuilt?" asked Keppler. "I still don't understand what this is or what we're looking for."

Priest walked down six steps into darkness before he turned and smiled up at them through the plastic faceplate of his mask. "The shoe factory was legitimate, at least at first. Ordinary structure, normal electrical needs. That changed, though, when this underground facility was rebuilt and repurposed near the end of the Cold War. This was the last great investment of money, resources, and technology in the hopes of salvaging the Soviet Union. Everyone knew that things were heading toward an inevitable collapse because of economic forces here and the rise of the Reagan military-industrial complex. The Soviets couldn't keep pace and they knew it. They were becoming resource poor, too, which is why they turned their attention to what can best be described as 'alternative sources' for raw materials."

"What is that supposed to mean?" asked Keppler.

Priest grinned at her. "That's what we're here to discover."

Boris made a face and laid his hand atop the rifle that was slung across his beefy shoulder. "'Discover,' *tovarisch*? We're in a radiation zone. I can feel my sperm curling up and dying inside my balls. I don't want to hear about 'discovering' anything. You said we were here to *recover* something. English may not be my mother tongue but I know the difference between discovery and recovery."

"Relax, my friend," said Priest, "call it a poor word choice. I know what we're looking for and I have a pretty good guess as to where it is."

Hiro mouthed the word 'guess.'

Keppler said, "If you know where it is, then let's get a move on."

But Priest did not immediately move. "Before we go down there," he said, gesturing behind him to whatever lay in the shadows below, "I want you to prepare yourselves."

Hiro automatically touched the seals of his suit. "Prepare for what?"

"For the impossible," said Priest.

And with that he turned and ran down the rest of the steps.

They stared after him. Hiro cupped his hands around his mouth and yelled, "You do understand that preparing for the impossible is a contradiction in terms?"

Priest's laugh floated up the stairs at them.

"That's just great," sighed the urban explorer. He looked at Rink and Keppler, and they all shrugged.

"At least it can't get any weirder than that," said Rink.

It was a joke, but it fell flat.

Boris said, "Shit."

They followed Priest down the stairs.

They caught up with him on a wide landing that had three doors. One was marked as a service closet and when they looked inside they saw brooms, mops, buckets, and shelves of cleaning supplies. The second was a security room that had a long bank of old fashioned monitors, clunky keyboards on a metal table, and primitive computers. Both of these rooms were abandoned and filled with the dust of decades. The third door, the farthest away from the stairs, was bigger and more strongly made. Hiro was able to pick the lock and open it in less than five minutes, but they soon discovered a second and much heavier door inside. It was two feet thick and made from titanium, with concealed hinges. A key code reader was mounted on the wall, but they ignored it. The thing wasn't necessary because the door stood ajar, blocked from closing by the thing that lay across the threshold.

"Jesus Christ," gasped Rink.

Keppler recoiled. "What the hell is *that*?"

It was gray and strange and looked entirely wrong. At first glance it looked like a huge and unusually thick canvas water hose, but that wasn't what it was. This was something organic, something that had been alive, and it was massive, bizarre and terrifying. The skin—if skin it was—was mottled with the faded marks of a dark pattern that was like rattlesnake skin. It was not smooth but instead showed the wrinkled sacs of what looked like pustules, and from the center of each of these was a leathery spike of hair or horn. The smallest of these spikes was an inch long and the largest were six inches. The hide was crisscrossed with lines and marks that looked uncomfortably like the scars of teeth and claws, but they were so big that whatever had left those marks must have been even more enormous than whatever this thing was.

Hiro, Priest and Keppler shined flashlight beams over the carcass, and slowly inched forward to examine it more closely. Rink hung far back, unwilling or unable to draw closer. Boris stood beside her, his rifle now held tightly in his hands.

"*Akógo chërta*," he breathed. "What the fuck is this bullshit?"

But Priest was only marginally less surprised that the rest of them, and shook his head slowly. He had been told the door would be blocked open, but his source hadn't said by *what*. The ancient texts he'd pored over, and the reams of commentary, had hinted at fantastic things but he had never once stood in the presence of it. Knowing that a thing exists and seeing it in the flesh were vastly different.

"I don't know," he said slowly, choosing the right lies and the right words of comfort to suit the moment, "but whatever it is—it's dead. It's not going to hurt us."

"But what *is* it?" insisted Boris.

"It's dead," said Priest, "and that's all that matters."

Hiro studied it without approaching. "Looks like it got crushed by the door."

Boris advanced cautiously toward it, keeping his barrel aimed at the center of its slack mass. The tentacle was caught a yard off the ground and drooped down on either side of the door. When Boris was a few feet away he lashed out with a kick, but all they heard was a dry rattle, like pieces of ivory in a leather bag. Dust puffed into the air and settled slowly.

Priest pushed Boris's gun barrel away and knelt. The thing was long and it lay sprawled thirty feet into the landing, with more of it vanishing inside. When he touched it some of it flaked away into dust.

Hiro edged over and aimed his flashlight inside. "It's torn off just a few feet on the other side."

Keppler looked nervously over her shoulder. "Yes, but torn off from *what*?"

-5-

Sam Hunter
Philadelphia, Pennsylvania

Acantha sold it to me.

She sold it pretty hard.

"The Unlearnable Truths were never stored together," she said. "Even those religious scholars who doubted—or claimed to doubt—their origins and nature did not risk creating a 'library' of such books. In church records there are accounts of catastrophic attempts to do just that. Three of them were stored in Pompeii, another four were in London in 1666. Do you know what happened in each place?"

"Yeah," I said as I fetched a fresh cup of coffee and slumped back into my chair. "A volcano and a big fire. I watch the History Channel."

"It became a duty of the Brotherhood of the Lock to keep the books separate and to keep them hidden. And, before you ask, this is why these particular books were never stored in the Vatican library. The cardinals overseeing the Brotherhood feared a disaster."

"Why not weight 'em down with rocks and drop 'em into the fucking ocean?" I asked.

"Oh no," she gasped. "That would never, ever do."

"Why not?"

"They would be found too easily in the depths."

"How? James Cameron going to grab them with that submarine thing he has?"

"There are things living in the deepest parts of the ocean that are sleeping, Mr. Hunter. If those books were dropped down they would cry out for those sleeping creatures and awaken them."

"Now you're just messing with me," I said.

"I wish," said Acantha.

"Balls."

"I know."

"Briny fish balls."

"It is a larger and stranger world than you think."

"Swell."

"Once it became clear that the Unlearnable Truths needed to be separated," continued Acantha, "Brotherhood teams took them to the ends of the earth and hid them away. Some, of course, had never been in the Brotherhood's hands, but these had also been hidden away."

"Hidden where?"

"It varies, of course. Some were buried along with saints or great warriors of the faith in the hopes that these champions would protect the world from the books. Others were hidden in inaccessible places and fiercely guarded by warrior monks, local tribes, or other sentries. This worked for many years...centuries in most cases, but that has changed. The development of archeological technologies and expeditionary equipment has left few places on our world inaccessible. The tombs of saints, kings and other historical figures have been looted or excavated, the protective seals broken in the process. Tribes and ethnic groups shift and change as national lines have been redrawn. During the twentieth and early twenty-first centuries the maps of the Middle East have been radically changed. Wars, ethnic genocide, and political instability have left some sacred sites completely abandoned or left them open to misuse. In Syria, Egypt, Iraq, Yemen, and Turkey the rise of Daesh—what you in America call ISIS or ISIL—have been actively seeking out any sacred site connected to any religion except their warped and perverted form of Islam. They think that by destroying temples or burning libraries they are eradicating other religions, but they are very wrong. They are destroying the protections that keep much older faiths from returning in force to our world."

"Okay," I said.

"Mr. Hunter," she said sharply, apparently having heard something in my tone, "skepticism of a thing does not mean that it is not real."

"Yeah, sorry. It's just that this is a lot to swallow."

"I'm not asking you to believe everything I'm saying," continued Acantha, "but since you have agreed to take this case you need to at least accept the possibility that this is real. Otherwise you may not apply yourself with the degree of commitment that has earned you the respect of the Limbus board of directors. We do not want you to do this strictly for the payday."

I sipped my coffee. "Okay, I hear you," I said. "I've got enough professionalism to guarantee that you'll get one hundred percent of my skills, energy, and enthusiasm. But actual belief isn't something that can be bought or sold."

The line was silent for a few moments. I swiveled my chair around to face the window. My view was of a bail bondsman, a leather bar, a tattoo parlor, and a diner. Yes, my office is in a cliché. A sad, low-rent stereotype of the kind of world-weary hard luck private investigator that looks great in movies. The truth is less charming. Most of my clients are half-crooked themselves, or they're desperately afraid people who are trying to break their own hearts by having me tail their spouses to prove that life absolutely sucks. Most of the people I meet in my job are lowlifes, scumbags, thieves, junkies, or people who are so lost that they wash up like flotsam on the streets of this part of Philadelphia. There's nothing noble about me or what I do. I don't believe in a whole lot even though I know for sure that there's more to the world than what can be measured or metered. The supernatural—or at least some of it—is real. *I'm* part of that world. My family has been part of it for a long, long time. But actual religion…? Jury's been out so long on that, at least for me, that I don't think they're ever coming in with a verdict. If God is up there, then He's either drunk, indifferent or bugfuck nuts, because no one in any religion has ever been able to make a case—at least to me—that makes real sense of the universe.

Not that I'm an atheist or even agnostic. I don't know what I am. I believe in something because I keep getting proof that there's *something* out there; but don't ask me to tell you what it is. Maybe the great god of the universe is a maniac in four-point restraints in a celestial loony bin.

The stuff Acantha was selling was pushing me to the edges of credulity. It sounded like Dan Brown and Salvador Dali went out and got blue-blind paralytic drunk one night and cooked this up in the wee hours over Jager shots.

"Very well," she said, "I suppose it's unreasonable to expect you to believe everything about this. At least in the absence of firsthand experience. But I would at least ask that you keep an open mind."

"I can promise that much," I said, wondering if it was too early to put a healthy slug of bourbon in my next cup of coffee. Decided it wasn't. "Tell me the rest."

-6-

Mr. Priest
Town of Poliske
Chernobyl Nuclear Power Plant Zone of Alienation
Kiev Oblast, Ukraine
Six Years Ago

The tentacle was desiccated and had clearly been there for years. Time, the severe dryness of the air down there and the hungry teeth of radiation had stripped it of nearly everything except its vague shape.

"Can't be a tentacle," said Boris firmly, nudging it again with his foot.

"Why not?" asked Rink, still unwilling to draw closer.

"It has bones. Listen." He kicked it again and the dry rattle was clear even through the material of their suits. "What the fuck kind of tentacle has bones? Octopuses don't have bones. Squids neither."

"And what the hell would an octopus be doing down here?" asked Hiro.

"No," insisted Boris, "I said *not* an octopus. Too many bones and too...big."

The whole section of severed tentacle was at least thirty feet long.

"Male giant squids can get to be over forty feet long," said Keppler.

"It's not a fucking squid," yelled Boris. "Enough with squids and octopuses. This thing is something else."

"Some kind of snake?" ventured Hiro.

Boris gave him a pitying look. "You been all over the world," he said acidly. "You ever see a fucking snake looks like that?"

Rink touched her throat with her hands. "Where's the rest of it?"

"Dead," said Keppler. "A long time ago."

"Then it can't hurt us, can it?" declared Priest, his patience with all of them wearing thin.

"No...I mean this was cut off of something else. Something much larger. Where is the rest of the animal?"

"Dead somewhere, I expect," said Priest. "Look, all of you—I admit that this is strange, but whatever it is...it's past tense, yes? It can't hurt us anymore than velociraptor bones can stand up and bite a paleontologist. Have some dignity, for God's sake."

No one said a word. After a moment Priest nodded.

"Come on," he said, "help me open the door. We need to get inside. We're almost there." No one moved. Not even Hiro. They stood staring at the tentacle until Priest gave another gunshot clap of his hands. "*Now!*"

They flinched and then inched forward, even Rink, and with great reluctance they steeled themselves, took up positions on one side of the carcass, gripped the lip of the massive door, and pulled. And pulled.

"It's stuck," gasped Keppler. "The hinges are rusted shut."

"Then pull harder, yes?"

They pulled harder. Boris slung his rifle and stepped around to put his shoulder against the inside edge. He screwed up his face and gave a roar like a bear.

The door moved.

So did the tentacle. As the gap widened it dropped and rattled. Boris jumped back and brought his gun up.

"No!" yelled Priest. "Don't, you idiot—it's the door, it's just the door."

The Russian eyed the length of dead gray flesh. "*Der'mó,*" he grumbled, but he lowered the gun.

They tried again. It moved. One stubborn, backbreaking inch at a time. Then it seemed to reach a point of acceptance and swung freely the rest of the way. They stepped back, panting and sweating.

Priest gave Hiro a light push on the shoulder. "You first."

The urban explorer removed a couple of chemical glow-sticks, snapped and shook them, and threw them inside. Then, with Boris close behind, he stepped over the threshold. The others crowded behind him, with Rink bringing up the rear. However as soon as they were all inside, Hiro looked around, saw a heavy tool box and lugged it to the doorway, positioning it so that it would create an even sturdier block against them being trapped.

"Just in case," he said, but no one argued against the caution. Certainly not Priest. He wanted to be here, but did not care to linger forever.

Inside they found more of the old fashioned computers, though most of these were more elaborate and expensive models used for high-level research. There were hundreds of them, big and small, on desks or freestanding. And there were machines of other kinds, design types that Priest had only ever seen in old books. He felt like he was in a museum of computer paleontology. Keppler's thoughts clearly mirrored his own because she walked along with her fingers trailing over the dusty keyboards and murmured, "Dinosaurs."

After a few minutes, Hiro stopped and turned to Priest. "Not that I want to downplay how good I am, but man...you don't even need me for this. I'm used to ruins, but it looks like they built this place to withstand a frigging nuke. If it wasn't for the, y'know, radiation and all, this place would be safe as Fort Knox. Nothing sketchy at all. Not even a hole in the floor. So far all I've done is pick a damn lock. I'm kind of useless on this job."

"You know what they say, Hiro," said Priest with a shrug. "It's like a condom. Better to have it and not need it than need it and not have it."

"Great. I'm a rubber. That'll look terrific on my business card."

"Besides," added Priest, "once we're done here there are a few other places I want to visit, and some of them will offer challenges more appropriate to your skills, yes?"

"Sure, dude. Whatever. Long as the check clears."

"What are we looking for?" asked Keppler nervously. "This place is enormous."

"I know," said Priest, beginning to walk faster now, moving along one of the walkways between the computers, breaking into a run, "but we're almost there. It's got to be here. It has to be."

"Stop," snapped Boris, stepping forward to put himself between the team and something up ahead.

"What is it?" asked Rink, shrinking back.

Ahead, only half visible in the dusty gloom, were several humped shapes.

"Let me look first," said the soldier, but Priest stopped him.

"No, it's okay. I think I know what that is."

Without a word of explanation Priest hurried forward, with Boris racing along to stay ahead of him, weapon ready. The others followed and then slowed to a stop as the humped shapes resolved themselves into large medical gurneys upon which machines of various unknown function were attached, wires trailing.

Rink came up last and then uttered a sharp cry as soon as she saw what was on each bed. The others stood staring in horror. Even Boris gave a strangled cry in gutter Russian.

There were seven beds.

Each one was occupied by a person. Or what had once been a person. The bodies were withered, the moisture leeched from their leathery skin, their eyes turned to milky kernels of dried rot, their hair nothing more than wisps as thin as spider webs. Electrodes had been drilled into their heads and others were attached at the wrists and heart and a dozen other places. Old-fashioned glass IV bottles hung from poles, the saline long since evaporated. Each body was strapped to the bed, and each had heavy manacles locked around their ankles.

The presence of seven restrained corpses was not what frightened the team.

No. It was the condition of each of them that made them stand around in abject horror.

"My god," breathed Keppler. "What *happened* to them?"

Priest did not answer. Inside his suit his body ran with sweat and a palsy of nervous excitement made his fingers twitch spasmodically.

The bodies were each twisted into impossible posture, limbs either rigid or twisted into nightmare shapes, backs arched, mouths open in silent, eternal screams.

"Who are these people?" asked Keppler. She stood staring down at the ankle chains.

"Dreamers," said Priest.

"That's not funny," said Rink.

"It wasn't meant to be," he said. "They were part of a special scientific project."

"Dreamers?" asked Keppler. "What is that supposed to mean? And…what kind of program?"

"Have you ever heard of remote viewing?" he asked.

She shrugged. "It's some kind of ESP nonsense, isn't it?"

"It's a bit more than that," said Priest. "It's a complex field of psychic expansion."

"Oh for god's sake," began Keppler, but Priest stalled her with a sharp look.

"Do you want to hear this or not?"

Keppler looked momentarily flustered, then cleared her throat. "I do, actually. Sorry."

Priest nodded, then glanced around at the others. "Look, I know there's a lot of pseudoscience in pop culture, but not all of it is actually fake. There are groups within various governments that have deliberately muddied the waters by encouraging some of the more outrageous speakers in a campaign of obfuscation, essentially letting the crazy ones endanger the credibility of anyone seeking the truth. Because of that, the real truth and any true attempt at public disclosure is lost."

Keppler nodded but said nothing. The others merely waited.

"The hype and nonsense make people think that all of this is just...silly. But it's not. I know it's not."

"How do you know?" asked Hiro.

"I have been briefed by people in the know," said Priest, but did not explain further.

The truth was that Oscar Bell was working with a science group hidden within the murky black budget waters of the Department of Defense. Bell's genius son, Prospero, had been trying to build a dimensional gateway which he called a God Machine, but which had proved to be deeply flawed. Some of the side-effects of those design errors, however, turned out to have a variety of uses, particularly for the espionage community. One of them was to greatly enhance psychic abilities in select people. Bell leased the technology to the military so they could research and weaponize it. This research fell under the umbrella of the Gateway Project that even the president and congress did not know about.

For years, however, the research limped along, hitting roadblocks at every turn. The problem, it was discovered, rested with the main device Prospero had designed. He called it a 'God Machine.' Other equally brilliant and equally mad scientists had attempted similar devices over the years. Nicola Tesla called his version an Orpheus Gate. Only recently Prospero Bell informed his father that in order to regulate the power of the God Machine he needed a code that had been carefully hidden in the pages of several ancient texts.

How these ancient books could connect with a sophisticated scientific device was something even Oscar Bell had not been able to coax out of his son. Not in any reliable way. Bell's son tried to convince his father that those texts were filled with knowledge and secrets brought to Earth billions of years ago by alien races.

"My son is maybe the smartest person alive on this planet right now," Bell had once told Priest, "but he's a grade-A fucking whackjob. He thinks he's an alien from another dimension and he's building that goddamn machine to try and go home."

Mad or not, Bell was willing to spend many millions to have Priest locate those books. The Unlearnable Truths. And the shadowy administrators of Gateway were hunting for them, too. They wanted to close Bell out of the project loop and take the God Machine and all of its useful side-effects away from the industrialist. True to their nature, they were doing it on the sly. They thought Bell didn't know that Gateway agents were already in the field. Bell was very smart and very connected.

And he had Mr. Priest.

Priest considered sharing some of this with his team, but he did not want to let them in on everything. There were parts of this that Priest did not even share with Bell. This was bigger than Bell thought, and bigger than anyone at Gateway knew. Priest had not yet decided how he wanted to use all of what he had so far discovered, and all of what he intended to find.

"What does it matter to you?" he asked calmly. "Either you accept my word or you don't." When Hiro said nothing else, Priest continued. "First, you have to understand that the military has been experimenting with this for years. Decades. Since before World War II. The American military, the Chinese, the Brits and a few others. Maybe everyone's government, to one degree or another. Hitler's Thule Society was definitely looking into psychic phenomena. So were the Russians. Remember I told you that this place was built in the twenties? That's what I mean. This isn't anything new, but a lot of time, money and effort has gone in to keeping it off the public radar, or making what leaks out appear to be crazy bullshit."

They all nodded.

"The research really intensified during the Cold War. Advances in computer and satellite technology boosted that along. Actually some of those advances came about because problems needed to be solved relative to projects like this. The space race was tied to this, too, but that's another story. We'll get to that later, I promise." Priest touched the desiccated cheek of one of the dead dreamers. "This facility was originally built to investigate, develop and weaponize tactical psychic potential."

"Right," said Hiro, "but what the hell *is* remote viewing?"

"Remote viewing," said Priest, "is the attempt to project the consciousness to another place in order to observe things. The goal is to create a new level of espionage that does not require the actual physical presence of a person. Just the consciousness."

Hiro laughed. "You're shitting me."

"I'm not, actually," said Priest. "Not even a little. Imagine the potential. Being able to send your best spies across miles, past guards and walls and locked doors. No secret would ever be safe."

"God," said Rink.

"This line of research has had a lot of names over the years. The phrase 'remote viewing' was actually coined in the '70s by two physicists at Stanford—Russell Targ and Harold Puthoff—but everyone was working on it long before that. The Russians called it 'remote control,' because it was always their intention to do more than look."

"Wait," said Hiro, "if this is supposed to be a spy program, then why are these guys chained to their beds?"

"Ah," said Priest, "that's because the attempts to explore remote viewing had a few, um, unexpected side effects, and some of those were quite dangerous. Some of the test subjects experienced psychological damage. Some shut down and went into comas. A few died. Well, quite a few, really. My guess is that these people were 'volunteers' from a gulag."

"'Volunteers'?"

"Figure of speech, yes? If you were in a Soviet gulag and someone said volunteer for this or we shoot you, what would you do? Oh, don't look so shocked. Using prisoners for medical experiments happens everywhere, including in your own country. Don't you ever watch the History Channel?"

Hiro played his flashlight over the faces of the dead. "What the Christ happened to them? Did the Chernobyl radiation do this?"

"No," said Keppler. "I don't think so. There's no sign of lesions. I think they may have been dead before the accident."

Rink crossed herself. "They look so scared," she said in a tiny voice.

Priest said, "Have you ever noticed that people make the same faces when they're in ecstasy as they do when they're in pain?"

Everyone stared at him.

"What?" Priest asked, genuinely surprised that they missed his point.

"Enough of this bullshit," growled Boris. "Is this what we came all this way to find? A bunch of dead people?"

"No," said Priest. He looked past them and saw the edge of something peeking out from around a corner. He began walking toward it and then broke into a run.

The others hurried to catch up. "Priest! What is it? What are we looking for?" called Keppler.

They rounded the corner and everyone stopped on a dime. Stopped and stared.

"*That*," breathed Priest.

They stood before a massive arch that rose thirty feet above them, and was made from metal inset with hundreds of dials and meters. Heavy cables hung from sockets and snaked along the floor. Nearby, monstrous condensers and generators rested on steel skids. Inside the arch was a flat panel of featureless gray, but as Hiro played his flashlight beam over the rim of the arch the beams flashed with intense reflected light.

"What the hell is *that*?" asked Boris, pointing to a row of huge faceted crystals socketed into the metal skin of the arch framework.

They all approached with great caution and greater wonder.

"Jesus," breathed Keppler, touching one of the crystals, "that looks like a ruby."

"Can't be," said Boris, shaking his head. "It's too big. Has to be fifty karats."

"Fifty-six point one-one-eight," said Priest.

Every head snapped around in his direction.

"What did you say?" asked Keppler.

"Every stone is exactly the same size. Ruby, garnet, emerald, sapphire, diamond. Each one is fifty-six point one-one-eight karats."

Boris cursed in Russian and English. Hiro was panting. Rink looked totally dazed.

"That can't be true," insisted Keppler. "Do you know how much that would have cost?"

"To the ruble," said Priest, nodding. "This project went a long way toward helping to bankrupt the Soviet Union."

"But *why?*" breathed Keppler. "Why throw so much money away on decoration? It's madness."

"It's *science*," corrected Priest. "These stones are used to regulate very specific frequencies of power. They're part of the device's failsafe system. Without them this whole facility would have been in real trouble when they shut down the power at Chernobyl."

"Looks pretty troubled to me," muttered Keppler. "From what I can see they had to abandon this place in a hurry. And there's that tentacle."

"It's not a fucking tentacle," growled Boris, but everyone ignored him.

Priest smiled. "Believe me when I tell you that if any of those crystals had been missing or damaged while this gate was active, then there would have been a disaster here a great deal worse than Chernobyl."

Despite his comment, the team clustered around the stones. Priest could almost taste their hunger for the hundreds of millions of dollars worth of gems. Radiation notwithstanding, they could each get massively wealthy and, big as they were, those stones could be carried out in three backpacks. Like the ones on the backs of Boris, Keppler and Hiro.

"This…is…*incredible*," said Keppler. She sounded like she was about to hyperventilate.

"You think that's something?" Priest said, teasing them. "Then take a look at *this*." He unclipped a multi-tool from his belt and stepped up to the arch, flicked open a flat-bladed screwdriver and gouged a long line across a metal panel. The gray paint curled away to reveal a different color, one that burned a fierce yellow.

"Oh my *god*…" breathed Rink. "You were telling me the truth. I…I thought you were just exaggerating so I'd sleep with you. But this is all true."

The others bent close and stared at the exposed yellow metal, then they stepped back and let their gaze travel over the entire massive structure.

"No way," said Hiro.

Boris said, "No *fucking* way."

"Yes," said Priest. "Every last ounce of it. Seventy-three tons of gold. Six tons of platinum, eight point nine tons of silver. All of it absolutely pure except for the nonconductive gray paint."

"And all of it radioactive," said Keppler. "How can we—?"

"Whoa, whoa, guys," said Hiro, cutting her off. "Jesus Christ, look at this!"

He raised his flashlight and aimed at the center of the metal panel inside the arch.

"What are we supposed to be looking at?" growled Boris, nervous and angry.

"I don't—" began Keppler, then she gasped. "Wait—*what*?"

Rink was equally shocked. She reached up and took hold of Hiro's wrist and moved it so that the beam traveled across the surface of the panel.

It took Boris a moment longer, and then he saw it, too. "*Oy blyad!*" he gasped.

The flashlight beam was visible in the dusty air. It was a stark white line between the lens and the wall, but there was something wrong with how it struck that flat gray metal. Because it *did not*. It simply did not illuminate the surface, nor did it bounce and scatter the light. The flashlight's beam simply vanished into it, like a straw stuck into mud. The light passed through the flat gray and was simply…*gone*.

"That's impossible," whispered Keppler.

Impossible or not, it was happening and they all stared blankly at it.

"My god, indeed," murmured Priest, his heart beginning to hammer in his chest. "It's still operational…"

Keppler turned sharply to him. "What do you mean 'operational'? What is this thing? How could it absorb light like that? It's impossible. What the hell have we found?"

Priest began to answer but then he saw something else and it froze his body but tore a cry from his throat.

"*God in heaven!*"

They all whirled and once more Boris brought up his gun.

Forty feet away, half shrouded in darkness, stood a pedestal. Priest raised his flashlight and played the beam over it, revealing that the pedestal was carved from some dark wood and fashioned into the shape of a hideous monster with a squat and lumpish body, stubby batlike wings, arms and legs that were vaguely humanoid, and a hideous head whose mouth was formed by dozens of writhing tentacles. It crouched there, arms outstretched to form a cradle upon which a book had been placed.

Rink cringed back from the horrific carving, raising a hand to shield her eyes from even looking at it. "No..." she whispered, and then began reciting an old Catholic prayer from her childhood.

Keppler and Hiro exchanged a look and then turned to Priest. Boris still pointed his gun at the thing as if the wooden monstrosity would somehow spring to life and attack with claws and tentacles.

"It's really here," murmured Priest and he felt a little faint. Even though he had spent many years as a younger man working with a group dedicated to locating, destroying or hiding away books such as this one, he had never before been in the actual presence of one. He'd seen pages, photographs, and held vials of ashes from some that had been destroyed. But this one was intact, and it looked pristine. The edges of the pages glinting with gold paint, the ink dark and legible despite its incredible age. "*Livre d'Eibon*," he said. "*The Book of Eibon.* God above." He looked over his shoulder at the others for a moment. "You can't imagine what this book contains. The fools who worked here tried to steal the code to make the God Machine function properly, but they probably disregarded the rest as the ramblings of a madman." He turned once more to face the book and took a few tentative steps closer to it. "This is the only surviving translation of the original text written by the great sorcerer Eibon, chief priest of the god Zhothaqquah. In those pages is the whole story of his life. Every secret he uncovered, every celestial being he encountered on his journeys to Cykranosh, through the Vale of Pnath, the planet Shaggai, and elsewhere. All of the veneration rites of Zhothaqquah are here, all of the formulae for potions and spells. So much...so much..." An erotic shiver rippled through him. "Scholars—those who believe in this book's existence at all—think that only a fragment of it remains, but here is the entire book."

"You want us to believe that this is—what?—a book of magic spells and shit?" asked Hiro. "Dude, you're out of your mind."

Priest ignored him.

"What's that?" asked Keppler, pointing to the pedestal. "Is that supposed to be the god he worshipped?"

Priest shook his head. "No. Zhothaqquah is the offspring of the god Yeb, and in sacred artwork is represented as a short, squat, furry toad. Don't laugh," he warned sharply. "You mock the elder gods at your peril, yes?"

Keppler turned away, probably to hide a smile.

"No," said Priest, as he nodded toward the pedestal, "that is something else entirely. This is the son of Yeb's twin, Nug." He moved to stand within a few feet of the pedestal and spread his arms wide. "And isn't he magnificent?"

"It's ugly," whispered Rink. "It's evil."

Priest walked a few steps closer, then stopped. "Evil?" he mused, tasting the word. "No, my dear, it's older than that."

"How can it be older than evil?" demanded Boris.

"Because evil is a concept developed by man," said Priest, touching the wooden tentacles, "and this one here…well, he is much older than us."

"'He'?" asked Hiro. "Who? That monster? Who are you talking about?"

Priest turned and looked at his companions. He smiled at them and he could feel that the smile on his face was strange. Wrong, somehow, though he could not see it. The others recoiled from him. Rink crossed herself. Then Priest turned back to the book and the magnificent pedestal on which it rested. He dropped very slowly to his knees and spread his arms wide.

And he said, *"Ph'nglui mglw'nafh Cthulhu R'lyeh wgah'nagl fhtagn. Iä! Iä!"*

-7-

Sam Hunter
Philadelphia, Pennsylvania

She gave me a lot of it. Probably not as much as she knew, but enough to make my head spin, and that had nothing to do with the Jack Daniels in my coffee.

"Okay, so this is some Indiana Jones bullshit," I told her. "Not sure I see any doorway for me to walk through. I mean, I'm flattered that you called and all—"

"No you're not," said Acantha.

"No I'm not," I agreed. "But I don't operate out of the country. Hell, I don't like going much outside of the tri-state area."

"Ah," she said, "my mistake. The problem is definitely coming your way."

"How so?"

"Some events are aligning in an unfortunate way. Or, an opportune way if we can act swiftly and correctly."

"You have a weird definition of 'swiftly,'" I said. "We've been on the phone for an hour."

She laughed. "The clock hasn't started ticking quite yet. But when it does, then you'll have to move fast."

"Uh huh."

"The team put together by Mr. Priest has acquired an alarming number of those books. And a competing team has also taken possession of some of them."

"Wait...*what* competing team? Are you talking about the Brotherhood of the Lock?"

"No," she said, "I'm talking about Closers."

"Closers? Never heard of them. Who are they?"

"Oh, they are a very dangerous group, Mr. Hunter," she said. "They are very highly trained special operators working for secret groups so deeply hidden inside the U.S. government that even the president is unaware of them. They are well-trained and well-funded by black budget dollars."

"Oh, that's just swell."

"They also have access to technology in the form of weapons, equipment and body armor that is far beyond anything you've seen. The source of that technology is something that has caused serious problems for a friend of yours."

"I don't have a lot of friends."

"An ally, then. Someone whose work has many times overlapped with projects being undertaken by Limbus."

"Who are we talking about?"

"Captain Joe Ledger of the Department of Military Sciences."

"Oh," I said. "Him."

Ledger was a kind of super Boy Scout with a strong dash of absolute fucking psychopath. Like me, he was a former cop, but unlike me he now ran with one of those 'we're-so-secret-if-we-told-you-we'd-have-to-kill-you' groups. Very James Bond. Very Mission

Impossible. When I did the Limbus gig in Pine Deep, Pennsylvania with the North Korean werewolf super soldiers, he was working the same case from another angle.

And, let's pause for a moment to discuss how absolutely fucking surreal my life is. I just said that I worked with a super spy to take down North Korean mad scientists who were creating werewolf super soldiers...and I'm not exaggerating. And you wonder why I drink?

"Are you still there?" asked Acantha.

"Yeah," I said, "but wishing I wasn't. Am I going to have to work with Ledger again?"

"Would you have a problem with that?"

"Yeah. He's a dick who's basically a standup comic with a gun. I'm not captain of his fan club."

"He's a good man," she said.

"So is Will Ferrell, but I don't want to go hunting bad guys with him, either."

"Point taken. And it's not an issue, I assure you. Captain Ledger is currently in the hospital in San Diego."

"Oh. Why? What happened? He crack a joke at the wrong time and somebody knocked his pearly white teeth out?"

"He's dying," she said, and left it at that.

That hit me pretty hard. A lot harder than I expected. Ledger was a bit of a dick, but he was on the side of the angels.

"Sorry," I said.

"The matter before us," she said after a moment, "is coming to a head in your own backyard. A groups of Closers is arriving in Philadelphia tonight to obtain a book in the collection of the University of Pennsylvania's folklore department. The book is *The Cloister Manifesto*, and it is arguably the rarest and most dangerous of the Unlearnable Truths. Dr. Holland, the professor who is studying it, does not know what it is because the text is written in a unique form of coded Aramaic. That's also why the book went missing for so long; it's been in various private collections under a number of names that don't hint at what it is. A rare book collector in Budapest had it among a collection of indecipherable curios for the last forty-six years, and he referred to it merely as the 'Latin book.' After that it was in an estate auction catalog as 'lot 561-F.' It was purchased in bulk with other items deemed curious but of little apparent value."

She laughed again. "It's a bit like people passing around and bidding on a nuclear bomb and thinking it's a doorstop or paperweight."

"And Dr. Holland got it?"

"From a friend of a friend of a colleague. Given to him as a Christmas present because it appeared to be Latin and Holland is a noted scholar of ancient Latin folkloric texts."

"Jesus."

"In point of fact," she said.

"What?"

"*The Cloister Manifesto* is very much connected with Jesus of Nazareth. It is why the Brotherhood of the Lock have sought it more aggressively than any of the other Unlearnable Truths. It is why the Closers will stop at nothing to get it. And it is why we need you to obtain that book at all costs."

"What do you mean? Why's that book so goddamned important?"

"For two reasons," said Acantha. "The first is that it contains a series of complex rituals for invoking a being of incalculable dark magic who would delight in consuming our entire world. A being hinted at in many religions but given a name in the Book of Revelation."

"Shit...please don't tell me you're talking about the antichrist."

"Yes," she said quietly, and once more I could hear the fear in her voice. "*The Cloister Manifesto* contains the rituals for bringing the antichrist into our world."

My throat went dry and my heart was hammering. I shouldn't be listening to this shit let alone believing it, but each time I'd done something for Limbus the world got bigger, stranger, and more terrifying. I did not think Acantha was lying to me now.

"You said there were two reasons...what's the other?"

There was a sound on the line. Did she catch her breath, or sob?

"*The Cloister Manifesto* is written in the blood of the man crucified on Golgotha," she said. "It is written in the blood of Jesus Christ."

-8-

Hiro Tsukino
Sicán Cave System

Nazca Desert
Southern Peru
Four Years Ago

Hiro hadn't understood why Priest had required them all to wear such clumsy outfits. They were modified versions of the heavy rubber and canvas rigs worn by firefighters and included thick gloves, boots and helmets with clear plastic visors. Emergency oxygen bottles were clipped to their backs, though Priest said they probably wouldn't need them.

The Peruvian sun was blistering hot despite the deep cold of the previous night. Deserts were like that, willing to torture and kill with extremes of temperature. The walk from where they'd parked their vehicle to this forgotten weed-choked gulley was filled with dangers, too, as if the landscape and the atmosphere were accomplices in premeditated murder. Without equipment, Hiro did not believe he could last more than a day out here. If the weather and terrain didn't kill him, the scorpions, spiders, biting lizards and poisonous plants would. How in hell the Sicán people ever thrived here for over six hundred years was a mystery. Bunch of masochists was the best Hiro could determine.

Luckily Mr. Priest had left nothing to chance, though, and outfitted them—as always—in the most advanced gear. Over-preparing so that there was no risk of ever being caught off guard with a need and no solution. Hiro appreciated that even if he didn't like having to test the boundaries of those preparations this often. Since joining Priest's little team of oddballs the urban explorer had found himself in several extreme locations. And not extreme in a fun way. Not like snowboarding down a sheer mountain or base jumping off a skyscraper in Dubai. But no, Priest dragged the team to the ass-end of the world. Different ass-ends, mused Hiro, if the metaphor would stretch that far. This place was a classic. They couldn't bring the truck closer than three miles. There was a road, but an earthquake thirty years ago had ripped it apart. And since it went from nowhere to nowhere, no one had seen fit to fix it. The team had to climb over boulders that had been thrust up by the seismic forces, and twice Hiro had to rig lines so that they could shimmy across deep chasms. It took hours to go those few miles.

During one of their many necessary breaks, Hiro took Keppler aside.

"This is nuts," he said quietly.

The nuclear scientist took a moment before replying. "It's no crazier than any of the last three jobs."

"No," he said, "I don't mean that part...though I wish Priest had told us more than 'we have to fetch a book.'"

"That's mostly what we've *been* doing," she said. "Except for Poliske."

They shared a smile about that. Each of them had been allowed to pry some of the massive jewels out of the God Machine. Those jewels were being treated now to remove as much radiation as possible, using a technique developed by one of Keppler's many uncles. The uncle was in for a hefty cut, of course, but there was plenty to go around. Sadly, the jewels could not be sold in their current form even though they would be worth much more that way. But the Soviets had laser-cut ID tags into them and once the cutters in Antwerp got the booty they'd have to cut those sections out. Currently Priest's organization was overseeing that process and the stones—in whole or part—would not be formally released to the team members until the whole mission was done. It was a three-year commitment but the payday at the end had a mind-numbing number of zeroes at the end of it.

"You know what's bugging the crap out of me," Hiro told Keppler, "is the geology of this place. Rink showed me the geophysical history of this region and I was surprised to see how many earthquakes they've had around here."

"So what? Earthquakes happen. What's the problem? Are they predicting another one or something?"

"No, that's just it," he said. "There shouldn't be *any* earthquakes here at all. There are no fault lines running anywhere near here. Not in this part of Peru. I checked with a geologist chick I used to date, had her look into it. She said this whole area is kind of freaky."

"Freaky?"

"Geologically speaking. She said that according to the structure and location of the tectonic plates this is supposed to be a stable region, and yet there've been over thirty quakes here in the last hundred years. Different universities have sent people to study it and they came up empty. They've used ground penetrating radar and all. No one understands it."

As he spoke it became clear to Hiro that Keppler either wasn't really listening or didn't really care about what he was saying. Lately she'd become more distant and cold; not that she'd been warm from the jump. But since the last couple of trips with Priest, Keppler had stopped acting like a scientist and tended to drift along in the boss man's wake. Even Rink—who had become jumpier and more fearful each time they went out—had more evident life force, and was more present than Keppler. Hiro wondered if Keppler had reached a limit or crossed some kind of line, on one side of which was the rational— if greedy—scientist and on the other was a mind unable to accept the things they'd all seen.

Boris was already over on the dark side, as far as Hiro saw it. After Poliske and a short but weird trip to a four thousand year old Arawak bat cult shrine in Aruba, the gruff Russian soldier had started treating Priest like some kind of holy man. Or a god. Or something. Hiro didn't have it all worked out yet, but it was starting to scare the crap out of him. Keppler had been stable at first, but now she was slipping into the weird, too.

"Hey," Hiro said, trying to reach the scientist, "we don't know what we're walking into."

That somehow struck a spark in Keppler and her eyes suddenly came to sharper focus. "There are a lot of people out there who can climb ropes and pick locks, Hiro. We both know that and I'm pretty sure that Priest knows it. I'm sure he'd find a replacement if you don't have the stomach for it." She paused and the glare in her eyes crystallized into something else, an expression he could not identify. "Courage requires vision, Hiro. Courage requires faith."

Hiro said, "What's that supposed to—"

But Keppler turned away and walked over to stand near Priest. For a moment Hiro was afraid that she was going to tell their team-leader about the conversation, but she didn't. Instead she just stood there, behind and to one side of him. It was then that Hiro became consciously aware of something he'd half noticed before. Like Boris, Keppler often stood in Priest's shadow. Not metaphorically and completely, but partly, even if it was only their foot or hand. It was something Boris had started doing after the trip to Poliske, and Hiro had assumed it was simply a bodyguard standing close to the person he was protecting. But it was more than that and Hiro now knew it. Boris would shift slowly around so as to be actually touched by Priest's shadow. Not always, but often enough that it was clearly not an accident. And now Keppler was doing it, too. It was starting to freak Hiro out. He tried to remember whether Rink ever did that.

No, he determined. Just the opposite. The more of these kinds of things they did, the more Rink kept herself at a distance. Not even within arm's reach most of the time.

Keppler stood close to Priest now, and she stared at him with an unusual and somewhat adoring intensity.

Priest turned to look at Hiro. "Everything is good, yes?"

"Yeah," he said diffidently, "it's all good. I guess I'm just a little bit on edge. Maybe it's the heat."

Priest gave him a smile that would have looked at home on the Joker from the Batman comics. Very happy in bad ways.

Fucking freak, thought Hiro.

"Okay," called Priest, climbing down from the small boulder on which he'd been sitting, "let's go."

They went.

Hiro did not like it one little bit, though.

Within twenty minutes of their last rest stop they reached the mouth of a narrow cleft. Hiro peered at the rock and decided that this was an old split, not the result of recent seismic activity. He wondered if that was good or bad.

The mouth of the cleft was nearly hidden by a tangle of water-starved shrubs and the twisted stumps of trees that had suffered from lack of nutrients and had grown into improbable goblin shapes. Lizards scuttled through the brush as they approached. Priest reached out with a heavily gloved hand and pushed some of the shrubs aside, revealing a slope that swept down and around out of sight. It was steep but walkable, but the entire way was protected by a strange type of thorn tree whose needles were a dark and threatening red that glistened with some kind of sap.

"Everyone keep your suit on," ordered Priest, pointing to a sticky wetness on the ends of the thorns. "See that? Do not under any circumstances touch it. It's a natural neurotoxin that will drop you in your tracks within two steps, yes? It won't actually kill you, but it takes six days to leave the bloodstream. Get stuck and you will lie out here and die of exposure."

"Unless something comes along to eat you," said Boris.

"Yes," said Priest with a smile, "unless that happens."

He used his booted toe to push a smaller bush out of the way. Beyond it lay a tangle of bones. A goat or something similar. And there were more bones along the path. Not all of them were animal bones. When Rink saw a pair of human skulls she cried out and shrank back. She almost fled to Priest's side, but caught herself and merely stepped backward. Priest didn't appear to notice, but Hiro did.

She's afraid of him, he thought. *Even wearing a protective suit, she's afraid to touch him. Fuck me.*

"Let's go," ordered Priest. "Everyone be careful. I can't afford to lose anyone at this point. Though…to be clear, if you fall, none of us will carry you back to the vehicles."

It was long past the time when Hiro thought comments like that were a joke. He caught Rink's eyes and from the terror in them it was clear she believed Priest, too. It was all about the mission. Nothing else was a priority or even a concern.

It took another twenty minutes to navigate the hundred yards of the cleft, and by the time they reached the bottom their suits were covered in scratches and dripping with the deadly sap. Along the way they saw bones of every description. From the delicate bones of hummingbirds to the heavy bones of wild cattle.

"God!" cried Rink as she recoiled from a skull. Hiro hurried over and saw that it was a human skull. Small. A young woman or a child.

Priest joined them. "Yes. Expect more of that."

It was all he would say. A single, cold statement of fact. Ugly in its honesty. Prophetic in its accuracy, because the closer they got to the end of the cleft the more human bones they were forced to step over. Dozens of dead people, and some of the bones looked like they'd been there for ages. Many years at least, if not centuries.

"Who are these people?" asked Rink.

Priest shrugged. "Pilgrims, some of them. Explorers. Opportunists." He paused. "Sacrifices. What does it matter?"

"It matters in how they died," said Rink. "And why."

"No, my dear, it does not. It only matters that they died trying to get to where we're going. It matters that they were unsuccessful."

"Hasn't anyone gotten to where we're going?" asked Keppler.

"And gotten out? No," said Priest, "we will be the first."

"Then how do you know it's going to still be there?" asked Rink.

Priest did not answer until they reached the very bottom. He stopped in front of a thick tangle of the thorn bushes and stood considering it for nearly two full minutes. Deep in the cleft it was stiflingly hot and Hiro considered attaching his oxygen supply. But then Priest turned toward them and the look in his eyes stopped Hiro from doing anything. His breath caught in his throat and once more he backed up a step, afraid of the mad, weird lights that glittered in this man's eyes.

"I *know* it's here because I can *feel* it."

"Feel it?" echoed Rink. Even through the thickness of her suit Hiro could see her shiver. It was one of those deep shudders that begins in the marrow and ripples outward. It almost provoked a sympathetic shiver in Hiro, but he managed—just barely managed—to keep control.

"Feel what, exactly?" Hiro asked.

Instead of answering directly, Priest turned and touched the tips of the thorns. "Can't you hear it singing?"

No one answered.

Priest stepped back and signaled to Boris.

"Burn it," he snapped.

Immediately the soldier unlimbered his pack and removed from it a small tank with a flexible leather hose and metal nozzle with a pistol grip. He flipped a switch to ignite a spark, then turned a dial to start the flow of flammable liquid. Then he raised the sprayer and pulled the trigger. Bright yellow flame whooshed out and a fireball engulfed the thorn bushes that stood in a cluster against the wall. Boris kept feeding fuel, kept spraying the fire until the bushes were blazing wildly. He only stopped when Priest nodded. Then Boris simply tossed the flamethrower into the weeds.

They stood watching the thorn bushes burn. They were rugged but dry and they burned with great heat and immediacy. The weeds turned black and began to curl, and then pieces began falling away trailing sparks. A few smaller fires ignited from the embers.

Keppler made to stamp them out but Priest stopped her.

"No," he said.

"This whole gulley will catch fire."

Priest considered, then shrugged. "Let it. It'll be easier for us to get out of here."

As the big clump of bushes burned away, Hiro could see that there was a second cleft behind it, this one tall and vertical. It had been completely hidden by the deadly plants.

"Clear it," said Priest, and Boris began kicking savagely at the thorn bushes, and they crumpled into burning debris. He kept kicking until the opening was completely free. Then he peered inside, stepped back and nodded to Priest.

The opening was too narrow for anyone to walk in normally, so Priest turned sideways and shimmied into it. He vanished into the heart of the mountain. Boris followed close behind, and then Keppler. Rink lingered a moment, though, and cast a worried look back at Hiro.

"What's in there?" Hiro asked.

Rink merely shook her head and followed the others.

Hiro peered inside and saw only a window narrow passage. A few distant scuffling sounds echoed back to him, muffled by the helmet he wore. Then he looked at the gully behind him. All of the bushes were smoking now and a few fires had taken hold. Soon all of this brush would be fully involved. If he waited here, protected by the mouth of the cleft, it would burn up and burn out soon. And then he could leave. Without the thorns in the way, and with his own skills at moving over rough terrain, he knew he could make it all the way back to the truck before anyone knew he'd fled.

He almost did that.

Almost.

Almost.

Was that what Priest had asked. *Can't you hear it singing*?

"Goddamn it," Hiro said to himself.

Then he went inside.

The passage was very curved and twisted like a snake, and in spots Hiro had to suck it in to squeeze through. He was amazed that the larger and bulkier Boris had managed it at all. He clicked on the helmet light and saw fresh scrapes on the stone, proof that the Russian soldier had not had an easy time of it.

Within a dozen yards, though, the passage widened and soon he was able to walk normally. At this point the walls changed from the simple roughness of rock that had been split open in the distant geologic past to something different. He paused, training his light on irregularities in the wall and saw that they were carvings. At first he had the irrational thought that they were Egyptian pictograms, but as he bent closer to inspect them he realized that they were not. These were strange markings, unlike anything he'd seen. Animals of many different kinds, strange buildings, exotic trees, and creatures clearly born in myth or madness. Tiny human figures knelt in humility or lay upon sacrificial altars. Some, dressed in odd garments, stood like priests, arms raised, daggers in their hands, heads thrown back in exultation. But what disturbed Hiro most was the representation of the gods these people seemed to be worshipping. He'd seen pictures of the local gods but these did not look like any of those. No, the gods of the people who had painstakingly chiseled these carvings untold years ago seemed better fitted to people who lived by remote seas or on isolated islands. The gods were massive and bulbous, with many trailing, twisting tentacles. Huge black eyes seemed to burn with intensity, even from the cold representation in the old rock.

They gathered around the pedestal and stared at the book.

Even closed and covered with a glass dome it looked wrong.

That's the word that came into Hiro's head. *Wrong.*

The book was as thick as one of the old illuminated Bibles. Hundreds, perhaps thousands of pages; the edges painted with gold. The cover was some kind of leather that was pale and wrinkled, and it looked uncomfortably like old skin. Human skin. Hiro's grandmother had skin like that in the months before she died of cancer. A jaundiced tinge and dark lines that almost looked like collapsed veins.

It was ugly and Hiro wanted no part of it. He stood a deliberate step back from it, glancing around at the others, seeing how the book impacted each of them. Keppler was confused, her precise scientific mind no doubt wrestling with the odd and intense emotions she must be feeling. Rink looked small and frightened, and maybe a little sick. Disgusted or nauseous with fear. Boris, on the other hand, tried to keep his soldier's stoicism in place, but his lips were wet and he was sweating badly. Priest was like a god to him and this was something the twisted scientist craved.

The words that sprang to Hiro's mind when he looked at Priest were all variations of the same thing. Hunger. Deep desire. An almost carnal lust to possess this book. There were weird lights in Priest's eyes and even his skin glowed with a vitality that seemed to restore some of the youth the man had lost since this series of adventures had begun. In that moment, as Priest stood there with his hands resting on the glass dome, he was young again. Youthful in a way that Hiro found deeply disturbing. It was how he imagined the *jikininki*, the insatiable Hungry Ghost of Japanese folklore, to look at the moment it feasted. And just as the *jikininki* invariably became ravenous within seconds of finishing its grisly feast, Hiro knew that even now, even at the moment of possessing something that fed one of Priest's deepest needs, the scientist would become hungry again for the next item on his list. And the next, and the next.

"Priest," said Rink in a hushed and frightened voice, "let's get it and get out of here. This place is—"

Priest wheeled on her and hissed her to silence. Actually hissed like a snake, and Hiro thought for a moment the man was going to strike her. Hiro pulled Rink backward out of reach.

"She's right," said Keppler. "We need to go."

The pedestal was in the middle of a vast chamber nearly half a mile beneath the ground. All around them were massive chunks of rock that had fallen from the ceiling. Once, many years ago, there had been more than fifty titanic granite pillars holding up the shadowy ceiling. Now more than thirty of them lay in heaps beneath piles of limestone that had fallen from the ceiling when the columns fell. Hiro had studied the geological reports of this region and was alarmed at the number of earthquakes despite the paucity of fault lines. This whole area was supposed to be stable and yet it had trembled over and over again.

It's the book, whispered a voice from the shadows of his mind. *The earth itself can't abide its presence.*

The thought was absurd. Dramatic and foolish. And yet Hiro knew that it was the truth. Impossible, but true.

He looked around at the destruction and saw that nothing had fallen inside the glow from the pedestal. Not a stone, not a flake of dust. The glass dome was as clean as if it had been newly polished.

Get out of here, whispered the voice. *Run now. Get away while you can. Go…go now.*

Hiro felt himself edge backward. One step, two. A third.

But then he stopped, caught between his fears and the promises he'd made to Priest. And his need for the money. Until his contract was completed the bulk of the money would not be released.

It is a horrible thing to know about oneself that in the end it is greed that matters more than conscience, faith, self-respect, self-preservation or even hope.

Fewer realizations stab as deep.

"Help me," said Priest as he approached the book.

Every single one of them followed.

-9-

Sam Hunter
Philadelphia, Pennsylvania

How do you even respond to what Acantha just told me?

I mean, seriously?

An hour ago I was wondering which credit card company I was going to have stiff in order to write a check to keep my office lights on. I was worrying about whether I needed to start buying pants a size larger because I like meatball subs more that I like doing crunches and sit-ups. I was worrying about calling back the woman I met at the diner the other night because I couldn't afford to take her on a real date.

Now I had to worry about stopping the end of the world. Seriously. End of the fucking world. The end times. The apocalypse. Whatever else they call it. Dropping the curtain. A strange woman from a sketchy organization needed me to go up against an order of religious maniacs and shadow government special operators to fetch a book written in the blood of Jesus.

Hey, it's not like I'm any kind of holy-roller. I grew up in the Twin Cities as part of a family that sometimes went to church on Christmas, almost never on Easter, and rarely thought about it much the rest of the year. Not atheists, not even sure we're agnostics. Just indifferent.

And now this.

I lowered the phone and started to cry.

Couldn't help it. Call me a girly man, call me a sissy. Whatever. But tell me how you'd react to that.

Go on. Tell me.

-10-

Hiro Tsukino
Tristan da Cunha
1750 Miles from South Africa
South Atlantic Ocean
Three Years Ago

It looked like a scene from hell.

Or, to Hiro's eyes, something from one of the big budget summer blockbusters. In either case it didn't look entirely real.

The island was burning.

A massive column of smoke corkscrewed up into the sky and everything on the windward side of the island was coated with hot gray ash. The team was upwind, safe for the moment unless the winds veered. The lack of any ash at all on this section of beach was only a small comfort. Red veins of lava cut crooked channels down the hill. The last aftershocks were hours past now, but none of the members of Mr. Priest's party believed that they were truly safe. Not even their leader, who Hiro had come to believe was as mad as the moon.

What amazed the urban explorer was the timing. They'd come here by boat and Priest had ordered the captain to drop anchor twenty miles offshore and wait. Eleven hours later the dormant volcano erupted and blew Queen Mary's Peak a thousand meters into the sky. It was only the second eruption in recorded history, and the first since 1961.

"How did you know?" demanded Keppler as their ship rocked in the churning sea.

Priest's only answer was a manic grin.

The explosion was abrupt and intense, but it was of strangely short duration. Even though smoke continued to rise, the flow of lava was not nearly as intense as Hiro thought it should be.

"They will be coming," Boris said. "The British will send ships and planes."

"Of course they will," agreed Priest, "but not in time."

The mission timetable was the only part of this that Hiro understood. Even in a mechanized age such as this, it would take time to get boots on the ground here. Tristan da Cunha and the four smaller islands of this archipelago were fifteen hundred miles from the continents of Africa and South America. It was one of the most remote inhabited places on earth. Help would come, aid and rescue and surveillance would all happen, but not in time. Not according to the schedule Priest had given them.

"Nine hours," he said. "We have a window of nine hours before anyone of real authority arrives here. We need to be done and gone before that."

"What about flyovers and satellite imaging?" asked Rink.

"I don't care about any of that. If they take our pictures be sure to give them a pretty smile."

Their ship, *The Nautilus*, was an ultra-modern dual-purpose craft whose hull was coated with the same radar deflecting materials as a stealth fighter. It was fast, with both diesel-electric and hydroplane engines, and it could close up and submerge to a depth of one hundred feet. The vessel was one of a new class of smuggler boats financed by billionaire drug lords. Hiro had no idea how Priest acquired it, but the damn thing could outrun anything except aircraft and in a pinch it could simply vanish into the ocean while the eyes of the world were still goggling at the inexplicable volcano.

Now they were on the island. The ship's crew—a collection of South African mercenaries who were probably a very short step away from being actual pirates—offloaded their gear. Five heavy-duty all-terrain vehicles stood on their fat, low-pressure tires. Gassed and ready.

While Priest was busy checking his instruments, Hiro Tsukino took Rink by the arm and pulled her gently into the shadows of a boulder. Hiro nodded to the tall man who kept taking them from one impossible place to another.

"What's going on with him?" Hiro asked, keeping his voice down. "He's getting freakier by the day."

She licked her lips. "He's always been a little, um…"

"A little what? Crazy? Bugfuck nuts?"

"I was going to say 'intense.'"

"Really? Intense? That's the best word for it?"

Rink looked away. He knew she was as worried as he was.

"Has he ever told you what his end game is? I mean…why are we doing this shit?"

"All I know," she said, "is that someone is paying him a lot of money to collect these books. Or to prove for certain that those that are believed to have been destroyed are actually gone for good. He has to know one way or another. That's the job."

"Right, but why?"

She shook her head.

"C'mon, Rink," insisted Hiro, "it's our asses on the line here, too. We're out in the middle of nowhere, which means we have to trust one another. Right now Boris and Keppler aren't high on my list of people I give much of a shit about. Aside from me you're the only one left who hasn't become a zombie. We have to stick together."

But Rink shook her head. "Priest knows what he's doing."

Hiro couldn't let it go, however. He shifted around to stand in front of her. "Maybe he does. Maybe he's the great genius of our age, but I need to know if I can trust his judgment. And I need to know what the fuck we're doing. What's our plan? What's our goal?"

"We're here to get the *Unaussprechlichen Kulten.* You know that."

"Okay, sure, fine...but do you know what the fucking *Unaussprechlichen Kulten* is or why Priest was hired to find it? 'Cause I sure as hell don't."

"Priest knows and that's all that matters."

"C'mon, Rink, don't jerk me off. Getting that device is another step in a process that he hasn't explained. He wants us to do this, and then he hinted that there were like a dozen other places we had to go, all of them remote, each of them every bit as dangerous as Poliske and Nazca. I know the papers all say that I'm an adrenaline junkie, and maybe that's true, but it's not as true as it used to be. I'm greedy, sure, but what good is making boatloads of cash if I'm dead? Or in jail somewhere."

"You can always opt out," said Rink. "No one's forcing you."

"Whoa, what the hell, Rink, what's with you? Why are you being like this? You know what I'm asking."

"You want to know what's going on, Hiro?" said a voice behind him. Hiro whirled to see Priest standing right there, with Keppler and Boris flanking him. "Why not ask me?"

Hiro licked his lips. Boris had his rifle slung in front of his chest, one hand resting on it. The Russian soldier had become devoted to Priest since Poliske, and Hiro wondered if the man thought that their patron was God almighty. Or something approximating that.

"Okay, fine," Hiro said, taking a shot at it, "what are we doing on this island? What's the *Unaussprechlichen Kulten*? What does it do or what's it good for? We're exactly in the middle of nowhere and you haven't told me what to expect."

Priest widened his eyes and lowered his voice. "Expect the unexpected."

Hiro gave that a beat, then said, "You do realize that not only is that a bullshit answer, it's literally impossible?"

Priest laughed then shrugged. "It was worth a try."

"I'm serious, man…"

"I know, I know." Priest nodded. "Okay, the *Unaussprechlichen Kulten* is one of the rarest books in the world. It was written by the philosopher and alchemist Friedrich Wilhelm von Junzt, and the first printed edition of it appeared in Düsseldorf in 1839. An English translation surfaced in 1845, but it was a deeply flawed translation. Some scholars argue that even Junzt's version is actually a translation of a much older work whose authorship is unknown. In either case, the original version is bound in heavy leather and fastened with iron clasps. There are also holy words and phrases carved into the covers by priests who sought to…shall we say 'contain' its secrets?" He grinned like a cat. "The Brotherhood of the Lock have managed to hunt down nearly all copies of it. Those copies were burned. However my sources tell me that the original is here on this island."

"Why?" asked Rink. "This is a weather research station. Why would they want an old book like that?"

Priest laughed. "No one on this island is studying the weather, my dear. This station is not unlike the base we found in Poliske. The British have been working on their own Orpheus Gate, but unlike the Soviets, they were smart enough not to conduct that research on their own soil. If something happened to this base, then the government could write it off and no one in the world would care. Or notice. After all, did any of you even know of this island before I told you about it? No? Of course not. That is the nature of discretion."

"You knew, though," said Hiro.

"It is my business to know these things," said Priest, still smiling.

"What's so important about the book?" asked Rink.

"Importance is such a relative thing, wouldn't you say?" He shrugged, though, and added, "The book contains highly detailed information about the rituals and beliefs of the cult of Ghatanothoa."

"Never heard of him," said Hiro.

"You wouldn't have," said Priest dryly. "The book also includes many important spells and useful invocations, and it is believed to hold clues necessary to locate items such as the Black Stone, the Smoke of Bisiall, the Mathematics of the Worm, and the location of the Temple of the Toad."

Hiro stared at him. "Are you just making shit up now?"

Priest laughed. "Hardly."

"This is nuts."

"I'm not asking you to believe in it, Hiro. All that I require is that you do what you are being paid to do. We're here to retrieve an artifact before British agents can arrive to take possession of it." He nodded toward the volcano. "And before that thing makes this whole trip an exercise in futility."

"How did you know about that before we even got here?" asked Hiro. "And don't tell me that you had insider information. If geologists knew it was about to blow then the Brits would have evacuated this base."

"True enough," said Priest, "but I'm afraid I prefer to keep the source of my information confidential per my agreement with my employer. What I can tell you is that it is directly related to a bungled attempt to open an Orpheus Gate. Our job is to get in, find the book and get out."

"Wait," insisted Hiro, "what *kind* of accident? Another meltdown? I need to know what we're walking into."

Keppler spoke up for the first time. "There's been no spike in radiation and the radiation here on the island is well within, even below, normal background levels."

Priest nodded. "Don't worry, Hiro, this is not a nuclear situation. The Soviets were the only group crazy enough to put their base near a reactor. The competing teams have learned from that error, yes?"

"Yeah, okay," conceded Hiro, "but we're still walking into an accident site with no idea what to expect?"

"We are," said Priest. "Should be exciting."

Before Hiro could reply to that Boris held up a hand. "Wait…" He touched the earbud he wore and listened, then looked at Priest.

"There's a ship inbound. British navy. They must have had one close. It'll be here in six hours."

Priest cursed and stared off toward the rocky shore as if he could see the craft.

"What kind of ship?" asked Rink. "Can they launch a helicopter?"

Boris spoke in rapid Russian to the captain of the *Nautilus*. Then he looked up. "No aircraft. They'll probably send a Zodiac. Figure six hours to get here, then fifteen minutes to put boots on the ground."

"Is that enough time?" asked Rink, touching Priest's arm with her fingertips.

"If we hurry," said Priest, and true to that he wheeled and set off toward the line of four-wheel ATVs that had been floated in by their ship's crew. Like most of the equipment for this run, Hiro knew that the ATVs would be abandoned. And like the other machines, weapons, and supplies, there were no identification numbers of any kind. Nothing could be traced, and certainly not back to the United States. Every single item had been purchased from foreign markets or specially manufactured for this trip. That was how Priest did everything, spending top dollar to be essentially invisible. That always impressed Hiro, but at the same time it added to the density of the secret walls Priest built around himself. And Hiro hated being on the outside of those walls. Absolutely hated it.

Now, though, even the time to complete their conversation about this mission had suddenly evaporated. Priest's original projection was a window of nine or ten hours.

Hiro traded a quick look with Keppler, who shrugged, snatched up her pack and ran to catch up. Hiro was the last one off the beach, but in his gut the worm of doubt was turning. Was this going to be another Poliske? Was the structure that upheld the world as he understood it going to lose another strut? If so, how soon would it fall and how hard would it land on him?

Thinking bleak and frightened thoughts, he ran to his ATV. Soon the whole team was roaring away from the frigid waters that lapped onto the brown and troubled sands.

-11-

Sam Hunter
Philadelphia, Pennsylvania

"Mr. Hunter...?"

I heard her voice rising from the cell phone that lay on my desk. I dug a tissue out of my pocket and wiped my eyes and blew my nose. My heart actually hurt. It felt like a big bruise inside my chest.

"Mr. Hunter," called Acantha, "are you still there?"

I picked up the phone. "No," I said. "I'm not sure I am."

"I'm sorry," she said, and I think she meant it.

"Tell me something, lady," I growled. "Why call me in on this? Even if Joe Ledger is circling the drain can't you call the people he works for? I got the impression they were the A-Team for this kind of shit. You can't put all this on someone like me."

"The Department of Military Sciences has been compromised," she said. "As have many of the groups who would normally handle something like this. And the few special projects groups we might otherwise call, such as Arklight, are dealing with matters of nearly equal importance."

"Equal to this? How the fuck can something be as bad as the frigging antichrist?"

"Oh, Mr. Hunter," she said softly, "you have no idea how truly large and frightening the world is."

"I beg to differ. I think I *do* know—"

"No," she said firmly, "you do not. And I hope you never find out."

"Well, let's be straight here, toots, every time you assholes call me it ups both my booze and therapy bills by an order of magnitude."

"Would you rather we crossed you off the list of people we trust?"

I wanted to throw the phone across the room. "Bite me."

There were a few long moments of silence on the line. "This is how it's going down," she said. "Maybe it's one of those completely random examples of arbitrary synchronicity or maybe it's fate—or whatever you personally choose to call it—but three separate teams are converging on Philadelphia right now. All three want to take possession of the *Manifesto* for different reasons."

"Three? Shit on toast, lady. The Brotherhood, the Closers and who else?"

"The third team is not composed of hostiles," she said quickly. "They are, in fact, on the run from the other two parties."

"Why?"

"They've managed to obtain one of the Unlearnable Truths and are trying to get it to Mr. Church, the man Joe Ledger works for. That process is complicated because, as I said, his organization has been compromised. Although Mr. Church is very much one of the good guys, he is dealing with deeply serious matters and therefore is unable to help."

"Who are these other players?" I asked.

"There are two of them," said Acantha. "A young man named Harry Bolt and a woman who is currently using the code name of Violin."

"Never heard of them."

"You wouldn't have. Mr. Bolt works for the CIA, though I'm afraid he is not the strongest player on their team."

"Meaning?"

She sighed. "Meaning, he's probably the most inept spy I've ever even heard of. He is also, however, lucky, which is why he's still alive. Part of that luck was encountering Violin during a botched mission in Europe. The Brotherhood wiped out Bolt's team, but Violin saved his life by eliminating the opposition."

"So, she's a fighter?"

"She is that and more. Violin is one of the most dangerous women you will ever meet unless you have the great misfortune to meet her mother," said Acantha, though again she did not elaborate. "Shortly after they escaped with the book, they were ambushed by a team of Closers. They managed to slip past them, though it was a messy affair, and now they are on the run. They have been on the run, in fact, for weeks. We believe Violin is trying to get Mr. Bolt and the book to Mr. Church."

"Who is running a compromised agency," I said.

"Yes."

"Well, fuck."

"Yes," she agreed.

"And this is a *different* book than the one at the U of P?"

"Yes. The book Violin and Mr. Bolt have in their possession is *De Vermis Mysteriis.*"

I tried to translate it. "Mysteries of Vermicelli...?"

"Mysteries of the Worm," she corrected.

"Oh. Right." I frowned.

"And that," she said, "is the second thing I need you to do."

"What is?"

"First you need to secure the *Manifesto*," said Acantha, "and then you need to steal the *De Vermis Mysteriis* from Violin and Harry Bolt."

"I—"

"Without them knowing you've taken it. That is of the utmost importance."

"How the hell am I supposed to do that?"

"Answer your door," she said.

"There's nobody at my—"

Somebody knocked on the door. I shot out of my chair and hurried across my office. My office is about the size of a phone booth, so it didn't take a lot of hurrying. I whipped the door open and nearly gave a FedEx guy a coronary. No, I hadn't shape-shifted but I had a kind of *look*, I guess. He yeeped. Seriously. That's the sound that came out of his mouth.

He had a big box on a hand-truck and a thick envelope tucked under his arm. I glared at him, snatched the electronic pad from his fingers, scrawled some approximation of my name, and jerked the envelope from him.

"Beat it," I said.

He beat it.

I took the box and the envelope inside and put them on my desk, extended one fingernail and exerted some lupine mojo to make it grow into a nice sharp point, and then cut open the box. Inside was a book. A massive old book. It was big, two feet long and eighteen inches wide and at least seven inches thick. It was securely sealed by six metal bands running laterally and two more going up and over. Each one was fastened with a small but sturdy padlock. The bands were covered with etchings and engravings of monsters with talons and teeth, prancing goats with too many heads, writhing squids, demon faces with hundreds of eyes, shapeless mounds with too many mouths and worms for hair.

I didn't dare touch it.

I heard Acantha calling my name and put the phone to my ear. "What the fuck?" I said.

"That," she told me, "is an exact replica of the *De Vermis Mysteriis.* It's safe to handle. We need you to substitute this for the one that Mr. Bolt and Violin are carrying with them. They will be going to the University of Pennsylvania because Violin will want to obtain the *Manifesto,* as well. She has only recently received intelligence that it is there. This is very important, Mr. Hunter, because Violin is taking an appalling risk to secure the *Manifesto* while trying to evade her pursuers. The fact that she is doing so is significant. She is risking much, because it's likely she will be a key player in events unfolding on the West Coast."

"And you know this how? Ouija board?"

She gave me a small, hard laugh. "Glib as it will sound, Mr. Hunter, it's fair to say that we at Limbus 'have our sources.'"

"Cute."

"Not really," she said with a sigh. "Knowledge of this kind does not make for a quiet or happy life."

I didn't know what to say to that so instead asked, "What makes you think Violin will bring the Worm book with her? Wouldn't she squirrel it away somewhere to keep it safe while she makes a run at the University?"

"Violin will never let that book out of her sight."

"And you want me to steal it from her and this Harry Bolt kid?"

"Yes," said Acantha, "and it is imperative that they do not know you've swapped them out."

"And this Violin chick is one of the most dangerous women on Earth?"

"One of the most dangerous people, male or female, yes."

"And there are two other teams converging at the same place and probably the same time?"

"Yes."

"One is an ancient order of killer monks?"

"Yes."

"And the other is a group of government killers with high-tech weapons?"

"Yes."

"And if I fuck this all up the world ends?"

"Yes."

I wanted so badly to bang my head on the hard top of my desk. Seemed like the best possible response to all this.

Acantha said, "Open the envelope."

I did. Inside were three items. The first was a ring of keys with an attached keycard for the University of Pennsylvania Museum. The second was a set of those little white cardboard things they give you at perfume stores so you can take scent samples home. I sniffed them. Nothing was Ralph Lauren or Chanel. Each of these carried a human scent. Acantha and her bosses at Limbus knew me a little too well. The third thing in the envelope was actually four things. Each identical. Crisp, clean bills wrapped in mustard colored paper bands. One hundred bills in each bundle. It wasn't the agreed twenty thousand dollars.

These were four bundles of one hundred dollars bills. New, but nonsequential.

Forty thousand dollars.

I wasn't sure I was breathing.

"Although we believe you would take this case entirely on its own merits," Acantha said quietly, "we feel that tangible incentives are always useful."

-12-

Hiro Tsukino
Tristan da Cunha
1750 Miles from South Africa
South Atlantic Ocean
Three Years Ago

Hiro dangled on a rope seventy meters down into a dark hole.

He still had plenty of line, but his light did not reach all the way to the bottom. The climbing harness he wore was one he'd brought with him from Tokyo. Secure, time-tested and familiar. Priest had recommended bringing one thousand meters of rope, which was a lot for what Hiro had understood was a climb into a building that was thirty-eight feet high and which had only one level of basement.

Like most of his assumptions whenever it came to an excursion with Priest, Hiro had been wrong in almost every way. Or, perhaps it was that there was no way to adequately predict the kinds of things they encountered.

The laboratory here on Tristan da Cunha was a small two-story affair built onto a rocky shelf that geologists had assured the builders was the most stable point on the island. Still close enough to the slumbering volcano to use geothermal energy to power the labs and equipment. Priest told them that the geologists had deemed the volcano sufficiently dormant to risk building a lab.

Hiro hoped those geologists had been here when the mountain blew. It would be nice to know they all got roasted.

The entire landscape was shattered. Roads were twisted out of shape, the government building and the fishing factory had been smashed to sticks, a cell-phone tower was bent in half and all of its equipment crushed, vehicles had been hurled onto improbable perches on the ruined slopes. On the flat plain between mountain and water was a garbage heap that had been the small cluster of red-roofed buildings that comprised the town. Now that tiny town with the grand name of the Tristan Settlement of Edinburgh of the Seven Seas was a smoking ruin half erased by lava. Calshot Harbor, which had been spared during the '61 eruption, had been covered by lava twelve feet thick, and the molten rock had oozed out into the water to create steaming islands. Charred stumps of boats littered the shore among thousands of dead rockhopper penguins and Atlantic petrels. A few bloated dolphin corpses bobbed in the foam.

Priest had skirted the destroyed town, not wanting to be caught up in any refugee confusions with the clock ticking like this, but he needn't have worried. If anyone had survived the disaster, they were not in sight.

According to the data Priest had provided there were supposed to be three hundred people on this island, not counting the twenty-six at the laboratory.

So, where were they?

Why had no one come to meet them when they'd landed on the beach? Survivors of a disaster usually fell upon potential rescuers and wept. Hiro had seen it firsthand. At very least someone would be left, someone would be signaling for help.

But there was no one.

It was the same at the lab, which was on the windward side on that supposedly unshakable shelf. Huge fissures cleaved the ground and one had cracked the laboratory open like a melon, collapsing the structure into two mounds of jagged debris. This crack ran deep and split the earth itself to a surprising depth.

It was hot as hell in that chasm, but even so it wasn't as hot as Hiro had expected.

This island had damn near torn itself to pieces, and yet the thermometer clipped to his rig said that it was only one hundred and eleven Fahrenheit.

Why?

How?

Where had the heat and lava gone?

He released some pressure on the figure-eight descender to drop a little faster. The chasm was deeply fractured and it revealed geological marvels that continued to astound and confuse him. The rock here should have been predominantly basalt from ancient lava flows separated by thin pyroclastic layers, and though he saw ample evidence of that, he also saw huge chunks of shattered crystal, like the massive selenite spears he'd climbed among in the Giant Crystal Cave in Naica, Mexico. Hiro was no scientist but he'd learned enough about geology to recognize when things were wrong. Crystals of this kind didn't form in active volcanoes. As far as he knew this kind of gypsum was more often found in meteor impact craters, like the ones on Devon Island in Canada. This island simply wasn't built to create crystal spears that had to have been three hundred feet long before the earthquake cracked them apart like rock candy.

Even this was not the greatest mystery Hiro contemplated as he went down, down, down.

Built into these walls, cut into the rock, was a man-made tube of concrete and steel. The laboratory had been a front for something bigger and stranger. This had to have taken months of work and millions of English pounds. There were power cables as thick as telephone poles running down into the darkness and at first Hiro thought that they were there to handle the load of geothermic heat converted to electricity, but again he noted the lack of intense heat. There was even a downdraft that pulled cooler air from above into the bottomless black, and that made no sense at all. Heat rises. So what, then, was happening here?

Machinery of exotic design had been built into slots in the walls, but now most of it was blackened, the guts torn open to spill broken wires.

"What are you seeing?"

The voice in his earbud was so sharp and clear that Hiro jerked as if Priest was somehow right behind him. He stopped his rate of descent.

"It's dark below," he said.

"Can you see the bottom?" asked Priest.

"No. Wait, let me drop some glow-sticks." Hiro removed two from a pouch on his thigh, snapped and shook them and watched as the green bars fell down into the chasm.

They fell for a long time.

Far too long.

He never saw them land. The green lights fell and fell, and then they were gone. Just like that.

"What the fuck?" he gasped and it came out almost as a whimper.

"What is it?"

"They're...gone. I mean, they're just gone."

There was a pause at the other end, then Priest said, "Shit."

"Shit? What do you mean 'shit'? What the fuck's happening?"

Priest said, "I think it's still open."

"*What's* still open? Christ, don't leave me hanging," he yelled, aware that it was a joke but not a funny one.

Another pause, longer this time. "Can you see the stairway?"

Hiro had to bite back an obscenity. Priest was never straight with him. Even in moments like this. But Hiro took a breath to calm himself—an action that had far less success than he would have liked—and turned slowly on his rope, aiming his powerful flashlight downward. Although the building above him had split apart and this shaft had cracked wider, the destruction was less severe the deeper he went. It was like a plant—the flowering destruction spread wide at the top but left the stem more or less intact. Another forty feet below him was a section that was hardly damaged at all, and yes, there was a steel platform bolted to the curved wall, and a set of metal stars that zigzagged down into blackness.

"I see it," he said.

"Can you get to it?" asked Priest.

Hiro wanted to tell him no. As much as he loved exploring ruins, there were too many things about this trip that did not make sense. There were too many variables and he was in no way sure that he could deal with new problems. Not with an active volcano and a completely unknown destination.

But he found himself answering that he could. "It's right below me."

"Does it look solid?"

Hiro lowered himself to a point just above the platform so he could study the wall. There were a few cracks down here, but none of them radiated out from the plates bolted to the walls. He swung carefully over and reached out with one hand to grasp the rail. With his other hand firm on the descender, he shook the rail. It did not budge. No dust fell from the bolt holes.

"I think it's secure."

"That's great," said Priest, sounding hugely relieved. "Get onto the platform. If the stairs are still safe, then go down one level. There's a door there with a keypad. I'll dictate the sequence."

"How do you—?" began Hiro, then stopped himself. He didn't need to know how Priest had obtained this information. He was clearly being bankrolled by someone with very deep pockets and the right connections. Money and power were the only things needed to get virtually anything. And clearly Priest had deep knowledge about what was going on here on this island. On it, and beneath it.

He hooked onto the rail and climbed over to stand on the platform. It was as solid as it looked. That was something. He kept his rope firmly attached to his rappelling rig, however. Trust was hard to come by in his line, and doubly so since Poliske.

Hiro crept down the steps, trying not to make a sound and failing. The tunnel seemed to magnify every noise. He reached the first landing without incident, though he didn't like the feel of the air. There was a steady stream of cool outside air blowing downward into the darkness, and no heat at all rising. To his fertile imagination it was like the slow inhalation of a dragon before he exhales his burning fire.

The landing had a recessed walkway of solid bedrock, at the end of which was a steel security door. Hiro unclipped his line and attached it to the rail. If things went badly he could run and grab that rope and even reattach it to his rig in mid-jump. That was something he'd done before. He was fast and agile and experienced.

He was also sweating heavily despite the cool downrush of air.

Fear keeps you sharp, he told himself. *So stay fucking sharp.*

"I'm down," he said into the mic He bent and examined the keypad. It was surprisingly high-tech for a lab way the hell out here. "I'm at the door and there are lights on it. The keypad still has power."

"Good," said Priest. Excitement made his voice sound clipped and high-pitched. "Enter this code in sequence with a one second pause between each number. Got it? Good. Here it is…23, 119, 7, 16, 11."

Hiro carefully tapped on the keypad. When he pressed the last number there was a click and a hydraulic hiss, and then the door slid sideways into the wall. A ball of heat instantly rolled out at him and Hiro staggered back, coughing at the awful stink that was carried with it.

"Jesus Christ!"

"What is it?" demanded Priest.

Hiro coughed and gagged, his stomach churning from the smell. It was truly vile, like rotting fish and wet mold and feces all swirling together and then amplified by the furnace heat. It was even worse than the corpse-choked mud flats that had once been fishing villages near Fukushima in the days after the tsunami. Worse than that. Worse than anything Hiro had ever experienced and he spun around and vomited onto the floor.

"*Hiro,*" growled Priest, "what's happening? Are you in? *Are you in?*"

After the first blast of fetid air the stench was less. Not gone by any stretch, but less. Hiro pulled off the World War II rising sun-patterned dew-rag he wore and wound it around his nose and mouth. He tottered forward, his eyes watering and his head aching from the assault on his senses

"I—I'm in," he gasped. "It's okay. I'm in."

But it wasn't okay.

Within a few steps Hiro knew that nothing in his world was likely to be 'okay' ever again.

Inside the doorway was a cavern that had been structurally reinforced with titanic struts of steel—massive pillars that were as big around as oak trees. Forty of them at least, upholding the roof and angled slantwise to reinforce the walls. Hiro goggled. He'd never seen structural engineering on this scale anywhere and the cost of building it must have been astronomical.

There were dozens of computer workstations enclosed in cubes of foot-thick clear plastic with steel reinforcing. Each workstation had a self-contained air supply and dedicated power lines. These cubes were empty and arranged in a wide semicircle and angled to face something that squatted on a trestle made from more of the heavy steel. It was round, segmented, and it angled downward into the heart of the mountain. Hiro's mouth went dry because he recognized—or thought he recognized—what this was. This technology had been all over the news the last few years.

It was an Orpheus Gate. A massive one, much bigger than the one in Poliske. Different in design, too. It reminded Hiro of pictures he'd seen of the Large Hadron Collider near Geneva, beneath the France-Switzerland border. This machine had to weigh a million tons. Maybe twice that much, and it filled a cavern that was incredibly vast.

What are they doing here? he thought. *What's this thing for?*

As if reading his thoughts, Priest's voice whispered in his ear. "You see it, don't you?"

"Y-yes." Hiro's throat felt like it was choked with dust. He stood there, his heart hammering as sweat poured down the sides of his face.

"What you are seeing is the world's most advanced accelerator technology married to an Orpheus Gate," continued Priest.

"Why...why...?"

It was all of the question Hiro could manage.

"Because, my friend," murmured Priest, "we will never save the human race by repairing our biosphere or colonizing the Moon or Mars."

"I don't understand."

"There are other worlds, Hiro. Countless worlds. And they are so close you can touch them." Priest's voice was filled with wonder, with awe. "The Orpheus Gate is a doorway to an infinite number of other worlds. Other *Earths*, yes? Worlds that are rich with all of the natural resources we could ever use in ten billion lifetimes. And they are all like ripe fruit for the plucking."

"That's impossible."

"No," said Priest, "it's merely difficult. There is a mathematical code hidden in the pages of the Unlearnable Truths. Find it, solve it, and you can align the Orpheus Gate so that it opens a doorway. Do it right, and the doorway is stable. Do it wrong, or try to align it without the *full* code, and you…well, you tend to blow things up."

"Jesus Christ."

"And, if you are very, very unlucky you also crack the wrong door open and *things* come out. You saw one of those things—or part of one—in Poliske. That was nothing. The smallest fragment. It is like seeing a thing and thinking that it is the worst imaginable horror and then learning that it is no more significant than a flea. There are so many things greater and more terrible than that," said Priest, his voice now a soft and eerie whisper.

Hiro closed his eyes. "Why did you bring us here, you maniac?"

"Shhh," soothed Priest, "this door is ajar but nothing has come through yet."

"How do you know?" demanded Hiro. "How can you possibly know if anything came through?"

"Because," said Priest, "you're still alive."

Hiro said nothing. He couldn't.

"Now," said Priest, "go and get me my book."

It took a lot for Hiro to continue. He stared into the mouth of the Orpheus Gate. Unlike the other one, this had a huge central diaphragm made of interlocking steel panels, like the shutter of a vast camera. Those panels had all been rolled back to reveal a massive glowing yellow light. It was like looking down the barrel of a long telescope to the surface of an alien sun.

But it was not a sun.

He looked around. The lab complex was spread out around and below him. All of the doors to all of the offices were open. Lights flickered on computer screens and along the surface of exotic machines. Every device in the lab was still functioning. Hiro was surrounded by the sound of computers and machinery laboring despite having no human guidance.

The humans were no longer manning those machines.

They were still in the lab, though.

All of them.

All that was left of them.

Rags of red flesh lying in pools of blood.

Pieces that had been discarded.

Hiro looked back at the red sun.

Which was not a sun.

He knew that even though his mind did not want to accept it. He knew what it was. He knew.

He did not start screaming until that massive, glowing orb at the other end of the collider blinked.

-13-

Sam Hunter
The University of Pennsylvania Museum
3260 South Street
Philadelphia, Pennsylvania

I drove downtown as the sun toppled out of sight behind the skyline. There was a little food cart near the museum that sold pretty good hotdogs. I'm a stress eater, so I bought three of them, loaded with peppers, onions, and relish. Lots of spicy mustard, and three cans of Coke. My digestive system hates me, and I haven't been on good speaking terms with my colon for years, but damn that stuff tasted pretty great. There's a lot of bullshit talk about baseball stadium hotdogs and Coney Island hotdogs, but that's just hype. Maybe it was true back in the sixties, but I wasn't born yet, so as far as I'm concerned it's ancient history. The best hotdogs come from those little stainless steel food carts owned by guys who don't speak a word of English but know how to boil meat. Their peppers are hot to the point of being toxic and the sodas are so cold they hurt your tongue.

I sat in my car and watched the street go dark. The food cart guy hitched up and drove off and the foot traffic dwindled. Tomorrow was Monday and it was a holiday. There wasn't a lot of Sunday traffic and this wasn't a residential part of town, so there weren't many pedestrians. I could feel the street go quiet. The sights and smells and warmth of humans ceased to be the dominant energy and the older, colder energy of concrete, asphalt, glass, metal and stone reclaimed the area. There were a few sentinel birds huddled close together on the edges of the big museum, but they were bored, weary pigeons and a few threadbare starlings.

The side door of the museum opened and three docents and a girl who probably ran the souvenir shop came out, said some goodbyes and went separate ways. Two toward the parking lot, one toward the subway, while the girl unchained a bike. I caught a glimpse of the security guard as he pulled the door shut from within.

After another five minutes I started my car and circled the building, then parked back where I'd been. Then I got out, pulled on the backpack with the fake version of the *Mysteries of the Worm* in it, and walked around the building. The first circuit had been to watch for watchers, but when I went walking I used my nose more than my eyes. The little pack of cardboard scent cards were in my pocket and I'd sniffed each one before getting out of the car. The average Joe can remember smells well enough to tell the difference between a rose and a marigold or a steak and a roast chicken. The canine and lupine sense of smell is a couple of million times more acute. My aunt Sophie liked to train me on it when I was a kid. She'd put a tiny drop of a scent in a little water and then freeze it. Sometimes she'd give me a whole bucket of ice cubes and I'd have to go through it to find the ones that had a scent, and then identify the scent. Or she'd give me a bucket where every cube had a different scent. It was a bitch but it was also fun. One cube might have a little dander from our dog, or some from the dog down the street. Another might have had a blade of grass dipped in it, or a micro drop of bacon grease. At first I was lousy at it, but it's one of those things you grow into. Now it was old hat, and it's one of those skills that always helped me when I was a cop in the Twin Cities, and it's been really useful as a P.I. here in Philly. They make jokes about detectives sniffing for clues, but for me it's truth in advertising.

While I walked I took the air, so to speak. Scents are particulate, so just walking down the street my nose vacuumed up thousands of things. Sounds disgusting, and maybe it is, but it's what it is. Next time you see a dog sniffing as it walks, bear in mind that Fido is learning everything about what happened on that street going all the way back to the last hard rain. People, animals, car exhausts, vermin, stuff on people's shoes, trash blown by the wind. That's the Internet for the nasally-inclined.

I was three quarters of the way around the big museum before I caught a whiff of anything. Faint…and a little strange. I stopped and allowed the scent to fill me. It was a female scent. Very female. Vital in the way that women are, which is entirely different from male vitality. There's a different chemistry and different physical potential in the blend of body oils, hormones, respiration, and pungencies. Which is not as creepy as it sounds. Not to me, anyway.

The scent matched one of the cards in my pocket. I liked the smell, but at the same time it gave me the willies. Not just because this was almost certainly Violin, the woman Acantha said was incredibly dangerous. No. What made the skin along my spine tingle was that the scent wasn't really human.

And I had no idea *what* it was.

Buried beneath her scent was a second and far less powerful scent. Male. Very human. Young. Harry Bolt? I could smell adrenaline and fear in large but equal quantities.

The smells were recent. Ten minutes, maybe, which meant they probably entered the building while I was doing my circuit.

I quickened my pace and was almost at a run by the time I reached the employee entrance. Acantha's keys were clearly marked and within a few seconds I was inside, standing in a short hallway with a time clock and card rack on one side and a bunch of city ordinance and inspection certificates in cheap frames on the other. The scent was stronger in here because there was no fresh breeze to dissipate it.

According to the timetable Acantha shared with me, Violin and Harry Bolt were always likely to get here first. In an ideal world they'd get the *Manifesto* and then haul ass out of here, maybe steal a car or go in disguise on a train or plane and head west. They'd gotten to the States aboard a series of commercial ships, the first of which took them to South America, then others that brought them incrementally to Baltimore. Not sure how they'd gotten here to Philly, but apparently stealing cars was in the skill sets of both Bolt and Violin. Fair enough. If they wanted to stay off the grid, though, then they might actually have to drive across country. Even with excellent fake IDs airports and train stations were risky. Between surveillance cameras, TSA, and fellow passengers who could be part of the bad guy network, you were also trapped. Trains and planes were boxes that weren't under your control. A car can make it in less than a week using the right roads and with two people tag-teaming on the driving. The fact that I hadn't seen a car outside didn't mean there wasn't one parked on a side street.

So far the only scents from the pack of cards were the two I'd followed inside. Good. I'm not a pussy and I don't mind a fight if the chips fall a certain way, but the two groups chasing this book, the Brotherhood of the Lock and the Closers, scared me a bit. I'll admit it. My family are the *benandanti*. That's not our surname; it's what we are. The *benandanti* are clans of lycanthropes who can trace their lines back to Etruscan days. Most of us are firmly on the side of the angels, so to speak. There are a few rogues and lone wolves, but not many. Not that we all try to live up to some of our more celebrated ancestors. My grandmother and a couple of my aunts are more exceptions to the rule. They always liked poking their snouts into things. My dad wasn't much of a troublemaker and he never did a thing for anyone unless it was helping them fill out their tax forms or coaching Little League. But in the past we had some real warriors. The problem is that we got serious pushback from people who should have been our allies. Our biggest enemy, strange as it seems, was the church. In their eyes we're monsters and as they see it there's only one kind of monster: the bad kind. A lot of my ancestors were hunted down, beheaded, hanged, burned or tortured to death by groups like the Inquisition. That doesn't inspire the warm fuzzies for hit squads like the Brotherhood, because they were tied to the Inquisition, in both history and approach.

So, sure, I'm not a fan.

Not a huge fan of any kind of religious fruitcake, actually. Doesn't matter which version of God they pray to, or claim to work for. Militancy and religion make for dangerous fanatics. And assholes like that have hung a lot of *benandanti* pelts on their walls over the last two thousand years.

As for the Closers…they were highly trained government agents with dangerous science fiction toys. I have teeth and claws. You know that old axiom about not taking a knife to a gunfight? Yeah, well that's how I felt.

Much as I hate to say it, I wished Joe Ledger was with me. Then I thought about what Acantha said. He was in a hospital in San Diego. He was dying.

Shit.

He was one of those guys who seemed to be painted with magic. The kind who might take some hits but would always be on his feet when the smoke cleared. Kind of scary to think that someone like him was off the field.

It wasn't very goddamn reassuring.

With those gloomy thoughts filling my head, I moved through the building.

Most of the place was dark except for small, dim security lights. I followed the scents and tried to not trip over my own feet. Wolves have decent night vision, but we're not cats. We have great peripheral vision, though, so we notice a lot, but there's this odd thing where we can't always pick out details of the stuff we see, especially at a distance. We're more movement sensitive. I sometimes wonder if our brains are so busy processing smells and, to a slightly lesser degree, sounds, that the eyesight doesn't get access to the same amount of mental computing. Not sure, and no one in my family has ever outed themselves to a doctor for a study.

So, I can't be entirely blamed for tripping over the body in the hall and falling flat on my face.

-14-

Hiro Tsukino
The Ritz-Cartlton, Dubai
The Walk, Dubai
United Arab Emirates
Eighteen Months Ago

The dreams were waiting for him every night. Dreams or maybe memories. He could never tell the difference and tried to escape from any certain knowledge. Booze helped. Pills, too. Sleeping pills and whatever else he could get. Rink had a few good connections and she kept him provided with whatever it took to help him through the night and to keep him functioning.

Priest still needed him. More and more often now that their shared project was accelerating. Priest's employer was putting a lot of pressure on him to obtain the last of the Unlearnable Truths.

Hiro tried not to calculate the cost of obtaining those books. Not the money spent, but the human cost. The cost to him as a person.

He knew without a doubt that this was going to drive him insane. Maybe kill him, too, but that might be a relief.

The dreams.

Goddamn those dreams.

If he didn't take the right pills or drink enough to drop him down into the black, then when he closed his eyes he found himself back in that lab, staring down the barrel of the Orpheus Gate. Seeing the eye.

Seeing the eye blink. Seeing it turn to look at him. Knowing that it was now aware of him.

Sometimes all he could do was scream, and sometimes, if the balance of pills was wrong, he screamed and screamed but could not scream himself awake.

As for the book...sure, he'd found it.

That part was easy because it was on a pedestal like the others had been. Waiting to be taken. Maybe wanting to be taken. After all, it, like all the others, contained that code and only when the code was deciphered and entered into an Orpheus Gate would the door swing all the way open.

The thing that had looked at him had known that. Wanted that.

It *let* him take the book.

Even so, it had played with him. Things had come out of the tunnel. They tried to take him, touch him, *own* him. He'd grabbed the book and ran and those things had followed.

That escape was the reason Priest had hired him. Hiro had whirled and fled, running as fast as he could out of the lab and onto the walkway, dodging obstacles, vaulting corpses, clambering along trailing wires, swinging from cables to handrails, grabbing for his climbing rope, attaching it to the rings on his harness, all the time screeching for Boris and Priest to pull him up. Screaming, crying, begging. Even before the slack line went taut Hiro flung himself off of the platform and into the shaft.

The tentacles very nearly caught him.

Nearly.

But the line jerked him upward as the winches drew him toward the ruined surface of the island.

Hiro never stopped screaming. Not even after he was out of the shaft and unbuckled from his harness. He did not stop screaming until Boris raised his rifle and slammed the stock full-force into Hiro's face.

It was worse in the darkness of unconsciousness, though.

Down there, trapped by concussion, he floated in a dark sea of nightmare. That sea was not empty and he was not alone. Slithery things rose from the depths and encircled him, igniting searing agony in his flesh and bones, filling his nostrils with the stink of rotting fish, and filling his mind with a chittering, endless cry from inhuman throats.

"Tekeli-li! Tekeli-li!"

That was what he'd heard down there. The cry had not come from the monster at the other end of the Gate.

No.

It had been a chorus raised by the dead. Every single corpse in the place had opened its mouth and shouted that cry.

"Tekeli-li! Tekeli-li!"

Sometimes, in the still of a long, bad night, Hiro realized that the voice crying out those words was his own.

-15-

Sam Hunter
The University of Pennsylvania Museum
3260 South Street
Philadelphia, Pennsylvania

I'm not an idiot, so let's clear that up right now. And, sure, I know I talk a lot about sense of smell and all that, but there was a bucket filled with water and bleach, and that'll cancel out any animal's sense of smell. Even my kind of animal.

No, I didn't smell the blood.

Not until I did a face plant in it.

So, it's not entirely my fault.

That said, I felt like the biggest freaking idiot in history. Sam Hunter, experienced investigator, *benandanti*, the guy Limbus had called to save the world.

Fuck me.

I tried to turn to catch the floor on my palms, but between surprise and the weight of the heavy book in my backpack, I was a micro-second too late and the cold marble banged my cheek. At least it wasn't my jaw; otherwise I'd be spitting teeth. My species regenerates after most injuries, but—weirdly—missing teeth don't always come back. Especially the older we get, and I was looking at middle age close enough to read the fine print.

Sharp agony detonated in my head and I rolled sideways as if I could roll away from the pain. That's when I realized two things. First, that I'd fallen into a fresh puddle of warm blood; and second, that the blood had all come from the security guard I'd seen letting the staff out.

That snapped me into a different gear and I changed as I rose. Not to full wolf, but to a useful half-and-half state that didn't rip my clothes to shit. The shift turned the dial on my senses all the way to eleven, sharpening my night vision a bit and doubling my sense of smell. The bleach punched me pretty hard, but halfway to wolf I could smell the blood, too. Hard not to, I guess, when I was now covered in it. Shit.

I quickly moved away from the corpse and crouched down, my back to a wall as I took in what the room and the moment had to tell me.

The guard's throat had been cut from ear to ear. A knife. The wound was too perfect for a claw. That was something. Was it Violin? As far as I could tell she and her companion were the only ones from Acantha's set of scent cards who'd entered the building.

If that was the case, though, it cast her in a different light. The guard was almost certainly an innocent. An unlucky bastard working a night shift whose very existence was inconvenient to someone else. That pissed me off. I may not be entirely human but I consider myself a humanist. When I found Violin and Harry Bolt I had some serious questions to ask them, and I had better like the answers or the guard wouldn't be the only corpse on the premises.

I removed my jacket and shirt, made sure there was nothing in the pockets, and dropped them. It had absorbed most of the blood. There was less on my pants and shoes. My undershirt was damp but not soaked. If there was time I'd come back to collect my stuff. I had a small-frame Glock on my belt if this turned into the O.K. Corral, but I seldom resort to gunplay. I have other weapons, and they're built in.

The hall was quiet but I strained to hear sounds from deeper inside the museum. Human ears wouldn't have heard what I heard.

A scuff of a shoe, the soft grunt of effort as someone did something in another room. The wheeze of someone who was getting out of breath.

As I moved away from the corpse and the bucketful of dirty water and bleach, I could still smell the blood from the security guy. There were other smells, too. Human smells—sweat, skin, hair, breath, cologne, deodorant, socks. Everything has a unique scent.

There were other odors, too. Some of them were museum smells. Too many visitors who brought the aromatic olio of their lives with them. Lots of kids with indifferent hygiene. Snacks. Dust and varnish. Cleaning products and air fresheners. The earthy smells of wood, metal and stone.

And two other things. One I couldn't identify and one I definitely could.

The strange smell was strong but not close and it was out of place. It was the kind of smell I'd expect to encounter on the docks, in a bad seafood restaurant or an aquarium where they don't change the filters often enough. Fish. A rotting, decaying stink. And yet...it wasn't a dead scent. That sounds like a contradiction, but that's what I smelled. Decay and vitality wrapped together in the same scent.

I'd only ever smelled something like this once before. It was on a case where I'd been asked to help save a kid from the monster in his closet. Yeah. Real kid, real closet, real monster. When I'd gone into the darkness of that closet I stepped into another place, and the fish stink was incredibly strong, and very much alive.

This was like that.

"Shit," I said to myself.

The other thing I smelled was blood on the air. There was a lot of it and it wasn't from the dead security guard. Someone else was bleeding, and I caught the faintest thump of a heart. Fading, though. Fading, going shallow, and then going silent.

Shit.

I ran.

I was pretty sure I knew what I'd find, and I hate when I'm right.

A woman in a functional staff uniform sat on the top step of a stairway that led to the basement. Cleaning rags were tucked into her pockets. She wore sensible shoes and her salt-and-pepper hair was up in a bun. Black, maybe fifty. A low-pay worker. Somebody's mother, maybe. Or a wife. A person in any case. Someone had used a knife on her, too. It was cold in the museum and steam rose from the red mouths of five stab wounds clustered around her heart. Her eyes were open, though, and I swear I caught the last, fleeting glimpse of a departing awareness. It was as if she looked at me and pleaded for help that I simply could not give. I could smell her death. There was nothing I could do but watch her die.

That, and maybe catch up with whoever killed her.

I knelt beside her. A wisp of hair had come loose from her bun and I smoothed it back. Then, for reasons I will never be able to understand or explain, I bent and kissed her on the forehead.

Saying goodnight? Or making a promise? You tell me, I'm no philosopher.

There was a sound downstairs. A lock clicking and a door opening. Then a woman's voice said, "Hurry up."

A young woman's voice. Violin?

I rose from where I'd knelt and began moving down the stairs. I didn't really understand what was happening. This wasn't playing out the way Acantha said it would. If Violin was supposed to be one of the good guys, that wasn't going to save her. Not if there was blood on her hands and on her knife.

No.

It wasn't going to save her at all.

With each step down to the basement I became less of a man and more of what I truly am.

-16-

Hiro Tsukino
Monastery of St. George of Koziba
Wadi Qelt, West Bank
Palestinian Territories
One Year Ago

"Are you sure you're up for this?" asked Rink.

Hiro Tsukino took a while before he answered. The simple truth was that he wasn't sure if he was up for it or not. In the two years since Tristan da Cunha he had become a shell of the man he'd been. Booze no longer even took the edge off of things. The pills helped, but that was a dead end run because every day he seemed to need more of them. It was only when Boris dragged him out of a crack house did Hiro even start to get clean. The beating Boris gave him was probably unnecessary, but the memory of it kept Hiro from escaping the expensive rehab center Priest put him in.

The new drugs, the non-addictive ones Priest acquired for him, helped the most. They let him sleep and if he dreamed, he didn't remember anything. No great burning eyes. No tentacles. None of that. The only lingering memory was the strange cry whose echoes had chased him up out of that shaft.

Tekeli-li! Tekeli-li!

Now, nearly two years later, it was the only part of that experience that refused to submerge into unreality. Everything else had become part of a fabric of delusion and hallucination that Hiro no longer accepted as part of his actual memories. Even though they *felt* like something he'd experienced, his therapists—Priest's therapists—comforted him into the belief that they were really ghosts from his days smoking meth. It was the damage from the crack that made him misremember them as older memories, or as memories at all.

Fantasies. Nothing more.

Tekeli-li! Tekeli-li!

That meaningless cry, though…it persisted.

To keep the shrinks from locking him away again, Hiro lied and told them he heard no inhuman voices shrieking in his head. As addicts and the insane often do, Hiro had become a very convincing liar.

Now he stood on a bridge that spanned a gorge that everyone around here, including the monks at the monastery, believed was the Valley of the Shadow. The actual one mentioned in Psalm 23.

Yea, though I walk through the valley of the shadow of death I will fear no evil.

But Hiro did fear this place. As he feared the evil things he had seen.

If 'evil' could even begin to describe that eye. He knew for sure it was not God's eye looking at him, and until last year Hiro did not believe in the Devil. Or God. Or anything. Although he had been raised nominally Shinto he never held a splinter of faith.

Until that eye.

Until that fucking eye.

It's just the drugs, he told himself.

Except that another voice answered that claim. Answered and mocked it.

Tekeli-li! Tekeli-li!

Tristan da Cunha was many thousands of miles away from where he now stood. A world and a year away, half buried behind drug-warped memories.

"Hiro—?" asked Rink, her voice filled with concern. He turned and looked at her. She looked so different from the elfin girl he'd met more than five years ago. Her face was lined with care and stress and there were shadows in her eyes. She, too, had seen things she shouldn't have. Not the eye, but other things.

You're a fucking bastard, Priest, thought Hiro. *You're going to kill us all.*

Tekeli-li!

He placed his hands against the stones that lined the precarious edge of the pilgrim road and leaned out to look down into the valley. The monastery was built in the sixth century, erected near a cave where some believed the prophet Elijah was fed by ravens. The Greek Orthodox monks who lived here kept the place open to tourists, which paid the bills. He wondered how big a check Priest had written to allow the team exclusive access to this place. The monks had agreed to wait in their cells for a full day, and the roads were blocked, ostensibly for repairs.

"Hiro," said Rink, taking a few steps toward him, "if you can't do this—"

"I'm fine," he said.

"Boris and Keppler can—"

"I said I'm fine," he snapped. But when he saw the hurt in her eyes, he sighed and softened it. "Really, Rink, I'm good. Just getting my bearings, you know?"

He wore his full rappelling rig, and the bulky Russian soldier stood a dozen yards away, arms folded, face filled with dislike and disdain. He certainly didn't think Hiro was ready for this. Neither did Keppler, who was at the far end of the bridge, fretting and fidgeting.

"Are you ready?" asked a voice, and Hiro turned to see Priest walking briskly toward him. The scientist continued to age rapidly and now looked sixty, though despite his rail-thin body and white hair he had unnatural vigor. Hiro never even saw him yawn let alone take a moment to rest. Strange fires burned in Priest's eyes and Hiro had begun to fear that look. Those fires reminded him far too much of another fiery eye.

Far too much.

"I guess so," said Hiro.

The wide wet smile on Priest's face twitched and a vertical line etched itself between his brows. "Either you're ready or you're not. Which is it?"

Hiro cleared his throat and pretended to check his gear. "Yeah, I'm good to go."

Priest nodded. He bent and looked down just as Hiro had done. "This place is incredible. The monastery is named for Gorgias of Koziba, the first monk who lived here. They canonized him, though I forget why. Doesn't matter. Who the fuck cares about someone who believed in the wrong god in the ass-end of the world, yes? All that matters are the scrolls."

"Why are they hidden in the cliff wall?" asked Hiro.

"This place was destroyed by the Persians in 614 A.D. They slaughtered the fourteen monks who lived here. I just saw their skulls. The monks showed me, they have them in niches in the walls. Fascinating, you can almost hear their screams. Anyway, Crusaders rebuilt the monastery in 1179, and then in 1878 a Greek monk named Kalinikos settled here and began a restoration that he finished in 1901. During World War II this place was targeted by Hitler's Thule Society—which, for the record, was not dissolved after 1930 as the history books insist. Nope, they just went into hiding, trying to find all sorts of occult objects and secrets to help win the war."

"Raiders of the Lost Ark," said Hiro absently.

Priest shrugged. "Pretty much. There's a lot of pop culture stuff about Hitler's obsession with the supernatural, but like most things there's a great deal of truth to it. The *Thule-Gesellschaft* was real enough, and they came here looking for a book that had been given to the monks to protect."

"What kind of book is it this time?" asked Hiro, though he was fairly certain he didn't want to know.

"Oh...something fun. Lot of pop culture about *that*, too. Pretty much everyone thinks it's totally fake. Something made up for horror stories, but that's a long way from the truth."

"How do you know it's real?" asked Hiro.

The grin on Priest's face was truly manic. "I've seen photographs of it. I've seen jpegs of old pictures taken of a few of its pages." He licked his lips as if tasting the last drop of a savory meal. "The book was in the Vatican library for over a century, but like a lot of dangerous knowledge it was removed during the war. Not because the pope was afraid Hitler would get it—though I guess he didn't want that—but because the Allies had heard about it and they sent an investigator to find it."

"Who?"

"I don't know his real name. There are a few references to him in some records I saw on my dad's computer. His code name was 'St. Germain.' He was a notorious pain in the ass, though. He wasn't trying to obtain the book to use it—as it was *meant* to be used. No, that lunatic wanted to destroy it. Fucking book burning psychopath."

Hiro, who had always been opposed to any kind of censorship, thought that maybe he'd like to take a match to any book that had Priest this deeply obsessed.

"Luckily," continued Priest, "the Catholics are big ones for not destroying anything that might have value, even books from other religions. Or maybe especially books from other religions. Know thy enemy, I guess. Whatever. They took the most dangerous books in their vaults and scattered them around the world. Most were eventually brought back to the Vatican and are locked away where even we can't get them." He sighed wistfully. "But this book—*Al Azif*—was believed lost. Only a handful of monks know that it's here, and the Orthodox monks are no friends of the Vatican crew. They didn't trust the Romans to keep it safe, or maybe they were afraid of anyone ever using it."

"Why didn't they burn it?"

Priest laughed. "That's just it, dude, you *can't* burn it. Not without knowing how. You can pour gasoline on it and drop a match and all you'll do is burn the gas. The book won't even get warm."

Hiro almost said, "Bullshit," but it died on his tongue. Most of his doubt had died down in the underground lab on Tristan da Cunha.

The scientist was caught up in his tale. "The monks were smart, though. They cut some niches in the wall below this bridge and stored the book inside. Then they sealed it up."

"And they told you all this?" asked Hiro.

Priest shrugged.

"If they are so dedicated to preserving the book, why are they letting us take it?"

Boris, who was close enough to overhear this, laughed. It was not a nice laugh. Hiro frowned and touched Priest's arm.

"Hey, they *are* letting us do this, right?"

"Mmmmm," said Priest, "not so much 'letting' us as 'not being able to give a shit.' Dumbasses thought we were here to shoot a documentary for the Discovery Channel."

Boris laughed again. A donkey bray. "More martyr skulls for the wall."

Hiro stared at the monastery. His touch turned into a grip and pulled Priest close. "What the fuck *did you do*?"

The Russian soldier stepped forward and swatted Hiro's hand away. He was not gentle about it. "Keep your fucking hands to yourself, you fucking junkie."

Priest jabbed Hiro in the chest with a stiff forefinger. "Remember your place, boy. Remember who pays your bills and gives you all those yummy pills."

"You *killed* them?"

"Martyred is a nicer word."

"Jesus Christ."

"That's what they said," laughed Priest. "And yet the Messiah failed to show up to save them. Talk about misplaced faith."

His hand suddenly shot out and caught Hiro by the throat. The grip was insanely strong. Way too strong. Hiro felt himself rising to his toes and nearly into the air. It was impossible for someone as skinny and withered as Priest to be this strong.

Impossible.

The fires in the scientist's eyes burned hot enough to sear Hiro's mind.

"Listen to me," said Priest. Now there was no laughter. Now there was only power in the madman's voice. A strange power that was in no way human. No way. It sounded old and alien. It was the voice of something else. Something Hiro would not dare name for fear of revealing it to be true. "Game time is over. You will crawl down this wall like the insect you are. You'll cut open the vault and remove the sacred book, and then you will bring *Al Azif* to me before the sun sets over this valley. You will do it quickly and you will do it correctly."

A stink filled the air and for a moment Hiro thought that it was his own bowels that had failed. But that wasn't it. There was the stench of rotting fish and it roiled in the air around Priest. The grip was crushing the life from Hiro, choking off his air. Darkness began crowding in and with it came hallucinations. Worms of darkness writhed at the edge of his vision and a voice that sounded like his own voice whispered strange words that Hiro was sure he had heard before.

Ugly, dangerous words in a language no man was meant to speak.

Ph'nglui mglw'nafh Cthulhu R'lyeh wgah'nagl fhtagn.

Hiro heard Rink crying out in fear, pleading with Priest to stop.

Then the crushing force was gone and Hiro sagged down. Ironically it was the killer, Boris, who kept him from plunging over the edge. Priest turned away as if to hide his face. Rink seemed torn as to whether to run to see if Hiro was okay or to go to her lover. Indecision rooted her to the spot.

The moment stretched and then leveled out as Hiro gasped in lungsful of air. He shoved himself away from Boris and stood panting in the middle of the bridge.

"You're a fucking maniac," he gasped and spat on the ground.

Priest turned, knelt, and rubbed his fingers through the spittle. His long, red tongue snuck out from between his teeth and licked the spit from his thin, white fingers.

"No," he said softly, "that's not what I am."

Hiro stumbled backward as Priest straightened, and he backed into Boris. Priest pointed to the edge.

"Do as you're told."

Rink was crying now. Keppler was as white as a ghost and had not advanced a single step forward during the whole encounter.

Hiro swallowed hard, fighting terror and disgust and confusion.

He took a step away from Boris, dragged in a steadying breath, and then walked to the edge. With trembling hands he checked his ropes and rappelling gear. Boris took up his position as anchor. And then Hiro stepped over the rail and went down.

Into the Valley of the Shadow.

-17-

Sam Hunter
The University of Pennsylvania Museum
3260 South Street
Philadelphia, Pennsylvania

The lights were off at the bottom of the stairs, the bulb smashed, the ground littered with glass. I had to step carefully and pick my way using whatever light followed me down from upstairs. I hadn't gone full wolf because I wanted my clothes intact. I had a spare set in the car but like an idiot I hadn't brought them inside with me. You'd think that after all this time I'd have thought that through.

Even so, I was more wolf than man. If you think that looks funny—a werewolf in shoes and K-Mart clothes wearing a backpack—maybe it does. You wouldn't think so if you saw me coming down those stairs, though. Pretty sure I wasn't wearing a 'let's all have a chuckle' expression. What was the phrase Shakespeare used? He had a lean and hungry look. Sure. Like that.

The stairs ended in a landing with halls going off in different directions. Most of them were lined with office doors. One hooked around and ended at a security door. My quarry went that way. The smell of blood was mingled with the rotting fish stink and it was a lot stronger down here.

The security door stood ajar and beyond it there was only darkness. I could smell the woman—Violin--and the less interesting smell of the man Acantha called Harry Bolt. One was clearly an alpha scent, and the other was... What's a good word? *Prey*? Yeah, close enough. Or, maybe late night snack if this thing kept going south.

The hinges on the security door creaked with all of the clichéd noise of a bad horror flick. Another thing I should have brought—WD-40.

I went through quickly and faded to one side, crouching low in the shadows in case someone decided to take a pot shot at whoever opened the door.

Nothing.

There was light at the far end of the hall. It spilled out of an open door. The rest of the hall seemed to be empty and the bloody footprints had mostly faded out. I couldn't see them anymore, but I could still smell the blood. You'd have to walk fifty miles to lose that scent from a nose like mine. Imagine how much fun it is when someone farts. Unlike actual dogs I am not a connoisseur of ass smells.

Blood was different. It spoke to something buried very deep inside my soul. It whispered to the wolf beneath my skin. My mom says that we were people who became wolves, but my grandmother disagrees. She says we were wolves who learned how to pretend to be human. None of us know for sure, but most of the time I think Granny was right.

I crept along the hallway. Yes, crept. I'm a monster. We tend to creep. It's a thing.

There were sounds coming from inside the open doorway. I paused to listen. Voices. There was a fresh odor of blood, too, and I could tell that it wasn't the blood of either the security guard or the cleaning lady. This was a different person. Everyone's blood has a uniqueness that's made up of the things they eat and their body chemistry.

The fish smell, though, was stronger than ever. It made my eyes water. And it also made the hairs on my back stand up. On some deep level below my human consciousness the wolf was reacting to something that scared it.

Which scared me.

I listened to the voices inside. A man's voice, young and frightened, yelled, "What the actual fuck?"

Another man's voice, older and clearly unafraid, laughed.

Then a woman's voice, accented and harsh, said, "Step away from that book."

To which the older man replied, "Kill her."

And, like an idiot, I rushed into the room.

-18-

Hiro Tsukino
The Fairy Chimneys of Cappadocia
Central Anatolia, Turkey
One Month Ago

"They're coming!" cried Rink. She drew her pistol and began backing quickly away from the tunnel mouth.

Hiro was just going over the edge of the hole and froze, one foot on the mouth of the vertical shaft and the other dangling over the sheer drop. He had a gun, too, but it was holstered and his hands were busy with his rappelling rope. He turned to where the others stood. Priest, as always, was flanked by Boris and Keppler. His worshippers. Both of them had rifles slung and when Priest nodded they brought the guns up.

"Wait," said Hiro, "they're just guards."

"What does that matter?" asked Priest.

"We don't have to kill them, for Christ's sake. We can disarm them or something."

Rink looked over her shoulder. She had her pistol out in a shaky two-handed grip and the sounds of men running echoed from beyond the chamber's rocky opening. They were in the fifth of six sub-chambers that had been cut into the living rock beneath one of the fairy chimneys. The lowest chamber was a shrine sanctified by the *Cappadocian Fathers*--Basil the Great, who was Bishop of Caesarea, and his younger brother, Gregory of Nyssa. Along with their friend, Gregory of Nazianzus, they had come here in the middle of the fourth century to bury one of the Unlearnable Truths. It had been a sacred and dangerous mission for the three men, and they had undertaken it with the help of a few trusted priests. The bones of those priests were rumored to be down in the last chamber. They had sacrificed themselves to serve as protectors of the evil book for all eternity. That had earned them the rare privilege of a kind of secret sainthood known only to a cabal hidden within the vast bureaucracy of the church.

Now that book was forty feet below them. The team had followed a series of maddening clues, false leads, dead ends, and obscure references to this remote part of Turkey, and had discovered the network of tunnels that were still protected by Vatican soldiers despite the religious and political unrest here. The Swiss Guardsmen who were coming this way were doing what they believed was a truly sacred duty. They had been told, Hiro knew, that this hidden shrine held the bones of Saint Joseph the Carpenter, the humble Nazarene who had been husband to Mary and stepfather to Jesus.

And, as far as Priest had determined, the bones of Joseph did, indeed, lie here, brought from Nazareth in secret and with the belief that a man capable of protecting the newborn Christ was up to the task of protecting the world from the *Eligoth Ministries.* That book was one of several long believed to have been destroyed but whose existence had been confirmed by Priest's many agents and contacts. The team had already collected two others like it, and when this was done they would begin the hunt for the last two of the Unlearnable Truths—*De Vermis Mysteriis* and the most dreadful of all, *The Cloister Manifesto.*

And then it would all be done. The three-year contract that had been expanded to six brutal years. All of the missions to places the rest of the world wanted to forget ever existed. The gradual loss of self—first to horror, then to fear and paranoia, and to the drugs that helped him get through each night and face each day. For Hiro it was no longer the big payday that kept him going. No, it was the knowledge that this was almost over. This job and two others...and done.

After these two, there were no more books to find.

Hiro was positive that Priest neither knew nor cared how many bodies they'd left behind, how many lives destroyed. Dozens of the Brotherhood, some of the Closers, and countless guards, museum staff, priests and monks, nuns, imams. And the innocent, too. Bystanders, passersby. People whose karma had put them in the path of Mr. Priest, and who had been swept away. First by Boris and over the last year by Keppler, who had somehow become less of the scientist she had been and was now a thug, a killer who carried a gun and slaughtered anyone who became an inconvenience or impediment to her master. To Priest.

And now the Swiss Guardsmen here. Men who protected a shrine that even Hiro respected. Joseph the Carpenter. If the Christian stories were true—and Hiro, a lapsed Shinto, was on the fence about that—then Joseph had been a good and simple man who been given a raw deal from God. To marry a girl he wasn't allowed to touch and raise the child she said belonged to God. Joseph was either the most gullible man in history, or he loved that girl, or he believed the story. No matter which was true, he had protected Mary and Jesus. Or so the stories told. And then, when his usefulness was done, he was pretty much written out of the rest of the Bible. Only tales from the Apocrypha—the lost and suspect books of the Bible—ever spoke of him.

When Priest told the team that this was Joseph's tomb, none of them doubted him. Priest had never been wrong before. Not once.

Somehow, coming here had done something to them all. Boris and Keppler had become even more like organic robots. Cold, efficient and scary. Rink had become less of a total mouse and had become harder. Not like the others, but in a different way. She carried weapons now and she no longer even tried to touch the man who had once been her lover. Hiro wondered if she was planning on killing Priest. If so, why hadn't she done it?

As for him, Hiro felt like he was living some kind of dream. More than once he wondered if he was in a coma somewhere and was merely dreaming all this. Or that he was dead and this was his Hell.

When this was over, he wondered how he would ever be able to return to the world. To any world.

All of this flashed through his brain in a moment as he leaned out from the edge of the hole. The guards were yelling as they approached, panic and outrage filling their shouts.

"Priest," he called, "don't. Please."

Rink turned at the sound of his voice and looked at him and then at Mr. Priest. As she turned, her gun turned with her. Not exactly pointing at the team leader, but there was a sense of dark promise in the way she held it.

Priest smiled his white, oily, merciless smile. The guards burst into the chamber.

Boris and Keppler opened up with their rifles and emptied their magazines into them. The bullets burned through the air on either side of Rink. Close. So close. She screamed and whatever courage she'd been summoning was smashed away, smashed down. Her gun fell from her hand, hit the edge of the hole and bounced past Hiro to vanish into darkness. The guards—four of them—juddered and danced as the bullets tore into them. Blood and flesh sprayed outward, splashing the rock walls. Gunfire filled the chamber and the acoustics turned everything into a madhouse of thunder. The iron and copper stink of blood permeated the air.

And then there was a sudden, terrible silence broken only by a kind of broken sigh as Rink sank slowly down to her knees and buried her face in her hands. Gunsmoke hung thick in the still air. Hiro's head throbbed from the memory of that thunder.

Then Priest spoke.

"Reload," he said, and his two slaves swapped out their magazines with emotionless precision.

No, not emotionless. As they performed that familiar action Hiro saw Keppler's face. Instead of the blank nothing that was usually there he saw a curl of lip and a glitter in the eye that told of a deep, hidden, erotic pleasure.

It was a horrible thing to see. It was worse to know, because it was the truest measure of how far Keppler had fallen.

Priest walked over to the fallen guards. One of them, despite a dozen awful wounds, was still alive. He was pathetically trying to crawl. Not to the safety of the corridor, but toward the hole. Toward the shrine he had given his life to protect.

Priest squatted down in front of him and used a hooked finger to raise the man's chin so he could look into the dying man's eyes. Priest spoke to him in a language Hiro did not recognize, and the man replied, his words slurred by the blood that bubbled from between his lips.

Then Priest did something that astonished and confused Hiro. He bent forward and kissed the man full on those bloody lips. The guard shuddered once and then collapsed down with the finality of death.

"God..." gasped Rink in disgust. She'd watched this from between the fingers of the hands covering her face. "What...what...?"

She was unable to finish the sentence.

Priest straightened. "Hiro," he said, "you're not going down there."

Boris instantly stepped forward, hooked a hand under Hiro's armpit and hauled him back onto solid ground.

"I don't understand," said Hiro. "What did he say to you?"

Instead of answering, Priest walked over to where Rink sat on her knees. He bent and gently pulled her hands away from her face. There was a smile on his face that was almost kind, though it was made hideous by the blood on his lips. He brushed her hair from her face and caressed her cheek.

"You're going to go down there, my pet," he said.

"No!" she cried.

But Keppler and Boris closed in on her and pulled Rink to her feet.

"I can't," she pleaded, but Priest only smiled as his slaves clipped the rappelling gear to the small woman. Rink caught Priest's sleeve. "Don't make me go down there."

"I'll do it," said Hiro, stepping forward, but Boris spun and pointed his rifle at Hiro's face.

"No," said Priest calmly, "Rink will go."

Rink began weeping and Keppler pulled her toward the edge of the shaft.

"Please..."

"You can rappel down," said Priest, "or you can fall. Take your pick."

The lack of mercy in Priest's face was evident and absolute.

Rink threw a desperate glance at Hiro, but there was nothing the urban explorer could do. Boris's dark eyes were as black and uncompromising as the open barrel of the rifle.

Hiro licked his lips. "It's okay, Rink," he said, forcing the words out, "you'll be okay."

"But—"

"You've done this a hundred times. It's not far. Just remember what I taught you and you'll be fine."

It hurt him to say those words, to become an accomplice in Priest's plan, but Hiro had no doubt at all that Priest would throw his former lover into the pit.

Rink turned to Priest. Tears still ran freely down her cheeks but she suddenly gave him a look of such venomous hatred that Hiro recoiled from it. "You're a monster," she said, spitting the words.

Priest only smiled.

Rink shook free of Keppler, took hold of the rope and pushed backward off the edge. Hiro slapped Boris' gun aside and went to the rim to watch her fall. The darkness seemed to swallow her at once.

"Be careful," he called after her.

Rink was gone.

Priest came over and stood next to Hiro, looking down, smiling.

"She's right," said Hiro quietly. "You are a monster."

The team leader put his hand on Hiro's shoulder and for a horrible moment Hiro thought Priest was going to push him in. But the hand remained steady. Heavy and oddly cold.

"The world is full of monsters."

Down below there was a sudden, terrible scream. It spiraled up out of the darkness, high-pitched and raw and wet.

"Rink!" cried Hiro, and he lunged for her rope, but Boris pulled him back. Hiro fought him, trying to reach the rope, needing to pull the poor woman out of the hole. But then the scream stopped.

Just like that.

They all froze and looked down into the silent blackness at the bottom of the shaft. The moment stretched to horrible tautness.

"Rink...?" whispered Hiro. "Oh god..."

Then there was a new sound from below.

Laughter.

Rink's voice. Laughing.

The laughter rose from the shaft and filled the still air, louder than the sound of gunfire. Louder than her screams. There was nothing sane about that laugh. There was nothing human about it. Not anymore.

And it went on and on and on...

-19-

Sam Hunter
The University of Pennsylvania Museum
3260 South Street
Philadelphia, Pennsylvania

Tableau.

There were a bunch of people in the room. One of them was dead. They stood in two groups on either side of a man who lay sprawled in a pool of fresh blood. The dead man wore khakis and a cardigan over a white dress shirt. A pair of cracked reading glasses lay next to him. From the picture I'd seen on the Internet, this was Dr. Holland.

Standing on the left of the corpse and closest to the door were two people who were as unalike as possible. The guy looked like a short, slightly dumpy version of Matt Damon. He wore a heavy backpack a lot like the one I wore, and he looked scared as hell. He held a pistol in a trembling hand. The woman was tall, slender, built like a dancer, with a brunette ponytail and eyes that were dark and dangerous.

Going out on a limb and guessing this was Harry Bolt and Violin.

Standing across from them was a group of five people. A tall, sinister-looking guy of about forty with black hair and a cruel mouth. He was flanked by a guy with a flat Russian face and dead eyes and a stocky blond woman with a hard mouth. They held AK-47s in their hands. To one side of them was a thin brunette woman and a Japanese guy. They had handguns.

None of them looked like what I expected either the Brotherhood of the Lock or the Closers to look like.

Sitting on a wheeled metal cart next to the corpse was a book. It was about the size of a phone book and bound in heavy wood inlaid with lapis and carnelian to form patterns of coiling tentacles. Stiff bands of cracked leather were wrapped around it and buckled securely.

Before I went into the room I turned back to human form. Much easier to handle the Glock that I pulled.

The people with guns were pointing them at each other. The doorway was at a right angle to them, so no one had a gun pointed at me.

"Fucking freeze!" I growled in my best cop voice.

And then everyone was pointing guns at me.

Fun times.

"Who the heck are you?" asked Harry Bolt.

Violin looked me up and down and I saw her nostrils flare and a look of surprise flash in her eyes. Somehow—don't ask me to explain it—she *knew* what I was. That was creepy as all fuck.

The tall guy with the dark hair also gave me an appraising stare. "My, my," he said. "We are an interesting little ménage, yes?"

That's when I saw that he wasn't holding a gun. He had a knife down at his side and the blade was slick with blood. A few things clicked into place for me. Maybe it wasn't Violin and Harry Bolt who'd killed those people. Maybe they, like me, were a few seconds late to a party that had already started. I mean, let's face it, the dark-haired guy looked like a villain from central casting, and his crew might as well have been wearing t-shirts that said 'henchman.'

"I know who you are," I said to Violin. "We have some friends in common. But who are these ass-clowns?"

"I have no freaking idea," said Harry.

"Esteban Santoro," said Violin.

"Oh, I haven't gone by that name in ages," said the super villain. He had a slight Spanish accent. Spain Spanish, not Mexican or Puerto Rican. "I am Mr. Priest to everyone who's anyone these days."

"Priest?" echoed Violin with a hollow laugh. "Is that supposed to be clever?"

Priest shrugged. "I considered 'acolyte,' but it doesn't scan as well. And, Mr. Church was already taken."

"Church?" Harry Bolt and I said it at the same time. Church was the name of Joe Ledger's boss. If there was an in-joke—and I'm pretty sure there was—it went sailing over my head.

I aimed my pistol at his face. His henchmen closed ranks around him, but I still had a shot if I wanted to take it. "You killed Dr. Holland?"

He shrugged.

"Why?"

Another shrug.

"You're here for the book, aren't you?"

Priest smiled. "I believe we are all here for the same thing. Perhaps we should draw lots. Or maybe we could play rock, paper, scissors, yes?"

"Who are you?" Harry asked me.

Without shifting either gaze or gun barrel away from Priest, I said, "I'm a friend of Joe Ledger."

Not exactly true, but close enough.

At the mention of Ledger's name I saw several interesting reactions. Violin cocked an intrigued eyebrow at me. Bolt looked confused. But Priest's face darkened with surprise and anger.

"Ledger," he said, spitting the name. "He's a dead man."

"Not yet," I said. Again, not exactly true. Not if Acantha was right. Didn't seem the time to share that info, though.

Violin's eyes flared for a moment and then she nodded. "Ah. I know who you are," she said with a faint smile. "Joseph told me about you. I believe you met in Pine Deep."

I grunted. "He told you about that?"

"He told me *everything* about it," she said, and she leaned on the word 'everything.' Balls. Not sure how I felt about that. I'd asked Ledger to keep all information about me on the DL. Either he was a Chatty Cathy or Violin shared a level of confidence that transcended Ledger's promises to me.

Priest looked past me to the door. "Is Ledger here? Are you part of his team? Does he now run with dogs?"

Calling a guy like me a dog is supposed to be an insult. Some of my relatives would throw down for something like that. I kind of like dogs, and I don't give much of a cartwheeling fuck what you call me, so I managed not to fly into a homicidal rage.

"First," I said, "go fuck yourself. Just putting that out there."

He inclined his head as if accepting that as an appropriate response.

"Second, who the fuck are you and why's it worth killing people to get some dumb book?"

"You know what the book is?" asked Priest.

"Maybe," I said.

"You know," he said, nodding. "Then you know that Violin and her pet monkey are hoping to destroy it. They are on the side of the angels."

Harry bristled, but Violin merely shrugged.

Priest's smile turned into a leer. "Yes, they are on the side of the angels. I, however, am not."

"Cool," I said. "Good line. Do you practice stuff like that in front of a mirror or does it just come to you?"

Violin warned, "Don't antagonize him..."

"I'm not," I said. "Though I just have to mention that you and your butt-buddies all smell like fish rectums."

Without turning toward his henchmen Priest started to say, "Kill—"

And then there was a shout from the hallway. Male voices and the sound of running. We all turned to see a bunch of men dressed in black pants, shirts and ski masks come crowding into the doorway. At least a half dozen of them, and they had guns, too. Swell.

They froze when they saw what was going on inside. Everyone looked at everyone, and then the first of the ski-mask crew pointed at Priest.

"Traitor," he snarled.

"Oh, shit," whined Harry. "The *Brotherhood*."

"Kill them," bellowed Priest, finally completing his sentence, but directing it at the newcomers.

Guns swiveled but before a single finger could pull a trigger there was a strange sound. A hollow *TOK!* And one of the Brotherhood thugs exploded. Or, at least his head did. It was very immediate and messy, and we were all showered with gore.

I wheeled and saw that there was another group of men pouring in from the far end of Dr. Holland's office. They wore black suits, white shirts and dark ties.

Closers.

I shared a microsecond glance with Violin. She looked scared and amused in equal portions. Her hands flashed and a pair of wicked fighting knives seemed to appear out of nowhere.

Every-damn-body else started firing guns.

Which is when everything went over the edge and down into crazy town.

-20-

Hiro Tsukino
The Fairy Chimneys of Cappadocia
Central Anatolia, Turkey
One Month Ago

It cost Hiro to go over the edge and drop down into the darkness. He knew that he should not go. He was certain it was the wrong call.

But Rink was down there and something had happened to her. Hiro did not have much humanity left in him, not after all that he had done as part of Priest's team. Although he'd never pulled a trigger, he was complicit in the deaths of so many. His soul was already scorched and stained with the shit of his own choices. His greed had damned him.

Rink, though, was an innocent. In Hiro's view, at least. Bullied and cowed by Priest, dominated by Boris and Keppler, swept along in a raging tide of dreadful choices. A victim of Priest rather than an accomplice.

Her mad laughter dwindled to a low, broken chuckle. There was no sanity left in it. No hope.

Hiro could not leave her down in the shadows like that.

So he went over the edge. Keppler lunged forward to stop him, but Hiro swatted her hands away.

"Let him go," said Priest coldly. "Let the brave knight rescue the beautiful princess."

Those mocking words seem to chase Hiro down into the blackness.

-21-

Crazy Town

There are words that fit. 'Clusterfuck' is the first one that comes to mind. Oh, and 'FUBAR'. That's an endlessly useful military acronym for 'fucked up beyond all redemption.'

I dove for the wall and swept my hand down across the light switch and plunged everything into darkness. A computer screen was on and the ghostly blue light traced the outlines of bodies in motion. It wasn't a strobe but with everyone in motion the effect was almost the same.

I saw Violin shove Harry Bolt out of the way as the Russian guy opened up with his automatic rifle. The hail of bullets tore into the leader of the Brotherhood, splashing his men with blood that looked black in the bad light.

Mr. Priest and his crew of zombie henchmen spread out, ducking low and firing at anything that moved. Half a dozen rounds from the Russian's gun struck one of the Closer's center mass, and although the dark-suited man staggered back he did not fall. Instead he caught his balance and brought up a very weird-looking handgun. Instead of a barrel it had a ring of metal prongs and when the Closer fired the gun there was that same *tok* sound. The Russian's body seemed to explode from within like a potato in a microwave if you don't poke holes in it. His arms and head were propelled away from his torso by streaks of fire.

"Holy shit!" I heard someone say and turned to see Harry Bolt dive for cover. There was another *tok* and the wall behind where he had been standing erupted into bright flame.

Violin did not retreat from the attackers but instead whirled toward the Brotherhood killers and waded into them, her knives gleaming like hot silver as she attacked. I have never in my life seen anyone fight like her. She was like a great dancer, with all of the posture and dignity of a prima ballerina and all of the lethality of a threshing machine. Her lithe body evaded bullets and blades as she moved among the larger, stronger male killers and cut them to pieces. Drops of blood seeded the air like thousands of black jewels. Men screamed and reeled away, clutching the stumps of arms or clawing at the holes where eyes or noses should have been. I don't know if it's even possible for carnage to have a kind of beauty, but if so, then Violin was an artist of destruction.

Mr. Priest was no slouch, either. He had a long knife in one hand and a snub-nosed pistol in another and was using the cover of desks, file cabinets, and work tables to make his way across the room toward the Closers. He shot one in the heart but it didn't put the man down. The guy hardly winced, in fact, which made me wonder what kind of body armor he had beneath his suit. Priest didn't burn up a lot of calories being either surprised or frustrated by that and put his next bullet through the bridge of the guy's nose. Nope, wasn't wearing body armor there. The heavy lead bullet made a small dot on the way in but exploded the back of the Closer's skull. The man behind him got an eyeful and mouthful of hair, skull fragments and brains. He reeled back, gagging and pawing the stuff away, and in that moment Priest stepped up and corkscrewed the point of his knife in the man's eye-socket.

Harry Bolt began crawling across the floor toward an object and I realized that in his panic he'd dropped his gun. Idiot. But as he reached it, the Japanese guy kicked it away and aimed his own gun at Harry's head.

So, fuck it.

I changed all the way. It's a violent process and it hurts like a motherfucker. It also tears the shit out of my clothes. They flew apart and my backpack thudded to the floor. When I was younger the process took minutes. Now I can do it in the space of a leap. One minute I'm a short, dorky-looking guy with thinning hair, and the next I'm a wolf.

A big, bad wolf.

-22-

Mr. Priest
The Fairy Chimneys of Cappadocia
Central Anatolia, Turkey
One Month Ago

Priest stood on the edge of the shaft, bent as far forward as safety would allow. If he lost balance, though, he knew Boris and Keppler would catch him. They were fully attuned to him, a connection that he treasured but did not yet fully understand. He knew that Hiro and Rink thought that it was his own mind, his own will, or perhaps some dark magic he possessed that bound the Russian soldier and the nuclear scientist to him.

How wrong they were.

They were not his slaves.

At best, they were on loan to him. At worst they were there to insure that he did not fail or stray from his mission. There were forces more powerful than Oscar Bell, the Gateway Project, or the United States Government, and they wanted those books found.

No…they wanted them liberated.

They wanted the knowledge in those books to be rediscovered. They wanted the voices of those tomes to speak after centuries—and in some cases millennia—of enforced silence.

Already some of those voices were speaking in Priest's head. They never left him, were never silent. Hiro was too dense to realize that his smiles were a screen. A façade. He never let them see the face he saw when he looked into his shaving mirror. When the smile was gone the terror was there.

The terror and…

It shamed Priest to know that there was joy there, too. A carnal delight whose shape and depth he shuddered to consider. Rink had glimpsed it only once, and that was why she now carried a gun. Not to defend herself against guards or monsters. She carried the gun because she was afraid of him. Of the touch of his hand and the appetites that were connected to his hands and tongue and cock. To the rapacious *other* who had taken up residence in his flesh on that first day in Poliske. Even Priest did not know its name. It was not one of the Elder Gods or the Great Old Ones. It was a slave to them, a worshipper or priest-spirit. Priest did not know what to call it.

All he knew was that it owned him.

Body and soul.

He could feel the tentacles of its energy wrapped around him. Probing tendrils of the thing entered him at every orifice and coiled around his heart. It knew everything about him. It shared knowledge with him, but only hints. Never the deepest truths. Enough, though. Enough to help him find the Unlearnable Truths. Enough to have limited precognition so that he could stay one step ahead of the Closers and the Brotherhood of the Lock.

Enough to keep him chained to the vehicle of this quest.

The ropes that trailed over the edge had been slack for long minutes and now they jerked, became taut.

"Pull them up," he said.

Boris took hold of Hiro's rope and Keppler grabbed Rink's. They braced their feet, squatted and then began reeling the others up, straining with the weight, pulling hand over hand as sweat burst from their pores. Boris was sturdy and muscular and he managed easily; but Keppler was half his size, and yet she worked without groan or complaint. Priest marveled at it. He knew that he could assign her any task and she would perform it with a kind of mechanical efficiency and inhuman dedication, even if it killed her.

So strange. Useful, but so very strange.

He watched without helping as the slaves pulled and pulled.

Hiro emerged first, pulling himself up even as Boris reeled in the line. When he reached the edge of the shaft Hiro snaked out a hand, caught the lip of rock, and hauled himself up. He rested on his knees and turned to watch Rink being pulled up. Priest could not see the urban explorer's face, but he saw Rink as she came into the light. Her hair was wild and soaked with sweat, and her eyes were filled with madness.

She was smiling in all the wrong ways.

Rink grabbed Keppler's proffered hand and swarmed over the edge to stand panting like a dog. The utility pack she wore strapped to her chest bulged and strained against its buckles. A dark joy leapt up in Priest's chest, though he knew it was not his own emotion. The *thing* that lived inside him exulted at the sight as Rink unbuckled her pack and removed a thick book bound in plates of ebony wood.

"You got it," cried Priest. "Give it to me."

Rink held the book, looking at the cover, on which complex designs had been painted in gold leaf. They were star charts overlaid with the precise shapes of a perverse twist on sacred geometry. Rink bent her head toward the book and laid her cheek against it, eyelids drifting shut. Her lips moved as she silently murmured a prayer to the book.

"Rink," said Priest sternly, "give me the book."

Without opening her eyes, Rink turned her face toward the book. Her mouth curled into a lascivious smile, and then her pink tongue slipped like a wriggling worm from between her lips. She licked the cover of the book, then stiffened her tongue so that just the tip of it traced a pentagonal shape. The sight of this sent waves of revulsion and erotic joy through Priest, both emotions coming in equal measure. He felt himself grow hard.

"Rink..." began Priest again, but before he could finish, Hiro took the book from her, turned and offered it to Priest.

Priest paused for a moment and then reached out to accept the black-bound *Eligoth Ministries*. As soon as his bare flesh touched it his heart spasmed with deep pain and his knees nearly buckled. He looked up from it to Hiro. The urban explorer's eyes were dark, his face expressionless.

"What happened down there?" asked Priest. "What did you see?"

Hiro smiled then. A broad, happy smile that pulled the corners of his mouth and exposed his wet teeth. His smile grew and grew and grew until Priest thought that it must soon rip the corners of Hiro's mouth.

"Stop that," he ordered.

Rink came up to stand beside Hiro. And after a moment Keppler and Boris joined them. The four of them in a line, and they all smiled at him.

They smiled and smiled and smiled.

Then Hiro reached out a hand and placed his palm flat against the book that Priest held.

He said, *"Ph'nglui mglw'nafh Cthulhu R'lyeh wgah'nagl fhtagn."*

-23-

Crazy Town

I roared as I slammed into the Japanese guy and sent him sprawling.

He was fast, though, and managed to twist away from my claws, but his aim was for shit. He fired two shots and both missed me by inches. I landed and swiped at him, knocking his gun from his hand, but he scrabbled backward out of reach. I turned to Harry and shifted enough of my face to allow me to speak.

"Hide!" I snarled.

Harry Bolt screamed like a girl and kicked me full in the face.

It rocked me sideways and I caught a glimpse of him crawling as fast as he could past me. Asshole.

I pivoted and slashed at him. Not to cut him, though. My nails sliced through the straps of his backpack and it slid around and fell off. Harry looked back and I saw him give it a moment of thought. Grab the pack or run away from the scary monster. I guess I expected him to run.

He didn't, though.

A sob of fear broke from his chest and he flopped forward to try and snatch the torn straps of his backpack.

Kid had some balls. No brains, but he did have stones. From the look of terrified surprise I think he was startled by what he was doing. It was a weirdly endearing thing. Here was a kid who was totally out of his mind with fear and clearly out of his depth with the violent madness going on around us, and yet he tried to do the right thing rather than the safe thing. Maybe there was something in him that he didn't yet recognize. A buried courage, or the makings of it, anyway.

Shame that I couldn't let him have his moment.

I bared my teeth at him—all wolf again—and snatched the bag away, flinging it behind me. I heard it thump against the one I'd dropped.

Harry dove after it at the same moment that the Japanese guy lunged at me. The collision sent all three of us toppling backward in a sprawl. They both used a lot of elbows, knees, fists, feet and knuckles.

I used teeth and claws.

The Japanese guy tried to make a real fight of it. He chopped me in the throat with an edge-hand blow. One of those good old-fashioned karate chops. A good one, too. And it hurt. I yelped—yes, werewolves yelp. Fuck you.—and fell sideways as the Japanese guy grabbed for Harry, caught his hair, yanked him away from the backpack and punched him in the face three times. Very hard. Blood erupted from Harry's nose, but even as he fell back bleeding he stuck his thumb in his attacker's eye. It burst the eye in a spectacularly ugly way. The Japanese man should have rolled away screaming. He didn't. Instead he opened his mouth and vomited on Harry.

Not puke. Nope. That would have almost been okay.

Instead a black mass of some oily muck came pouring out. At first I thought it was blood but then it burst apart and became something else.

It became a mass of oily black tentacles.

Yeah.

Deal with that.

The tentacles wrapped around Harry Bolt's face and probed at him, trying to enter his mouth and nostrils and ears. Harry screamed and I can't blame him one bit.

I got to all fours and darted my head forward to clamp my teeth around the tentacles at the point where they erupted from the Japanese guy's mouth. I bit down hard and felt rubbery tissue and something that crunched like bones. The taste was appalling. It was like biting fish that had been sitting in the sun for a couple of days. A smell both dead and alive with wrongness. I bit all the way through, though, and then jerked my head to one side, ripping as much of them away as I could.

Harry flopped back and immediately began slapping at his face to remove the dying ends of the tentacles. He screamed and screamed.

I was busy with the Japanese man—if he was even still a man. He went wild with either pain or fury, or both, and came at me like Bruce Lee on a bad day. Kicks and punches, and a dozen kinds of chop-socky moves that I've never seen. And they all damn well hurt.

But, let's face it, I'm a werewolf, so I get to play that card. And I played it hard.

As he went after me I went for him. No need for the details, but the bottom line is that when they bury him it'll be a closed casket.

He tasted fucking awful. Even the human parts.

Jeez.

A body crashed down beside me and I saw that it was one of the Brotherhood goons. Or what Violin had left after going all Ginsu knife on him. The wolf in me was impressed. Maybe the human guy, too. She was one hell of a woman.

Harry Bolt was still being hysterical, so I took the moment to shift to a mostly human form and do half of the job I was sent here to do. I quickly opened my backpack, removed the fake book, swapped it out for the one in Harry's pack, and tossed my pack out of sight behind an overturned desk. Then as I rose I kind of kicked the other pack toward Harry. It hit him and he stopped swatting at his face—which was long-since clear of any of the tentacle bits—and looked at what had hit his shoulder. His eyes went wide and he grabbed it, hugging the thing to his chest as he knee-walked away from the melee.

Feeling a little smug, I wolfed out and rushed at the Closers. No way I wanted to get involved in the fight between Violin and the Brotherhood. Not only didn't she need my help, she looked like she was enjoying herself. Who am I to be a killjoy?

The battle between Priest and his two remaining goons and the Closers was hot and bloody. The blond woman was down, her head and right arm gone. The other woman, the petite brunette, had a Closer down and was doing the same nasty mouth tentacle soul kiss with him that the Japanese guy had tried on Harry. The Closer's body thrashed and twitched and blood sprayed out his eyes, nostrils and ears. The woman's body trembled as if she was having the mother of all orgasms. I could smell it, too. She was definitely having a sexual encounter with the guy she was killing. And, hey, I dig porn as much as the next fellow, but that's a kind of kinky that is six miles beyond weirdsville.

One of the Closers swung his metal-pronged gun thingy in my direction and I flung myself sideways as it went *tok!* The air around me went instantly white hot and I could smell my fur burning. I rolled over and over to put it out, then wheeled on the guy, teeth bared, really fucking pissed. He tried to take a second shot but I took his hand off at the wrist instead. The guy screamed and staggered, blood shooting from the ragged stump. He collided with another Closer hard enough to spoil the man's aim and the shot hit the ceiling. Burning plaster rained down on us and the heat triggered the fire alarm. Suddenly all the sprinklers kicked in and now we were having the world's most violent wet t-shirt contest.

Good times.

I rose up under the shooter and gutted him. Then pivoted and went for Mr. Priest.

He saw me coming and snapped a kick at me that caught me in exactly the way you don't want to be caught. A shockingly hard shot with the point of a steel-reinforced toe on the hinge of my jaw.

It hurt.

It hurt a whole damn lot.

I staggered sideways and the bastard kicked me again, this time hitting my ribs at an angle that sent a shockwave through my lungs and diaphragm. It was almost like he understood how to fight a werewolf. We don't have a lot of vulnerabilities but we're not indestructible. My grandmother and aunts taught me how to fight my own kind, because not all werewolves are *benandanti*. Most, in fact, aren't. If you know how to attack in just the right way, even a human can cripple us. Sure, we'll heal, but not always fast enough.

Priest kicked again and again, breaking things, sending shocks through my heart, hitting nerve clusters on my spine.

Yeah, he knew what he was doing. He laughed while he did it, too, and said a lot of very vile things in Spanish. I know just enough of that language to understand the gist of what he was saying.

I fled from the attack. Running, falling, crawling.

Priest followed me, kicking at my balls hard enough to lift me off the ground.

Balls are balls are balls. Find me any creature—human, animal or monster—who can shake off a full-power steel-toed kick to the nutsack and I will worship him as a god.

In the moment, though, I prayed to whatever gods may be to take me from a world of hurt and bring me sweetly into any dimension, including death, where I could not feel my balls.

Priest laughed out loud, the sound of it magnified by a moment of silence as no one fired a gun or screamed. It froze the whole room for a second, and all eyes turned toward him.

He flung away his empty pistol and snatched the *Manifesto* from the cart, then he turned quickly and rushed at Harry Bolt, who had taken that unfortunate moment to peer out from behind his cover.

Violin was on the wrong side of the room, and as soon as Priest moved the whole dance began again. Guns roared and men died. So did the little brunette, who was down on all fours over her victim. A line of heavy caliber bullets stitched her from hip to temple. She died quickly and badly. Four of the Brotherhood closed in around Violin and I lost sight of her, while the last three of the Closers went stomping across the floor after Priest. One of them fired his gun, but Priest ducked, warned by some sense or awareness. The air above him shimmered and the doorway burst into flames, sending a hail of burning splinters into the backs of the men attacking Violin.

I shifted back to human form and rose naked and sick to trembling feet. Then I vomited onto the floor as pain and nausea punched their way from my groin to my gut. I staggered, caught myself on the corner of a filing cabinet. The cool metal was the only steadying thing in my world. I gripped it hard and then forced myself back into wolfshape.

The transition was agonizing.

It was also healing.

Not entirely, but enough so that the pain no longer crippled me. Instead it fueled my rage.

Snarling, I pelted across the room to where Priest was kicking the shit out of Harry Bolt. The young agent was putting up a fight, though, holding onto the backpack with one hand and trying to Jackie Chan his way out of the moment. Maybe in a bar fight or an attempted mugging the kid might have won. But he was fighting a guy who'd just kicked a werewolf's ass--*my* ass--and that is kind of saying a lot.

Priest hit him from thirty different directions. His arms and legs were blurs and the sound of those blows was like a butcher chopping up a cow carcass.

Before I could even close the five steps to reach him, Harry went down, his eyes rolling up, blood pouring from his nose, his limbs completely slack. He went down and he went out.

I leapt into the air to try and hit Priest from the blind side and maybe break his back. It's a good move that I've done before.

Priest crouched, spun and smashed me aside with the backpack.

I fell hard but came up quick, but by then Priest was heading for the burning doorway. One of the Brotherhood guys tried to stop him, but Priest slashed him diagonally across the face then foot-swept him so that he fell into my path. I dodged, but then the floor under me exploded and like an after echo I heard a double *tok-tok!*

I fell to one side, again having to smother flames.

A hand closed around my ruff and pulled me up, and I very nearly took the arm attached to it, but then realized it was Violin.

"Get the books," she snapped.

We had another microscopic moment of connection and I got a flash of something behind her eyes. Something very, very old and dangerous. When she smiled I saw that her teeth were sharper than they were before.

Holy shit.

Then she was fighting. The Brotherhood and the Closers tried to kill her and kill each other. Violin just wanted to kill all of them.

She looked happy about it. So I left her to it.

I ran through flames into the hallway and followed Priest's scent. He had blood on his shoes and the stink of rotting fish filled the air. I could have followed him blind.

He made it all the way to the employee exit before I caught up with him. I couldn't see the *Manifesto*, but since the backpack was thicker now, it wasn't hard to put two-and-two together.

I put on a burst of speed and then hurled myself at him. Priest turned and tried another kick at my snout, but it was too late. My weight was already committed to the jump and midway through it I turned into a man. The new configuration made the kick land on my shoulder rather than my jaw. It hurt, but it wasn't the pinpoint precision that he needed to stop me.

I barreled into him and we hit the service door with crushing impact. His hip struck the crashbar and we went spilling out onto the pavement. The backpack went flying into the street, where it burst apart. The fake *Der Vermis Mysteriis* went skidding under a parked car, while *The Cloister Manifesto* flew straight up in the air. Priest dove for the fake worm book and I scrambled up, shapeshifted back to human and went long to catch a touchdown pass with the *Manifesto*.

Priest rose, clutching the other book. He tried to kick my hands to make me drop the *Manifesto*, but I turned, took the shockingly painful blow on my hip and simultaneously flung the book in through the open doorway. Then I dodged a second kick as I jumped and slapped both hands against the door, slamming it shut. I turned and leaned back against it, hearing the lock click shut.

As a human I am not protected against the cold, and the sidewalk was frigid. Cold air blew knives across my skin. I changed halfway back to wolf, still standing on two feet, but now they had leathery pads and long claws. I flexed my claws and snarled at him. My body was trembling from pain and damage and I wasn't sure how long I could stay on my feet. Priest looked ready to rumble, though, but uncertainty flickered in his eyes. He'd have to get through me and get inside the door. I don't know how he'd managed it earlier, but if he had to pick the lock it was going to take time and we both knew I wasn't going to make it easy for him.

Impasse. We stared at each other, both ready to continue the fight but uncertain how to proceed. Mr. Priest had the fake book and me and a locked door were between him and the real *Manifesto*.

Priest held the book in his hands and stared hot nuclear death at me. Not sure I've ever had anyone focus that much pure hatred in my direction, and I have three ex-wives.

"You'll scream for this," he said. "You will burn in a pit of fire and beg to die."

"Stick it up your ass," I said, gasping from the cold.

"Open that door and I may let you live."

"Suck my dick," I suggested. My legs were a half-second away from giving out and there was a bell ringing in my head from his earlier kicks. Even with the healing abilities I'd inherited I was all the way out on the ragged edge of collapse.

Then Priest suddenly straightened and looked down at the book he held. His eyes went big and round and his mouth slowly opened.

"No…" he breathed. "God…no…"

Overhead in a cloudless winter sky there was a heavy rumble of thunder. Lightning forked above us, but it was as red as blood.

Then two tears, every bit as red as that lightning, broke from the corners of Priest's eyes and fell down his cheeks.

"No…" he said again. I saw the horrible realization come into his eyes. He knew that what he held was a fake. Both books were inside the museum. He would have to get through me and through Violin to retrieve them, and if he'd seen that woman fight he would have to know that even with his skills, she'd turn him into cold cuts.

"You're done," I said, and it came out as a wheeze.

Priest let the backpack fall from his hands. It thumped onto the ground and lay there, inert and useless.

Another bolt of red lightning ripped across the skies chased by heavy thunder. Priest pointed a finger at me.

"You are cursed," he said and my heart nearly froze when he spoke because it wasn't his voice. Whoever or whatever spoke through him did so in a voice as heavy and deep as the rolling thunder. "You are damned."

I tried to speak, but couldn't. My mouth would not work at all.

"We know you, wolf," spoke that voice. "We know you and we have marked you. Look for us in your dreams and despair, for we are coming for you."

The words were melodramatic, corny, bad scripting from a cheap pulp horror story. That's what I told myself later.

But in the moment?

Shit.

My heart was hammering so bad I was afraid it would explode in my chest. Despite the cold there was sweat pouring down my face and chest and thighs.

Mr. Priest backed away from me, still pointing his finger. Then he turned and walked away.

I could have gone after him. I could have caught up to him.

Sure.

Yeah, I could have.

Like hell.

-24-

Sam Hunter
Philadelphia, Pennsylvania

I kept a spare set of car keys in a magnetic box in the wheel well of my car, and extra clothes in the back. I changed into sweats and sneakers, then grabbed some tools and picked the lock on the museum door. The *Manifesto* was on the floor where I'd thrown it. I propped the door open and ran the damned thing over to my car and stowed it in a heavy corrugated steel lockbox. Then I took the backpack inside and made my way downstairs.

Violin was kneeling beside Harry Bolt, doing some kind of massage thing to wake him up. She paused and looked across the sea of corpses that lay between us.

"*Benandanti?*" she asked.

"*Benandanti,*" I agreed.

She nodded. I held out the backpack and she came and took it. She weighed it in her hands and nodded. Harry Bolt got to his feet and looked like a schoolyard kid who'd been roughed up by bullies. He had tear streaks on his face.

Violin glanced at the metal cart and back to me. "The other book?"

"That's mine," I said.

"For who?" she asked.

I almost lied, but didn't. "Limbus."

Violin studied me for a long, long time. "Fill a trash barrel with holly and hawthorn wood. Douse it with kerosene from a church. Any church. Strike a match at first light."

"You want me to destroy it?"

"Yes."

"Not give it to Limbus?"

She wiped blood from her cheek. "Not to anyone."

"What about the other book?"

She almost smiled and shrugged. "Maybe one day I'll build a similar pyre."

"Same way?"

"There's only one truly good way," she said. There was a look of barely controlled horror and disgust in her eyes, and it was clear it came from a deep and total awareness of what those books are. And what they could do. Maybe of what Priest *would* have done if he'd stolen one or both.

Harry Bolt stumbled over and stood beside her, then flinched when his senses cleared enough to realize who I was.

"Holy shit!" he cried and flinched backward.

"Shhh," soothed Violin. "There are no enemies here."

With that, she turned and steered a trembling, shambling Harry Bolt out of the room. I stood and watched them go, my head full of a thousand questions, but my heart knowing that those answers would never be mine.

I could hear them all the way up the stairs and I waited for the bang of the security door.

The museum settled into a tomblike stillness.

Everywhere I looked there was death. Grotesque and appalling. I had no idea in the world how the police and forensics teams were going to make sense of this. And, frankly, I didn't care.

The backpack I'd brought with me was where I'd left it, hidden behind a desk, soaked in blood. Intact.

I bent and picked it up, and felt a wave of sickness wash through me. I was glad I couldn't see the cover and didn't need to touch it again with my own flesh. It was such an ugly thing.

Acantha would want it and the *Manifesto*.

That's what she was paying me for.

I stepped over the bodies and parts of bodies and went upstairs and out the door and to my car. All the time wondering where the hell I was going to find holly and hawthorn wood and church kerosene this late at night.

There was one last rumble of thunder.

We know you, wolf. We know you and we have marked you. Look for us in your dreams and despair, for we are coming for you.

I started the engine and turned on the radio. Found some hillbilly rock and turned it all the way up. Loud enough to block out the thunder. Loud enough to block out the whispers in my head.

I tried not to be afraid.

I tried real hard.

But you can't win every fight.

Goth Chicks

-1-

I Hate Missing persons cases. Given a choice between trying to find a missing kid and having my nuts pounded flat with a mallet, I'd go for the mallet.

The effect is nearly the same. Your balls get busted either way.

Except that if the missing person is a teenage runaway your heart gets broken, too.

Case in point.

-2-

I was having lunch at the Heaven Street Diner. Usual place, usual spot at the counter. Rueben with extra everything, side of fries, coffee. Usual lunch. The TV above the bar had a ballgame on, but nobody I cared about was playing, and the guys who were playing were doing a piss-poor job of it. So I read a book. It was one of those self-help things written by someone a couple of tiers down from Tony Robbins. The title wasn't *How Not to be a Total Dickhead,* but it might as well have been. That was the message. Since I can be a dickhead, in full or in part, and didn't want anyone to feel compelled to chisel that onto my tombstone when I went, I thought I'd better read at least some of it.

And I was waiting for someone.

He came in when I had just finished a chapter called, I shit you not, *The Jackass Principle.* I saw him in the mirror behind the counter. Tall guy in his fifties, iron gray hair, hero chin, wide-receiver shoulders and a five thousand dollar watch. If Captain America from the movies retired and went into business, he'd look like this guy. Couldn't be more out of place in a diner on Heaven Street. He looked around with gray, calculating eyes, and could probably price everything and everyone in the joint to within plus or minus five bucks. He had a good poker face so he didn't let his disappointment show. Not too much, at least.

There were eight people in the bar and I was the only one who didn't look like he –or she—was out on bail for petty theft or there to meet their dealer. It's that kind of diner. So he came straight over to me.

"Mr. Hunter?" he said.

I swiveled a quarter turn on my counter stool. "Mr. Smith?" I said.

He held out his hand. "Jonah Smith."

I shook it but didn't stand to do it. Hard hand. The kind that's done hard work. A ridge of shooter's calluses on the inside of the big knuckle of his right index finger. Handgun man, and he had a lot of military in his posture, build and bearing. Officer, or ex-officer. Not some grunt humping battle rattle through the sand.

"May I?" he asked and didn't wait for permission from me or anyone as he slid onto the next stool. The waitress, Ivy, came over and gave him as frank and calculating an appraisal as he'd given the whole place. Probably as accurate, too.

"Coffee?" she asked.

"Please. Black, no sugar."

She produced a thick porcelain cup and saucer, poured, gave me a brief look, and wandered away. Ivy wasn't one for chitchat when it looked like someone was there to do business. She's a very good waitress.

"Thanks for meeting me," said Smith.

I nodded. "You were very mysterious on the phone. What can I do for you?"

"Right to it? That's fine, that's good. I would like to hire you to find someone."

"Skip trace?"

"Pardon?"

"Was this person out on bail and failed to make a court date?"

"No."

"You're not an attorney?"

"What? No. Why would you ask?" said Smith.

"Ninety-nine percent of my missing person's work is bail skips, which means that lawyers usually hire me. Way you're dressed, you could be with one of the better law firms."

"Would a top lawyer meet you in a diner all the way down here?" he asked, amused.

"Depends on how quiet he wanted things to be. Lot of times a lawyer wants his client fetched back home before the cops and the courts get worked up. If everything's hunky-dory they go for better P.I.s and ask them to come to their offices."

Smith nodded. "Understood. But, no. I'm not a lawyer, though I was referred to you by an attorney with whom I play golf. Alfred Pederson of Pederson—"

"—Bailey and Schmidt, yeah, I know Al. He's a dick."

"He is, in fact, a dick," agreed Smith. "And he cheats at golf."

"But you play with him?"

"I enjoy taking money away from him. Those golf games are good for ten thousand a year, and it's easy money. Add to that the fact that he's senior partner in a firm that handles a considerable chunk of my holdings, and there we are."

"What holdings?"

He shrugged. "I am a defense contractor," he said. "My various companies manufacture airplane missile guidance systems, submarine missile defense systems, and drone air-to-air targeting systems."

"You blow shit up," I said.

"I blow a lot of shit up," he said.

We drank some coffee. "So who's missing?" I asked. "One of your people sneak off with designs for a nuke?"

"I don't deal with nuclear weapons," he said in a way that made me think he did. "And if this was corporate espionage or someone within my organization I have internal security people who would handle it."

Ivy came by, poured our cups full and left again.

"How many times do I have to ask who's missing before you just come right out and tell me?" I said.

Smith sighed. "My daughter is missing."

And he started to cry.

I said, "Ah, shit."

-3-

We moved to a booth in the back.

Smith had a hell of a lot of control but it was pretty obvious that if he was so far out on a limb that he was down in this part of town talking to a guy like me, then a lot of serious dials had already been turned on him. His control was habit and discipline but it was a mask. Ivy brought our coffees over and left us alone. The other people at the diner know that when I'm in booth eight that it was business. We understand each other.

I gave Smith a little time to get his shit together. He did. He didn't apologize for his emotions, which is good. Apologies of that kind are bullshit.

"Her name is—was—Catherine."

"Was?"

"It was Cathy when she was little. Then Kate in middle school, then Cat in high school. Until she dropped out. After that it was Bellatrix for a while. Like the character from the—"

"Harry Potter books. Sure, Bellatrix LeStrange."

"That was a phase. And it's when she started dying her hair black and wearing a lot of white makeup."

"She's Goth?"

"I suppose. But when I asked her that she said that calling her 'Goth' was no different than calling her heterosexual. Not sure what that means. Maybe she's gay, I don't know. We stopped having real conversations a long time ago. Right around the time she changed her name again. This time it's Pollydorry." He spelled it. "When I asked her what it meant she told me to go read a book, but I can't find one by that name."

"It's a play on John Polidori, a nineteenth century writer," I said.

"Never heard of him."

"He was the personal physician for the poet George Gordon, Lord Byron," I explained. "Polidori and Byron were friends with

Percy and Mary Shelley. They were all in Switzerland at some villa and they decided to all write ghost stories. I think it was Byron's idea, but it's been too long since I took English Lit in college. Anyway, Percy Shelley wrote a poem, Byron wrote part of a novel, Mary Shelley started writing *Frankenstein*, and Polidori wrote a short story called *'The Vampyre'* that my professor said was where the modern vampire story was born. Or at least the first romantic vampire story. Way the hell back in 1819 or thereabout. If your daughter's running with the Goth crowd, then a name like Pollydorry makes sense. The name has ties to the old vampire stuff, it's ironic or sarcastic or maybe an in-joke."

"Whatever," he said. "It was the Pollydorry version of her that dropped out of school, cleaned out her bank accounts and ran away."

"How old is she?"

"Twenty."

"Not a minor. Seems to me she's allowed to *be* lost."

"I want to find my daughter, Mr. Hunter."

I looked at him over the rim of my cup. "How hard you try to find her?"

Smith stiffened. "What kind of question is that?"

"The kind private investigators being asked to find daddy's little girl ought to ask," I said.

Smith thought about it for a while, his gray eyes searching my face and then shifting down to look at his coffee cup. After a while he nodded. "Maybe not hard enough."

"Any idea why she ran?" I asked, settling back in my corner of the booth.

"She hates me," he said.

"Why?"

"Why do kids ever hate their parents?"

"Offhand," I said, "I can give you about three hundred good answers."

He bristled. "Look, we may not have been the happiest family in history, but we got along. We had a good life and no one wanted for anything."

"What about love, affection and approval?" I asked.

"Are you trying to be offensive?"

"Only a little," I admitted. "What I'm mostly doing is trying to get past the brochure version of your life and read the actual details.

There are a lot of runaways in this country. One in seven kids between the ages of ten and eighteen run away at some point in their lives. About two million teens run away every year. Running away *after* high school is a much lower statistic. Poverty, abuse, abandonment, family tension, divorce, and drug addiction are all major causes in all age groups. You tell me you had a happy home. You have money, which suggests that poverty wasn't a factor. That leaves a lot of other causes."

"She's emotionally disturbed."

"Is that a clinical diagnosis or your own opinion?"

"Both."

"Disturbed in what way?"

"Stunted emotional growth, a tendency toward rebellious behavior…"

"Those are bullshit. I'm emotionally stunted, according to my ex-wives, and my former employers at the Minneapolis Police Department claimed I had rebellious tendencies."

"So far, Mr. Hunter, I'm leaning toward agreeing," said Smith.

I smiled and gestured toward the door with my coffee cup. "Feel free to fuck off, Mr. Smith."

He didn't get up. Instead he drummed his fingers very slowly on the tabletop. "This isn't going well."

I shrugged.

"Can we start again?"

"Sure," I said. "Let's start with the truth. Why'd your daughter run away?"

I watched his face as he worked out how to say it, and I could tell that it cost him, though I didn't know why. He was a bit of a pompous asshole but I wasn't getting the child molester vibe from him. Not to say that I'm always right about that, but I'm right enough of the time.

Finally he said, "If I tell you the truth, will you agree to find her?"

"That depends on what that truth is, and if finding her is going to put your daughter in any danger."

"You don't even know her," said Smith, "why would you care?"

I let him read the expression on my face. He did and he got the right message and gave me another nod.

"I don't want her hurt, God knows," he said. "I love her, even if she doesn't think so. I've always loved her. I loved her mother, too. Very much."

"Past tense?" I suggested.

"Nora died six years ago," he said, and there was genuine pain in his voice. "She used to ride. Loved horses, you understand. Had a dozen of them and she competed in amateur show jumping all over the country. Never all that good at it, but enthusiastic, and she donated to equine organizations. She was part of a group of amateurs giving an exhibition in Lexington, Kentucky in the days leading up to the big national show jumping competition. Her horse took the fence wrong and Nora fell off and the fucking horse fell on top of her. Half a ton of scared, thrashing horse coming down on a woman who was barely five foot two and one hundred and fifteen pounds. Broke Nora's neck and back. She was in a coma for eleven months. I brought in specialists from all over to try and help her. The very best people. And I even tried some, um, *experimental* treatments, but the damage was too severe and some of the specialists were hard to find. By the time I could arrange to bring them here, the tissue deterioration was too extensive. There was too much irreparable damage to her spinal cord and brain. My wife died on Christmas morning."

"That's pretty horrible," I said. "I'm sorry for your loss."

He nodded. "I loved my wife, Mr. Hunter. We had the kind of romance they write books about. Teen sweethearts, first loves, storybook wedding, honeymoon in paradise, lots of passion, lots of laughs, and a deep friendship. There was supposed to be a happily ever after, but that fucking horse…"

"How many kids?"

"Just the one," he said. "Cathy. Or Pollydorry. Stupid goddamn name. We wanted more kids but Nora had a couple of miscarriages and we decided to stop trying. Cathy had a lot of friends, so there was always kid noise and laughter in the house. It was nice."

"Until it wasn't," I said. "What changed the frequency?"

"Puberty, mostly," said Smith. "It hit my daughter hard. She went from a skinny eleven year old to a twelve year old who looked twenty. Lots of boobs and hips, long legs, the works and absolutely no idea how to deal with the sudden and intense attention from boys and men of all ages. I had to fire a cook and a yardman from the household staff because of things they said to her, and I knocked one of my oldest friends on his ass for cracking a joke about her. It was unfair to Cathy, too, because from that point on she had no chance of growing up ordinary. She was sexualized by everyone 24/7 and eventually she stopped trying to fight it and bought into it. Maybe it was a defensive reaction, but she started dressing in increasingly more provocative ways. Everything was low-cut, see-through or tight. We had horrible fights about the outfits she wanted to wear on dates when she was fifteen and sixteen. We found out that a girl she knew got a prescription for birth control pills and was giving them to Cathy. It was like that. Day in and day out."

I sipped my coffee, picturing it, but wondering what version of that story Pollydorry would tell. Didn't say anything though.

"When she was in senior year of high school," continued Smith, "she started going in the other direction."

"Goth?"

"No. Girls. She started going out on dates with girls. At first I didn't think much of it. I thought she was simply hanging out with other girls for, you know, protection. Safety in numbers, like that. Then I found out that she was sneaking those girls into the house and they were sometimes sleeping over. One of the maids walked in at the wrong time. Cathy and I had a hell of a fight about it."

"About her exploring her own sexuality?"

"No, and don't be smug. I'm not one of those Luddites who thinks homosexuality is either an aberration or a choice. I get it. And if Cathy came and told me she was a lesbian, I'd deal. Sure, I'd have been bummed because who doesn't want grandkids some day, especially with Nora gone. No, what bothered me was how careless she was being. Not locking her door seemed to be more of a set-up than an accident, because she'd sometimes go further and leave her bedroom door open. You know how disturbing that is when you're a father and you hear your daughter and some other girl moaning like that? Loud enough to hear all the way downstairs. And out at the pool. Swimming naked with other girls, making out on the beach chairs."

"Okay, I get the picture. She was trying to make a point."

"She was trying to hurt me."

"Or get your attention," I said. "Your wife was dead by this point, right? How emotionally available were you for Pollydorry?"

He took about five seconds too long answering that. "I was processing my grief."

"So was she. Life doesn't come with a set of instructions."

"Oh, very wise, thank you so much."

"So, long story short, you were dealing with your own shit, Pollydorry wasn't getting fed emotionally, you two didn't connect on the right points, and she bugged out. What else am I missing?"

Jonah Smith finished his coffee and stared at me for a long, long time. "I married into Nora's family as much as I married her. Her father was the money. I took over his companies and tripled them in size, but after the old man died Nora was the majority stockholder. I own twelve percent of the company. The rest of the shares are held in trust. When Cathy turns twenty-one she will inherit."

"And there we go," I said. "How much cash are we talking about?"

Smith's smile looked physically painful. "Including all holdings in subsidiary companies, real estate, the art collections, Nora's jewelry, and what's in the bank? Let's call it sixteen point three."

"Million? Wow."

"No," he said. "Billion."

I said, "Oh shit."

He said, "I need Cathy to come back to the family. I need her to sign papers that will allow me to continue to manage and grow the family business. I'm not asking her to sign away any of her stocks. She'll retain controlling interest insofar as her inheritance goes, but I need to have some freedom of action to grow the company. There are some major—and I do mean *major*—contracts coming up that I want to bid on, but I can't without her signature on the right statements of authority. It's in her own best interests, because even if she never cashes in a single share she could spend a million dollars a day of her own money and it wouldn't even tickle the family business."

"Wow," I said. "Does she know this?"

"She has some idea, but probably lacks perspective. She didn't do herself any favors by running away. She's barely touched what's sitting in her checking account. At most she takes five grand a month, and usually only half that. She's living small when she could be living like the queen of the world."

"Maybe she doesn't want to be queen."

"She would if she understood."

"Maybe she's happy living the way she does."

"I refuse to believe that," said Smith.

"Okay. Do you have any idea where she is?"

"Only in general. She withdraws money from ATMs and occasionally at branches of the bank we use. All in the Philadelphia area, and mostly in Center City and Old City, South Street, Headhouse Square. Like that." He named the bank and gave me a list of the branches she's hit. The list also included her debit card numbers.

"This is useful," I said, folding the list and tucking a corner under my coffee cup.

"Right now she's lost somewhere in the bullshit Goth culture," said Smith, "and her lowlife friends can see my regular investigators coming a mile off. My people have caught a whiff of her now and again but that's it. I heard that you're more familiar with that scene and can find people like my daughter, even if she's hiding out with junkies, whores and the scum of the goddamn earth. Is that blunt enough for you, Mr. Hunter? I need someone like you to find my daughter and bring her home."

"Well," I said, "ain't love grand?"

"Will you do it?" he asked, reaching into his jacket pocket to produce a checkbook and a gold pen. "I can tell by your expression that you think I'm a disingenuous asshole."

"*Elitist* asshole," I corrected.

"Elitist asshole," he agreed. "I am. However even my eleven percent of that stock will allow me to write a check that's larger than your level of disapproval. Tell me what number will get this done."

"Five grand," I said.

"Okay," he said, and began to write.

"Per day," I added. His pen paused. "Five days in advance, nonrefundable."

He looked at me. "Are you fucking with me?"

"Of course I am," I said, "but I'm also serious as a heart attack."

Smith snorted, but he wrote the check. I watched. Twenty-five grand was enough to make me tingle in my special parts. He tore off the check and handed it to me. If he had tried that bullshit of snatching it away to make me lunge for it, the way some dickheads do, I'd have dragged him out into the alley and stomped him unconscious. Not joking.

I placed the check on the table between us.

"There are conditions," I said.

"I figured there would be."

"Pollydorry has to want to come home."

"Agreed."

"She has to be told why you want her home."

"Agreed."

"And if she tells a different story, like maybe you're one of the guys who got handsy with her—"

"Not a chance," he said.

"—if she tells me that and I believe her, we're going to have a different kind of conversation and you won't like it much at all."

"Don't threaten me, Mr. Hunter. My security team is second to none."

"Fuck your security team."

He looked for the false bravado in my eyes and did not find it. I wasn't kidding, and he was enough of a poker player to know when someone is bluffing.

"You think pretty highly of yourself," he said.

"So do you."

He took a letter from his other jacket pocket. It had his contact information and clipped to it was a data sheet on Catherine Smith, including social security numbers, physical description, list of last known associates, and a photo of a pretty girl in a red and white striped corset, black spandex miniskirt, lots of black eyeliner and red-black lipstick glaring at the camera. Looking defensive. Looking unhappy.

Smith left without saying another word. I sat for a moment and had another cup of coffee, staring into the eyes of Pollydorry.

-4-

There was a pretty strong Goth scene here in Philadelphia, mostly in the stretch from Spring Garden Street down to Bainbridge. A few elsewhere. I knew them all. Most of them weren't permanent, except for the Coffin Factory, Descent and Xanax. The rest were regular event nights when the Goth crowd took over other venues. *Fusion by Intrepid* was at Emerald City on Fridays, *Fast, Cheap and Out of Control* was held at Fluid on Sundays, and *Sex Dwarf* was at that same place every third Friday. Like that. Some were pure Goth, but most drew mingled crowds from the Glam and Punk people, and some strays who did not define themselves in any way that mattered to anyone but themselves. I could relate.

All told there were a couple of dozen places where you could make that scene. Fewer if you were under twenty-one and had shitty cards. Pollydorry had probably not been carded since she was fifteen. The date on the photo her father gave me was from three years ago, which meant she'd been seventeen when it was taken, but she looked twenty-seven.

Even though I can move among that crowd I don't belong to it. They know it and I know it. I'm tolerated because I don't judge and because I've helped out a few people here and there, and word gets around. Sometimes I get help on a case now and then, especially if resolving that case gets someone they care about out of a jam, or keeps the bad guys from preying on the innocents.

And there are a lot of innocents among the Goths. More than you'd guess. Sure, they rock the funeral clothes and vampire chic, and a lot of the music is either loud enough to sterilize an elk or moody to the point of requiring a suicide watch. There's that. Just like there's piercings and skin art and provocative clothing and even some kinky sex. That's there, but you'd have to be blind, stupid or have your head up your ass not to understand what's really going on. The Goth kids are on the fringe because a lot of them have been pushed there. By heavy-handed parents, by sexual abuse, by being ignored, by having their individuality questioned and criticized. We —society—inflict all sorts of injuries on people and then blame them for having scars. We sexualize and exploit and then condemn them for being the living representations of our own desires. We use them and then blame them for having been used.

The movement isn't a movement. Not really. It's not one unified population but rather islands in a stormy sea. You can trace it back to the sixties, when music critic John Stickney met with Jim Morrison in a dusty old wine cellar and said that was the perfect setting for *The Doors'* 'Gothic rock,' but the movement was really already in motion by then. Formless, nameless, peopled by the kids who didn't want to be part of the Establishment world of their parents but weren't as optimistic as the hippies. Some of them used their music to speak in private conversations to whomever was able to listen. I listened, too. I sat in the dark and played my *Souxsie and the Banshees* and *Joy Division* albums and wondered how someone like me could ever hope to fit into the world, and knew that the answer was simple: I couldn't. I never would. And never did.

I wasn't part of that crowd anymore. I did my time and the tidal forces of my life took me to other waters. I became a cop in the Twin Cities, and that broke my heart in different ways. I failed at being a husband, and wore those scars, too. Then I drifted east and got my private investigator's ticket here in Philly, but it didn't lift me out of the shadows. It couldn't, because changing mailing addresses didn't change who and what I was. In the Goth world, and in the larger less well-defined fringe community, I was allowed to be myself. Some of the people there even know about me. They know about the wolf. And they're good with it, because they know what the wolf is, what he wants, how he feeds, and who he feeds on.

Ivy knows. A few others. Enough of them so that I don't feel as alone as I used to feel.

So, when I decided to go looking for Pollydorry I knew that there were people I could approach. People who might know.

My first stop was a strip club called, god help me, *ViXXXens*. The place isn't exactly a Goth hangout, but some of the dancers were a mix of somber Goth and the less genuine depressed 'Candy Goth.' Besides, I had friends in this place. I parked a couple of blocks away, put on my ancient leather Indian Motorcycle jacket because the nights were getting cold and I don't have a lot of meat on me. A couple of guys in business suits were at the door, fishing in their wallets for the ten-dollar cover. One of them produced a fifty and waited impatiently for the doorman to make change from a wad that would have choked a rhino. The doorman was taking his time with it, licking his thumb before peeling off a series of fives.

"Come on, man, can we put some spin on this?" complained the man with the fifty. "I'm freezing my nuts off."

The doorman looked up at him. He was a dwarf with a shaved head and precisely trimmed black goatee. He wore a three-button polo shirt over a long-sleeved thermal undershirt. The polo had the club's logo—a silhouette of a naked woman with improbably large and gravity-resistant breasts—on the left chest and below that was his name: PUNCH.

Punch smiled. "You made me lose count, sport," he said, put the fives back onto the roll and started counting again. Slower.

The business guy did not push the issue. Even though he and his buddy were tall and looked fit, and even though the doorman was a dwarf, there was no doubt in anybody's mind how a scuffle between them would end. Punch was built like a gorilla. Short legs, massive shoulders, long arms, and lots of muscle. He looked like he could bench-press a Volvo. I've only ever seen him fight twice. Both times it was over in a couple of seconds. I don't know if Punch ever studied martial arts, but somewhere along the way he'd learned how to punch really fast and really hard and in very bad places. He smiled a lot, even while waiting for the ambulance to take away whoever was stupid enough to make jokes about him, or—much worse—anyone who put their hands on one of the women who worked at the club. Aside from what I've seen firsthand there are a lot of stories about Punch, and I do not think any of them are exaggerated. You'd have to be really stupid or very drunk to think pissing him off was the most important thing on your to-do list.

The two businessmen stood and shivered and waited for their change. As Punch handed the cash over he said to them what he says to everyone.

"Be nice."

They mumbled something and went in. Punch shoved his roll of bills into his pants pocket and smiled at me. "It's the Big Bad Wolf," he said. "Huffing and puffing and blowing any houses down lately?"

We shook hands. He had a grip like an industrial vice but his skin was always surprisingly soft. He told me that it was all about moisturizing. The ladies appreciated soft hands.

"'Sup, Punch," I said. "How're things?"

He shrugged. "Things are things."

Punch always said that. I could hear the bass notes of the music thumping from inside. Some kind of electronica shit. I love music and I try not to be a total middle aged dick about it, but I'm pretty sure there was only ever one EDM track, that it's the exact same track on every album in that genre ever made, that it's two hours long, and everyone who goes to clubs is too hammered to realize that it's always that same music. I also think it was composed, played and recorded by robots, with no human intervention of any kind. If I was ever captured by agents of a foreign power and they wanted to torture secrets out of me by blasting that shit, I'd start spilling my guts thirty seconds in. I once asked Punch how he could stand it and he gave me a ten minute speech about the electronic dance music scene, its history, the key performers, and the nuances of song structure. So, he's either insane or he was fucking with me.

Another customer came up, handed a ten, and vanished inside. Looked like a schoolteacher. Didn't meet anyone's eyes. Punch added the money to his roll with a philosophical sigh.

"Married guy," he said.

"I know," I said.

"You see him take his ring off?"

"Nope."

"Smelled the sweat from where it had been?"

"Yup."

"You're a creepy motherfucker," said Punch. "You know that, right?"

"Been told once or twice."

Punch glanced around, saw the street was empty.

"What's the what, Sam?" he asked. "You on a case?"

"Yeah. Missing girl."

He cocked an eyebrow. "Underage?"

"No."

"A close relative need one of her kidneys?"

"No."

"Then why would I help you?"

I told him the whole story. He listened, pausing only to take cover money from an old guy who looked like George Carlin and chase off two teenage boys who had fake I.D.

When I was done talking Punch leaned against the wall counting his money and thinking about it.

"Guess you better tell me what kind of conversation you want to have with her."

"Just that," I said. "A conversation. Her old man's check cleared, so I'm paid either way. And you know me, Punch, I don't strong arm anyone. If she wants to come home, I'll be happy to facilitate that under any conditions she wants to set. If she doesn't want to come home, I'll ask if she'll let me take a video on my phone of her saying that. End of story."

"What if her old man wants to know where you found her?"

"That's Pollydorry's call. She gets to set the rules. Same as always with me," I said.

Punch had to think about it some more. I did not push it. Sure, I know that if I wolfed out I could tear him apart, but in all other circumstances he would hand me my ass. And, besides, Punch was one of the genuine good guys. We've backed each other's play a few times, which makes him family, which makes him part of my pack.

That's how it works. With certain clients and with certain other people they become part of my unofficial pack. My New Agey second ex-wife would call it my 'soul family.' Whatever. Pack works for me. It appeals to the wolf that lives beneath my skin. Whenever someone fucks with my pack the wolf comes out to play and he does not play nice.

"You ain't been down here much lately," said Punch.

"No. What of it?"

"You been reading the news?" he asked. "You hear about the gang stuff?"

"Sure. Some kind of small scale drug war, as I understand it. Why? What's that have to do with the girl?"

"Been nine guys killed over the last sixteen years," he said.

"And...?"

"And maybe the crowd Pollydorry runs with been around each time. Not saying they're involved. Actually," he admitted, "I don't know the whole story. It's just that her name's come up a couple times and you might not be the only one looking for her."

"Who else?"

"It's complicated," said Punch, looking pained. "I just got back from a couple weeks in New England so I'm a little out of touch. Went up for the apple festival."

With anyone else I'd have made a joke about that, but since I didn't want to get my scrotum punched into orbit I held my tongue.

"What I'm hearing is a bit freaky," continued Punch. "If this is a gang war then it's not playing out like any I ever saw. Been hits on both sides, but there've been hits outside of the gangs, too. Bad hits, too. Blood on the streets and hair on the walls, if you can dig me. But no theme to it."

"Theme?"

"Sure. With gangs there's always this need to let blood tell a story. Someone's a snitch and you cut his tongue out and nail it to his head. Someone's fucking someone else's girl and you cut his dick off and sew it into his mouth. Someone's skimming the take and he loses his hands. Like that. That's internal shit. When it's gang to gang it's all about showing how fucking intense they are. Handcuffing a guy to the steering wheel of his car, pouring gasoline on his crotch and tossing in a match. Not too much gas, either, because they want him to scream a long time, and they make videos of it. Or they get one of the higher-ups and hang him from his ankles and skin him alive. Seen that twice when the Jamaicans and the Puerto Ricans were tussling over the action on South Street. And there's that new thing the biker gangs are doing. Drawing and quartering, but instead of tying someone's arms and legs to four horses they chain him to four Harleys, then they drag the pieces around until they fall off the chain. It's all about big drama, about making the victims suffer in big ways, and about how it creates a legend on the streets."

"Fuck me," I said.

"You been out of the cop stuff so long you ain't seen how it's changed, Sam. Bet you don't run into that shit as a P.I."

"Not that shit, but shit," I said, and he thought about it, then nodded.

"Fair enough. You get the weird shit. The fucking Stephen King shit. On the streets, though, it's the Wild Wild West."

"But you say this isn't like that?"

Punch shook his head. "Nah. Mind you, it's every bit as nasty, but this is closer to Hannibal Lecter shit than gang drama."

"How so?" I asked, interested.

"Lots of dead bodies but not enough parts."

"Come again?"

"What I said, Sam. Whoever's been doing these killings has taken parts of the victims with him. Or with them, whatever."

"For what? Trophies?"

"Maybe. When gangs cut something off they put it up on display. It's all about making a point, establishing their narrative, if you can dig that."

"Sadly, I can."

"Some of these recent killings, though," said Punch, "are total splatter scenes and the killers have been walking off with body parts. Cops been keeping it all on the downlow 'cause they want to hold back details to help weed out cranks."

"I know that routine," I said. "Do you know which body parts? Someone cutting heads or are they going old school and collecting ears? I had a former Spec Ops guy once back in the Cities who took ears. Picked up the habit in Afghanistan."

"No," said Punch, "hearts."

"What?"

"Whoever's killing those poor sons-a-bitches cuts their hearts out and walks off with that shit. How's that for some Halloween stuff right there?"

"I love this town," I said, meaning I damn well did not. Punch nodded.

"That's all I know, 'cept that Pollydorry's name came up as a possible witness. Not sure what that means, though."

"Who'd know the bottom line on this?"

Punch hedged then nodded to the club entrance. "Her ladyship."

I thanked him and offered him a twenty spot. He shook it off. "Not selling you anything today, Sam. Just give me your word that you ain't cruising around here for a snatch and grab on behalf of dear old dad."

"Hey, man, who you talking to?"

He laughed. "Yeah, okay. Had to say it, though."

He offered a fist and I bumped it and went inside.

-5-

'Her ladyship,' as Punch often called her, was the owner of *ViXXXens* as well as one of the dancers. Well, former dancer. Never learned her real name, but everyone calls her Juicy.

She lives with Punch. Has for years. Some folks think they're a couple. Some think they're both gay and that their cohabitation is some kind of cover. Others think they're brother and sister. Personally I don't care. I wouldn't care if all of that was true at once. Punch and Juicy were in the extended family of my pack.

Juicy was working behind the bar, mixing drinks and flirting with the customers. She's north of thirty and maybe north of forty, but not where it showed. Tall, natural blonde, with unnatural curves. Gravity has no claim on that woman and she's paid a lot to insure that. She's pure Candy Goth and dressed for it from head to toe. Pigtails with hot pink ribbons, skintight black skirt with a pattern of red kissy lips and a bustier in alternating vertical red, black and pink stripes from which the half moons of her breasts always threatened — but never actually managed — to spill out. Knee high pink and black socks, boots that laced to right below her knees, and fingerless gloves studded with chrome spikes. I knew that she also had a bunch of small knives and spikes concealed in her clothes and she was scorpion quick with them. If you fucked with Juicy you'd be lucky to only have Punch wail on you because Juicy doesn't take prisoners and she has no mercy at all. Not for assholes, at least. When it came to the women who worked the club, and the others who swam in her protected waters, she was possessive, motherly and lethal.

I bellied up to the bar and ordered a Jack and ginger. She poured it but didn't try to hold a conversation with that much noise bashing everyone. When I caught her eye I ticked my head toward the back room. She held up five fingers and I nodded. I took four minutes finishing my drink and then wandered over to the short hall that led to her office. Another bartender came to fill Juicy's post and she followed me back.

Her office was soundproofed and as soon as she had the door closed Juicy removed the wax earplugs she wore. She kissed my cheek, waved me to a chair, poured a couple of drinks — Jack, no ginger this time — handed me one and sank into the big leather swivel behind the desk. We toasted, drank, sighed.

"You haven't been down here in a while," she said.

"Been busy."

Juicy had shrewd blue eyes. "You're looking for someone."

I nodded.

"Runaway?"

"Kind of." And I told her the same story I told Punch. When I mentioned Pollydorry's name I saw shutters drop behind those blue eyes. She listened without interruption, rolling the whiskey glass back and forth between her palms.

"Like I told Punch," I said, "I want to tell her I'm looking for her and ask if she wants to go home and sign some papers."

"And if she doesn't?"

"Then she doesn't, but her family company starts falling apart."

She poured herself more whiskey and slid the bottle across the desk to me, but I shook my head.

I said, "Punch told me about some stuff that's been happening. Someone killing people and taking hearts as souvenirs? That's extreme even for this part of town. Is this gang stuff? Punch didn't think so. And he said that Pollydorry's involved somehow, but said I had to ask you about it. So, this is me asking."

Juicy sipped her drink and looked up at the ceiling. She took so long to answer that I didn't think she was going to. When she did speak her voice was quiet and distant.

"Ten years ago," she began, "I used to run with the crowd over at the Coffin Factory. You know them?"

"Sure," I said. "They're the post-Anne Rice crowd. Victorian clothes, very dark music, and a vampire fetish."

"It's more than a fetish. They worshipped them. Called them the Dark Ones, the Lonely Ones, the Lonely Angels. Like that. They had this idealized view that vampires were like angels, that they were immortals who watched humanity and sometimes intervened on our behalf."

"They haven't been doing a very good job of it," I joked.

"Hush. Listen. My niece, Lolly, was part of that crowd, too. She ached for the day when a real vampire would enter her life and give her the dark gift, the bite and the exchange of blood that would elevate her to the status of immortal. Think about that, Sam. Think about what it would mean to some of these kids. The lost ones. The lonely and discarded ones. Immortality, eternal youth, eternal beauty, freedom from pain, from sickness. They would become too powerful to be hurt by all the things that had hurt them in their lives. They would rise above the versions of themselves that had become disappointments to their families and, more importantly, disappointments to themselves. Instead of having to wear the clothes and makeup of darkness they would *become* the darkness. Powerful, undying, perfect."

"Sure," I said, "but I've met vampires and they're not like that."

"No," she said, still not looking at me, "they're not. Vampires are not beautiful even if they look pretty. They're not generous, they don't protect, and they don't care. They are parasites that take. They are the ultimate rapists, Sam, because they take breath and blood, hope and trust, beauty and life and all they give in return is pain, betrayal and death."

I sat there for a moment, then reached for the bottle and poured a fresh slug. Juicy nodded and we both drank. Then she looked over at me.

"You never met Lolly, did you?"

"No. I thought she died."

"She did. Must have been right before you moved to Philly."

"Should I even ask what happened to her?"

"Pretty sure you already know. There's a longer version of the story, but you should know that you're not the only one out there kicking the asses of the things that go bump in the night. Lolly did her part, and it cost her."

"Fucking vampires," I sighed.

"Fucking vampires," she agreed.

We drank.

"How's this get us to Pollydorry?" I asked.

"People are getting hurt out there, Sam. Some of them are people I couldn't give a dry fart about. Some of the gangbangers who are getting chopped up? That's someone taking out the garbage. Sometimes it's the other gangs, sometimes, well..." She shrugged. "But some of my people are getting hurt, too. The disenfranchised ones, the fringe dwellers. People like Punch and me, and maybe you."

"Like Pollydorry, too?"

"Yes. She's walking in the shadows and she thinks she can handle whatever's hiding there."

"You mean vampires?"

"Maybe. I don't actually know for sure. Them, or something scarier."

"From the name she chose I figure she's cruising with some of the fang-gang crowd. The wannabes."

Juicy took a moment on that. "Not exactly," she said. "It's an attempt at irony."

"How?"

She shook her head. "Doesn't matter. Most kids don't actually know what irony is. She picked her name to make a statement, to be contrary."

"You lost me."

Juicy set her glass down, took a pen from her desk drawer and scribbled a note on a sheet of printer paper, then signed it with a flourish. She folded the sheet and held it for a moment, chewing her lower lip as she considered.

"I'm trusting you with this, Sam," she said. "This is a note from me to her. It's me saying that you're safe. That you're a friend."

"Okay."

"Before I give it to you, I need you to give me your word on something."

"Such as what?" I asked.

"Such as if she asks for help, you give it."

"That's always a given."

"You say that, but you don't know what kind of help she might ask for."

"She's your friend, right? That makes her part of the family," I said.

Juicy smiled a sad smile. "Sometimes family can be...*challenging*."

I smiled right back. "Everyone I'm related to by blood is a fucking werewolf, honey. I can roll with the whole challenging thing."

Even though she already knew that about me, hearing me say it made her twitch. She reached across the desk and placed the folded page within reach.

"You've always been one of the good guys," she said.

"I try."

"I'm glad that you never confuse 'good' with 'nice.'"

"Yeah, well." I finished off my drink, took the note, and stood up. "Thanks, Juicy. I owe you one."

"There are no debts in the family, Sam," she said. "You above all should know that."

We looked at each other for a long time, having a conversation on some level so deep that I wasn't sure what we were saying. But I found myself nodding.

-6-

The address was for a place called *Borgo Pass*. Cute.

The doorman looked like Lurch from the *Addams Family*. The crowd going in and out was a mix of Goth and wasted junkie-types. No one looked happy or healthy. Most of the people looked dazed to one degree or another. I could smell cocaine, crystal meth, fifteen different kinds of weed, some heroin, and a few of those designer drugs that keep floating around. *Flakka* and *Eclipse*. Like that. Lots of booze smells. Lots of sex smells, too, and a ton of the chemical signatures of emotions like fear, depression, despair, envy, hate, and passion. Very little love, though, which has its own special scent. Lots of need. Not a lot of hope.

I was going to need to go binge watch some fucking Disney films by the time the night was over. Some Ben and Jerry's, some *Frozen*, and maybe read *Rebecca of Sunnybrook Farm*. I have a tendency toward depression as it is, and my life path hasn't exactly taken me through sunny meadows of wildflowers. But Jesus H.T. Ignatius Christ on a moped, the vibe I got from the crowd at *Borgo Pass* would have driven the Dalai Lama to hard liquor and bad choices.

The doorman asked me for a twenty and stamped my hand. I went inside, looking out of place and feeling stupid. I had twenty years on most of the people here. I wondered if maybe I should wolf out a little. Some hair, some fangs and claws. Who knows, I might fit in better.

The inside of the club was like an S&M orgy as painted by Hieronymus Bosch. People were having painful sex right out in the open. Whipping. Cutting. Bleeding. It wasn't sexy though they were all trying hard to sell it as that. This is ugly, painful and desperate. Most of the people here were willing victims to others who identified as 'masters,' and there was every kind of using and abusing in the book. The motif was black and white, with blood as the only real color. I saw a couple engaged in blood play. The 'donor' was a young woman dressed in sexy Goth clothing but clearly looking self-conscious and terrified. A nearly naked man loomed over her, wearing a studded jockstrap and leather bands around his torso, legs and arms. He wore a set of fake metal fangs attached to his teeth like a dental retainer. The fangs dripped with blood and there were fresh bleeding bites on the girl's arm, breasts and throat.

I have to admit that part of me wanted to beat the shit out of the guy, but the woman was here willingly and this was their thing. Who was I, except a prude and an outsider? This wasn't mine to judge.

So I moved on, working my way through the madness. I was absolutely sure that about a hundred health regulations were being shredded in here, not to mention fire codes. Whoever owned this joint had to be paying the local cops to look the other way because any assistant district attorney five days out of law school could put half of the clientele and *all* of the staff away for years.

I drifted.

Tried really hard not to judge. Failed a lot.

Then I saw her.

She was in a little alcove at the back of the club, sprawled on a sofa with a lot of cushions spilling onto the floor. There were two other women with her and seven men, all of them dressed for fun and games. I moved in that direction, but I took my time, trying to blend in enough so that she wouldn't spot me and mark me for what I was. Jonah Smith had said his daughter could always spot his guys. So I changed my body language, moved slower, affected to look inward and disaffected. I stopped at the bar and bought a glass of dark red wine.

Pollydorry Smith was something, and I can see why she ran into troubles as a kid. You know Sofia Vergara from that show, *Modern Family*? Imagine her at twenty. Now think about what it would be like for a girl one year into puberty looking like that. If we humans were a better class of people there wouldn't be even the possibility of sexualizing a little kid. We're not that classy. Some are, most aren't. Sure, you can argue that seeing curves like hers triggers biological reactions hardwired into our genetic need to procreate, blah, blah, blah. One of the points of our claim to being civilized is that we are supposed to have control over our base impulses. We actually do, despite what you read in the transcripts of rape cases. I was a cop and I know for a fact that no one has ever really been 'driven to it,' and no amount of bullshit is ever going to sell me on the whole 'look how she was dressed' or 'she was asking for it' fucktard rationalization.

So, looking at Pollydorry I can see how some of the men in her life—peers and adults—found some way to blame her for being sexually appealing and tried to use that against her. It's tragic and cheap and, saddest of all, commonplace. Am I ranting? Fucking right I'm ranting. I've taken sexually abused kids from the hands of abusive parents; I've helped scrape them off the streets after they've crashed and burned because they couldn't deal with what happened to them. I've volunteered hundreds of hours at women's shelters. A lot of cops do. Those who give a shit. I give a shit.

As I stood there pretending to drink my wine I watched the men fawn and paw over Pollydorry and the other women. They were all dressed in the dark blacks and bright hues of the Candy Goth tribe. Lots of skin showing. Lots of white teeth when they smiled. Beer bottles and cocktail glasses all around them, and a haze of pot smoke.

Then I shifted my attention to the seven men.

That they were predators was obvious. I could tell that much even without my wolf senses. They looked like a bunch of white and Latino guys trying to pass themselves off as hip hop gangstas. The clothes, the chains and Rolexes and gold rings and all that. But I could see the gang and prison tats peeking out from cuffs and collars and open shirts. The ink smelled wrong and I realized that it wasn't real. It smelled like India ink, and a little like paint, and I thought, *who the fuck paints on fake tattoos to come into an S & M club?*

I edged closer so I could smell more. My sense of smell is, well let's face it, supernatural. Even when I'm in human form it's ten times better than a bloodhound's. When I go full wolf it has no parallel in nature. Ditto for eyesight. When I'm a wolf I can see full color as well as infrared and ultraviolet. The downside is that only a lycanthrope brain can process that much input. As a human I can take in a lot but can't process everything to the same minute degree.

What I smelled wasn't at all right. No sir, no way.

I smelled dead meat.

Alive. But dead.

Fucking vampires.

-7-

What I couldn't tell was how many vampires I was looking at. At least one or two of the people in that alcove were still alive. The rest weren't, and in human form I couldn't tell which was which. Maybe the three women were all alive. Maybe some of them were turned and one or more of the men were alive. In either case I was looking at a dinner party.

Whoever the vamps were, they were a lot closer to Pollydorry and the other women than I was. Vampires are fast as fuck. Hard to hurt, harder to kill. If I was dumb enough to make a move on them it would guarantee a bloodbath and Papa Smith would be buying a coffin for his daughter.

Unless she was a vampire.

The dynamic of the group wasn't apparent. For all I knew Pollydorry could be the ringleader of a vampire crew. My wishful thinking that she was a total innocent kept trying to talk me out of that thought, but she was the one laughing the loudest, waving for more drinks, flirting outrageously, making crude jokes about the charms of her two friends. No matter how much I didn't want to believe it, Pollydorry seemed to be working hard to pimp the other women to the men, and they were responding like a pack of dogs.

I sipped and watched and tried to come up with some plausible way for me to crash the party. If I'd planned this better I'd have brought some changes of clothes and a makeup kit, but I hadn't expected to need that stuff. My fault for not taking this as seriously as I should have.

Fate, though, has a way of intervening in strange and perverse ways. Proof that the gods love to be entertained and give us endless opportunities to be clowns in their ongoing circus.

A waiter who looked like an emaciated version of Johnny Depp appeared and bent to say something to Pollydorry. A huge smile blossomed on her face and she sat up and declared that the *real* party was just about to start.

"Everybody grab your drinks," she yelled. "The limo's outside!"

Everyone in her group staggered to their feet and they moved in a tightly-knit bunch down a hall that led to a back door. I tried to follow but a very, very large bouncer stepped into my path.

"Private party, sport," he said.

The guy was roughly the size of Nebraska and looked like he was made from slabs of granite, barbed wire and attitude. The name stitched onto his shirt was 'Fluffy,' but I didn't get the in-joke.

No way I could take him without going wolf, but since he was just a guy—a very large Planet of the Apes-looking motherfucker—doing his job, there was no reason to do him harm. Without going wolf he could fold me like origami paper.

I turned around and made my way as quickly as possible to the front exit. A woman dressed like Wednesday Addams was in my way, so I gave her my wine glass, blew her a kiss and slipped past. I hurried past Lurch, ran down the street to the first alley, cut left, found that it was a dead-end, spun and ran out, raced to the end of the block and hauled ass all the way around to the back. As a wolf I can run all day, but in my human form I am seriously out of fucking shape. I was puffing like an octogenarian at the homestretch of the Boston Marathon by the time I saw the back-end of the club come into sight past rows of greasy dumpsters. There was one weak yellow light in the back alley and it spilled its yellow glow down on a big, black stretch limo. The crowd of laughing partiers were stumbling their way toward the open back door, which was held open by a tall, wiry guy in driver's livery.

"We're going to have us some *fun*," growled one of the men, and everyone laughed.

And in the next moment Pollydorry suddenly pushed back from a man who had his arm around her waist with one hand cupping her ass. She spun and with a flick of her wrist snapped the four-inch blade of a lock-knife into place and then slashed one of the other women across the throat.

The woman gaped in shock and clamped her hands to her throat but she was too late to stop the jet of bright red blood shot like a geyser over the heads of the whole crowd. Everyone screamed. Everyone staggered back.

Pollydorry stood there with the knife in her hand and a wicked smile on her face and no trace of sanity in her eyes.

I skidded to a stop ten feet from the crowd and watched as the woman she'd slashed sank slowly to her knees, blood pumping steadily but less forcefully as her body emptied itself. Some of the blood splashed on Pollydorry's shoes.

"What the fuck?" gasped the tallest of the men.

Three of the other men dove hands inside their jackets to pull guns. The driver produced an ugly little Czech machine pistol from god knows where. Maybe he pulled it out of his ass. He swung it toward Pollydorry and opened up.

I was moving by then.

Running, leaping, changing. My clothes ripped apart and I felt as if I was being torn in half as well. The change hurts. It really fucking hurts. Doesn't take long but every cell of my body was torn apart and reorganized into a new form, with new senses that were so much keener and able to feel all of that pain.

But the wolf was who and what I needed to be.

I hit the driver hard. Real hard. Teeth and claws, mass and velocity. I crushed him against the side of the car and took his arm off at the elbow and ripped his throat out because I didn't want to hear him scream.

I landed and whirled and watched madness unfold around me.

It was a fight of two against seven.

All seven of the men were vampires. Hard to see that a little while ago, easy to see—and smell—now. The woman who'd been slashed was down on all fours and if the world was normal she'd be dead.

The world was never normal.

She wasn't dead.

She snarled up at Pollydorry and I saw the fangs grow and grow. Long, needle-like fangs. More like a snake's than a bat's. Her eyes turned black and all ten of her fingernails burst off in sprays of blood as black talons curved out and down. Not sure what in the world she was, but she wasn't human, and she came up off the floor and charged at Pollydorry as a shriek of mingled pain and fury burst from her mouth.

The woman with Pollydorry, an Asian gal with platform shoes, pulled a pair of collapsible fighting sticks from the sides of her bustier, shook them out and pushed a button that made electric sparks dance from the tips. Pollydorry had her knife and as I watched she drew what looked like a perfume bottle from her waistband. I knew what it was before she sprayed it. The smell was so distinctive. And so appropriate.

Two of the vampires rushed as her and Pollydorry sprayed them in the face with a mixture of bleach and garlic. They screamed and staggered, and she drove at them, slashing the blade with impressive speed, demonic fury, and professional competence. Deep, horrific wounds opened up in their faces, hands, chests, groins.

The Asian woman knew some kind of Filipino martial arts. Escrima, I think. She kicked and evaded and battered and clubbed at the vampires who tried to drag her down.

Whatever the hell this was, it was playing out like an ambush. Pollydorry and the Asian woman had lured the vampires out here and were trying to take them all down. It was impressive, it was admirable, and it was suicidal. Maybe they'd overestimated their own skills or underestimated the vampires, or both, but they were going to lose this fight. Two vampires were down, one was jolted by the shock rods, but the others were spreading out like a pack of hyenas. I tried to make this all fit in my head. Was Pollydorry crazy? Or was she on some kind of vigilante kick? And who were these vampires to her? Why do this? Why take these kinds of risks? The only reason they weren't dead yet is that they were using some of the vampires as shields against the ones who had guns. How long could that last? Two seconds? Three?

Questions, questions, questions, and no damn time at all to get answers.

There were two human women fighting a pack of vampires and I was a benandanti. I'd already accepted Pollydorry into my extended pack, which meant her fight—even if I didn't understand it—was mine.

So, fuck it.

I attacked.

Two of the vampires turned toward me, raising their guns, and fired.

Here's the thing about werewolves and bullets. Bullets hurt. They hurt like fuck. They do not, however, do shit to stop a werewolf. What they do is trigger an even deeper primal rage. It's something that goes all the way back to the earliest and most dangerous version of our species. It calls the *canis dirus* out of the darkest part of our genetic heritage. The Dire Wolf does not play nice. It has no 'dog' in it at all. It has no compassion. It roamed the forests and competed with the saber-toothed cat for prey, and sometimes it ate the damn cats. These guys woke that part of me.

Bad call.

I felt a blackness come over me. I heard a sound in my ears like something ripping and there were fireworks in my mind. My body changed again, shifting more mass to my jaws and my chest. I hit the two vampires so hard they flew apart like dogs. Arms and legs and bones disintegrating as I tore into them. Guns flew into the air with hands still holding them.

Pollydorry saw this and screamed, reading the moment wrong. She sprayed me with the bleach-garlic mixture, and it hurt worse than the bullets. I almost—*almost*—turned on her. It was close. I rose up and swatted the bottle from her hand and one of my claws gashed the inside of her forearm. She shrieked and stumbled backward, and one of the vampire leaped on her and drove her down to the ground, his mouth snapping at the welling blood.

I moved in, but another vampire kicked me in the throat hard enough to flip me onto my back and dim the lights of the whole world.

"*Vlkodlak*," he sneered, using the Czech word for werewolf as he dove at me with the monster woman with him. Suddenly claws and fangs were slashing and tearing at me.

Then Pollydorry tackled the male vampire like a linebacker, hitting him under the armpit and crashing him over onto his side. He tried to bite her, but she drove the point of her knife up under his jaw, pinning his mouth shut.

I was busy with the snakelike female vampire. She was exceptionally—dishearteningly—strong and fast, and there was some kind of venom in her bite that burned. I could feel parts of me trying to go dead even as my lycanthropic constitution struggled to fight the effects. It was some kind of powerful neurotoxin. She darted her head forward to try and take me by the throat, but I moved in faster, going for the fast target. My jaws clamped around her windpipe and I snapped shut with eighteen hundred pounds of pressure. Her throat, which had somehow healed from Pollydorry's knife cut, disintegrated between my jaws. It tore the whole mass of it away. And ate it.

Her body went limp, but I scrambled to all fours and took a second bigger bite, crunching through the whole spine. Her head rolled away and I wheeled around just as the Asian woman drove the point of a shock rod into the eye of one of the other vampires. Never saw that trick before. Didn't know a direct electrical shock would do much to a vampire. Apparently shoving the goddamn thing through the eye and into the brain does the trick. Who knew? The vampire dropped like a sack of disconnected parts.

I was up and turned to see Pollydorry kneeling on the vampire she'd spiked. The knife was still in place but she'd produced another and was chopping the living shit out of the vamp's face while he thrashed and moaned. And died.

The other vampires tried to make a fight of it.

Tried.

Not succeeded.

We killed them all.

-8-

And then it was the three of us. Pollydorry, the Asian woman, and me, standing in a lake of blood, surrounded by parts and inert bodies, each of us breathing heavy, each of us still caught in that high realm of ultimate commitment to killing without fear of dying.

They had seen me fight alongside them, but they held their weapons ready to shift the focus of their war.

So I shifted first. In form.

Which meant that I was suddenly a very naked guy covered in blood.

They stood their ground, weapons still in their hands.

I reached down and slowly, carefully stripped the pants off of one of the dead vampires. And put them on. One does not like to wave one's dick around in moments like that.

I said, "I'm a friend of Juicy's."

They stared at me.

"She told me where to find you."

Nothing.

"I'm a friend."

Nothing.

I walked without haste over to the dead driver, fished in his pocket for the keys, picked up the remains of my clothes, and then went around to the driver's side. "Cops are going to be here soon. There's going to be a crowd. How about we go somewhere where we can talk?"

I didn't expect them to agree.

I expected them to bolt and run.

I could smell their fear, their doubt. Their rage.

They got into the car.

-9-

We drove to *ViXXXens*. Punch saw us and let us in the back door. Juicy met us there. She sent me off to one of the bathrooms to clean up, found a pair of sweats for me. I took my time, standing under a spray hot enough to cook lobsters, letting the heat wash the tension out of me. Letting time help my body process the adrenaline. And the bullets.

Yeah, there's this thing that happens. The bullets work their way through my system. It looks like I had huge boils and then they pop and the slugs fall out. Takes about ten minutes from the time it starts until the wounds scab over. It hurts so bad I had to stuff a washcloth in my mouth to stifle the screams.

When I came out of the shower Punch was sitting on a folding chair reading a copy of *Glamour Magazine,* a pair of half-moon glasses perched on his crooked snub nose.

"They're waiting for you in her ladyship's office," he said.

"Okay."

He studied me. "Looks like you had yourself a night."

"I could use a couple Advil."

"And a bottle of bourbon?"

"To wash them down, sure."

We smiled at each other as if that was funny. I followed up there without saying another word.

The Asian woman's name was Dish. That's all the name I ever got. Juicy introduced me to her and Pollydorry. Punch closed the door and leaned against it. Five of us in the room. I drank a lot of Juicy's whiskey. Pollydorry and Dish didn't. They stared at me with cold, lethal eyes.

"You want to take me back to my dad?" said Pollydorry after a long time.

"Want to? No. Hired to? Sure."

"I'll cut your balls off if you try."

I sighed and leaned back in my chair putting my heels on the corner of Juicy's desk. "I'm not going to try," I said. "If you want to go, then cool. If you don't, also cool."

"He'll make you try," she said.

I looked at her. "You saw what happened in the alley. You think he could make me do anything?"

She thought about that. Dish took her hand and held it. Nearly a full minute peeled itself bit by bit from the clock on the wall.

"What are you?" asked Dish.

"I'm what you think I am," I said.

More silence.

"My dad wants me to sign the papers, doesn't he?" asked Pollydorry.

"That's what he told me. He said it would be in your best interest, too."

"He doesn't know what's best for me. He never has."

"I got that impression," I said.

"All he cares about is the family business. Making bombs and missile systems and all that. He gets a hard on every time he closes a deal. That's where he gets all his thrills. Making weapons, helping people fight wars. Killing."

"Seems to me you don't mind spilling blood, too," I said, and from the look of disappointment on the faces of the two young women I knew that I'd said the wrong thing. Before anyone could reply I held up a hand. "Look, it's been a rough night and I've had a lot to drink, so if I'm off base set me straight. I don't know what the heck's going on. I was hired to look for you and you were described as a societal dropout and runaway. Your father painted you as an over-sexualized irresponsible person with all sorts of emotional issues. He said you dove into the Goth crowd as a way of protesting or acting out or whatever. Frankly I don't give a microwaved fuck what he thinks. I come down here and the word on the street is that there's a gang war and that someone's killing people and cutting their hearts out. Then Juicy tells me that there are vampires hunting in the Goth scene and that maybe you're mixed up with them. She doesn't know exactly how, but she cares about you and she helped me find you. She wouldn't have done that if she thought I was going to try and strong arm you. Juicy knows me pretty well and she knows where I stand when it all comes down to being real. So, I *did* find you and you're partying with a bunch of vampires and then you go outside with them and go all *Buffy the Vampire Slayer* on them. So, bottom line is that I'm confused as a motherfucker. I've been bitten, shot and kicked. Every molecule of my body hurts and my head hurts even worse trying to figure this out. So...instead of sitting there and glaring at me, how about you tell me what the hell is going on."

I think we sat through four whole minutes of solid silence before Pollydorry spoke.

"My mother broke her neck falling off a horse, did my dad tell you that?"

"He did."

She nodded. "Bet he didn't tell you about all the stuff he tried to keep her alive long enough to sign those papers."

"He said that he brought in specialists from all over the world."

"'Specialists,'" said Pollydorry, spitting the word. Her face twisted into an ugly sneer. "You met one of those specialists tonight. The ugly bitch with the snake teeth."

"What?"

Pollydorry nodded. "When Dad couldn't save her with ordinary medicine he sent his people to find vampires. Yeah. Be with that. He thought that they might be able to turn her, make her immortal. Bring her back to life—or whatever—and she'd be so grateful that she'd do anything for Dad. Sign papers, whatever. Dad paid them a ton of money, too. His own money. He brought a bunch of them over, and after Mom died they stayed. They decided they liked it here. They brought over some of their friends, too. Now there's a bunch of them in Philly and some in New York and Baltimore. Trenton, too, I think. They're starting to tear apart the gang structure all up and down the East Coast because they want to run things. A vampire mob. Almost funny when you say it out loud."

"No," I said, "it's not."

"No," said Dish.

"No," said Pollydorry.

Punch stood there shaking his head. Juicy poured me another shot.

"When they tried to turn my mom," said Pollydorry, "it didn't work. Not really. It woke her up, it enhanced her senses, it made her able to feel again, but it couldn't heal the damage to her spine." Tears broke and rolled down her cheeks. "I would sit by the side of her bed, day after day, listening to her scream. She kept screaming and kept screaming and kept screaming…"

"What did you do?" I asked, my voice choked.

She looked at me with the coldest, saddest eyes in town. And I knew what she did.

"Jesus," I whispered.

She nodded. Dish got up and hugged her and stood there with her arm wrapped around Pollydorry's shoulders.

"I dropped out," said Pollydorry. "Of course I did. I ran. I found Dish and made some friends down here. I was with other kids who ran. With a whole community of people who'd run. We all ran here and found each other."

Dish kissed her on the top of the head, then she looked at me. "I was seeing a girl named Chiclet," she said. "She was a waitress at one of the clubs. Vampire Goth, you know? She had this vampire fetish. And...and one day she found a real vampire. I found her later."

She was weeping too, but her jaw was tight and small muscles flexed and bunched at the corners of it.

"There were five of us," said Pollydorry. "Dish, a girl named Phoebe, and two guys, Ringo and Jax. We were all...alike, you know? We'd all run from something, we'd all found something, and we all had it taken away."

I nodded.

"So, what can you do? Either you keep running or you get eaten. Or you fight."

I said nothing.

"I'm so fucking tired of running," she said. "I'm so tired of being nothing to anyone. And I'm so tired of losing the people I care about."

She leaned her head against Dish.

"So we fight," said Pollydorry. "We took some martial arts classes. We know people who can get us weapons. And we fight."

"How many have you killed?" I asked.

"Counting tonight? Fifteen."

"Holy shit."

She shrugged. "There are a lot more of them. We can't really win. We know that. We'll die, too. Like Chiclet and Jax and Ringo."

"You can stop fighting. You've done some damage."

"Not enough," said Dish.

"Not enough," said Pollydorry. "They're feeding off of us. They see us as freaks, as cattle. They know that we love the dark stuff, that we like to crowd the edges, and that's where they hunt. They're trying to make us look like fools for being who we are. They think Goth is just an affectation, that it has no meaning. That we have no meaning other than what they can take from us." She shook her head. A strong, definite movement that was as much filled with ferocity as it was with acceptance of her own inevitable failure. "If I don't do this—if *we* don't—who will?"

I sipped my bourbon and looked at her and then at the wall above her.

"Your father wants you home to sign the papers," I said. "I think you should go home."

"Jesus, have you heard a *word* I said—?"

I held up a hand. "I didn't say go home and sign his papers. I know some lawyers. Some good ones. Lawyers who know this part of the world and who owe me favors. I think we should talk to them. Maybe let them draw up new papers. Break up your father's company. Give him the little pieces and then get rid of him, close him out. Take the rest of the money and use it."

"To do what?" she demanded. "Live in a big house and—"

"No," I said. "Your family made its money on war. You're fighting a war. Use the money to help you win your fight."

The room went silent again.

"Think about it. Weapons, training, surveillance equipment, fuck, even hire some mercenaries. You can go to actual war with these bloodsuckers. You could win the war."

"Maybe it can't be won," said Punch.

"Maybe it can't," I said, "but we don't know that. No one's ever done something like this before. No one would ever see it coming."

Pollydorry looked up at Dish. It was the first time either of them smiled since we got here. They were not very nice smiles. But then Pollydorry glanced over at me. "And what do you get out of all of this?"

"A phone call," I said.

"A phone call?"

"Sure. Every once in a while pick up the phone and say, 'Hey Sam, there's something big going down. You want in?'"

"It's not even your fight," said Juicy.

"Right," agreed Pollydorry, "why would you even care?"

I finished my drink. "Because every once in a while I like to be on the winning side."

I stood up. Nobody else got up, nobody shook hands. I nodded to them and they nodded back and I left.

Outside it was cool and the stars were burning in the night sky. I could feel the moon off somewhere behind the buildings, waiting to fill the world with its pure, cold light. I stuffed my hands into the pockets of the borrowed sweat pants and walked back to my car.

Feeling, oddly, less alone than I have in a long, long time.

JONATHAN MABERRY is a NY Times bestselling novelist, five-time Bram Stoker Award winner, and comic book writer. He writes the Joe Ledger thrillers, the Rot & Ruin series, the Nightsiders series, the Dead of Night series, as well as standalone novels in multiple genres. His novels include KILL SWITCH, the 8th in his best-selling Joe Ledger thriller series; VAULT OF SHADOWS, a middle-grade sf/fantasy mash-up; and MARS ONE, a standalone teen space travel novel. He is the editor of many anthologies including THE X-FILES, SCARY OUT THERE, OUT OF TUNE, and V-WARS. His comic book works include, among others, *CAPTAIN AMERICA*, the Bram Stoker Award-winning *BAD BLOOD, ROT & RUIN, V-WARS*, the NY Times best-selling *MARVEL ZOMBIES RETURN*, and others. His books EXTINCTION MACHINE, MARS ONE, anf V-WARS are in development for TV/film. A board game version of V-WARS was released in early 2016. He is the founder of the Writers Coffeehouse, and the co-founder of The Liars Club. Prior to becoming a full-time novelist, Jonathan spent twenty-five years as a magazine feature writer, martial arts instructor and playwright. He was a featured expert on the History Channel documentary, *Zombies: A Living History* and a regular expert on the TV series, *True Monsters*. He is one third of the very popular and mildly weird Three Guys With Beards pop-culture podcast. Jonathan lives in Del Mar, California with his wife, Sara Jo. www.jonathanmaberry.com

WHISTLING

PAST THE

GRAVEYARD

AND OTHER STORIES

JONATHAN MABERRY

NEW YORK TIMES BESTSELLING AUTHOR

INTRODUCTION BY *NEW YORK TIMES* BESTSELLER SCOTT SIGLER

www.ingramcontent.com/pod-product-compliance
Lightning Source LLC
Chambersburg PA
CBHW020928020726
47495CB00002B/401